William Makepeace Thackeray

Novels

Volume X.

William Makepeace Thackeray

Novels
Volume X.

ISBN/EAN: 9783337024055

Printed in Europe, USA, Canada, Australia, Japan

Cover: Foto ©Andreas Hilbeck / pixelio.de

More available books at **www.hansebooks.com**

NOVELS

BY

WILLIAM MAKEPEACE THACKERAY.

IN TWELVE VOLUMES.
VOLUME X.

THE ADVENTURES OF PHILIP

ON HIS WAY THROUGH THE WORLD.

VOL. I.

LONDON:
SMITH, ELDER, & CO., 15 WATERLOO PLACE.
1877.

THE

ADVENTURES OF PHILIP

ON HIS WAY THROUGH THE WORLD;

SHEWING

WHO ROBBED HIM, WHO HELPED HIM, AND WHO PASSED HIM BY:

TO WHICH IS NOW PREFIXED

A SHABBY GENTEEL STORY.

By W. M. THACKERAY.

WITH ILLUSTRATIONS BY FREDERICK WALKER AND BY THE AUTHOR

IN TWO VOLUMES.

VOL. I.

LONDON:

SMITH, ELDER & CO., 15 WATERLOO PLACE.

1877.

ADVERTISEMENT.

WHEN the "Shabby Genteel Story" was first reprinted with other
stories and sketches by Mr. Thackeray, collected together under the
title of "Miscellanies," the following note was appended to it :—

> It was my intention to complete the little story, of which only the first part is
> here written. Perhaps novel-readers will understand, even from the above
> chapters, what was to ensue. Caroline was to be disowned and deserted by her
> wicked husband : that abandoned man was to marry somebody else : hence, bitter
> trials and grief, patience and virtue, for poor little Caroline, and a melancholy
> ending—as how should it have been gay? The tale was interrupted at a sad
> period of the writer's own life. The colours are long since dry ; the artist's hand
> is changed. It is best to leave the sketch, as it was when first designed seventeen
> years ago. The memory of the past is renewed as he looks at it—
>
> *die Bilder froher Tage*
> *Und manche liebe Schatten steigen auf.*
>
> W. M. T.

LONDON, *April* 10*th*, 1857.

Mr. Brandon, a principal character in this story, figures prominently
in "The Adventures of Philip," under his real name of Brand
Firmin ; Mrs. Brandon, his deserted wife, and her father, Mr. Gann,
are also introduced ; therefore the "Shabby Genteel Story" is now
prefixed to "The Adventures of Philip."

CONTENTS.

A SHABBY GENTEEL STORY.

THE ADVENTURES OF PHILIP.

LIST OF PLATES.

A SHABBY GENTEEL STORY.

A

SHABBY GENTEEL STORY.

CHAPTER I.

AT that remarkable period when Louis XVIII. was restored a second time to the throne of his fathers, and all the English who had money or leisure rushed over to the Continent, there lived in a certain boarding-house at Brussels a genteel young widow, who bore the elegant name of Mrs. Wellesley Macarty.

In the same house and room with the widow lived her mamma, a lady who was called Mrs. Crabb. Both professed to be rather fashionable people. The Crabbs were of a very old English stock, and the Macartys were, as the world knows, County Cork people; related to the Sheenys, Finnigans, Clancys, and other distinguished families in their part of Ireland. But Ensign Wellesley Mac, not having a shilling, ran off with Miss Crabb, who possessed the same independence; and after having been married about six months to the lady, was carried off suddenly, on the 18th of June, 1815, by a disease very prevalent in those glorious times—the fatal cannon-shot morbus. He, and many hundred young fellows of his regiment, the Clonakilty Fencibles, were attacked by this epidemic on the same day, at a place about ten miles from Brussels, and there perished. The ensign's lady had accompanied her husband to the Continent, and about five months after his death brought into the world two remarkably fine female children.

Mrs. Wellesley's mother had been reconciled to her daughter by this time—for, in truth, Mrs. Crabb had no other child but her runaway Juliana, to whom she flew when she heard of her destitute condition. And, indeed, it was high time that some one should come to the young widow's aid; for as her husband did not leave money, nor anything that represented money, except a number of tailors' and bootmakers' bills, neatly docketed, in his writing-desk, Mrs. Wellesley was in danger of starvation, should no friendly person assist her.

Mrs. Crabb, then, came off to her daughter, whom the Sheenys, Finnigans, and Clancys refused, with one scornful voice, to assist. The fact is, that Mr. Crabb had once been butler to a lord, and his lady a lady's-maid; and at Crabb's death, Mrs. Crabb disposed of the "Ram" hotel and posting-house, where her husband had made three thousand pounds, and was living in genteel ease in a country town, when Ensign Macarty came, saw, and ran away with Juliana. Of such a connexion, it was impossible that the great Clancys and Finnigans could take notice; and so once more widow Crabb was compelled to share with her daughter her small income of a hundred and twenty a year.

Upon this, at a boarding-house in Brussels, the two managed to live pretty smartly, and to maintain an honourable reputation. The twins were put out, after the foreign fashion, to nurse, at a village in the neighbourhood; for Mrs. Macarty had been too ill to nurse them; and Mrs. Crabb could not afford to purchase that most expensive article, a private wet-nurse.

There had been numberless tiffs and quarrels between mother and daughter when the latter was in her maiden state; and Mrs. Crabb was, to tell the truth, in nowise sorry when her Jooly disappeared with the ensign,—for the old lady dearly loved a gentleman, and was not a little flattered at being the mother to Mrs. Ensign Macarty. Why the ensign should have run away with his lady at all, as he might have had her for the asking, is no business of ours; nor are we going to rake up old stories and village scandals, which insinuate that Miss Crabb ran away with *him*, for with these points the writer and the reader have nothing to do.

Well, then, the reconciled mother and daughter lived once more together, at Brussels. In the course of a year, Mrs. Macarty's sorrow had much abated; and having a great natural love of dress, and a tolerably handsome face and person, she was induced, without much reluctance, to throw her weeds aside, and to appear in the most becoming and varied costumes which her means and ingenuity could furnish. Considering, indeed, the smallness of the former, it was agreed on all hands that Mrs. Crabb and her daughter deserved wonderful credit,—that is, they managed to keep up as respectable an appearance as if they had five hundred a year; and at church, at tea-parties, and abroad in the streets, to be what is called quite the gentlewomen. If they starved at home, nobody saw it; if they patched and pieced, nobody (it was to be hoped) knew it; if they bragged about their relations and property, could any one say them nay? Thus they lived, hanging on with desperate energy to the skirts of genteel society; Mrs. Crabb, a sharp woman, rather respected her daughter's superior rank; and Mrs. Macarty did not quarrel so much as heretofore with her mamma, on whom herself and her two children were entirely dependent.

While affairs were at this juncture, it happened that a young Englishman, James Gann, Esq., of the great oil-house of Gann, Blubbery and Gann (as he took care to tell you before you had been an hour in his company),—it happened, I say, that James Gann, Esq., came to Brussels for a month, for the purpose of perfecting himself in the French language; and while in that capital went to lodge at the very boarding-house which contained Mrs. Crabb and her daughter. Gann was young, weak, inflammable; he saw and adored Mrs. Wellesley Macarty; and she, who was at this period all but engaged to a stout old wooden-legged Scotch regimental surgeon, pitilessly sent Dr. M'Lint about his business, and accepted the addresses of Mr. Gann. How the young man arranged matters with his papa the senior partner, I don't know; but it is certain that there was a quarrel, and afterwards a reconciliation; and it is also known that James Gann fought a duel with the surgeon,—receiving the Æsculapian fire, and discharging his own bullet into the azure skies. About nine thousand times in the course of his after-years did Mr. Gann narrate the history of the combat; it enabled him to go through life with the reputation of a man of courage, and won for him, as he said with pride, the hand of his Juliana; perhaps this was rather a questionable benefit.

One part of the tale, however, honest James never did dare to tell, except when peculiarly excited by wrath or liquor; it was this: that on the day after the wedding, and in the presence of many friends who had come to offer their congratulations, a stout nurse, bearing a brace of chubby little ones, made her appearance; and these rosy urchins, springing forward at the sight of Mrs. James Gann, shouted affectionately, "*Maman! maman!*" at which the lady, blushing rosy red, said, "James, these two are yours;" and poor James well nigh fainted at this sudden paternity so put upon him. "Children!" screamed he, aghast; "whose children?" at which Mrs. Crabb, majestically checking him, said, "These, my dear James, are the daughters of the gallant and good Ensign Macarty, whose widow you yesterday led to the altar. May you be happy with her, and may these blessed children" (tears) "find in you a father, who shall replace him that fell in the field of glory!"

Mrs. Crabb, Mrs. James Gann, Mrs. Major Lolly, Mrs. Piffler, and several ladies present, set up a sob immediately; and James Gann, a good-humoured, soft-hearted man, was quite taken aback. Kissing his lady hurriedly, he vowed that he would take care of the poor little things, and proposed to kiss them likewise; which caress the darlings refused with many roars. Gann's fate was sealed from that minute; and he was properly henpecked by his wife and mother-in-law during the life of the latter. Indeed, it was to Mrs. Crabb that the stratagem of the infant concealment was due; for when her daughter innocently proposed to have or to see the children, the old lady strongly pointed out the folly of such an arrangement, which might, perhaps, frighten away Mr. Gann from the delightful matri-monial trap into which (lucky rogue!) he was about to fall.

Soon after the marriage, the happy pair returned to England, occupying the house in Thames Street, City, until the death of Gann senior; when his son, becoming head of the firm of Gann and Blubbery, quitted the dismal precincts of Billingsgate and colonized in the neighbourhood of Putney; where a neat box, a couple of spare bed-rooms, a good cellar, and a smart gig to drive into and out from town, made a real gentleman of him. Mrs. Gann treated him with much scorn, to be sure, called him a sot, and abused hugely the male companions that he brought down with him to Putney. Honest James would listen meekly, would yield, and would bring down a brace more friends the next day, with whom he would discuss his accustomed number of bottles of port. About this period, a daughter was born to him, called Caroline Brandenburg Gann; so named after a large mansion near Hammersmith, and an injured queen who lived there at the time of the little girl's birth, and who was greatly compassioned and patronized by Mrs. James Gann, and other ladies of distinction. Mrs. James *was* a lady in those days, and gave evening-parties of the very first order.

At this period of time, Mrs. James Gann sent the twins, Rosalind Clancy and Isabella Finnigan Wellesley Macarty, to a boarding-school for young ladies, and grumbled much at the amount of the half-years' bills which her husband was called upon to pay for them; for though James discharged them with perfect good-humour, his lady began to entertain a mean opinion indeed of her pretty young children. They could expect no fortune, she said, from Mr. Gann, and she wondered that he should think of bringing them up expensively, when he had a darling child of his own, for whom he was bound to save all the money that he could lay by.

Grandmamma, too, doted on the little Caroline Brandenburg, and vowed that she would leave her three thousand pounds to this dear infant; for in this way does the world show its respect for that most respectable thing prosperity. Who in this life get the smiles, and the acts of friendship, and the pleasing legacies?—The rich. And I do, for my part, heartily wish that some one would leave me a trifle—say twenty thousand pounds—being perfectly confident that some one else would leave me more; and that I should sink into my grave worth a plum at least.

Little Caroline then had her maid, her airy nursery, her little carriage to drive in, the promise of her grandmamma's consols, and that priceless treasure—her mamma's undivided affection. Gann, too, loved her sincerely, in his careless, good-humoured way; but he determined, notwithstanding, that his step-daughters should have something handsome at his death, but—but for a great BUT.

Gann and Blubbery were in the oil line,—have we not said so? Their profits arose from contracts for lighting a great number of streets in London; and about this period GAS came into use. Gann and Blubbery appeared in the *Gazette;* and, I am sorry to say, so bad had been the management of Blubbery,—so great the extravagance of both partners and their ladies,—that they only paid their creditors fourteenpence halfpenny in the pound.

When Mrs. Crabb heard of this dreadful accident—Mrs. Crabb, who dined thrice a week with her son-in-law; who never would have been allowed to enter the house at all had not honest James interposed his good nature between her quarrelsome daughter and herself —Mrs. Crabb, I say, proclaimed James Gann to be a swindler, a villain, a disreputable, tipsy, vulgar man, and made over her money to the Misses Rosalind Clancy and Isabella Finnigan Macarty; leaving poor

little Caroline without one single maravedi. Half of one thousand five
hundred pounds allotted to each was to be paid at marriage, the other
half on the death of Mrs. James Gann, who was to enjoy the interest
thereof. Thus do we rise and fall in this world—thus does Fortune
shake her swift wings, and bid us abruptly to resign the gifts (or rather
loans) which we have had from her.

How Gann and his family lived after their stroke of misfortune,
I know not; but as the failing tradesman is going through the process
of bankruptcy, and for some months afterwards, it may be remarked
that he has usually some mysterious means of subsistence—stray spars
of the wreck of his property, on which he manages to seize, and to
float for a while. During his retirement, in an obscure lodging in
Lambeth, where the poor fellow was so tormented by his wife as to
be compelled to fly to the public-house for refuge, Mrs. Crabb died;
a hundred a year thus came into the possession of Mrs. Gann; and
some of James's friends, who thought him a good fellow in his prosperity, came forward, and furnished a house, in which they placed
him, and came to see and comfort him. Then they came to see
him not quite so often; then they found out that Mrs. Gann was
a sad tyrant, and a silly woman; then the ladies declared *her* to be
insupportable, and *Gann* to be a low, tipsy fellow : and the gentlemen
could but shake their heads, and admit that the charge was true.
Then they left off coming to see him altogether; for such is the way
of the world, where many of us have good impulses, and are generous
on an occasion, but are wearied by perpetual want, and begin to
grow angry at its importunities—being very properly vexed at the
daily recurrence of hunger, and the impudent unreasonableness of
starvation. Gann, then, had a genteel wife and children, a furnished
house, and a hundred pounds a year. How should he live? The
wife of James Gann, Esq., would never allow him to demean himself
by taking a clerk's place ; and James himself, being as idle a fellow
as ever was known, was fain to acquiesce in this determination of
hers, and to wait for some more genteel employment. And a curious
list of such genteel employments might be made out, were one
inclined to follow this interesting subject far ; shabby compromises
with the world, into which poor fellows enter, and still fondly talk of
their " position," and strive to imagine that they are really working .
for their bread.

Numberless lodging-houses are kept by the females of families who have met with reverses : are not "boarding-houses, with a select musical society, in the neighbourhood of the squares," maintained by such? Do not the gentlemen of the boarding-houses issue forth every morning to the City, or make believe to go thither, on some mysterious business which they have? After a certain period, Mrs. James Gann kept a lodging-house (in her own words, received "two inmates into her family "), and Mr. Gann had his mysterious business.

In the year 1835, when this story begins, there stood in a certain back-street in the town of Margate a house, on the door of which might be read, in gleaming brass, the name of Mr. GANN. It was the work of a single smutty servant-maid to clean this brass plate every morning, and to attend as far as possible to the wants of Mr. Gann, his family, and lodgers; and his house being not very far from the sea, and as you might, by climbing up to the roof, get a sight between two chimneys of that multitudinous element, Mrs. Gann set down her lodgings as fashionable; and declared on her cards that her house commanded "a fine view of the sea."

On the wire window-blind of the parlour was written, in large characters, the word OFFICE; and here it was that Gann's services came into play. He was very much changed, poor fellow! and humbled; and from two cards that hung outside the blind, I am led to believe that he did not disdain to be agent to the "London and Jamaica Ginger-Beer Company," and also for a certain preparation called "Gaster's Infants' Farinacio, or Mothers' Invigorating Substi-tute,"—a damp, black, mouldy, half-pound packet of which stood in permanence at one end of the " office " mantelpiece; while a fly-blown ginger-beer bottle occupied the other extremity. Nothing else indicated that this ground-floor chamber was an office, except a huge black inkstand, in which stood a stumpy pen, richly crusted with ink at the nib, and to all appearance for many months enjoying a sinecure.

To this room you saw every day, at two o'clock, the *employé* from the neighbouring hotel bring two quarts of beer; and if you called at that hour, a tremendous smoke, and smell of dinner, would gush out upon you from the "office," as you stumbled over sundry battered tin dish-covers, which lay gaping at the threshold. Thus had that great bulwark of gentility, the dining at six o'clock, been broken in; and the reader must therefore judge that the house of Gann was in a demoralised state.

Gann certainly was. After the ladies had retired to the back-parlour (which, with yellow gauze round the frames, window-curtains, a red silk cabinet piano, and an album, was still tolerably genteel), Gann remained, to transact business in the office. This took place in the presence of friends, and usually consisted in the production of a bottle of gin from the corner cupboard, or, mayhap, a *litre* of brandy, which was given by Gann with a knowing wink, and a fat finger placed on a twinkling red nose : when Mrs. G. was out, James would also produce a number of pipes, that gave this room a constant and agreeable odour of shag tobacco.

In fact, Mr. Gann had nothing to do from morning till night. He was now a fat, bald-headed man of fifty ; a dirty dandy on week-days, with a shawl-waistcoat, a tuft of hair to his great double chin, a snuffy shirt-frill, and enormous breast-pin and seals : he had a pilot-coat, with large mother-of-pearl buttons, and always wore a great rattling telescope, with which he might be seen for hours on the sea-shore or the pier, examining the ships, the bathing-machines, the ladies' schools as they paraded up and down the esplanade, and all other objects which the telescopic view might give him. He knew every person connected with every one of the Deal and Dover coaches, and was sure to be witness to the arrival or departure of several of them in the course of the day ; he had a word for the ostler about "that grey mare," a nod for the "shooter" or guard, and a bow for the dragsman ; he could send parcels for nothing up to town ; had twice had Sir Rumble Tumble (the noble driver of the Flash-o'-lightning-light-four-inside-post-coach) "up at his place," and took care to tell you that some of the party were pretty considerably "sewn up," too. He did not frequent the large hotels ; but in revenge he knew every person who entered or left them ; and was a great man at the "Bag of Nails" and the "Magpie and Punchbowl," where he was president of a club ; he took the bass in "Mynheer Van Dunk," "The Wolf," and many other morsels of concerted song, and used to go backwards and forwards to London in the steamers as often as ever he liked, and have his "grub," too, on board. Such was James Gann. Many people, when they wrote to him, addressed him James Gann, Esq.

His reverses and former splendours afforded a never-failing theme of conversation to honest Gann and the whole of his family ; and it may be remarked that such pecuniary misfortunes, as they

are called, are by no means misfortunes to people of certain disposi-
tions, but actual pieces of good luck. Gann, for instance, used to
drink liberally of port and claret, when the house of Gann and
Blubbery was in existence, and was henceforth compelled to imbibe
only brandy and gin. Now he loved these a thousand times more
than the wine; and had the advantage of talking about the latter,
and of his great merit in giving them up. In those prosperous days,
too, being a gentleman, he could not frequent the public-house as he
did at present; and the sanded tavern-parlour was Gann's supreme
enjoyment. He was obliged to spend many hours daily in a dark
unsavoury room in an alley off Thames Street; and Gann hated
books and business, except of other people's. His tastes were low;
he loved public-house jokes and company; and now being fallen,
was voted at the "Bag of Nails" and the "Magpie" before mentioned a tip-top fellow and real gentleman, whereas he had been
considered an ordinary vulgar man by his fashionable associates at
Putney. Many men are there who are made to fall, and to profit by
the tumble.

As for Mrs. G., or Jooly, as she was indifferently called by her
husband, she, too, had gained by her losses. She bragged of her
former acquaintances in the most extraordinary way, and to hear
her you would fancy that she was known to and connected with half
the peerage. Her chief occupation was taking medicine, and mend·
ing and altering her gowns. She had a huge taste for cheap finery,
loved raffles, tea-parties, and walks on the pier, where she flaunted
herself and daughters as gay as butterflies. She stood upon her
rank, did not fail to tell her lodgers that she was "a gentlewoman,"
and was mighty sharp with Becky the maid, and poor Carry, her
youngest child.

For the tide of affection had turned now, and the "Misses
Wellesley Macarty" were the darlings of their mother's heart, as
Caroline had been in the early days of Putney prosperity. Mrs. Gann
respected and loved her elder daughters, the stately heiresses of
1,500*l.*, and scorned poor Caroline, who was likewise scorned (like
Cinderella in the sweetest of all stories) by her brace of haughty,
thoughtless sisters. These young women were tall, well-grown, black-
browed girls, little scrupulous, fond of fun, and having great health
and spirits. Caroline was pale and thin, and had fair hair and meek
grey eyes; nobody thought her a beauty in her moping cotton

gown; whereas the sisters, in flaunting printed muslins, with pink scarfs, and artificial flowers, and brass *ferronnières*, and other fallals, were voted very charming and genteel by the Ganns' circle of friends. They had pink cheeks, white shoulders, and many glossy curls stuck about their shining foreheads, as damp and as black as leeches. Such charms, madam, cannot fail of having their effect; and it was very lucky for Caroline that she did not possess them, for she might have been rendered as vain, frivolous, and vulgar, as these young ladies were.

While these enjoyed their pleasures and tea-parties abroad, it was Carry's usual fate to remain at home, and help the servant in the many duties which were required in Mrs. Gann's establishment. She dressed that lady and her sisters, brought her papa his tea in bed, kept the lodgers' bills, bore their scoldings if they were ladies, and sometimes gave a hand in the kitchen if any extra piecrust or cookery was required. At two she made a little toilet for dinner, and was employed on numberless household darnings and mendings in the long evenings, while her sisters giggled over the jingling piano, mamma sprawled on the sofa, and Gann was over his glass at the club. A weary lot, in sooth, was yours, poor little Caroline! since the days of your infancy, not one hour of sunshine, no friendship, no cheery playfellows, no mother's love; but that being dead, the affections which would have crept round it, withered and died too. Only James Gann, of all the household, had a good-natured look for her, and a coarse word of kindness; nor, indeed, did Caroline complain, nor shed many tears, nor call for death, as she would if she had been brought up in genteeler circles. The poor thing did not know her own situation; her misery was dumb and patient; it is such as thousands and thousands of women in our society bear, and pine, and die of; made up of sums of small tyrannies, and long indifference, and bitter wearisome injustice, more dreadful to bear than any tortures that we of the stronger sex are pleased to cry *Ai! Ai!* about. In our intercourse with the world—(which is conducted with that kind of cordiality that we see in Sir Harry and my lady in a comedy—a couple of painted, grinning fools, talking parts that they have learned out of a book,)—as we sit and look at the smiling actors, we get a glimpse behind the scenes from time to time; and alas for the wretched nature that appears there!—among women especially, who deceive even more than men, having more to hide, feeling more, living more than we who have our business, pleasure, ambition, which carries us abroad. Ours are the great strokes of misfortune, as they are called, and theirs the small miseries. While the male thinks, labours, and battles without, the domestic woes and wrongs are the lot of the women; and the little ills are so bad, so infinitely fiercer and bitterer than the great, that I would not change my condition—no, not to be Helen, Queen Elizabeth, Mrs. Coutts, or the luckiest she in history.

Well, then, in the manner we have described lived the Gann family. Mr. Gann all the better for his " misfortunes," Mrs. Gann little the worse; the two young ladies greatly improved by the circumstance, having been cast thereby into a society where their expected three thousand pounds made great heiresses of them; and poor Caroline, as luckless a being as any that the wide sun shone upon. Better to be alone in the world and utterly friendless, than to have sham friends and no sympathy; ties of kindred which bind one as it were to the corpse of relationship, and oblige one to bear through life the weight and the embraces of this lifeless, cold connexion.

I do not mean to say that Caroline would ever have made use of this metaphor, or suspected that her connexion with her mamma and sisters was anything so loathsome. She felt that she was ill-treated, and had no companion; but was not on that account envious, only humble and depressed, not desiring so much to resist as to bear injustice, and hardly venturing to think for herself. This tyranny and humility served her in place of education, and formed her manners, which were wonderfully gentle and calm. It was strange to see such a person growing up in such a family; the neighbours spoke of her with much scornful compassion. " A poor half-witted thing," they said, " who could not say bo! to a goose; " and I think it is one good test of gentility to be thus looked down on by vulgar people.

It is not to be supposed that the elder girls had reached their present age without receiving a number of offers of marriage, and been warmly in love a great many times. But many unfortunate occurrences had compelled them to remain in their virgin condition. There was an attorney who had proposed to Rosalind; but finding that she would receive only 750*l.* down, instead of 1500*l.*, the monster had jilted her pitilessly, handsome as she was. An apothecary, too, had been smitten by her charms; but to live in a shop

was beneath the dignity of a Wellesley Macarty, and she waited for
better things.   Lieutenant Swabber, of the coast-guard service, had
lodged two months at Gann's ; and if letters, long walks, and town-
talk could settle a match, a match between him and Isabella must
have taken place. Well, Isabella was not married ; and the lieutenant,
a colonel in Spain, seemed to have given up all thoughts of her.
She meanwhile consoled herself with a gay young wine-merchant,
who had lately established himself at Brighton, kept a gig, rode out
with the hounds, and was voted perfectly genteel ; and there was a
certain French marquess, with the most elegant black mustachios,
who had made a vast impression upon the heart of Rosalind, having
met her first at the circulating library, and afterwards, by the most
extraordinary series of chances, coming upon her and her sister daily
in their walks upon the pier.

Meek little Caroline, meanwhile, trampled upon though she was,
was springing up to womanhood ; and though pale, freckled, thin,
meanly dressed, had a certain charm about her which some people
might prefer to the cheap splendours and rude red and white of the
Misses Macarty. In fact we have now come to a period of her
history when, to the amaze of her mamma and sisters, and not
a little to the satisfaction of James Gann, Esquire, she actually
inspired a passion in the breast of a very respectable young man.

CHAPTER II.

HOW MRS. GANN RECEIVED TWO LODGERS.

IT was the winter season when the events recorded in this history
occurred ; and as at that period not one out of a thousand lodging-
houses in Margate are let, Mrs. Gann, who generally submitted
to occupy her own first and second floors during this cheerless
season, considered herself more than ordinarily lucky when circumstances occurred which brought no less than two lodgers to her
establishment.

She had to thank her daughters for the first inmate ; for, as these
two young ladies were walking one day down their own street,
talking of the joys of the last season, and the delight of the raffles and

singing at the libraries, and the intoxicating pleasures of the Vauxhall balls, they were remarked and evidently admired by a young gentleman who was sauntering listlessly up the street.

He stared, and it must be confessed that the fascinating girls stared too, and put each other's head into each other's bonnet, and giggled and said, "Lor'!" and then looked hard at the young gentleman again. Their eyes were black, their cheeks were very red. Fancy how Miss Bélla's and Miss Linda's hearts beat when the gentleman, dropping his glass out of his eye, actually stepped across the street, and said, "Ladies, I am seeking for lodgings, and should be glad to look at those which I see are to let in your house."

"How did the conjuror know it was our house?" thought Bella and Linda (they, always thought in couples). From the very simple fact that Miss Bella had just thrust into the door a latch-key.

Most bitterly did Mrs. James Gann regret that she had not on her best gown when a stranger—a stranger in February—actually called to look at the lodgings. She made up, however, for the slovenliness of her dress by the dignity of her demeanour; and asked the gentleman for references, informed him that she was a gentlewoman, and that he would have peculiar advantages in her establishment; and, finally, agreed to receive him at the rate of twenty shillings per week. The bright eyes of the young ladies had done the business; but to this day Mrs. James Gann is convinced that her peculiar dignity of manner, and great fluency of brag regarding her family, have been the means of bringing hundreds of lodgers to her house, who but for her would never have visited it.

"Gents," said Mr. James Gann, at the "Bag of Nails" that very evening, "we have got a new lodger, and I'll stand glasses round to his jolly good health!"

The new lodger, who was remarkable for nothing except very black eyes, a sallow face, and a habit of smoking cigars in bed until noon, gave his name George Brandon, Esq. As to his temper and habits, when humbly requested by Mrs. Gann to pay in advance, he laughed and presented her with a bank-note, never quarrelled with a single item in her bills, walked much, and ate two mutton-chops per diem. The young ladies, who examined all the boxes and letters of the lodgers, as young ladies will, could not find one single document relative to their new inmate, except a tavern-bill of the "White Hart," to which the name of George Brandon, Esquire, was prefixed. Any other papers which might elucidate his history, were locked up in a Bramah box, likewise marked G. B. ; and though these were but unsatisfactory points by which to judge a man's character, there was a something about Mr. Brandon which caused all the ladies at Mrs. Gann's to vote he was quite a gentleman.

When this was the case, I am happy to say it would not unfrequently happen that Miss Rosalind or Miss Isabella would appear in the lodger's apartments, bearing in the breakfast-cloth, or blushingly appearing with the weekly bill, apologizing for mamma's absence, " and hoping that everything was to the gentleman's liking."

Both the Misses Wellesley Macarty took occasion to visit Mr. Brandon in this manner, and he received both with such a fascinating ease and gentleman-like freedom of manner, scanning their points from head to foot, and fixing his great black eyes so earnestly on their faces, that the blushing creatures turned away abashed, and yet pleased, and had many conversations about him.

"Law, Bell," said Miss Rosalind, "what a chap that Brandon is ! I don't half like him, I do declare !" Than which there can be no greater compliment from a woman to a man.

"No more do I neither," says Bell. "The man stares so, and says such things ! Just now, when Becky brought his paper and sealing-wax—the silly girl brought black and red too—I took them up to ask which he would have, and what do you think he said ? "

"Well, dear, what ? " said Mrs. Gann.

" ' Miss Bell,' says he, looking at me, and with such eyes ! ' I'll keep everything: the red wax, because it's like your lips ; the black wax, because it's like your hair ; and the satin paper, because it's like your skin ! ' Wasn't it genteel ? "

"Law, now !" exclaimed Mrs. Gann.

" Upon my word, I think it's very rude !" said Miss Lindy; "and if he'd said so to me, I'd have slapped his face for his imperence !" And much to her credit, Miss Lindy went to his room ten minutes after to see if he *would* say anything to her. What Mr. Brandon said, I never knew ; but the little pang of envy which had caused Miss Lindy to retort sharply upon her sister, had given place to a pleased good-humour, and she allowed Bella to talk about the new lodger as much as ever she liked.

And now if the reader is anxious to know what was Mr. Brandon's character, he had better read the following letter from him. It was addressed to no less a person than a viscount; and given, perhaps, with some little ostentation to Becky, the maid, to carry to the post. Now Becky, before she executed such errands, always showed the letters to her mistress or one of the young ladies (it must not be supposed that Miss Caroline was a whit less curious on these matters than her sisters); and when the family beheld the name of Lord Viscount Cinqbars upon the superscription, their respect for their lodger was greater than ever it had been :—

> "MARGATE, *February*, 1835.

"MY DEAR VISCOUNT,—For a reason I have, on coming down to Margate, I with much gravity informed the people of the 'White Hart' that my name was Brandon, and intend to bear that honourable appellation during my stay. For the same reason (I am a modest man, and love to do good in secret), I left the public hotel immediately, and am now housed in private lodgings, humble, and at a humble price. I am here, thank heaven, quite alone. Robinson Crusoe had as much society in his island, as I in this of Thanet. In compensation I sleep a great deal, do nothing, and walk much, silent, by the side of the roaring sea, like Calchas, priest of Apollo.

"The fact is, that until papa's wrath is appeased, I must live with the utmost meekness and humility, and have barely enough money in my possession to pay such small current expenses as fall on me here, where strangers are many and credit does not exist. I pray you, therefore, to tell Mr. Snipson the tailor, Mr. Jackson the bootmaker, honest Solomonson the discounter of bills, and all such friends in London and Oxford as may make inquiries after me, that I am at this very moment at the city of Munich in Bavaria, from which I shall not return until my marriage with Miss Goldmore, the great Indian heiress ; who, upon my honour, will have me, I believe, any day for the asking.

"Nothing else will satisfy my honoured father, I know, whose purse has already bled pretty freely for me, I must confess, and who has taken the great oath that never is broken, to bleed no more unless this marriage is brought about. Come it must. I can't work, I can't starve, and I can't live under a thousand a year.

"Here, to be sure, the charges are not enormous ; for your edification, read my week's bill :—

'George Brandon, Esquire,

　　　　　　　　　　　　　　'To Mrs. James Gann.

	£	s.	d.
A week's lodging	1	0	0
Breakfast, cream, eggs	0	9	0
Dinner (fourteen mutton-chops)	0	10	6
Fire, boot-cleaning, &c.	0	3	6
	£2	3	0

'Settled, Juliana Gann.'

"Juliana Gann! Is it not a sweet name? it sprawls over half the paper. Could you but see the owner of the name, my dear fellow! I love to examine the customs of natives of all countries, and upon my word there are some barbarians in our own less known, and more worthy of being known, than Hottentots, wild Irish, Otaheiteans, or any such savages. If you could see the airs that this woman gives herself; the rouge, ribands, rings, and other female gimcracks that she wears; if you could hear her reminiscences of past times, 'when she and Mr. Gann moved in the very genteelest circles of society;' of the peerage, which she knows by heart; and of the fashionable novels, in every word of which she believes, you would be proud of your order, and admire the intense respect which the *canaille* show towards it. There never was such an old woman, not even our tutor at Christchurch.

"There is a he Gann, a vast, bloated old man, in a rough coat, who has met me once, and asked me, with a grin, if my mutton-chops was to my liking? The satirical monster! What *can* I eat in this place but mutton-chops? A great bleeding beef-steak, or a filthy, reeking *gigot à l'eau*, with a turnip poultice? I should die if I did. As for fish in a watering-place, I never touch it; it is sure to be bad. Nor care I for little sinewy, dry, black-legged fowls. Cutlets are my only resource; I have them nicely enough broiled by a little humble companion of the family, (a companion, ye gods, in *this* family!) who blushed hugely when she confessed that the cooking was hers, and that her name was Caroline. For drink I indulge in gin, of which I consume two wine-glasses daily, in two tumblers of cold water; it is the only liquor that one can be sure to find genuine in a common house in England.

"This Gann, I take it, has similar likings, for I hear him occasionally at midnight floundering up the stairs (his boots lie dirty in the passage)—floundering, I say, up the stairs, and cursing the candlestick, whence escape now and anon the snuffers and extinguisher, and with brazen rattle disturb the silence of the night. Thrice a week, at least, does Gann breakfast in bed—sure sign of pridian intoxication; and thrice a week, in the morning, I hear a hoarse voice roaring for 'my soda-water.' How long have the rogues drunk soda-water?

"At nine, Mrs. Gann and daughters are accustomed to breakfast; a handsome pair of girls, truly, and much followed, as I hear, in the quarter. These dear creatures are always paying me visits—visits with the tea-kettle, visits with the newspaper (one brings it, and one comes for it); but the one is always at the other's heels, and so one cannot show oneself to be that dear, gay seducing fellow that one has been, at home and on the Continent. Do you remember *cette chère marquise* at Pau? That cursed conjugal pistol-bullet still plays the deuce with my shoulder. Do you remember Betty Bundy, the butcher's daughter? A pretty race of fools are we to go mad after such women, and risk all—oaths, prayers, promises, long wearisome courtships—for what?—for vanity, truly. When the battle is over, behold your conquest! Betty Bundy is a vulgar country wench; and *cette belle marquise* is old, rouged, and has false hair. *Vanitas vanitatum!* what a moral man I will be some day or other!

"I have found an old acquaintance (and be hanged to him!), who has come to lodge in this very house. Do you recollect at Rome a young artist, Fitch by name, the handsome gaby with the large beard, that mad Mrs. Carrickfergus was doubly mad about? On the second floor of Mrs. Gann's house dwells this youth. His beard brings the *gamins* of the streets trooping and yelling about him; his fine braided coats have grown somewhat shabby now; and the poor fellow is, like your humble servant (by the way, have you a 500 franc billet to spare?)—like your humble servant, I say, very low in pocket. The young Andrea bears up gaily, however; twangles his guitar, paints the worst pictures in the world, and pens sonnets to his imaginary mistress's eyebrow. Luckily the rogue did not know my name, or I should have been compelled to unbosom to him; and when I called out to him, dubious as to my name, 'Don't you know me? I met you in Rome. My name is Brandon,' the painter was perfectly satisfied, and majestically bade me welcome.

"Fancy the continence of this young Joseph—he has absolutely run away from Mrs. Carrickfergus! 'Sir,' said he, with some hesitation and blushes, when I questioned him about the widow, 'I was compelled to leave Rome in consequence of the fatal fondness of that woman. I am an 'andsome man, sir,—I know it—all the chaps in the Academy want me for a model; and that woman, sir, is sixty. Do you think I would ally myself with her; sacrifice my happiness for the sake of a creature that's as hugly as an 'arpy? I'd rather starve, sir. I'd rather give up my hart and my 'opes of rising in it than do a haction so di*shhh*honourable.'

"There is a stock of virtue for you! and the poor fellow half-starved. He lived at Rome upon the seven portraits that the Carrickfergus ordered of him, and, as I fancy, now does not make twenty pounds in the year. O rare chastity! O wondrous silly hopes! *O motus animorum, atque O certamina tanta!—pulveris exigui jactu*, in such an insignificant little lump of mud as this! Why the deuce does not the fool marry the widow? His betters would. There was a captain of dragoons, an Italian prince, and four sons of Irish peers, all at her feet; but the Cockney's beard and whiskers have overcome them all. Here my paper has come to an end; and I have the honour to bid your lordship a respectful farewell.

"G. B."

Of the young gentleman who goes by the name of Brandon, the reader of the above letter will not be so misguided, we trust, as to have a very exalted opinion. The noble viscount read this document to a supper-party in Christchurch, in Oxford, and left it in a bowl of milk-punch; whence a scout abstracted it, and handed it over to us. My lord was twenty years of age when he received the epistle, and had spent a couple of years abroad, before going to the university, under the guardianship of the worthy individual who called himsel*f* George Brandon.

Mr. Brandon was the son of a half-pay colonel, of good family, who, honouring the great himself, thought his son would vastly benefit by an acquaintance with them, and sent him to Eton, at cruel charges upon a slender purse. From Eton the lad went to Oxford, took honours there, frequented the best society, followed with a kind of proud obsequiousness all the tufts of the university, and left it owing exactly two thousand pounds. Then there came storms at home; fury on the part of the stern old "governor;" and final payment of the debt. But while this settlement was pending, Master George had contracted many more debts among bill-discounters, and was glad to fly to the Continent as tutor to young Lord Cinqbars, in whose company he learned every one of the vices in Europe; and having a good natural genius, and a heart not unkindly, had used these qualities in such an admirable manner as to be at twenty-seven utterly ruined in purse and principle—an idler, a spendthrift, and a glutton. He was free of his money; would spend his last guinea for a sensual gratification; would borrow from his neediest friend; had no kind of conscience or remorse left, but believed himself to be a good-natured devil-may-care fellow; had a good deal of wit, and indisputably good manners, and a pleasing, dashing frankness in conversation with men. I should like to know how many such scoundrels our universities have turned out; and how much ruin has been caused by that accursed system which is called in England "the education of a gentleman." Go, my son, for ten years to a public school, that "world in miniature;" learn "to fight for yourself" against the time when your real struggles shall begin. Begin to be selfish at ten years of age; study for other ten years; get a competent knowledge of boxing, swimming, rowing, and cricket, with a pretty knack of Latin hexameters and a decent smattering of Greek plays,—do this and a fond father shall bless you—bless the two thousand pounds which he has spent in acquiring all these benefits for you. And, besides, what else have you not learned? You have been many hundreds of times to chapel, and have learned to consider the religious service performed there as the vainest parade in the world. If your father is a grocer, you have been beaten for his sake, and have learned to be ashamed of him. You have learned to forget (as how should you remember, being separated from them for three-fourths of your time?) the ties and natural affections of home. You have learned, if you have a kindly heart and an open hand, to compete with associates much more wealthy than yourself; and to consider money as not much, but honour—the honour of dining and consorting with your betters—as a great deal. All this does the public-school and college boy learn; and woe be to his knowledge!

Alas, what natural tenderness and kindly clinging filial affection is he taught to trample on and despise! My friend Brandon had gone through this process of education, and had been irretrievably ruined by it—his heart and his honesty had been ruined by it, that is to say; and he had received, in return for them, a small quantity of classics and mathematics—pretty compensation for all he had lost in gaining them!

But I am wandering most absurdly from the point; right or wrong, so nature and education had formed Mr. Brandon, who is one of a considerable class. Well, this young gentleman was established at Mrs. Gann's house; and we are obliged to enter into all these explanations concerning him, because they are necessary to the right understanding of our story—Brandon not being altogether a bad man, nor much worse than many a one who goes through a course of regular selfish swindling all his life long, and dies religious, resigned, proud of himself, and universally respected by others; for this eminent advantage has the getting-and-keeping scoundrel over the extravagant and careless one.

One day, then, as he was gazing from the window of his lodging-house, a cart, containing a vast number of easels, portfolios, wooden cases of pictures, and a small carpet-bag that might hold a change of clothes, stopped at the door. The vehicle was accompanied by a remarkable young fellow—dressed in a frock-coat covered over with frogs, a dirty turned-down shirt-collar, with a blue satin cravat, and a cap placed wonderfully on one ear—who had evidently hired apartments at Mr. Gann's. This new lodger was no other than Mr. Andrew Fitch; or, as he wrote on his cards, without the prefix,

ANDREA FITCH.

Preparations had been made at Gann's for the reception of Mr. Fitch, whose aunt (an auctioneer's lady in the town) had made arrangements that he should board and lodge with the Gann family. and have the apartments on the second floor as his private rooms. In these, then, young Andrea was installed. He was a youth of a poetic temperament, loving solitude; and where is such to be found

more easily than on the storm-washed shores of Margate in winter?
Then the boarding-house keepers have shut up their houses and
gone away in anguish ; then the taverns take their carpets up, and
you can have your choice of a hundred and twenty beds in any one
of them ; then but one dismal waiter remains to superintend this
vast echoing pile of loneliness, and the landlord pines for summer ;
then the flys for Ramsgate stand tenantless beside the pier ; and
about four sailors, in pea-jackets, are to be seen in the three principal
streets ; in the rest, silence, closed shutters, torpid chimneys enjoying
their unnatural winter sinecure—not the clack of a patten echoing
over the cold dry flags !

This solitude had been chosen by Mr. Brandon for good reasons
of his own ; Gann and his family would have fled, but that they had
no other house wherein to take refuge ; and Mrs. Hammerton, the
auctioneer's lady, felt so keenly the kindness which she was doing to
Mrs. Gann, in providing her with a lodger at such a period, that she
considered herself fully justified in extracting from the latter a bonus
of two guineas, threatening on refusal to send her darling nephew to
a rival establishment over the way.

Andrea was here then, in the loneliness that he loved,—a fantastic
youth, who lived but for his art ; to whom the world was like the
Coburg Theatre, and he in a magnificent costume acting a principal
part. His art, and his beard and whiskers, were the darlings of his
heart. His long pale hair fell over a high polished brow, which
looked wonderfully thoughtful ; and yet no man was more guiltless of
thinking. He was always putting himself into attitudes ; he never
spoke the truth ; and was so entirely affected and absurd, as to be
quite honest at last : for it is my belief that the man did not know
truth from falsehood any longer, and was when he was alone, when
he was in company, nay, when he was unconscious and sound asleep
snoring in bed, one complete lump of affectation. When his apartments on the second floor were arranged according to his fancy, they
made a tremendous show. He had a large Gothic chest, in which
he put his wardrobe (namely, two velvet waistcoats, four varied satin
under ditto, two pairs braided trousers, two shirts, half-a-dozen false
collars, and a couple of pairs of dreadfully dilapidated Blucher
boots). He had some pieces of armour ; some China jugs and
Venetian glasses ; some bits of old damask rags, to drape his doors
and windows : and a rickety lay figure, in a Spanish hat and cloak,

over which slung a long Toledo rapier, and a guitar, with a riband of
dirty sky-blue.

Such was our poor fellow's stock in trade. He had some volumes
of poems—" Lalla Rookh," and the sterner compositions of Byron .
for, to do him justice, he hated " Don Juan," and a woman was in
his eyes an angel; a *h*angel, alas! he would call her, for nature and
the circumstances of his family had taken sad Cockney advantages
over Andrea's pronunciation.

The Misses Wellesley Macarty were not, however, very squeamish
with regard to grammar, and, in this dull season, voted Mr. Fitch an
elegant young fellow. His immense beard and whiskers gave them
the highest opinion of his genius; and before long the intimacy
between the young people was considerable, for Mr. Fitch insisted
upon drawing the portraits of the whole family. He painted
Mrs. Gann in her rouge and ribands, as described by Mr, Brandon ;
Mr. Gann, who said that his picture would be very useful to the artist,
as every soul in Margate knew him ; and the Misses Macarty (a neat
group, representing Miss Bella embracing Miss Linda, who was
pointing to a pianoforte.)

" I suppose you'll do my Carry next ?" said Mr. Gann, expressing
his approbation of the last picture.

" Law, sir," said Miss Linda, " Carry, with her red hair !—it
would be *ojus*."

" Mr. Fitch might as well paint Becky, our maid," said Miss
Bella.

" Carry is quite impossible, Gann," said Mrs. Gann ; " she hasn't
a gown fit to be seen in. She's not been at church for thirteen
Sundays in consequence."

" And more shame for you, ma'am," said Mr. Gann, who liked his
child ; " Carry *shall* have a gown, and the best of gowns." And
jingling three and twenty shillings in his pocket, Mr. Gann determined to spend them all in the purchase of a robe for Carry. But
alas, the gown never came ; half the money was spent that very
evening at the " Bag of Nails."

" Is that—that young lady, your daughter ?" said Mr. Fitch, surprised, for he fancied Carry was a humble companion of the family.

" Yes, she is, and a very good daughter, too, sir," answered
Mr. Gann. *Fetch* and Carry I call her, or else Carryvan—she's so
useful. Ain't you, Carry ?"

"I'm very glad if I am, papa," said the young lady, who was blushing violently, and in whose presence all this conversation had been carried on.

"Hold your tongue, miss," said her mother; "you are very expensive to us, that you are, and need not brag about the work you do. You would not live on charity, would you, like some folks?" (here she looked fiercely at Mr. Gann); "and if your sisters and me starve to keep you and some folks, I presume you are bound to make us some return."

When any allusion was made to Mr. Gann's idleness and extravagance, or his lady showed herself in any way inclined to be angry, it was honest James's habit not to answer, but to take his hat and walk abroad to the public-house; or if haply she scolded him at night, he would turn his back and fall a-snoring. These were the only remedies he found for Mrs. James's bad temper, and the first of them he adopted on hearing these words of his lady, which we have just now transcribed.

Poor Caroline had not her father's refuge of flight, but was obliged to stay and listen; and a wondrous eloquence, God wot! had Mrs. Gann upon the subject of her daughter's ill-conduct. The first lecture Mr. Fitch heard, he set down Caroline for, a monster. Was she not idle, sulky, scornful, and a sloven? For these and many more of her daughter's vices Mrs. Gann vouched, declaring that Caroline's misbehaviour was hastening ,her own death, and finishing by a fainting-fit. In the presence of all these charges, there stood Miss Caroline, dumb, stupid, and careless; nay, when the fainting-fit came on, and Mrs. Gann fell back on the sofa, the unfeeling girl took the opportunity to retire, and never offered to smack her mamma's hands, to give her the smelling-bottle, or to restore her with a glass of water.

One stood close at hand; for Mr. Fitch, when this first fit occurred, was sitting in the Gann parlour, painting that lady's portrait; and he was making towards her with his tumbler, when Miss Linda cried out, "Stop! the water's full of paint;" and straightway burst out laughing. Mrs. Gann jumped up at this, cured suddenly, and left the room, looking somewhat foolish.

"You don't know Ma," said Miss Linda, still giggling; "she's always fainting."

"Poor thing!" cried Fitch; "very nervous, I suppose?"

"Oh, very!" answered the lady, exchanging arch glances with Miss Bella.

"Poor dear lady!" continued the artist; "I pity her from my hinmost soul. Doesn't the himmortal bard of Havon observe, how sharper than a serpent's tooth it is to have a thankless child? And is it true, ma'am, that that young woman has been the ruin of her family?"

"Ruin of her fiddlestick!" replied Miss Bella. "Law, Mr. Fitch, you don't know Ma yet; she is in one of her tantrums."

"What, then, it *isn't* true?" cried simple-minded Fitch. To which neither of the young ladies made any answer in words, nor could the little artist comprehend why they looked at each other, and burst out laughing. But he retired pondering on what he had seen and heard; and being a very soft young fellow, most implicitly believed the accusations of poor dear Mrs. Gann, and thought her daughter Caroline was no better than a Regan or Goneril.

A time, however, was to come when he should believe her to be a most pure and gentle Cordelia; and of this change in Fitch's opinions we shall speak in Chapter III.

CHAPTER III.

A SHABBY GENTEEL DINNER, AND OTHER INCIDENTS OF A LIKE NATURE.

MR. BRANDON's letter to Lord Cinqbars produced, as we have said, a great impression upon the family of Gann; an impression which was considerably increased by their lodger's subsequent behaviour: for although the persons with whom he now associated were of a very vulgar, ridiculous kind, they were by no means so low or ridiculous that Mr. Brandon should not wish to appear before them in the most advantageous light; and, accordingly, he gave himself the greatest airs when in their company, and bragged incessantly of his acquaintance and familiarity with the nobility. Mr. Brandon was a tuft-hunter of the genteel sort; his pride being quite as slavish, and his haughtiness as mean and cringeing, in fact, as poor Mrs. Gann's stupid wonder and respect for all the persons whose names are written with titles before them. O free and happy Britons, what a miserable, truckling, cringeing race ye are !

The reader has no doubt encountered a number of such swaggerers in the course of his conversation with the world—men of a decent middle rank, who affect to despise it, and herd only with persons of the fashion. This is an offence in a man which none of us can forgive ; we call him tuft-hunter, lickspittle, sneak, unmanly ; we hate, and profess to despise him. I fear it is no such thing. We envy Lickspittle, that is the fact ; and therefore hate him. Were he to plague us with the stories of Jones and Brown, our familiars, the man would be a simple bore, his stories heard patiently ; but so soon as he talks of my lord or the duke, we are in arms against him. I have seen a whole merry party in Russell Square grow suddenly gloomy and dumb, because a pert barrister, in a loud, shrill voice, told a story of Lord This or the Marquis of That. We all hated that man ; and I would lay a wager that every one of the fourteen persons assembled round the boiled turkey and saddle of mutton (not to mention side-dishes from the pastrycook's opposite the British Museum)—I would wager, I say, that every one was muttering inwardly, " A plague on that fellow ! he knows a lord, and I never spoke to more than three in the whole course of my life." To our betters we can reconcile ourselves, if you please, respecting them very sincerely, laughing at their jokes, making allowance for their stupidities, meekly suffering their insolence ; but we can't pardon our equals going beyond us. A friend of mine who lived amicably and happily among his friends and relatives at Hackney, was on a sudden disowned by the latter, cut by the former, and doomed in innumerable prophecies to ruin, because he kept a footboy,—a harmless little blowsy-faced urchin, in light snuff-coloured clothes, glistering over with sugar-loaf buttons. There is another man, a great man, a literary man, whom the public loves, and who took a sudden leap from obscurity into fame and wealth. This was a crime ; but he bore his rise with so much modesty, that even his brethren of the pen did not envy him. One luckless day he set up a one-horse chaise ; from that minute he was doomed.

" Have you seen his new carriage ? " says Snarley.

" Yes," says Yow ; " he's so consumedly proud of it, that he can't see his old friends while he drives."

"Ith it a donkey-cart," lisps Simper, "thith gwand cawwaige? I always thaid that the man, from hith thtile, wath fitted to be a vewy dethent cothtermonger."

"Yes, yes," cries old Candour, "a sad pity indeed!—dreadfully extravagant, I'm told—bad health—expensive family—works going down every day—and now he must set up a carriage forsooth!"

Snarley, Yow, Simper, Candour, hate their brother. If he is ruined, they will be kind to him and just; but he is successful, and woe be to him!

*   *   *   *   *

This trifling digression of half a page or so, although it seems to have nothing to do with the story in hand, has, nevertheless, the strongest relation to it; and you shall hear what.

In one word, then, Mr. Brandon bragged so much, and assumed such airs of superiority, that after a while he perfectly disgusted Mrs. Gann and the Misses Macarty, who were gentlefolks themselves, and did not at all like his way of telling them that he was their better. Mr. Fitch was swallowed up in his hart as he called it, and cared nothing for Brandon's airs. Gann, being a low-spirited fellow, completely submitted to Mr. Brandon, and looked up to him with deepest wonder. And poor little Caroline followed her father's faith, and in six weeks after Mr. Brandon's arrival at the lodgings had grown to believe him the most perfect, finished, polished, agreeable of mankind. Indeed, the poor girl had never seen a gentleman before, and towards such her gentle heart turned instinctively. Brandon never offended her by hard words; insulted her by cruel scorn, such as she met with from her mother and her sisters; there was a quiet manner about the man quite different to any that she had before seen amongst the acquaintances of her family; and if he assumed a tone of superiority in his conversation with her and the rest, Caroline felt that he *was* their superior, and as such admired and respected him.

What happens when in the innocent bosom of a girl of sixteen such sensations arise? What has happened ever since the world began?

I have said that Miss Caroline had no friend in the world but her father, and must here take leave to recall that assertion;—a friend she most certainly had, and that was honest Becky, the smutty maid, whose name has been mentioned before. Miss Caroline had learned, in the course of a life spent under the tyranny of her mamma, some of the notions of the latter, and would have been very much offended to call Becky her friend : but friends, in fact, they were ; and a great comfort it was for Caroline to descend to the calm kitchen from the stormy back-parlour, and there vent some of her little woes to the compassionate servant of all work.

When Mrs. Gann went out with her daughters, Becky would take her work and come and keep Miss Caroline company ; and if the truth must be told, the greatest enjoyment the pair used to have was in these afternoons, when they read together out of the precious greasy, marble-covered volumes that Mrs. Gann was in the habit of fetching from the library. Many and many a tale had the pair so gone through. I can see them over " Manfrone ; or the One-handed Monk "—the room dark, the street silent, the hour ten—the tall, red, lurid candlewick waggling down, the flame flickering pale upon Miss Caroline's pale face as she read out, and lighting up honest Becky's goggling eyes, who sat silent, her work in her lap : she had not done a stitch of it for an hour. As the trap-door slowly opens, and the scowling Alonzo, bending over the sleeping Imoinda, draws his pistol, cocks it, looks well if the priming be right, places it then to the sleeper's ear, and—*thunder-under-under*—down fall the snuffers ! Becky has had them in her hand for ten minutes, afraid to use them. Up starts Caroline, and flings the book back into her mamma's basket. It is that lady returned with her daughters from a tea-party, where two young gents from London have been mighty genteel indeed.

For the sentimental, too, as well as for the terrible, Miss Caroline and the cook had a strong predilection, and had wept their poor eyes out over " Thaddeus of Warsaw " and the " Scottish Chiefs." Fortified by the examples drawn from those instructive volumes, Becky was firmly convinced that her young mistress would meet with a great lord some day or other, or be carried off, like Cinderella, by a brilliant prince, to the mortification of her elder sisters, whom Becky hated. And when, therefore, the new lodger came, lonely, mysterious, melancholy, elegant, with the romantic name of George Brandon—when he wrote a letter directed to a lord, and Miss Caroline and Becky together examined the superscription, such a look passed between them as the pencil of Leslie or Maclise could alone describe for us. Becky's orbs were lighted up with a preternatural look of wondering wisdom ; whereas, after an instant, Caroline dropped hers, and blushed, and said, " Nonsense, Becky ! "

" *Is* it nonsense ? " said Becky, grinning and snapping her fingers with a triumphant air ; " the cards comes true ; I knew they would. Didn't you have king and queen of hearts three deals running? What did you dream about last Tuesday, tell me that ? "

But Miss Caroline never did tell, for her sisters came bouncing down the stairs, and examined the lodger's letter. Caroline, however, went away musing much upon these points; and she began to think Mr. Brandon more wonderful and beautiful every day.

In the meantime, while Miss Caroline was innocently indulging in her inclination for the brilliant occupier of the first floor, it came . to pass that the tenant of the second was inflamed by a most romantic passion for her.

For, after partaking for about a fortnight of the family dinner, and passing some evenings with Mrs. Gann and the young ladies, Mr. Fitch, though by no means quick of comprehension, began to perceive that the nightly charges that were brought against poor Caroline could not be founded upon truth. " Let's see," mused he to himself. " Tuesday, the old lady said her daughter was bringing her grey hairs with sorrow to the grave, because the cook had not boiled the potatoes. Wednesday, she said Caroline was an assassin, because she could not find her own thimble. Thursday, she vows Caroline has no religion, because that old pair of silk stockings were not darned. And this can't be," reasoned Fitch, deeply. " A gal haint a murderess because her Ma can't find her thimble. A woman that goes to slap her grown-up daughter on the back, and before company too, for such a paltry thing as a hold pair of stockings, can't be surely a-speaking the truth." And thus gradually his first impression against Caroline wore away. As this disappeared, pity took possession of his soul— and we know what pity is akin to ; and, at the same time, a corresponding hatred for the oppressors of a creature so amiable.

To sum up, in six short weeks after the appearance of the two gentlemen, we find our chief *dramatis personæ* as follows :

> CAROLINE, an innocent young woman, in love with BRANDON.
>
> FITCH, a celebrated painter, almost in love with CAROLINE.
>
> BRANDON, a young gentleman, in love with himself.

At first he was pretty constant in his attendance upon the Misses Macarty when they went out to walk, nor were they displeased at his attentions; but he found that there were a great number of Margate beaux—ugly, vulgar fellows as ever were—who always followed in the young ladies' train, and made themselves infinitely more agreeable than he was. These men Mr. Brandon treated with a great deal of scorn : and, in return, they hated him cordially. So did the ladies speedily : his haughty manners, though quite as impertinent and free, were not half so pleasant to them as Jones's jokes or Smith's charming romps; and the girls gave Brandon very shortly to understand that they were much happier without him. "Ladies, your humble," he heard Bob Smith say, as that little linendraper came skipping to the door from which they were issuing. "The sun's hup and trade is down; if you're for a walk, I'm your man." And Miss Linda and Miss Bella each took an arm of Mr. Smith, and sailed down the street. "I'm glad you ain't got that proud gent with the glass hi," said Mr. Smith; "he's the most hillbred, supercilious beast I ever see."

"So he is," says Bella.

"Hush !" says Linda.

The "proud gent with the glass hi" was at this moment lolling out of the first-floor window, smoking his accustomed cigar ; and his eyeglass was fixed upon the ladies, to whom he made a very low bow. It may be imagined how fond he was of them afterwards, and what looks he cast at Mr. Bob Smith the next time he met him. Mr. Bob's heart beat for a day afterwards; and he found he had business in town.

But the love of society is stronger than even pride ; and the great Mr. Brandon was sometimes fain to descend from his high station and consort with the vulgar family with whom he lodged. But, as we have said, he always did this with a wonderfully condescending air, giving his associates to understand how great was the honour he did them.

One day, then, he was absolutely so kind as to accept of an invitation from the ground-floor, which was delivered in the passage by Mr. James Gann, who said, "It was hard to see a gent eating mutton-chops from week's end to week's end ; and if Mr. Brandon had a mind to meet a devilish good fellow as ever was, my friend Swigby, a man who rides his horse, and has his five hundred a year to spend, and to eat a prime cut out of as good a leg of pork (though he said it) as ever a knife was stuck into, they should dine that day at three o'clock sharp, and Mrs. G. and the gals would be glad of the honour of his company."

The person so invited was rather amused at the terms in which Mr. Gann conveyed his hospitable message; and at three o'clock made his appearance in the back-parlour, whence he had the honour of conducting Mrs. Gann (dressed in a sweet yellow *mousseline de laine*, with a large red turban, a *ferronnière*, and a smelling-bottle attached by a ring to a very damp, fat hand) to the "office," where the repast was set out. The Misses Macarty were in costumes equally tasty: one on the guest's right hand; one near the boarder, Mr. Fitch—who, in a large beard, an amethyst velvet-waistcoat, his hair fresh wetted, and parted accurately down the middle to fall in curls over his collar, would have been irresistible if the collar had been a little, little whiter than it was.

Mr. Brandon, too, was dressed in his very best suit; for though he affected to despise his hosts very much, he wished to make the most favourable impression upon them, and took care to tell Mrs. Gann that he and Lord So-and-so were the only two men in the world who were in possession of that particular waistcoat which she admired: for Mrs. Gann was very gracious, and had admired the waistcoat, being desirous to impress with awe Mr. Gann's friend and admirer, Mr. Swigby—who, man of fortune as he was, was a constant frequenter of the club at the "Bag of Nails."

About this club and its supporters Mr. Gann's guest, Mr. Swigby, and Gann himself, talked very gaily before dinner; all the jokes about all the club being roared over by the pair.

Mr. Brandon, who felt he was the great man of the party, indulged himself in his great propensities without restraint, and told Mrs. Gann stories about half the nobility. Mrs. Gann conversed knowingly about the Opera; and declared that she thought Taglioni the sweetest singer in the world.

"Mr.—a—Swigby, have you ever seen Lablache dance?" asked Mr. Brandon of that gentleman, to whom he had been formally introduced.

"At Vauxhall is he?" said Mr. Swigby, who was just from town.

"Yes, on the tight-rope; a charming performer."

On which Mr. Gann told how he had been to Vauxhall when

the princes were in London ; and his lady talked of these knowingly. And then they fell to conversing about fireworks and rack-punch ; Mr. Brandon assuring the young ladies that Vauxhall was the very pink of the fashion, and longing to have the honour of dancing a quadrille with them there.   Indeed, Brandon was so very sarcastic, that not a single soul at table understood him.

The table, from Mr. Brandon's plan of it, which was afterwards sent to my Lord Cinqbars, was arranged as follows :—

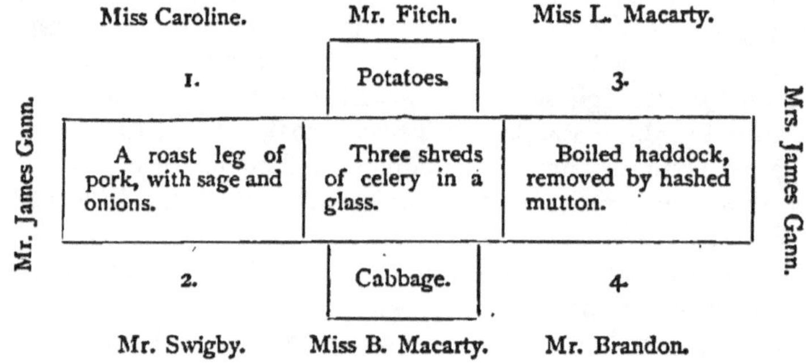

Miss Caroline.	Mr. Fitch.	Miss L. Macarty.
1.	Potatoes.	3.
A roast leg of pork, with sage and onions.	Three shreds of celery in a glass.	Boiled haddock, removed by hashed mutton.
2.	Cabbage.	4.
Mr. Swigby.	Miss B. Macarty.	Mr. Brandon.

(Mr. James Gann at the left end of the table; Mrs. James Gann at the right end.)

1 and 2 are pots of porter; 3, a quart of ale, Mrs. Gann's favourite drink ; 4, a bottle of fine old golden sherry, the real produce of the Uva grape, purchased at the " Bag of Nails " Hotel for 1*s.* 9*d.* by Mr. J. Gann.

Mr. Gann. " Taste that sherry, sir.   Your 'ealth, and my services to you, sir.   That wine, sir, is given me as a particular favour by my—ahem !—my wine-merchant, who only will part with a small quantity of it, and imports it direct, sir, from—ahem !—from——"

Mr. Brandon. " From Xeres, of course.   It is, I really think, the finest wine I ever tasted in my life—at a commoner's table, that is."

Mrs. Gann. " Oh, in course, a commoner's table !—we have no titles, sir, (Mr. Gann, I will trouble you for some more crackling,) though my poor dear girls are related, by their blessed father's side, to some of the first nobility in the land, I assure you."

Mr. Gann. " Gammon, Jooly my dear.   Them Irish nobility, you know, what are they ?   And besides, it's my belief that the gals are no more related to them than I am."

Miss Bella (to Mr. Brandon, confidentially). "You must find that poor Par is sadly vulgar, Mr. Brandon."

Mrs. Gann. "Mr. Brandon has never been accustomed to such language, I am sure; and I entreat you will excuse Mr. Gann's rudeness, sir."

Miss Linda. "Indeed, I assure you, Mr. Brandon, that we've high connexions as well as low; as high as some people's connexions, per'aps, though we are not always talking of the nobility." This was a double shot: the first barrel of Miss Linda's sentence hit her stepfather, the second part was levelled directly at Mr. Brandon. "Don't you think I'm right, Mr. Fitch?"

Mr. Brandon. "You are quite right, Miss Linda, in this as in every other instance; but I am afraid Mr. Fitch has not paid proper attention to your excellent remark: for, if I don't mistake the meaning of that beautiful design which he has made with his fork upon the tablecloth, his soul is at this moment wrapped up in his art."

This was exactly what Mr. Fitch wished that all the world should suppose. He flung back his hair, and stared wildly for a moment, and said, "Pardon me, madam: it is true my thoughts were at that moment far away in the regions of my hart." He was really thinking that his attitude was a very elegant one, and that a large garnet ring which he wore on his forefinger must be mistaken by all the company for a ruby.

"Art is very well," said Mr. Brandon; "but with such pretty natural objects before you, I wonder you were not content to think of them."

"Do you mean the mashed potatoes, sir?" said Andrea Fitch, wondering.

"I mean Miss Rosalind Macarty," answered Brandon, gallantly, and laughing heartily at the painter's simplicity. But this compliment could not soften Miss Linda, who had an uneasy conviction that Mr. Brandon was laughing at her, and disliked him accordingly.

At this juncture, Miss Caroline entered and took the place marked as hers, to the left hand of Mr. Gann, vacant. An old rickety wooden stool was placed for her, instead of that elegant and commodious Windsor chair which supported every other person at table; and by the side of the plate stood a curious old battered tin mug, on which the antiquarian might possibly discover the inscription of the word " Caroline." This, in truth, was poor Caroline's mug and stool, having been appropriated to her from childhood upwards; and here it was her custom meekly to sit, and eat her daily meal.

It was well that the girl was placed near her father, else I do believe she would have been starved; but Gann was much too good-natured to allow that any difference should be made between her and her sisters. There are some meannesses which are too mean even for man—woman, lovely woman alone, can venture to commit them. Well, on the present occasion, and when the dinner was half over, poor Caroline stole gently into the room and took her ordinary place. Caroline's pale face was very red; for the fact must be told that she had been in the kitchen helping Becky, the universal maid; and having heard how the great Mr. Brandon was to dine with them upon that day, the simple girl had been showing her respect for him, by compiling, in her best manner, a certain dish, for the cooking of which her papa had often praised her. She took her place, blushing violently when she saw him, and if Mr. Gann had not been making a violent clattering with his knife and fork, it is possible that he might have heard Miss Caroline's heart thump, which it did violently. Her dress was somehow a little smarter than usual; and Becky the maid, who brought in that remove of hashed mutton which has been set down in the bill of fare, looked at her young lady with a good deal of complacency, as, loaded with plates, she quitted the room. Indeed, the poor girl deserved to be looked at: there was an air of gentleness and innocence about her that was apt to please some persons, much more than the bold beauties of her sisters. The two young men did not fail to remark this; one of them, the little painter, had long since observed it.

"You are very late, miss," cried Mrs. Gann, who affected not to know what had caused her daughter's delay. "You're always late!" and the elder girls stared and grinned at each other knowingly, as they always did when mamma made such attacks upon Caroline, who only kept her eyes down upon the tablecloth, and began to eat her dinner without saying a word.

"Come, my dear," cried honest Gann, "if she is late you know why. A girl can't be here and there too, as I say; can they, Swigby?"

"Impossible!" said Swigby.

"Gents," continued Mr. Gann, " our Carry, you must know, has been downstairs, making the pudding for her old pappy ; and a good pudding she makes, I can tell you."

Miss Caroline blushed more vehemently than ever ; the artist stared her full in the face ; Mrs. Gann said, " Nonsense " and " stuff," very majestically ; only Mr. Brandon interposed in Caroline's favour.

" I would sooner that my wife should know how to make a pudding," said he, " than how to play the best piece of music in the world ! "

" Law, Mr. Brandon ! I, for my part, wouldn't demean myself by any such kitchen-work ! " cries Miss Linda.

" Make puddens, indeed ; it's ojous ! " cries Bella.

" For you, my loves, of course ! " interposed their mamma. " Young women of your family and circumstances is not expected to perform any such work. It's different with Miss Caroline, who, if she does make herself useful now and then, don't make herself near so useful as she should, considering that she's not a shilling, and is living on our charity, like some other folks."

Thus did this amiable woman neglect no opportunity to give her opinions about her husband and daughter. The former, however, cared not a straw ; and the latter, in this instance, was perfectly happy. Had not kind Mr. Brandon approved of her work ; and could she ask for more ?

" Mamma may say what she pleases to-day," thought Caroline. " I am too happy to be made angry by her."

Poor little mistaken Caroline, to think you were safe against three women ! The dinner had not advanced much further, when Miss Isabella, who had been examining her younger sister curiously for some short time, telegraphed Miss Linda across the table, and nodded, and winked, and pointed to her own neck ; a very white one, as I have before had the honour to remark, and quite without any covering, except a smart necklace of twenty-four rows of the lightest blue glass beads, finishing in a neat tassel. Linda had a similar ornament of a vermilion colour ; whereas Caroline, on this occasion, wore a handsome new collar up to the throat, and a brooch, which looked all the smarter for the shabby frock over which they were placed. As soon as she saw her sister's signals, the poor little thing, who had only just done fluttering and blushing, fell to this same work over again. Down went her eyes once more, and her face and neck lighted up to the colour of Miss Linda's sham cornelian.

"What's the gals giggling and ogling about?" said Mr. Gann, innocently.

"What is it, my darling loves?" said stately Mrs. Gann.

"Why, don't you see, Ma?" said Linda. "Look at Miss Carry! I'm blessed if *she has not got on Becky's collar and brooch* that Sims the pilot gave her!"

The young ladies fell back in uproarious fits of laughter, and laughed all the time that their mamma was thundering out a speech, in which she declared that her daughter's conduct was unworthy a gentlewoman, and bid her leave the room and take off those disgraceful ornaments.

There was no need to tell her; the poor little thing gave one piteous look at her father, who was whistling, and seemed indeed to think the matter a good joke; and after she had managed to open the door and totter into the passage, you might have heard her weeping there, weeping tears more bitter than any of the many she had shed in the course of her life. Down she went to the kitchen, and when she reached that humble place of refuge, first pulled at her neck and made as if she would take off Becky's collar and brooch, and then flung herself into the arms of that honest scullion, where she cried and cried till she brought on the first fit of hysterics that ever she had had.

This crying could not at first be heard in the parlour, where the young ladies, Mrs. Gann, Mr. Gann, and his friend from the "Bag of Nails" were roaring at the excellence of the joke. Mr. Brandon, sipping sherry, sat by, looking very sarcastically and slyly from one party to the other; Mr. Fitch was staring about him too, but with a very different expression, anger and wonder inflaming his bearded countenance. At last, as the laughing died away and a faint voice of weeping came from the kitchen below, Andrew could bear it no longer, but bounced up from his chair and rushed out of the room exclaiming,—

"By Jove, it's too bad!"

"What does the man mean?" said Mrs. Gann.

He meant that he was from that moment over head and ears in love with Caroline, and that he longed to beat, buffet, pummel, thump, tear to pieces, those callous ruffians who so pitilessly laughed at her.

" What's that chop wi' the beard in such tantrums about?" said the gentleman from the " Bag of Nails."

Mr. Gann answered this query by some joke, intimating that "per'aps Mr. Fitch's dinner did not agree with him," at which these worthies roared again.

The young ladies said, " Well, now, upon my word ! "

" Mighty genteel behaviour truly ! " cried mamma ; " but what can you expect from the poor thing ? "

Brandon only sipped more sherry, but he looked at Fitch as the latter flung out of the room, and his countenance was lighted up by a more unequivocal smile.

*   *   *   *   *   *

These two little adventures were followed by a silence of some few minutes, during which the meats remained on the table, and no signs were shown of that pudding upon which poor Caroline had exhausted her skill. The absence of this delicious part of the repast was first remarked by Mr. Gann ; and his lady, after jangling at the bell for some time in vain, at last begged one of her daughters to go and hasten matters.

" BECKY ! " shrieked Miss Linda from the hall, but Becky replied not. " Becky, are we to be kept waiting all day ? " continued the lady in the same shrill voice. " Mamma wants the pudding ! "

" TELL HER TO FETCH IT HERSELF ! " roared Becky, at which remark Gann and his facetious friend once more went off into fits of laughter.

" This is too bad ! " said Mrs. G., starting up ; " she shall leave the house this instant ! " and so no doubt Becky would, but that the lady owed her five quarters' wages ; which she, at that period, did not feel inclined to pay.

Well, the dinner at last was at an end ; the ladies went away to tea, leaving the gentlemen to their wine ; Brandon, very condescendingly, partaking of a bottle of port, and listening with admiration to the toasts and sentiments with which it is still the custom among persons of Mr Gann's rank of life to preface each glass of wine. As thus :—

Glass 1. " Gents," says Mr. Gann, rising, " this glass I need say nothink about. Here's the king, and long life to him and the family ! "

3—2

Mr. Swigby, with his glass, goes knock, knock, knock on the table; and saying gravely, "The king!" drinks off his glass, and smacks his lips afterwards.

Mr. Brandon, who had drunk half his, stops in the midst and says, "Oh, ' the king!'"

Mr. Swigby. "A good glass of wine that, Gann my boy!"

Mr. Brandon. "Capital, really; though, upon my faith, I'm no judge of port."

Mr. Gann (smacks). "A fine fruity wine as ever I tasted. I suppose you, Mr. B., are accustomed only to claret. I've 'ad it, too, in my time, sir, as Swigby there very well knows. I travelled, sir, *sure le Continong,* I assure you, and drank my glass of claret with the best man in France, or England either. I wasn't always what I am, sir."

Mr. Brandon. "You don't look as if you were."

Mr. Gann. "No, sir. Before that —— gas came in, I was head, sir, of one of the fust 'ouses in the hoil-trade, Gann, Blubbery & Gann, sir—Thames Street, City. I'd my box at Putney, as good a gig and horse as my friend there drives."

Mr. Swigby. "Ay, and a better too, Gann, I make no doubt."

Mr. Gann. "Well, *say* a better. I *had* a better, if money could fetch it, sir; and I didn't spare that, I warrant you. No, no, James Gann didn't grudge his purse, sir; and had his friends around him, as he's 'appy to 'ave now, sir. Mr. Brandon, your 'ealth, sir, and may we hoften meet under this ma'ogany. Swigby my boy, God bless you!"

Mr. Brandon. "Your very good health."

Mr. Swigby. "Thank you, Gann. Here's to you, and long life and prosperity and happiness to you and yours. Bless you, Jim my boy; heaven bless you! I say this, Mr. Bandon—Brandon—what's your name—there ain't a better fellow in all Margate than James Gann,—no, nor in all England. · Here's Mrs. Gann, gents, and the family. MRS. GANN!" (*drinks.*)

Mr. Brandon. "MRS. GANN. Hip, hip, hurrah!" (*drinks.*)

Mr. Gann. "Mrs. Gann, and thank you, gents. A fine woman, Mr. B.; ain't she now? Ah, if you'd seen 'er when I married her! Gad, she *was* fine then—an out and outer, sir! *Such* a figure!"

Mr. Swigby. "You'd choose none but a good 'un, I war'nt. Ha, ha, ha!"

Mr. Gann. " Did I ever tell you of my duel along with the regi mental doctor? No ! Then I will. I was a young chap, you see, in those days ; and when I saw her at Brussels—(*Brusell*, they call it)—I was right slick up over head and ears in love with her at once. But what was to be done ? There was another gent in the case—a regimental doctor, sir—a reg'lar dragon. ' Faint heart,' says I, ' never won a fair lady,' and so I made so bold. She took me, sent the doctor to the right about. I met him one morning in the park at Brussels, and stood to him, sir, like a man. When the affair was over, my second, a leftenant of dragoons, told me, ' Gann,' says he, ' I've seen many a man under fire—I'm a Waterloo man,' says he,— · ' and have rode by Wellington many a long day ; but I never, for coolness, see such a man as you.' Gents, here's the Duke of Wellington and the British army !" (*the gents drink.*)

Mr. Brandon. " Did you kill the doctor, sir ? "

Mr. Gann. " Why, no, sir ; I shot in the hair."

Mr. Brandon. " Shot him in the hair ! Egad, that was a severe shot, and a very lucky escape the doctor had of it ? Whereabout in the hair ? a whisker, sir ; or, perhaps, a pig-tail ? "

Mr. Swigby. " Haw, haw, haw ! shot'n in the *hair*—capital, capital ! "

Mr. Gann, who has grown very red. " No, sir, there may be some mistake in my pronounciation, which I didn't expect to have laughed at, at my hown table."

Mr. Brandon. " My dear sir ! I protest and vow——"

Mr. Gann. " Never mind it, sir. I gave you my best, and did my best to make you welcome. If you like better to make fun of me, do, sir. That may be the *genteel* way, but hang me if it's *hour* way ; is it, Jack ? *Our* way ; I beg your pardon, sir."

Mr. Swigby. " Jim, Jim ! for heaven's sake !—peace and harmony of the evening—conviviality—social enjoyment—didn't mean it—did you mean anything, Mr. What-d'-ye-call-'im ? "

Mr. Brandon. " Nothing, upon my honour as a gentleman ! "

Mr. Gann. " Well, then, there's my hand !" and good-natured Gann tried to forget the insult, and to talk as if nothing had occurred: but he had been wounded in the most sensitive point in which a man can be touched by his superior, and never forgot Brandon's joke. That night at the club, when dreadfully tipsy, he made several speeches on the subject, and burst into tears many times. The pleasure of the evening was quite spoiled; and, as the conversation became rapid and dull, we shall refrain from reporting it. Mr. Brandon speedily took leave, but had not the courage to face the ladies at tea; to whom, it appears, the reconciled Becky had brought that refreshing beverage.

CHAPTER IV.

IN WHICH MR. FITCH PROCLAIMS HIS LOVE, AND MR. BRANDON PREPARES FOR WAR.

FROM the splendid hall in which Mrs. Gann was dispensing her hospitality, the celebrated painter, Andrea Fitch, rushed forth in a state of mind even more delirious than that which he usually enjoyed. He looked abroad into the street: all there was dusk and lonely; the rain falling heavily, the wind playing Pandean pipes and whistling down the chimney-pots. "I love the storm," said Fitch, solemnly; and he put his great Spanish cloak round him in the most approved manner (it was of so prodigious a size that the tail of it, as it twirled over his shoulder, whisked away a lodging-card from the door of the house opposite Mr. Gann's.) "I love the storm and solitude," said he, lighting a large pipe filled full of the fragrant Oronooko; and thus armed, he passed rapidly down the street, his hat cocked over his ringlets.

Andrea did not like smoking, but he used a pipe as a part of his profession as an artist, and as one of the picturesque parts of his costume; in like manner, though he did not fence, he always travelled about with a pair of foils; and quite unconscious of music, nevertheless had a guitar constantly near at hand. Without such properties a painter's spectacle is not complete; and now he determined to add to them another indispensable requisite—a mistress. "What great artist was ever without one?" thought he. Long, long had he sighed for some one whom he might love, some one to whom he might address the poems which he was in the habit of making. Hundreds of such fragments had he composed, addressed to Leila, Ximena, Ada—imaginary beauties, whom he courted in dreamy verse. With what joy would he replace all those by a real charmer of flesh and blood! Away he went, then, on this evening—the tyranny of Mrs. Gann towards poor Caroline having awakened all his sympathies in the gentle girl's favour—determined now and for ever to make her the mistress of his heart. Monna-Lisa, the Fornarina, Leonardo, Raphael—he thought of all these, and vowed that his Caroline should be made famous and live for ever on his canvas. While Mrs. Gann was preparing for her friends, and enter taining them at tea and whist; while Caroline, all unconscious of the love she inspired, was weeping upstairs in her little garret; while Mr. Brandon was enjoying the refined conversation of Gann and Swigby, over their glass and pipe in the office, Andrea walked abroad by the side of the ocean; and, before he was wet through, walked himself into the most fervid affection for poor persecuted Caroline. The reader might have observed him (had not the night been very dark, and a great deal too wet to allow a sensible reader to go abroad on such an errand) at the sea-shore standing on a rock, and drawing from his bosom a locket which contained a curl of hair tied up in riband. He looked at it for a moment, and then flung it away from him into the black boiling waters below him.

"No other 'air but thine, Caroline, shall ever rest near this 'art!" he said, and kissed the locket and restored it to its place. Light-minded youth, whose hair was it that he thus flung away? How many times had Andrea shown that very ringlet in strictest confidence to several brethren of the brush, and declared that it was the hair of a dear girl in Spain whom he loved to madness? Alas! 'twas but a fiction of his fevered brain; every one of his friends had a locket of hair, and Andrea, who had no love until now, had clipped this precious token from the wig of a lovely lay-figure, with cast-iron joints and a card-board head, that had stood for some time in his atelier. I don't know that he felt any shame about the proceeding, for he was of such a warm imagination that he had grown to believe that the hair did actually come from a girl in Spain, and only parted with it on yielding to a superior attachment.

This attachment being fixed on, the young painter came home wet through; passed the night in reading Byron; making sketches, and burning them; writing poems to Caroline, and expunging them with pitiless india-rubber. A romantic man makes a point of sitting up all night, and pacing his chamber; and you may see many a composition of Andrea's dated "Midnight, 10th of March, A. F.," with his peculiar flourish over the initials. He was not sorry to be told in the morning, by the ladies at breakfast, that he looked dreadfully pale ; and answered, laying his hand on his forehead and shaking his head gloomily, that he could get no sleep : and then he would heave a huge sigh; and Miss Bella and Miss Linda would look at each other, and grin according to their wont. He was glad, I say, to have his woe remarked, and continued his sleeplessness for two or three nights ; but he was certainly still more glad when he heard Mr. Brandon, on the fourth morning, cry out, in a shrill angry voice, to Becky the maid, to give the gentleman upstairs his compliments—Mr. Brandon's compliments—and tell him that he could not get a wink of sleep for the horrid trampling he kept up. "I am hanged if I stay in the house a night longer," added the first floor sharply, "if that Mr. Fitch kicks up such a confounded noise !" Mr. Fitch's point was gained, and henceforth he was as quiet as a mouse ; for his wish was not only to be in love, but to let every-body know that he was in love, or where is the use of a *belle passion ?*

So, whenever he saw Caroline, at meals, or in the passage, he used to stare at her with the utmost power of his big eyes, and fall to groaning most pathetically. He used to leave his meals untasted, groan, heave sighs, and stare incessantly. Mrs. Gann and her eldest daughters were astonished at these manœuvres; for they never suspected that any man could possibly be such a fool as to fall in love with Caroline. At length the suspicion came upon them, created immense laughter and delight ; and the ladies did not fail to rally Caroline in their usual elegant way. Gann, too, loved a joke (much polite waggery had this worthy man practised in select inn-parlours for twenty years past), and would call poor Caroline "Mrs. F. ;" and say that, instead of *Fetch* and Carry, as he used to name her, he should style her *Fitch* and Carry for the future ; and laugh at this great pun, and make many others of a similar sort, that set Caroline blushing.

Indeed, the girl suffered a great deal more from this raillery than at first may be imagined ; for after the first awe inspired by Fitch's whiskers had passed away, and he had drawn the young ladies' pictures, and made designs in their albums, and in the midst of their jokes and conversation had remained perfectly silent, the Gann family had determined that the man was an idiot: and, indeed, were not very wide of the mark. In everything except his own peculiar art honest

Fitch *was* an idiot ; and as upon the subject of painting, the Ganns, like most people of their class in England, were profoundly ignorant, it came to pass that he would breakfast and dine for many days in their company, and not utter one single syllable. So they looked upon him with extreme pity and contempt, as a harmless, good-natured, crack-brained creature, quite below them in the scale of intellect, and only to be endured because he paid a certain number of shillings weekly to the Gann exchequer. Mrs. Gann in all companies was accustomed to talk about her idiot. Neighbours and children used to peer at him as he strutted down the street; and though every young lady, including my dear Caroline, is flattered by having a lover, at least they don't like such a lover as this. The Misses Macarty (after having set their caps at him very fiercely, and quarrelled concerning him on his first coming to lodge at their house) vowed and protested now that he was no better than a chimpanzee ; and Caroline and Becky agreed that this insult was as great as any that could be paid to the painter. "He's a good creature, too," said Becky, "crack-brained as he is. Do you know, miss, he gave me half a sovereign to buy a new collar, after that business t'other day?"

"And did—Mr.——,— did the first floor say anything?" asked Caroline.

"Didn't he! he's a funny gentleman, that Brandon, sure enough ; and when I took him up breakfast next morning, asked about Sims the pilot, and what I gi'ed Sims for the collar and brooch,—he, he!"

And this was indeed a correct report of Mr. Brandon's conversation with Becky; he had been infinitely amused with the whole transaction, and wrote his friend the viscount a capital facetious account of the manners and customs of the native inhabitants of the Isle of Thanet.

And now, when Mr. Fitch's passion was fully developed—as far, that is, as sighs and ogles could give it utterance—a curious instance of that spirit of contradiction for which our race is remarkable was seen in the behaviour of Mr. Brandon. Although Caroline, in the depths of her little silly heart, had set him down for her divinity, her wondrous fairy prince, who was to deliver her from her present miserable durance, she had never by word or deed acquainted Brandon with her inclination for him, but had, with instinctive modesty, avoided him more sedulously than before. He, too, had never bestowed a thought upon her. How should such a Jove as Mr. Brandon, from the cloudy summit of his fashionable Olympus, look down and perceive such an humble, retiring being as poor little Caroline Gann? Thinking her at first not disagreeable, he had never, until the day of the dinner, bestowed one single further thought upon her; and only when exasperated by the Miss Macartys' behaviour towards him, did he begin to think how sweet it would be to make them jealous and unhappy.

" The uncouth grinning monsters," said he, "with their horrible court of Bob Smiths and Jack Joneses, daring to look down upon me, a gentleman,—me, the celebrated *mangeur des cœurs*—a man of genius, fashion, and noble family! If I could but revenge myself on them ! What injury can I invent to wound them."

It is curious to what points a man in his passion will go. Mr. Brandon had long since, in fact, tried to do the greatest possible injury to the young ladies; for it had been, at the first dawn of his acquaintance, as we are bound with much sorrow to confess, his fixed intention to ruin one or the other of them. And when the young ladies had, by their coldness and indifference to him, frustrated this benevolent intention, he straightway fancied that they had injured him severely, and cast about for means to revenge himself upon them.

This point is, to be sure, a very delicate one to treat,—for in words, at least, the age has grown to be wonderfully moral, and refuses to hear discourses upon such subjects. But human nature, as far as I am able to learn, has not much changed since the time when Richardson wrote and Hogarth painted, a century ago. There are wicked Lovelaces abroad, ladies, now as then, when it was considered no shame to expose the rogues ; and pardon us, therefore, for hinting that such there be. Elegant acts of *rouerie*, such as that meditated by Mr. Brandon, are often performed still by dashing young men of the world, who think no sin of an *amourette*, but glory in it, especially if the victim be a person of mean condition. Had Brandon succeeded (such is the high moral state of our British youth), all his friends would have pronounced him, and he would have considered himself, to be a very lucky, captivating dog ; nor, as I believe, would he have had a single pang of conscience for the rascally action which he had committed. This supreme act of scoundrelism has man permitted to himself—to deceive women.

When we consider how he has availed himself of the privilege so created by him, indeed one may sympathize with the advocates of woman's rights who point out this monstrous wrong. We have read of that wretched woman of old whom the pious Pharisees were for stoning incontinently; but we don't hear that they made any outcry against *the man* who was concerned in the crime. Where was he? Happy, no doubt, and easy in mind, and regaling some choice friends over a bottle with the history of his success.

Being thus injured then, Mr. Brandon longed for revenge. How should' he repay these impertinent young women for slighting his addresses? "*Pardi,*" said he; "just to punish their pride and insolence, I have a great mind to make love to their sister."

He did not, however, for some time condescend to perform this threat. Eagles such as Brandon do not sail down from the clouds in order to pounce upon small flies, and soar airwards again, contented with such an ignoble booty. In a word, he never gave a minute's thought to Miss Caroline, until further circumstances occurred which caused this great man to consider her as an object somewhat worthy of his remark.

The violent affection suddenly exhibited by Mr. Fitch, the painter, towards poor little Caroline was the point which determined Brandon to begin to act.

"My dear Viscount" (wrote he to the same Lord Cinqbars whom he formerly addressed)—"Give me joy; for in a week's time it is my intention to be violently in love,—and love is no small amusement in a watering-place in winter.

"I told you about the fair Juliana Gann and her family. I forgot whether I mentioned how the Juliana had two fair daughters, the Rosalind and the Isabella; and another, Caroline by name, not so good-looking as her half-sisters, but, nevertheless, a pleasing young person.

"Well, when I came hither, I had nothing to do but to fall in love with the two handsomest; and did so, taking many walks with them, talking much nonsense; passing long dismal evenings over horrid tea with them and their mamma: laying regular siege, in fact, to these Margate beauties, who, according to the common rule in such cases, could not, I thought, last long.

"Miserable deception! disgusting aristocratic blindness!" (Mr. Brandon always assumed that his own high birth and eminent position were granted.) "Would you believe it, that I, who have seen, fought, and conquered in so many places, should have been ignominiously defeated here? Just as American Jackson defeated our Peninsular veterans, I, an old Continental conqueror too, have been overcome by this ignoble enemy. These women have entrenched themselves so firmly in their vulgarity, that I have been beaten back several times with disgrace, being quite unable to make an impression. The monsters, too, keep up a dreadful fire from behind their entrenchments; and besides have raised the whole country against me : in a word, all the snobs of their acquaintance are in arms. There is Bob Smith, the linendraper; Harry Jones, who keeps the fancy tea-shop; young Glauber, the apothecary; and sundry other persons, who are ready to eat me when they see me in the streets; and are all at the beck of the victorious Amazons.

"How is a gentleman to make head against such a *canaille* as this?—a regular *jacquerie*. Once or twice I have thought of retreating; but a retreat, for sundry reasons I have, is inconvenient. I can't go to London; I am known at Dover; I believe there is a bill against me at Canterbury; at Chatham there are sundry quartered regiments whose recognition I should be unwilling to risk. I must stay here—and be hanged to the place—until my better star shall rise.

"But I am determined that my stay shall be to some purpose; and so to show how persevering I am, I shall make one more trial upon the third daughter,—yes, upon the third daughter, a family Cinderella, who shall, I am determined, make her sisters *crever* with envy. I merely mean fun, you know—not mischief,—for Cinderella is but a little child : and, besides, I am the most harmless fellow breathing, but must have my joke. Now, Cinderella has a lover, the bearded painter of whom I spoke to you in a former letter. He has lately plunged into the most extraordinary fits of passion for her, and is more mad than even he was before. Woe betide you, O painter! I have nothing to do : a month to do that nothing in; in that time, mark my words, I will laugh at that painter's beard. Should you like a lock of it, or a sofa stuffed with it? there is beard enough : or should you like to see a specimen of poor little Cinderella's golden ringlets? Command your slave. I wish I had paper enough to write you an account of a grand Gann dinner at which I assisted, and of a scene which there took place; and how Cinderella was dressed out, not by a fairy, but by a charitable kitchen-maid, and was turned out of the room by her indignant mamma, for appearing in the scullion's finery. But my *forte* does not lie in such descriptions of polite life. We drank port, and toasts after dinner : here is the *menu*, and the names and order of the eaters."

*　　　*　　　*　　　*　　　*　　　*

The bill of fare has been given already, and need not, therefore, be again laid before the public.

"What a fellow that is!" said young Lord Cinqbars, reading the letter to his friends, and in a profound admiration of his tutor's genius.

"And to think that he was a reading man too, and took a double first," cried another; "why, the man's an Admirable Crichton."

"Upon my life, though, he's a little too bad," said a third, who was a moralist. And with this a fresh bowl of milk-punch came reeking from the college butteries, and the jovial party discussed that.

CHAPTER V.

CONTAINS A GREAT DEAL OF COMPLICATED LOVE-MAKING.

THE Misses Macarty were excessively indignant that Mr. Fitch should have had the audacity to fall in love with their sister; and poor Caroline's life was not, as may be imagined, made much the happier by the envy and passion thus excited. Mr. Fitch's amour was the source of a great deal of pain to her. Her mother would tauntingly say, that as both were beggars, they could not do better than marry; and declared, in the same satirical way, that she should like nothing better than to see a large family of grandchildren about her, to be plagues and burdens upon her, as her daughter was. The short way would have been, when the young painter's intentions were manifest, which they pretty speedily were, to have requested him immediately to quit the house; or, as Mr. Gann said, " to give him the sack at once;" to which measure the worthy man indignantly avowed that he would have resort. But his lady would not allow of any such rudeness; although, for her part, she professed the strongest scorn and contempt for the painter. For the painful fact must be stated : Fitch had a short time previously paid no less a sum than a whole quarter's board and lodging in advance, at Mrs. Gann's humble request, and he possessed his landlady's receipt for that sum; the mention of which circumstance silenced Gann's objections at once. And indeed, it is pretty certain that, with all her taunts to her daughter and just abuse of Fitch's poverty, Mrs. Gann in her heart was not altogether averse to the match. In the first place, she loved match-making; next, she would be glad to be rid of her daughter at any rate; and, besides, Fitch's aunt, the auctioneer's wife, was rich, and had no children; painters, as she had heard, make often a great deal of money, and Fitch might be a clever one, for aught she knew. So he was allowed to remain in the house, an undeclared but very assiduous lover; and to sigh, and to moan, and make verses and portraits of his beloved, and build castles in the air as best he might. Indeed our humble Cinderella was in a very curious position. She felt a tender passion for the first floor, and was adored by the second floor, and had to wait upon both at the summons of the bell of either; and as the poor little thing was compelled not to notice any of the sighs and glances which the painter bestowed upon her, she also had schooled herself to maintain a quiet demeanour towards Mr. Brandon, and not allow him to discover the secret which was labouring in her little breast.

I think it may be laid down as a pretty general rule, that most romantic little girls of Caroline's age have such a budding sentiment as this young person entertained; quite innocent of course; nourished and talked of in delicious secrecy to the *confidante* of the hour. Or else what are novels made for? Had Caroline read of Valancourt and Emily for nothing, or gathered no good example from those five tear-fraught volumes which describe the loves of Miss Helen Mar and Sir William Wallace? Many a time had she depicted Brandon in a fancy costume, such as the fascinating Valancourt wore; or painted herself as Helen, trying a sash round her knight's cuirass, and watching him forth to battle. Silly fancies, no doubt; but consider, madam, the poor girl's age and education; the only instruction she had ever received was from these tender, kind-hearted, silly books: the only happiness which Fate had allowed her was in this little silent world of fancy. It would be hard to grudge the poor thing her dreams; and many such did she have, and impart blushingly to honest Becky, as they sate by the humble kitchen-fire.

Although it cost her heart a great pang, she had once ventured to implore her mother not to send her upstairs to the lodgers' rooms, for she shrunk at the notion of the occurrence that Brandon should discover her regard for him; but this point had never entered Mrs. Gann's sagacious head. She thought her daughter wished to avoid Fitch, and sternly bade her do her duty, and not give herself such impertinent airs; and, indeed, it can't be said that poor Caroline was very sorry at being compelled to continue to see Brandon. To do both gentlemen justice, neither ever said a word unfit for Caroline to hear. Fitch would have been torn to pieces by a thousand wild horses rather than have breathed a single syllable to hurt her feelings; and Brandon, though by no means so squeamish on ordinary occasions, was innately a gentleman, and from taste rather than from virtue, was carefully respectful in his behaviour to her.

As for the Misses Macarty themselves, it has been stated that they had already given away their hearts several times; Miss Isabella being at this moment attached to a certain young wine-merchant, and to Lieutenant or Colonel Swabber of the Spanish service; and Miss Rosalind having a decided fondness for a foreign nobleman, with black mustachios, who had paid a visit to Margate. Of Miss Bella's lovers, Swabber had disappeared; but she still met the wine-merchant pretty often, and it is believed had gone very nigh to accept him. As for Miss Rosalind, I am sorry to say that the course of her true love ran by no means smoothly: the Frenchman had turned out to be not a marquess, but a billiard-marker; and a sad, sore subject the disappointment was with the neglected lady.

We should have spoken of it long since, had the subject been one that was much canvassed in the Gann family; but once when Gann had endeavoured to rally his stepdaughter on this unfortunate attachment (using for the purpose those delicate terms of wit for which the honest gentleman was always famous), Miss Linda had flown into such a violent fury, and comported herself in a way so dreadful, that James Gann, Esquire, was fairly frightened out of his wits by the threats, screams, and imprecations which she uttered. Miss Bella, who was disposed to be jocose likewise, was likewise awed into silence; for her dear sister talked of tearing her eyes out that minute, and uttered some hints, too, regarding love-matters personally affecting Miss Bella herself, which caused that young lady to turn pale-red, to mutter something about " wicked lies," and to leave the room immediately. Nor was the subject ever again broached by the Ganns. Even when Mrs. Gann once talked about that odious French impostor, she was stopped immediately, not by the lady concerned, but by Miss Bella, who cried, sharply, " Mamma, hold your tongue, and don't vex our dear Linda by alluding to any such stuff." It is most probable that the young ladies had had a private conference, which, beginning a little fiercely at first, had ended amicably: and so the marquess was mentioned no more.

Miss Linda, then, was comparatively free (for Bob Smith, the linendraper, and young Glauber, the apothecary, went for nothing); and, very luckily for her, a successor was found for the faithless Frenchman, almost immediately.

This gentleman was a commoner, to be sure; but had a good estate of five hundred a year, kept his horse and gig, and was, as Mr. Gann remarked, as good a fellow as ever lived. Let us say at once that the new lover was no other than Mr. Swigby.   From the day when he had been introduced to the family he appeared to be very much attracted by the two sisters ; sent a turkey off his own farm, and six bottles of prime Hollands, to Mr. and Mrs. Gann, in presents ; and, in ten short days after his first visit, had informed his friend Gann that he was violently in love with two women whose names he would never—never breathe.   The worthy Gann knew right well how the matter was ; for he had not failed to remark Swigby's melancholy, and to attribute it to its right cause.

Swigby was forty-eight years of age, stout, hearty, gay, much given to drink, and had never been a lady's man, or, indeed, passed half-a-dozen evenings in ladies' society.   He thought Gann the noblest and finest fellow in the world.   He never heard any singing like James's, nor any jokes like his ; nor had met with such an accomplished gentleman or man of the world.   "Gann has his faults," Swigby would say at the "Bag of Nails ;" "which of us has not?—but I tell you what, he's the greatest trump I ever see."   Many scores of scores had he paid for Gann, many guineas and crown-pieces had he lent him, since he came into his property some three years before.   What were Swigby's former pursuits I can't tell. What need we care? Hadn't he five hundred a year now, and a horse and gig?   Ay, that he had.

Since his accession to fortune, this gay young bachelor had taken his share (what he called "his whack ") of pleasure ; had been at one —nay, perhaps, at two—public-houses every night ; and had been tipsy, I make no doubt, nearly a thousand times in the course of the three years.   Many people had tried to cheat him ; but, no, no ! he knew what was what, and in all matters of money was simple and shrewd.   Gann's gentility won him ; his bragging, his *ton*, and the stylish tuft on his chin.   To be invited to his house was a proud moment ; and when he went away, after the banquet described in the last chapter, he was in a perfect ferment of love and liquor.

"What a stylish woman is that Mrs. Gann !" thought he, as he tumbled into bed at his inn ; fine she must have been as a gal ! fourteen stone now, without saddle or bridle, and no mistake.   And them Miss Macartys. Jupiter ! what spanking, handsome, elegant creatures !—real elegance in both on 'em ! Such hair !—black's the word—as black as my mare ; such cheeks, such necks, and shoulders !" At noon he repeated these observations to Gann himself, as he walked up and down the pier with that gentleman, smoking Manilla cheroots.

He was in raptures with his evening.   Gann received his praises with much majestic good-humour.

"Blood, sir !" said he, "blood's everything ! Them gals have been brought up as few ever have.   I don't speak of myself; but their mother—their mother's a lady, sir.   Show me a woman in England as is better bred or knows the world more than my Juliana !"

"It's impawssible," said Swigby.

"Think of the company we've kep', sir, before our misfortunes— the fust in the land.   Brandenburg House, sir,—England's injured queen.   Law bless you ! Juliana was always there."

"I make no doubt, sir ; you can see it in her," said Swigby, solemnly.

"And as for those gals, why, ain't they related to the fust families in Ireland, sir ?—In course they are.   As I said before, blood's every-thing; and those young women have the best of it: they are connected with the reg'lar old noblesse."

"They have the best of everythink, I'm sure," said Swigby, "and deserve it, too," and relapsed into his morning remarks.   "What creatures ! what elegance ! what hair and eyes, sir !—black, and all's black, as I say.   What complexion, sir !—ay, and what *makes*, too ! Such a neck and shoulders I never see !"

Gann, who had his hands in his pockets (his friend's arm being hooked into one of his), here suddenly withdrew his hand from its hiding-place, clenched his fist, assumed a horrible knowing grin, and gave Mr. Swigby such a blow in the ribs as well nigh sent him into the water.   "You sly dog !" said Mr. Gann, with inexpressible em-phasis ; "you've found *that* out, too, have you ?   Have a care, Joe my boy,—have a care."

And herewith Gann and Joe burst into tremendous roars of laughter, fresh explosions taking place at intervals of five minutes during the rest of the walk.   The two friends parted exceedingly happy ; and when they met that evening at "The Nails" Gann drew Swigby mysteriously into the bar, and thrust into his hand a triangular piece of pink paper, which the latter read :—

"Mrs. Gann and the Misses Macarty request the honour and pleasure of Mr. Swigby's company (if you have no better engagement) to tea to-morrow evening, at half-past five.
"*Margaretta Cottage, Salamanca Road North,*
　　　Thursday evening."

The faces of the two gentlemen were wonderfully expressive of satisfaction as this communication passed between them. And I am led to believe that Mrs. Gann had been unusually pleased with her husband's conduct on that day, for honest James had no less than thirteen and sixpence in his pocket, and insisted, as usual, upon standing glasses all round. Joe Swigby, left alone in the little parlour behind the bar, called for a sheet of paper, a new pen and a wafer, and in the space of half-an-hour concocted a very spirited and satisfactory answer to this note; which was carried off by Gann, and duly delivered. Punctually at half-past five Mr. Joseph Swigby knocked at Margaretta Cottage door, in his new coat with glistering brass-buttons, his face clean-shaved, and his great ears shining over his great shirt-collar delightfully bright and red.

What happened at this tea-party it is needless here to say; but Swigby came away from it quite as much enchanted as before, and declared that the duets sung by the ladies in hideous discord, were the sweetest music he had ever heard. He sent the gin and the turkey the next day; and, of course, was invited to dine.

The dinner was followed up on his part by an offer to drive all the young ladies and their mamma into the country; and he hired a very smart barouche to conduct them. The invitation was not declined; and Fitch, too, was asked by Mr. Swigby, in the height of his good-humour, and accepted with the utmost delight. "Me and Joe will go on the box," said Gann. "You four ladies and Mr. Fitch shall go inside. Carry must go bodkin; but she ain't very big."

"Carry, indeed, will stop at home," said her mamma; "she's not fit to go out."

At which poor Fitch's jaw fell; it was in order to ride with her that he had agreed to accompany the party; nor could he escape now, having just promised so eagerly.

"Oh, don't let's have that proud Brandon," said the young ladies, when the good-natured Mr. Swigby proposed to ask that gentleman; and therefore he was not invited to join them in their excursion : but he stayed at home very unconcernedly, and saw the barouche and its load drive off. Somebody else looked at it from the parlour-window with rather a heavy heart, and that some one was poor Caroline. The day was bright and sunshiny; the

spring was beginning early; it would have been pleasant to have
been a lady for once, and to have driven along in a carriage with
prancing horses. Mr. Fitch looked after her in a very sheepish,
melancholy way; and was so dismal and silly during the first part
of the journey, that Miss Linda, who was next to him, said to her
papa that she would change places with him; and actually mounted
the box by the side of the happy, trembling Mr. Swigby. How
proud he was, to be sure! How knowingly did he spank the horses
along, and fling out the shillings at the turnpikes!

"Bless you, *he* don't care for change!" said Gann, as one of the
toll-takers offered to render some coppers; and Joe felt infinitely
obliged to his friend for setting off his amiable qualities in such
a way.

O mighty Fate, that over us miserable mortals rulest supreme,
with what small means are thy ends effected!—with what scornful
ease and mean instruments does it please thee to govern mankind!
Let each man think of the circumstances of his life, and how its lot
has been determined. The getting up a little earlier or later, the
turning down this street or that, the eating of this dish or the other,
may influence all the years and actions of a future life. Mankind
walks down the left-hand side of Regent Street instead of the right,
and meets a friend who asks him to dinner, and goes, and finds the
turtle remarkably good, and the iced punch very cool and pleasant;
and, being in a merry, jovial, idle mood, has no objection to a social
rubber of whist—nay, to a few more. glasses of that cool punch. In
the most careless, good-humoured way, he loses a few points; and
still feels thirsty, and loses a few more points; and, like a man of
spirit, increases his stakes, to be sure, and just by that walk down
Regent Street is ruined for life. Or he walks down the right-hand
side of Regent Street instead of the left, and, good heavens! who is
that charming young creature who has just stepped into her carriage
from Mr. Fraser's shop, and to whom and her mamma Mr. Fraser
has made the most elegant bow in the world? It is the lovely
Miss Moidore, with a hundred thousand pounds, who has remarked
your elegant figure, and regularly drives to town on the first of the
month, to purchase her darling Magazine. You drive after her as
fast as the hack-cab will carry you. She reads the Magazine the
whole way. She stops at her papa's elegant villa at Hampstead,
with a conservatory, a double coach-house, and a park-like paddock.

4—2

As the lodge-gate separates you from that dear girl, she looks back just once, and blushes. *Erubuit, salva est res.* She has blushed, and you are all right. In a week you are introduced to the family, and pronounced a charming young fellow of high principles. In three weeks you have danced twenty-nine quadrilles with her, and whisked her through several miles of waltzes. In a month Mrs. O'Flaherty has flung herself into the arms of her mother, just having come from a visit to the village of Gretna, near Carlisle; and you have an account at your banker's ever after. What is the cause of all this good fortune?—a walk on a particular side of Regent Street. And so true and indisputable is this fact, that there's a young north-country gentleman with whom I am acquainted, that daily paces up and down the above-named street for many hours, fully expecting that such an adventure will happen to him; for which end he keeps a cab in readiness at the corner of Vigo Lane.

Now, after a dissertation in this history, the reader is pretty sure to know that a moral is coming; and the facts connected with our tale, which are to be drawn from the above little essay on fate, are simply these :—1. If Mr. Fitch had not heard Mr. Swigby invite *all* the ladies, he would have refused Swigby's invitation, and stayed at home. 2. If he had not been in the carriage, it is quite certain that Miss Rosalind Macarty would not have been seated by him on the back seat. 3. If he had not been sulky, she never would have asked her papa to let her take his place on the box. 4. If she had not taken her papa's place on the box, not one of the circumstances would have happened which did happen; and which were as follows :—

1. Miss Bella remained inside.

2. Mr. Swigby, who was wavering between the two, like a certain animal between two bundles of hay, was determined by this circumstance, and made proposals to Miss Linda, whispering to Miss Linda : "Miss, I ain't equal to the like of you ; but I'm hearty, healthy, and have five hundred a year. Will you marry me?" In fact, this very speech had been taught him by cunning Gann, who saw well enough that Swigby would speak to one or other of his daughters. And to it the young lady replied, also in a whispering, agitated tone, "Law, Mr. S. ! What an odd man ! How can you?" And, after a little pause, added, "*Speak to mamma.*"

3. (And this is the main point of my story.) If little Caroline

had been allowed to go out, she never would have been left alone
with Brandon at Margate. When Fate wills that something should
come to pass, she sends forth a million of little circumstances to
clear and prepare the way.

In the month of April (as indeed in half-a-score of other months
of the year) the reader may have remarked that the cold north-east
wind is prevalent; and that when, tempted by a glimpse of sunshine,
he issues forth to take the air, he receives not only it, but such
a quantity of it as is enough to keep him shivering through the rest
of the miserable month. On one of these happy days of English
weather (it was the very day before the pleasure-party described in
the last chapter) Mr. Brandon cursing heartily his country, and
thinking how infinitely more congenial to him were the winds and
habits prevalent in other nations, was marching over the cliffs near
Margate, in the midst of a storm of shrill east wind which no
ordinary mortal could bear, when he found perched on the cliff, his
fingers blue with cold, the celebrated Andrea Fitch, employed in
sketching a land or a sea scape on a sheet of grey paper.

"You have chosen a fine day for sketching," said Mr. Brandon,
bitterly, his thin aquiline nose peering out livid from the fur collar
of his coat.

Mr. Fitch smiled, understanding the allusion.

"An hartist, sir," said he, "doesn't mind the coldness of the
weather. There was a chap in the Academy who took sketches
twenty degrees below zero in Hiceland—Mount 'Ecla, sir! *E* was the
man that gave the first hidea of Mount 'Ecla for the Surrey
Zoological Gardens."

"He must have been a wonderful enthusiast!" said Mr. Brandon;
"I fancy that most would prefer to sit at home, and not numb their
fingers in such a freezing storm as this!"

"Storm, sir!" replied Fitch, majestically; "I live in a storm, sir!
A true hartist is never so 'appy as when he can have the advantage
to gaze upon yonder tempestuous hocean in one of its hangry
moods."

"Ay, there comes the steamer," answered Mr. Brandon; "I can
fancy that there are a score of unhappy people on board who are not
artists, and would wish to behold your ocean quiet."

"They are not poets, sir: the glorious hever-changing expression
of the great countenance of Nature is not seen by them. I should

consider myself unworthy of my hart, if I could not bear a little privation of cold or 'eat for its sake. And besides, sir, whatever their hardships may be, such a sight hamply repays me; for, although my private sorrows may be (has they are) tremendous, I never can look abroad upon the green hearth and hawful sea, without in a measure forgetting my personal woes and wrongs; for what right has a poor creature like me to think of his affairs in the presence of such a spectacle as this? I can't, sir; I feel ashamed of myself; I bow my 'ead and am quiet. When I set myself to examining hart, sir (by which I mean nature), I don't dare to think of anything else."

"You worship a very charming and consoling mistress," answered Mr. Brandon, with a supercilious air, lighting and beginning to smoke a cigar; "your enthusiasm does you credit."

"If you have another," said Andrea Fitch, "I should like to smoke one, for you seem to have a real feeling about hart, and I was a-getting so deucedly cold here, that really there was scarcely any bearing of it."

"The cold is very severe," replied Mr. Brandon.

"No, no, it's not the weather, sir!" said Mr. Fitch; "it's here, sir, here" (pointing to the left side of his waistcoat).

"What! you, too, have had sorrows?"

"Sorrows, sir! hagonies—hagonies, which I have never unfolded to any mortal! I have hendured halmost hevery thing. Poverty, sir, 'unger, hobloquy, 'opeless love! but for my hart, sir, I should be the most miserable wretch in the world!"

And herewith Mr. Fitch began to pour forth into Mr. Brandon's ears the history of some of those sorrows under which he laboured, and which he communicated to every single person who would listen to him.

Mr. Brandon was greatly amused by Fitch's prattle, and the latter told him under what privations he had studied his art: how he had starved for three years in Paris and Rome, while labouring at his profession; how meanly jealous the Royal Academy was which would never exhibit a single one of his pictures; how he had been driven from the Heternal City by the attentions of an immense fat Mrs. Carrickfergus, who absolutely proposed marriage to him; and how he was at this moment (a fact of which Mr. Brandon was already quite aware) madly and desperately in love with one of the most beautiful maidens in this world. For Fitch, having a mistress to his heart's desire, was boiling with impatience to have a confidant; what, indeed, would be the joy of love, if one were not allowed to speak of one's feelings to a friend who could know how to sympathise with them? Fitch was sure Brandon did, because Brandon was the very first person with whom the painter had talked since he had come to the resolution recorded in the last chapter.

"I hope she is as rich as that unlucky Mrs. Carrickfergus, whom you treated so cruelly?" said the confidant, affecting entire ignorance.

"Rich, sir? no, I thank heaven, she has not a penny!" said Fitch.

"I presume, then, you are yourself independent," said Brandon, smiling; "for in the marriage state, one or the other of the parties concerned should bring a portion of the filthy lucre."

"Haven't I my profession, sir?" said Fitch, majestically, having declared five minutes before that he starved in his profession. "Do you suppose a painter gets nothing? Haven't I horders from the first people in Europe?—commissions, sir, to hexecute 'istory-pieces, battle-pieces, haltar-pieces?"

"Master-pieces, I am sure," said Brandon, bowing politely; "for a gentleman of your astonishing genius can do no other."

The delighted artist received this compliment with many blushes, and vowed and protested that his performances were not really worthy of such high praise; but he fancied Mr. Brandon a great connoisseur, nevertheless, and unburdened his mind to him in a manner still more open. Fitch's sketch was by this time finished; and, putting his drawing implements together, he rose, and the gentlemen walked away. The sketch was hugely admired by Mr. Brandon, and when they came home, Fitch, culling it dexterously out of his book, presented it in a neat speech to his friend, "the gifted hamateur."

"The gifted hamateur" received the drawing with a profusion of thanks, and so much did he value it, that he had actually torn off a piece to light a cigar with, when he saw that words were written on the other side of the paper, and deciphered the following :—

"SONG OF THE VIOLET.
" A humble flower long time I pined,
Upon the solitary plain.
And trembled at the angry wind,
And shrunk before the bitter rain.

> And, oh ! 'twas in a blessed hour,
>   A passing wanderer chanced to see
> And, pitying the lonely flower,
>   To stoop and gather me.
>
> " I fear no more the tempest rude,
>   On dreary heath no more I pine,
> But left my cheerless solitude,
>   To deck the breast of Caroline.
> Alas ! our days are brief at best,
>   Nor long I fear will mine endure,
> Though shelter'd here upon a breast
>   So gentle and so pure.
>
> " It draws the fragrance from my leaves,
>   It robs me of my sweetest breath ;
> And every time it falls and heaves,
>   It warns me of my coming death.
> But one I know would glad forego
>   All joys of life to be as I ;
> An hour to rest on that sweet breast,
>   And then, contented, die.
>
>   " ANDREA."

When Mr. Brandon had finished the perusal of these verses, he laid them down with an air of considerable vexation. "Egad !" said he, "this fellow, fool as he is, is not so great a fool as he seems; and if he goes on this way, may finish by turning the girl's head. They can't resist a man if he but presses hard enough—I know they can't !" And here Mr. Brandon mused over his various experience, which confirmed his observation, that be a man ever so silly, a gentlewoman will yield to him out of sheer weariness. And he thought of several cases in which, by the persevering application of copies of verses, young ladies had been brought from dislike to sufferance of a man, from sufferance to partiality, and from partiality to St. George's, Hanover Square. "A ruffian who murders his *h*'s to carry off such a delicate little creature as that !" cried he in a transport : "it shall never be if I can prevent it !" He thought Caroline more and more beautiful every instant, and was himself by this time almost as much in love with her as Fitch himself.

Mr. Brandon, then, saw Fitch depart in Swigby's carriage with no ordinary feelings of pleasure. Miss Caroline was not with them. "Now is my time !" thought Brandon; and, ringing the bell, he inquired with some anxiety, from Becky, where Miss Caroline was? It must be confessed that mistress and maid were at their usual occupation, working and reading novels in the back-parlour. Poor Carry! what other pleasure had she?

She had not gone through many pages, or Becky advanced many stitches in the darning of that tablecloth which the good housewife, Mrs. Gann, had confided to her charge, when an humble knock was heard at the door of the sitting-room, that caused the blushing Caroline to tremble and drop her book, as Miss Lydia Languish does in the play.

Mr. George Brandon entered with a very demure air. He held in his hand a black satin neck-scarf, of which a part had come to be broken. He could not wear it in its present condition, that was evident; but Miss Caroline was blushing and trembling a great deal too much to suspect that this wicked Brandon had himself torn his own scarf with his own hands one moment before he entered the room. I don't know whether Becky had any suspicions of this fact, or whether it was only the ordinary roguish look which she had when anything pleased her, that now lighted up her eyes and caused her mouth to expand smilingly, and her fat red cheeks to gather up into wrinkles.

"I have had a sad misfortune," said he, "and should be very much obliged indeed to Miss Caroline to repair it." (Caroline was said with a kind of tender hesitation that caused the young woman, so named, to blush more than ever.) "It is the only stock I have in the world, and I can't go barenecked into the streets; can I, Mrs. Becky?"

"No, sure," said Becky.

"Not unless I was a celebrated painter, like Mr. Fitch," added Mr. Brandon, with a smile, which was reflected speedily upon the face of the lady whom he wished to interest. "Those great geniuses," he added, "may do anything."

"For," says Becky, "hee's got enough beard on hees faze to keep hees neck warm!" At which remark, though Miss Caroline very properly said, "For shame, Becky!" Mr. Brandon was so convulsed with laughter, that he fairly fell down upon the sofa on which Miss Caroline was seated. How she startled and trembled, as he flung his arm upon the back of the couch! Mr. Brandon did not attempt to apologize for what was an act of considerable impertinence, but continued mercilessly to make many more jokes concerning poor Fitch, which were so cleverly suited to the comprehension of the maid and the young mistress, as to elicit a great number of roars of laughter from the one, and to cause the other to smile in spite of herself. Indeed, Brandon had gained a vast reputation with Becky in his morning colloquies with her, and she was ready to laugh at any single word which it pleased him to utter. How many of his good things had this honest scullion carried downstairs to Caroline? and how pitilessly had she contrived to *estropier* them in their passage from the drawing-room to the kitchen?

Well, then, while Mr. Brandon "was a-going on," as Becky said, Caroline had taken his stock, and her little fingers were occupied in repairing the damage he had done to it. Was it clumsiness on her part? Certain it is that the rent took several minutes to repair: of them the *mangeur de cœurs* did not fail to profit, conversing in an easy, kindly, confidential way, which set our fluttering heroine speedily at rest, and enabled her to reply to his continual queries, addressed with much adroitness and an air of fraternal interest, by a number of those pretty little timid whispering yeses and noes, and those gentle, quick looks of the eyes, wherewith young and modest maidens are wont to reply to the questions of seducing young bachelors. Dear yeses and noes, how beautiful you are when gently whispered by pretty lips!—glances of quick innocent eyes, how charming are you!—and how charming the soft blush that steals over the cheek, towards which the dark lashes are drawing the blue-veined eyelids down. And here let the writer of this solemnly declare, upon his veracity, that he means nothing but what is right and moral. But look, I pray you, at an innocent, bashful girl of sixteen: if she be but good, she must be pretty. She is a woman now, but a girl still. How delightful all her ways are! How exquisite her instinctive grace! All the arts of all the Cleopatras are not so captivating as her nature. Who can resist her confiding simplicity, or fail to be touched and conquered by her gentle appeal to protection?

All this Mr. Brandon saw and felt, as many a gentleman educated in this school will. It is not because a man is a rascal himself, that he cannot appreciate virtue and purity very keenly; and our hero did feel for this simple, gentle, tender, artless creature, a real respect and sympathy—a sympathy so fresh and delicious, that he was but too glad to yield to it and indulge in it, and which he mistook, probably, for a real love of virtue, and a return to the days of his innocence.

Indeed, Mr. Brandon, it was no such thing. It was only because vice and debauch were stale for the moment, and this pretty virtue new. It was only because your cloyed appetite was long unused to this simple meat that you felt so keen a relish for it; and I thought of you only the last blessed Saturday, at Mr. Lovegrove's, "West India Tavern," Blackwall, where a company of fifteen epicures, who had scorned the turtle, pooh-poohed the punch, and sent away the whitebait, did-suddenly and simultaneously make a rush upon— a dish of *beans and bacon.* And if the assiduous reader of novels will think upon some of the most celebrated works of that species, which have lately appeared in this and other countries, he will find, amidst much debauch of sentiment and enervating dissipation of intellect, that the writers have from time to time a returning appetite for inno- cence and freshness, and indulge us with occasional repasts of beans and bacon. How long Mr. Brandon remained by Miss Caroline's side I have no means of judging ; it is probable, however, that he stayed a much longer time than was necessary for the mending of his black-satin stock. I believe, indeed, that he read to the ladies a great part of the " Mysteries of Udolpho," over which they were engaged ; and interspersed his reading with many remarks of his own, both tender and satirical. Whether he was in her company half-an-hour or four hours, this is certain, that the time slipped away very swiftly with poor Caroline ; and when a carriage drove up to the door, and shrill voices were heard crying, " Becky !" " Carry !" and Rebecca the maid starting up, cried, " Lor', here's missus !" and Brandon jumped rather suddenly off the sofa, and fled up the stairs —when all these events took place, I know Caroline felt very sad indeed, and opened the door for her parents with a very heavy heart.

Swigby helped Miss Linda off the box with excessive tenderness. Papa was bustling and roaring in high good-humour, and called for "hot water and tumblers immediately." Mrs. Gann was gracious ; and Miss Bell sulky, as she had good reason to be, for she insisted upon taking the front seat in the carriage before her sister, and had lost a husband by that very piece of obstinacy.

Mr. Fitch, as he entered, bestowed upon Caroline a heavy sigh and a deep stare, and silently ascended to his own apartment. He was lost in thought. The fact is, he was trying to remember some verses regarding a violet, which he had made five years before, and which he had somehow lost from among his papers. So he went up-stairs, muttering,

> " A humble flower long since I pined
> Upon a solitary plain ——"

CHAPTER VI.

DESCRIBES A SHABBY GENTEEL MARRIAGE, AND MORE LOVE-MAKING.

IT will not be necessary to describe the particulars of the festivities which took place on the occasion of Mr. Swigby's marriage to Miss Macarty. The happy pair went off in a postchaise and four to the bridegroom's country-seat, accompanied by the bride's blushing sister; and when the first week of their matrimonial bliss was ended, that worthy woman, Mrs. Gann, with her excellent husband, went to visit the young couple. Miss Caroline was left, therefore, sole mistress of the house, and received especial cautions from her mamma as to prudence, economy, the proper management of the lodgers' bills, and the necessity of staying at home.

Considering that one of the gentlemen remaining in the house was a declared lover of Miss Caroline, I think it is a little surprising that her mother should leave her unprotected ; but in this matter the poor are not so particular as the rich; and so this young lady was con-signed to the guardianship of her own innocence, and the lodgers' loyalty : nor was there any reason why Mrs. Gann should doubt the latter. As for Mr. Fitch, he would have far preferred to be torn to pieces by ten thousand wild horses, rather than to offer to the young woman any unkindness or insult; and how was Mrs. Gann to suppose that her other lodger was a whit less loyal? that he had any partiality for a person of whom he always spoke as a mean, insignificant little baby? So, without any misgivings, and in a one-horse fly with Mr. Gann by her side, with a bran new green coat and gilt buttons, Juliana Gann went forth to visit her beloved child, and console her in her married state.

And here, were I allowed to occupy the reader with extraneous matters, I could give a very curious and touching picture of the Swigby *ménage*. Mrs. S., I am very sorry to say, quarrelled with her husband on the third day after their marriage,—and for what, pr'thee? Why, because he would smoke, and no gentleman ought to smoke. Swigby, therefore, patiently resigned his pipe, and with it one of the quietest, happiest, kindest companions of his solitude. He was a different man after this; his pipe was as a limb of his body. Having on Tuesday conquered the pipe, Mrs. Swigby on Thursday did battle with her husband's rum-and-water, a drink of an odious smell, as she very properly observed; and the smell was doubly odious, now that the tobacco-smoke no longer perfumed the parlour-breeze, and counteracted the odours of the juice of West India sugar-canes. On Thursday, then, Mr. Swigby and rum held out pretty bravely. Mrs. S. attacked the punch with some sharp-shooting, and fierce charges of vulgarity; to which S. replied, by opening the battery of oaths (chiefly directed to his own eyes, however), and loud protestations that he would never surrender. In three days more, however, the rum-and-water was gone. Mr. Swigby, defeated and prostrate, had given up that stronghold; his young wife and sister were triumphant; and his poor mother, who occupied her son's house, and had till now taken her place at the head of his table, saw that her empire was for ever lost, and was preparing suddenly to succumb to the imperious claims of the mistress of the mansion.

All this, I say, I wish I had the liberty to describe at large, as also to narrate the arrival of majestic Mrs. Gann; and a battle-royal which speedily took place between the two worthy mothers-in-law. Noble is the hatred of ladies who stand in this relation to each other; each sees what injury the other is inflicting upon her darling child; each mistrusts, detests, and to her offspring privily abuses the arts and crimes of the other. A house with a wife is often warm enough; a house with a wife and her mother is rather warmer than any spot on the known globe; a house with two mothers-in-law is so excessively hot, that it can be likened to no place on earth at all, but one must go lower for a simile. Think of a wife who despises her husband, and teaches him manners; of an elegant sister, who joins in rallying him (this was almost the only point of union between Bella and Linda now,—for since the marriage, Linda hated her sister consumedly). Think, I say, of two mothers-in-law,—one, large, pompous, and atrociously genteel,—another coarse and shrill, determined not to have her son put upon,—and you may see what a happy fellow Joe Swigby was, and into what a piece of good luck he had fallen.

What would have become of him without his father-in-law? Indeed one shudders to think; but the consequence of that gentleman's arrival and intervention was speedily this:—About four o'clock, when the dinner was removed, and the quarrelling used commonly to set in, the two gents took their hats, and sallied out; and as one has found when the body is inflamed that the application of a stringent medicine may cause the ill to disappear for a while, only to return elsewhere with greater force; in like manner, Mrs. Swigby's sudden victory over the pipe and rum-and-water, although it had caused a temporary cessation of the evil of which she com- plained, was quite unable to stop it altogether; it disappeared from one spot only to rage with more violence elsewhere. In Swigby's parlour, rum and tobacco odours rose no more (except, indeed, when Mrs. Gann would partake of the former as a restorative); but if you could have seen the "Half-Moon and Snuffers" down the village; if you could have seen the good dry skittle-ground which stretched at the back of that inn, and the window of the back parlour which superintended that skittle-ground; if the hour at which you beheld these objects was evening, what time the rustics from their toils released, trolled the stout ball amidst the rattling pins (the oaken pins that standing in the sun did cast long shadows on the golden sward); if you had remarked all this, I say, you would have also seen in the back-parlour a tallow candle twinkling in the shade, and standing on a little greasy table. Upon the greasy table was a pewter porter-pot, and to the left a teaspoon glittering in a glass of gin; close to each of these two delicacies was a pipe of tobacco; and behind the pipes sat Mr. Gann and Mr. Swigby, who now made the "Half-Moon and Snuffers" their usual place of resort, and forgot their married cares.

In spite of all our promises of brevity, these things have taken some space to describe; and the reader must also know that some short interval elapsed ere they occurred. A month at least passed away before Mr. Swigby had decidedly taken up his position at the little inn : all this time, Gann was staying with his son-in-law, at the latter's most earnest request; and Mrs. Gann remained under the same roof at her own desire. Not the hints of her daughter, nor the

broad questions of the dowager Mrs. Swigby, could induce honest
Mrs. Gann to stir from her quarters. She had had her lodgers'
money in advance, as was the worthy woman's custom; she knew
Margate in April was dreadfully dull, and she determined to enjoy
the country until the jovial town season arrived. The Canterbury
coachman, whom Gann knew, and who passed through the village,
used to take her cargo of novels to and fro; and the old lady made
herself as happy as circumstances would allow. Should anything
of importance occur during her mamma's absence, Caroline was
to make use of the same conveyance, and inform Mrs. Gann in a
letter.

Miss Caroline looked at her papa and mamma, as the vehicle
which was to bear them to the newly married couple moved up the
street; but, strange to say, she did not feel that heaviness of heart
which she before had experienced when forbidden to share the
festivities of her family, but was on this occasion more happy than
any one of them,—so happy, that the young woman felt quite
ashamed of herself; and Becky was fain to remark how her mistress's
cheek flushed, and her eyes sparkled (and turned perpetually to the
door), and her whole little frame was in a flutter.

"I wonder if he will come," said the little heart; and the eyes
turned and looked at that well-known sofa-corner, where *he* had been
placed a fortnight before. He looked exactly like Lord Byron, that
he did, with his pale brow, and his slim bare neck; only not half
so wicked—no, no. She was sure that her—her Mr. B——, her
Bran——, her *George*, was as good as he was beautiful. Don't let us
be angry with her for calling him George; the girl was bred in an
humble sentimental school; she did not know enough of society
to be squeamish; she never thought that she could be his really,
and gave way in the silence of her fancy to the full extent of her
affection for him.

She had not looked at the door above twenty-five times—that is
to say, her parents had not quitted the house ten minutes—when,
sure enough, the latch did rattle, the door opened, and, with a faint
blush on his cheek, divine George entered. He was going to make
some excuse, as on the former occasion; but he looked first into
Caroline's face, which was beaming with joy and smiles; and the
little thing, in return, regarded him, and—made room for him on the
sofa. O sweet instinct of love! Brandon had no need of excuses,

but sate down, and talked away as easily, happily, and confidentially, and neither took any note of time. Andrea Fitch (the sly dog!) witnessed the Gann departure with feelings of exultation, and had laid some deep plans of his own with regard to Miss Caroline. So strong was his confidence in his friend on the first floor, that Andrea actually descended to those apartments, on his way to Mrs. Gann's parlour, in order to consult Mr. Brandon, and make known to him his plan of operations.

It would have made your heart break, or, at the very least, your sides ache, to behold the countenance of poor Mr. Fitch, as he thrust his bearded head in at the door of the parlour. There was Brandon lolling on the sofa, at his ease; Becky in full good-humour; and Caroline, always absurdly inclined to blush, blushing at Fitch's appearance more than ever! She could not help looking from him slyly and gently into the face of Mr. Brandon. That gentleman saw the look, and did not fail to interpret it. It was a confession of love—an appeal for protection. A thrill of delightful vanity shot through Brandon's frame, and made his heart throb, as he noticed this look of poor Caroline. He answered it with one of his own that was cruelly wrong, cruelly triumphant, and sarcastic; and he shouted out to Mr. Fitch, with a loud, disconcerted tone, which only made that young painter feel more awkward than ever he had been. Fitch made some clumsy speech regarding his dinner,—whether that meal was to be held, in the absence of the parents, at the usual hour, and then took his leave.

The poor fellow had been pleasing himself with the notion of taking this daily meal *tête-à-tête* with Caroline. What progress would he make in her heart during the absence of her parents! Did it not seem as if the first marriage had been arranged on purpose to facilitate his own? He determined thus his plan of campaign. He would make, in the first place, the most beautiful drawing of Caroline that ever was seen. "The conversations I'll 'ave with her during the sittings," says he, "will carry me a pretty long way; the drawing itself will be so beautiful, that she can't resist that. I'll write her verses in her halbum, and make designs hallusive of my passion for her." And so our pictorial Alnaschar dreamed and dreamed. He had, ere long, established himself in a house in Newman Street, with a footman to open the door. Caroline was upstairs, his wife, and her picture the crack portrait of the Exhibition. With her by his side,

Andrea Fitch felt he could do anything. Half-a-dozen carriages at his door,—a hundred guineas for a Kit-Cat portrait. Lady Fitch, Sir Andrew Fitch, the President's chain,—all sorts of bright visions floated before his imagination; and as Caroline was the first precious condition of his preferment, he determined forthwith to begin, and realise that.

But O disappointment! on coming down to dinner at three o'clock to that charming *tête-à-tête*, he found no less than four covers laid on the table, Miss Caroline blushing (according to custom) at the head of it; Becky, the maid, grinning at the foot; and Mr. Brandon sitting quietly on one side, as much at home, forsooth, as if he had held that position for a year.

The fact is, that the moment after Fitch retired, Brandon, inspired by jealousy, had made the same request which had been brought forward by the painter; nor must the ladies be too angry with Caroline, if, after some scruples and struggles, she yielded to the proposal. Remember that the girl was the daughter of a boarding-house, accustomed to continual dealings with her mamma's lodgers, and up to the present moment thinking herself as safe among them as the young person who walked through Ireland with a bright gold wand, in the song of Mr. Thomas Moore. On the point, however, of Brandon's admission, it must be confessed, for Caroline's honour, that she did hesitate. She felt that she entertained very different feelings towards him to those with which any other lodger or man had inspired her, and made a little movement of resistance at first. But the poor girl's modesty overcame this, as well as her wish. Ought she to avoid him? Ought she not to stifle any preference which she might feel towards him, and act towards him with the same indifference which she would show to any other person in a like situation? Was not Mr. Fitch to dine at table as usual, and had she refused him? So reasoned she in her heart. Silly little cunning heart! it knew that all these reasons were lies, and that she *should* avoid the man; but she was willing to accept of any pretext for meeting, and so made a kind of compromise with her conscience. Dine he should; but Becky should dine too, and be a protector to her. Becky laughed loudly at the idea of this, and took her place with huge delight.

It is needless to say a word about this dinner, as we have already described a former meal; suffice it to say, that the presence of

Brandon caused the painter to be excessively sulky and uncomfortable; and so gave his rival, who was gay, triumphant, and at his ease, a decided advantage over him. Nor did Brandon neglect to use this to the utmost. When Fitch retired to his own apartments—not jealous as yet, for the simple fellow believed every word of Brandon's morning conversation with him—but vaguely annoyed and disappointed, Brandon assailed him with all the force of ridicule; at all his manners, words, looks, he joked mercilessly; laughed at his low birth, (Miss Gann, be it remembered, had been taught to pique herself upon her own family,) and invented a series of stories concerning his past life which made the ladies—for Becky, being in the parlour, must be considered as such—conceive the greatest contempt and pity for the poor painter.

After this, Mr. Brandon would expatiate with much eloquence upon his own superior attractions and qualities. He talked of his cousin, Lord So-and-so, with the easiest air imaginable; told Caroline what princesses he had danced with at foreign courts; frightened her with accounts of dreadful duels he had fought; in a word, "posed" before her as a hero of the most sublime kind. How the poor little thing drank in all his tales; and how she and Becky (for they now occupied the same bedroom) talked over them at night!

Miss Caroline, as Mr. Fitch has already stated, had in her possession, like almost every young lady in England, a little square book called an album, containing prints from annuals; hideous designs of flowers; old pictures of faded fashions, cut out and pasted into the leaves; and small scraps of verses selected from Byron, Landon, or Mrs. Hemans; and written out in the girlish hand of the owner of the book. Brandon looked over this work with a good deal of curiosity—for he contended, always, that a girl's disposition might be learned from the character of this museum of hers—and found here several sketches by Mr. Fitch, for which, before that gentleman had declared his passion for her, Caroline had begged. These sketches the sentimental painter had illustrated with poetry, which, I must confess, Caroline thought charming, until now, when Mr. Brandon took occasion to point out how wretchedly poor the verses were (as indeed was the fact), and to parody them all. He was not unskilful at this kind of exercise, and at the drawing of caricatures, and had soon made a dozen of both parodies and drawings, which reflected cruelly upon the person and the talents of the painter.

What now did this wicked Mr. Brandon do? He, in the first place, drew a caricature of Fitch; and, secondly, having gone to a gardener's near the town, and purchased there a bunch of violets, he presented them to Miss Caroline, and wrote Mr. Fitch's own verses before given into her album. He signed them with his own initials, and thus declared open war with the painter.

CHAPTER VII.

WHICH BRINGS A GREAT NUMBER OF PEOPLE TO MARGATE BY THE STEAMBOAT.

THE events which this history records began in the month of February. Time had now passed, and April had arrived, and with it that festive season so loved by schoolboys, and called the Easter holidays. Not only schoolboys, but men, profit by this period of leisure,—such men, especially, as have just come into enjoyment of their own cups and saucers, and are in daily expectation of their whiskers—college men, I mean,—who are persons more anxious than any others to designate themselves and each other by the manly title.

Among other men, then, my Lord Viscount Cinqbars, of Christ Church, Oxon, received a sum of money to pay his quarter's bill, and having written to his papa that he was busily engaged in reading for the "little-go," and must, therefore, decline the delight he had promised himself of passing the vacation at Cinqbars Hall,—and having, the day after his letter was despatched, driven to town tandem with young Tom Tufthunt, of the same university,—and having exhausted the pleasures of the metropolis—the theatres, the Cider-cellars, the Finish, the station-houses, and other places which need by no means be here particularised,—Lord Cinqbars, I say, growing tired of London at the end of ten days, quitted the metropolis somewhat suddenly: nor did he pay his hotel bill at Long's before his departure ; but he left that document in possession of the landlord, as a token of his (my Lord Cinqbars') confidence in his host.

Tom Tufthunt went with my lord, of course (although of an

aristocratic turn in politics, Tom loved and respected a lord as much as any democrat in England). And whither do you think this worthy pair of young gentlemen were bound? To no less a place than Margate; for Cinqbars was filled with a longing to go and see his old friend Brandon, and determined, to use his own elegant words, "to knock the old buck up."

There was no adventure of consequence on board the steamer which brought Lord Cinqbars and his friend from London to Margate, and very few passengers besides. A wandering Jew or two were set down at Gravesend; the Rev. Mr. Wackerbart, and six unhappy little pupils whom the reverend gentleman had pounced upon in London, and was carrying back to his academy near Herne Bay; some of those inevitable persons of dubious rank who seem to have free tickets, and always eat and drink hugely with the captain; and a lady and her party, formed the whole list of passengers.

The lady—a very fat lady—had evidently just returned from abroad. Her great green travelling-chariot was on the deck, and on all her imperials were pasted fresh large bills, with the words INCE'S BRITISH HOTEL, BOULOGNE-SUR-MER; for it is the custom of that worthy gentleman to seize upon and plaster all the luggage of his guests with tickets, on which his name and residence are inscribed,— by which simple means he keeps himself perpetually in their recollection, and brings himself to the notice of all other persons who are in the habit of peering at their fellow-passengers' trunks, to find out their names. I need not say what a large class this is.

Well; this fat lady had a courier, a tall whiskered man, who spoke all languages, looked like a field-marshal, went by the name of Donnerwetter, and rode on the box; a French maid, Mademoiselle Augustine; and a little black page, called Saladin, who rode in the rumble. Saladin's whole business was to attend a wheezy, fat, white poodle, who usually travelled inside with his mistress and her fair *compagnon de voyage*, whose name was Miss Runt. This fat lady was evidently a person of distinction. During the first part of the voyage, on a windy, sunshiny April day, she paced the deck stoutly, leaning on the arm of poor little Miss Runt; and after they had passed Gravesend, when the vessel began to pitch a good deal, retired to her citadel, the travelling-chariot, to and from which the steward, the stewardess, and the whiskered courier were continually running with supplies—of sandwiches first, and afterwards of very hot brandy-and-water : for the truth must be told, it was rather a rough afternoon, and the poodle was sick ; Saladin was as bad ; the French maid, like all French maids, was outrageously ill ; the lady herself was very unwell indeed ; and poor dear sympathizing Runt was qualmish.

"Ah, Runt !" would the fat lady say in the intervals, "what a thing this malady de mare is !   Oh, mong jew !   Oh—oh !"

"It is, indeed, dear madam," said Runt, and went "Oh—oh !" in chorus.

"Ask the steward if we are near Margate, Runt."   And Runt did, and asked this question every five minutes, as people do on these occasions.

"Issy Monsieur Donnerwetter : ally dimandy ung pew d'o sho poor mwaw."

"Et de l'eau de fie afec, n'est-ce-bas, Matame ? " said Mr. Donnerwetter.

"Wee, wee, comme vous vouly."

And Donnerwetter knew very well what "comme vous vouly" meant, and brought the liquor exactly in the wished-for state.

"Ah, Runt, Runt ! there's something even worse than sea-sickness.   Heigh-ho !"

"Dear, dear Marianne, don't flutter yourself," cries Runt, squeezing a fat paw of her friend and patroness between her own bony fingers. "Don't agitate your nerves, dear.   I know you're miserable ; but haven't you got a friend in your faithful Runty ? "

"You're a good creater, that you are," said the fat lady, who seemed herself to be a good-humoured old soul ; "and I don't know what I should have done without you.   Heigh-ho !"

"Cheer up, dear ! you'll be happier when you get to Margate : you know you will," cried Runt, very knowingly.

"What do you mean, Elizabeth ? "

"You know very well, dear Marianne.   I mean that there's some one there will make you happy ; though he's a nasty wretch, that he is, to have treated my darling, beautiful Marianne so."

"Runt, Runt, don't abuse that best of men.   Don't call me beautiful—I'm not, Runt ; I have been, but I ain't now ; and oh ! no woman in the world is assy bong poor lui."

"But an angel is ; and you are, as you always was, an angel,— as good as an angel, as kind as an angel, as beautiful as one."

"Ally dong," said her companion, giving her a push; "you flatter me, Runt, you know you do."

"May I be struck down dead if I don't say the truth; and if he refuses you, as he did at Rome,—that is, after all his attentions and vows, he's faithless to you,—I say he's a wretch, that he is; and I *will* say he's a wretch, and he *is* a wretch—a nasty, wicked wretch!"

"Elizabeth, if you say that, you'll break my heart, you will! Vous casserez mong pover cure." But Elizabeth swore, on the contrary, that she would die for her Marianne, which consoled the fat lady a little.

A great deal more of this kind of conversation took place during the voyage; but as it occurred inside a carriage, so that to hear it was very difficult, and as possibly it was not of that edifying nature which would induce the reader to relish many chapters of it, we shall give no further account of the ladies' talk : suffice it to say, that about half-past four o'clock the journey ended, by the vessel bringing up at Margate Pier. The passengers poured forth, and hied to their respective homes or inns. My Lord Cinqbars and his companion (of whom we have said nothing, as they on their sides had scarcely spoken a word the whole way, except "deuce-ace," "quater-tray," "sizes," and so on,—being occupied ceaselessly in drinking bottled stout and playing backgammon,) ordered their luggage to be conveyed to "Wright's Hotel," whither the fat lady and suite followed them. The house was vacant, and the best rooms in it were placed, of course, at the service of the new comers. The fat lady sailed out of her bed-room towards her saloon, just as Lord Cinqbars, cigar in mouth, was swaggering out of his parlour. They met in the passage; when, to the young lord's surprise, the fat lady dropped him a low curtsey, and said,—

"Munseer le Vecomte de Cinqbars, sharmy de vous voir. Vous vous rappelez de mwaw, n'est-ce pas? Je vous ai vew à Rome—shay l'ambassadure, vous savy."

Lord Cinqbars stared her in the face, and pushed by her without a word, leaving the fat lady rather disconcerted.

"Well, Runt, I'm sure," said she, "he need not be so proud; I've met him twenty times at Rome, when he was a young chap with his tutor."

"Who the devil can that fat foreigner be?" mused Lord Cinqbars.

" Hang her, I've seen her somewhere ; but I'm cursed if I understand a word of her jabber." And so, dismissing the subject, he walked on to Brandon's.

"Dang it, it's a strange thing !" said the landlord of the hotel ; " but both my lord and the fat woman in number nine have asked their way to Mother Gann's lodging,"—for so did he dare to call that respectable woman !

It was true : as soon as number nine had eaten her dinner, she asked the question mentioned by the landlord ; and, as this meal occupied a considerable time, the shades of evening had by this time fallen upon the quiet city ; the silver moon lighted up the bay, and, supported by a numerous and well-appointed train of gas-lamps, illuminated the streets of a town,—of autumn eves so crowded and so gay ; of gusty April nights, so desolate. At this still hour (it might be half-past seven,) two ladies passed the gates of "Wright's Hotel," "in shrouding mantle wrapped, and velvet cap." Up the deserted High Street toiled they, by gaping rows of empty bathing-houses, by melancholy Jolly's French bazaar, by mouldy pastrycooks, blank reading-rooms, by fishmongers who never sold a fish, mercers who vended not a yard of riband—because, as yet, the season was not come,—and Jews and Cockneys still remained in town. At High Street's corner, near to Hawley Square, they passed the house of Mr. Fincham, chemist, who doth not only healthful drugs supply, but likewise sells cigars—the worst cigars that ever mortal man gave threepence for.

Up to this point, I say, I have had a right to accompany the fat lady and Miss Runt ; but whether, on arriving at Mr. Fincham's, they turned to the left, in the direction of the "Royal Hotel," or to the right, by the beach, the bathing-machines, and queer rickety old row of houses, called Buenos Ayres, no power on earth shall induce me to say ; suffice it, they went to Mrs. Gann's. Why should we set all the world gadding to a particular street, to know where that lady lives ? They arrived before that lady's house at about eight o'clock. Every house in the street had bills on it except hers (bitter mockery, as if anybody came down at Easter !) and at Mrs. Gann's house there was a light in the garret, and another in the two-pair front. I believe I have not mentioned before, that all the front windows were bow or bay-windows ; but so much the reader may know.

The two ladies, who had walked so far, examined wistfully the plate on the door, stood on the steps for a short time, retreated, and conversed with one another.

"Oh, Runty!" said the stouter of the two, "he's here—I know he's here, mong cure le dee—my heart tells me so." And she put a large hand upon a place on her left side, where there once had been a waist.

"Do you think he looks front or back, dear?" asked Runt. "P'raps he's not at home."

"That—that's his croisy," said the stout person; "I know it is;" and she pointed with instinctive justice to the two-pair. "Ecouty!" she added, "he's coming; there's some one at that window. Oh, mong jew, mong jew! c'est André, c'est lui!"

The moon was shining full on the face of the bow-windows of Mrs. Gann's house; and the two fair spies, who were watching on the other side, were, in consequence, completely in shadow. As the lady said, a dark form was seen in the two-pair front; it paced the room for a while, for no blinds were drawn. It then flung itself on a chair; its head on its hands; it then began to beat its brows wildly, and paced the room again. Ah! how the fat lady's heart throbbed as she looked at all this!

She gave a piercing shriek—almost fainted! and little Runt's knees trembled under her, as with all her might she supported, or rather pushed up, the falling figure of her stout patroness,—who saw at that instant Fitch come to the candle with an immense pistol in his hand, and give a most horrible grin as he looked at it, and clasped it to his breast.

"Unhand me, Runt; he's going to kill himself! It's for me! I know it is—I will go to him! Andrea, my Andrea!" And the fat lady was pushing for the opposite side of the way, when suddenly the second-floor window went clattering up, and Fitch's pale head was thrust out.

He had heard a scream, and had possibly been induced to open the window in consequence; but by the time he had opened it he had forgotten everything, and put his head vacantly out of the window, and gazed, the moon shining cold on his pale features.

"Pallid horb!" said Fitch, "shall I ever see thy light again? Will another night see me on this hearth, or view me, stark and cold, a lifeless corpse?" He took his pistol up, and slowly aimed it at a chimney-pot opposite. Fancy the fat lady's sensations, as she beheld her lover standing in the moonlight, and exercising this deadly weapon.

"Make ready—present—fire!" shouted Fitch, and did instantaneously, not fire off, but lower his weapon. "The bolt of death is sped!" continued he, clapping his hand on his side. "The poor painter's life is over! Caroline, Caroline, I die for thee!"

"Runt, Runt, I told you so!" shrieked the fat lady. "He is dying for me, and Caroline's my second name."

What the fat lady would have done more, I can't say; for Fitch, disturbed out of his reverie by her talking below, looked out, frowning vacantly, and saying, "Ulloh! we've hinterlopers 'ere!" suddenly banged down the window, and pulled down the blinds.

This gave a check to the fat lady's projected rush, and disconcerted her a little. But she was consoled by Miss Runt, promised to return on the morrow, and went home happy in the idea that her Andrea was faithful to her.

Alas, poor fat lady! little did you know the truth. It was Caroline Gann Fitch was raving about; and it was a part of his last letter to her, to be delivered after his death, that he was spouting out of the window.

Was the crazy painter going to fight a duel, or was he going to kill himself? This will be explained in the next chapter.

CHAPTER VIII.

WHICH TREATS OF WAR AND LOVE, AND MANY THINGS THAT ARE NOT TO BE UNDERSTOOD IN CHAP. VII.

FITCH'S verses, inserted in a previous chapter of this story, (and of which lines, by the way, the printer managed to make still greater nonsense than the ingenious bard ever designed,) had been composed many years before; and it was with no small trouble and thought that the young painter called the greater part of them to memory again, and furbished up a copy for Caroline's album. Unlike the love of most men, Andrea's passion was not characterized by jealousy and watchfulness, otherwise he would not have failed to perceive certain tokens of intelligence passing from time to time between Caroline and Brandon, and the lady's evident coldness to himself. The fact is, the painter was in love with being in love,—entirely absorbed in the consideration of the fact that he, Andrea Fitch, was at last enamoured; and he did not mind his mistress much more than Don Quixote did Dulcinea del Toboso.

Having rubbed up his verses, then, and designed a pretty emblematical outline which was to surround them, representing an arabesque of violets, dewdrops, fairies, and other objects, he came down one morning, drawing in hand ; and having informed Caroline, who was sitting very melancholy in the parlour, pre-occupied, with a pale face and red eyes, and not caring twopence for the finest drawing in the world,—having informed her that he was going to make in her halbum a humble hoffering of his hart, poor Fitch was just on the point of sticking in the drawing with gum, as painters know very well how to do, when his eye lighted upon a page of the album, in which nestled a few dried violets and —his own verses, signed with the name of George Brandon.

"Miss Caroline—Miss Gann, mam !" shrieked Fitch, in a tone of voice which made the young lady start out of a profound reverie, and cry, nervously,—"What in heaven is the matter ? "

"These verses, madam—a faded violet—word for word, gracious 'eavens ! every word !" roared Fitch, advancing with the book.

She looked at him rather vacantly, and as the violets caught her eye, put out her hand, and took them. " Do you know the hawthor, Miss Gann, of ' The faded Violets ?' "

"Author ? O yes ; they are—they are George's !" She burst into tears as she said that word ; and, pulling the little faded flowers to pieces, went sobbing out of the room.

Dear, dear little Caroline ! she has only been in love two months, and is already beginning to feel the woes of it !

It cannot be from want of experience—for I have felt the noble passion of love many times these forty years, since I was a boy of twelve (by which the reader may form a pretty good guess of my age),—it cannot be, I say, from want of experience that I am unable to describe, step by step, the progress of a love-affair ; nay, I am perfectly certain that I could, if I chose, make a most astonishing and heart-rending *liber amoris ;* but, nevertheless, I always feel a vast repugnance to the following out of a subject of this kind, which

I attribute to a natural diffidence and sense of shame that prevent me from enlarging on a theme that has in it something sacred—certain arcana which an honest man, although initiated into them, should not divulge.

If such coy scruples and blushing delicacy prevent one from passing the threshold even of an honourable love, and setting down, at so many guineas or shillings per page, the pious emotions and tendernesses of two persons chastely and legally engaged in sighing, ogling, hand-squeezing, kissing, and so forth (for with such outward signs I believe that the passion of love is expressed),—if a man feel, I say, squeamish about describing an innocent love, he is doubly disinclined to describe a guilty one ; and I have always felt a kind of loathing for the skill of such geniuses as Rousseau or Richardson, who could paint with such painful accuracy all the struggles and woes of Eloise and Clarissa,—all the wicked arts and triumphs of such scoundrels as Lovelace.

We have in this history a scoundrelly Lovelace in the person going by the name of George Brandon, and a dear, tender, innocent, yielding creature on whom he is practising his infernal skill ; and whether the public feel any sympathy for her or not, the writer can only say, for his part, that he heartily loves and respects poor little Caroline, and is quite unwilling to enter into any of the slow, painful, wicked details of the courtship which passed between her and her lover.

Not that there was any wickedness on *her* side, poor girl ! or that she did anything but follow the natural and beautiful impulses of an honest little female heart, that leads it to trust and love, and worship a being of the other sex, whom the eager fancy invests with all sorts of attributes of superiority. There was no wild, conceited tale that Brandon told Caroline which she did not believe,—no virtue which she could conceive or had read of in novels with which she did not endow him. Many long talks had they, and many sweet, stolen interviews, during the periods in which Caroline's father and mother were away making merry at the house of their son-in-law ; and while she was left under the care of her virtue and of Becky the maid. Indeed, it was a blessing that the latter was left in the joint guardianship. For Becky, who had such an absurd opinion of her young lady's merits as to fancy that she was a fit wife for any gentleman of the land, and that any gentleman might be charmed and fall in love with her, had some instinct, or possibly some experience, as to the passions and errors of youth, and warned Caroline accordingly. "If he's really in love, Miss, and I think he be, he'll marry you; if he won't marry you, he's a rascal, and you're too good for him, and must have nothing to do with him." To which Caroline replied, that she was sure Mr. Brandon was the most angelic, high-principled of human beings, and that she was sure his intentions were of the most honourable description.

We have before described what Mr. Brandon's character was. He was not a man of honourable intentions at all. But he was a gentleman of so excessively eager a temperament, that if properly resisted by a practised coquette, or by a woman of strong principles, he would sacrifice anything to obtain his ends,—nay, marry to obtain them; and, considering his disposition, it is only a wonder that he had not been married a great number of times already; for he had been in love perpetually since his seventeenth year. By which the reader may pretty well appreciate the virtue or the prudence of the ladies with whom hitherto our inflammable young gentleman had had to do.

The fruit, then, of all his stolen interviews, of all his prayers, vows, and protestations to Caroline, had been only this,—that she loved him; but loved him as an honest girl should, and was ready to go to the altar with him when he chose. He talked about his family, his peculiar circumstances, his proud father's curse. Little Caroline only sighed, and said her dearest George must wait until he could obtain his parent's consent. When pressed harder, she would burst into tears, and wonder how one so good and affectionate as he could propose to her anything unworthy of them both. It is clear to see that the young lady had read a vast number of novels, and knew something of the nature of love; and that she had a good principle and honesty of her own, which set her lover's schemes at naught: indeed, she had both these advantages,—her education, such as it was, having given her the one, and her honest nature having endowed her with the other.

On the day when Fitch came down to Caroline with his verses, Brandon had pressed these unworthy propositions upon her. She had torn herself violently away from him, and rushed to the door; but the poor little thing fell before she could reach it, screaming in a fit of hysterics, which brought Becky to her aid, and caused Brandon to leave her, abashed.   He went out ; she watched him go, and stole up into his room, and laid on his table the first letter she had ever written to him.   It was written in pencil, in a trembling, school-girl hand, and contained simply the following words :—

"George, you have almost broken my heart.   Leave me if you will, and if you dare not act like an honest man.   If ever you speak to me so again as you did this morning, I declare solemnly before heaven, I will take poison.

"C."

Indeed, the poor thing had read romances to some purpose ; without them, it is probable, she never would have thought of such a means of escape from a lover's persecutions ; and there was something in the girl's character that made Brandon feel sure that she would keep her promise.   How the words agitated him !   He felt a violent mixture of raging disappointment and admiration, and loved the girl ten thousand times more than ever.

Mr. Brandon had scarcely finished the reading of this document, and was yet agitated by the various passions which the perusal of it created, when the door of his apartment was violently flung open, and some one came in.   Brandon started, and turned round, with a kind of dread that Caroline had already executed her threat, and that a messenger was come to inform him of her death.   Mr. Andrea Fitch was the intruder.   His hat was on—his eyes were glaring ; and if the beards of men did stand on end anywhere but in poems and romances, his, no doubt, would have formed round his countenance a bristling auburn halo.   As it was, Fitch only looked astonishingly fierce, as he stalked up to the table, his hands behind his back.   When he had arrived at this barrier between himself and Mr. Brandon, he stopped, and, speechless, stared that gentleman in the face.

"May I beg, Mr. Fitch, to know what has procured me the honour of this visit?" exclaimed Mr. Brandon, after a brief pause of wonder.

"Honour !—ha, ha, ha !" growled Mr. Fitch, in a most sardonic, discordant way—"*honour !*"

"Well, sir, honour or no honour, I can tell you, my good man, it certainly is no pleasure !" said Brandon, testily.   "In plain English, then, what the devil has brought you here?"

Fitch plumped the album down on the table close to Mr. Brandon's nose, and said, " *That* has brought me, sir—that halbum, sir ; or, I ask your pardon, that a—album—ha, ha, ha !"

"Oh, I see !" said Mr. Brandon, who could not refrain from a smile. "It was a cruel trick of mine, Fitch, to rob you of your verses ; but all's fair in love."

"Fitch, sir ! don't Fitch me, sir ! I wish to be hintimate honly with men of h-honour, not with forgers, sir ; not with 'artless miscreants ! Miscreants, sir, I repeat ; vipers, sir ; b—b—b—blackguards, sir !"

" Blackguards, sir !" roared Mr. Brandon, bouncing up ; " blackguards, you dirty cockney mountebank ! Quit the room, sir, or I'll fling you out of the window !"

"Will you, sir ? try, sir ; I wish you may get it, sir. I'm a hartist, sir, and as good a man as you. Miscreant, forger, traitor, come on !"

And Mr. Brandon *would* have come on, but for a circumstance that deterred him ; and this was, that Mr. Fitch drew from his bosom a long, sharp, shining, waving poniard of the middle ages, that formed a part of his artistical properties, and with which he had armed himself for this encounter.

"Come, on, sir !" shrieked Fitch, brandishing this fearful weapon. " Lay a finger on me, and I bury this blade in your treacherous 'art. Ha ! do you tremble ?"

Indeed, the aristocratic Mr. Brandon turned somewhat pale.

" Well, well," said he, " what do you want? Do you suppose I am to be bullied by your absurd melodramatic airs ! It was, after all, but a joke, sir, and I am sorry that it has offended you. Can I say more ?—what shall I do ?"

"You shall hapologize ; not only to me, sir, but you shall tell Miss Caroline, in my presence, that you stole those verses from me, and used them quite unauthorised by me."

" Look you, Mr. Fitch, I will make you another set of verses quite as good, if you like ; but what you ask is impossible."

" I will 'asten myself, then, to Miss Caroline, and acquaint her with your dastardly forgery, sir. I will hopen her heyes, sir !"

" You may hopen her heyes, as you call them, if you please : but I tell you fairly, that the young lady will credit me rather than you ; and if you swear ever so much that the verses are yours, I must say that——"

" Say what, sir ? "

" Say that you *lie*, sir ! " said Mr. Brandon, stamping on the ground. " I'll make you other verses, I repeat ; but this is all I can do, and now go about your business ! "

" Curse your verses, sir ! liar and forger yourself ! Hare you a coward as well, sir ? A coward ! yes, I believe you are ; or will you meet me to-morrow morning like a man, and give me satisfaction for this hinfamous hinsult ? "

" Sir," said Mr. Brandon, with the utmost stateliness and scorn, " if you wish to murder me as you do the king's English, I won't balk you. Although a man of my rank is not called upon to meet a blackguard of your condition, I will, nevertheless, grant you your will. But have a care ; by heavens, I won't spare you, and I can hit an ace of hearts at twenty paces ! "

" Two can play at that," said Mr. Fitch, calmly ; " and if I can't hit a hace of 'arts at twenty paces, I can hit a man at twelve, and to-morrow I'll try." With which, giving Mr. Brandon a look of the highest contempt, the young painter left the room.

What were Mr. Brandon's thoughts as his antagonist left him ? Strange to say, rather agreeable. He had much too great a contempt for Fitch to suppose that so low a fellow would ever think seriously of fighting him, and reasoned with himself thus :—

" This Fitch, I know, will go off to Caroline, tell her the whole transaction, frighten her with the tale of a duel, and then she and I shall have a scene. I will tell her the truth about those infernal verses, menace death, blood, and danger, and then——"

Here he fell back into a charming reverie ; the wily fellow knew what power such a circumstance would give him over a poor weak girl, who would do anything rather than that her beloved should risk his life. And with this dastardly speculation as to the price he should ask for refraining from meeting Fitch, he was entertaining himself ; when, much to his annoyance, that gentleman again came into the room.

" Mr. Brandon," said he, " you have insulted me in the grossest and cruellest way."

" Well, sir, are you come to apologize ? " said Brandon sneeringly.

" No, I'm not come to apologize, Mr. Aristocrat : it's past that. I'm come to say this, sir, that I take you for a coward ; and that, unless you will give me your solemn word of honour not to mention

a word of this quarrel to Miss Gann, which might prevent our
meeting, I will never leave you till we *do* fight ! "

"This is outrageous, sir! Leave the room, or by heavens I'll
not meet you at all ! "

"Heasy, sir; easy, I beg your pardon, I can force you to that ! "

"And how, pray, sir ? "

"Why, in the first place, here's a stick, and I'll 'orsewhip you ;
and here are a pair of pistols, and we can fight now ! "

"Well, sir, I give you my honour," said Mr. Brandon, in a
diabolical rage ; and added, " I'll meet you to-morrow, not now ; and
you need not be afraid that I'll miss you ! "

" Hadew, sir," said the chivalrous little Fitch ; "bon giorno, sir,
as we used to say at Rome." And so, for the second time, he left
Mr. Brandon, who did not like very well the extraordinary courage
he had displayed.

"What the deuce has exasperated the fellow so ? " thought
Brandon.

Why, in the first place, he had crossed Fitch in love ; and, in the
second, he had sneered at his pronunciation and his gentility, and
Fitch's little soul was in a fury which nothing but blood would allay :
he was determined, for the sake of his hart and his lady, to bring
this proud champion down.

So Brandon was at last left to his cogitations ; when, confusion !
about five o'clock came another knock at his door.

" Come in ! " growled the owner of the lodgings.

A sallow, blear-eyed, rickety, undersized creature, tottering
upon a pair of high-heeled lacquered boots, and supporting himself
upon an immense gold-knobbed cane, entered the room with his hat
on one side and a jaunty air. It was a white hat with a broad brim,
and under it fell a great deal of greasy lank hair, that shrouded the
cheek-bones of the wearer. · The little man had no beard to his chin,
appeared about twenty years of age, and might weigh, stick and all,
some seven stone. If you wish to know how this exquisite was
dressed, I have the pleasure to inform you that he wore a great sky-
blue embroidered satin stock, in the which figured a carbuncle that
looked like a lambent gooseberry. He had a shawl-waistcoat of
many colours ; a pair of loose blue trousers, neatly strapped to
show his little feet : a brown cut-away coat with brass buttons, that
fitted tight round a spider waist ; and over all a white or drab

surtout, with a sable collar and cuffs, from which latter on each hand peeped five little fingers covered with lemon-coloured kid gloves. One of these hands he held constantly to his little chest: and, with a hoarse thin voice, he piped out,

"George my buck! how goes it?"

We have been thus particular in our description of the costume of this individual (whose inward man strongly corresponded with his manly and agreeable exterior), because he was the person whom Mr. Brandon most respected in the world.

"CINQBARS!" exclaimed our hero: "why, what the deuce has brought you to Margate?"

"Fwendship, my old cock!" said the Honourable Augustus Frederick Ringwood, commonly called Viscount Cinqbars, for indeed it was he. "Fwendship and the *City of Canterbuwy* steamer!" and herewith his lordship held out his right-hand forefinger to Brandon, who enclosed it most cordially in all his. "Wathn't it good of me, now, George, to come down and conthole you in thith curthed, thtupid place—hay now?" said my lord, after these salutations.

Brandon swore he was very glad to see him, which was very true, for he had no sooner set his eyes upon his lordship, than he had determined to borrow as much money from him as ever he could induce the young nobleman to part with.

"I'll tell you how it wath, my boy: you thee I wath thtopping at Long'th, when I found, by Jove, that the governor wath come to town! Cuth me if I didn't meet the infarnal old family dwag, with my mother, thithterth, and all, ath I wath dwiving a hack-cab with Polly Tomkinth in the Pawk! Tho when I got home, 'Hang it!' thayth I to Tufthunt, 'Tom my boy,' thaith I, 'I've just theen the governor, and must be off!' 'What, back to Ockthford?' thaith Tom. 'No,' thaith I, 'that *won't* do. Abroad—to Jewicho—anywhere. Egad, I have it! I'll go down to Margate and thee old George, that I will.' And tho off I came the very next day; and here I am, and thereth dinner waiting for uth at the hotel, and thixth bottleth of champagne in ithe, and thum thalmon: tho you mutht come."

To this proposition Mr. Brandon readily agreed, being glad enough of the prospect of a good dinner and some jovial society, for he was low and disturbed in spirits, and so promised to dine with his friend at the "Sun."

The two gentlemen conversed for some time longer. Mr. Brandon was a shrewd fellow, and knew perfectly well a fact of which, no doubt, the reader has a notion—namely, that Lord Cinqbars was a ninny; but, nevertheless, Brandon esteemed him highly as a lord We pardon stupidity in lords; nature or instinct, however sarcastic a man may be among ordinary persons, renders him towards men of quality benevolently blind : a divinity hedges not only the king, but the whole peerage.

" That's the girl, I suppose," said my lord, knowingly winking at Brandon : " that little pale girl, who let me in, I mean. A nice little filly, upon my honour, Georgy my buck !"

" Oh—that—yes—I wrote, I think, something about her," said Brandon, blushing slightly; for, indeed, he now began to wish that his friend should make no comments upon a young lady with whom he was so much in love.

" I suppose it's all up now?" continued my lord, looking still more knowing. " All over with her, hay? I saw it was by her looks, in a minute."

" Indeed you do me a great deal too much honour. Miss—ah, —Miss Gann is a very respectable young person, and I would not for the world have you to suppose that I would do anything that should the least injure her character."

At this speech, Lord Cinqbars was at first much puzzled; but, in considering it, was fully convinced that Brandon was a deeper dog than ever. Boiling with impatience to know the particulars of this delicate intrigue, this cunning diplomatist determined he would pump the whole story out of Brandon by degrees; and so, in the course of half an hour's conversation that the young men had together, Cinqbars did not make less than forty allusions to the subject that interested him. At last Brandon cut him short rather haughtily, by begging that he would make no further allusions to the subject, as it was one that was excessively disagreeable to him.

In fact, there was no mistake about it now. George Brandon was in love with Caroline. He felt that he was while he blushed at his friend's alluding to her, while he grew indignant at the young lord's coarse banter about her.

Turning the conversation to another point, he asked Cinqbars about his voyage, and whether he had brought any companion with him to Margate; whereupon my lord related all his feats in London, how he had been to the watchhouse, how many bottles of champagne he had drunk, how he had "milled" a policeman, &c. &c. ; and he concluded by saying that he had come down with Tom Tufthunt, who was at the inn at that very moment smoking a cigar.

This did not increase Brandon's good-humour; and when Cinqbars mentioned his friend's name, Brandon saluted it mentally with a hearty curse. These two gentlemen hated each other of old. Tufthunt was a small college man of no family, with a foundation fellowship; and it used to be considered that a sporting fellow of a small college was a sad, raffish, disreputable character. Tufthunt, then, was a vulgar fellow, and Brandon a gentleman, so they hated each other. They were both toadies of the same nobleman, so they hated each other. They had had some quarrel at college about a disputed bet, which Brandon knew he owed, and so they hated each other; and in their words about it Brandon had threatened to horsewhip Tufthunt, and called him a "sneaking, swindling, small college snob;" and so little Tufthunt, who had not resented the words, hated Brandon far more than Brandon hated him. The latter only had a contempt for his rival, and voted him a profound bore and vulgarian.

So, although Mr. Tufthunt did not choose to frequent Mr. Brandon's rooms, he was very anxious that his friend, the young lord, should not fall into his old bear-leader's hands again, and came down to Margate to counteract any influence which the arts of Brandon might acquire.

"Curse the fellow!" thought Tufthunt in his heart (there was a fine reciprocity of curses between the two men); "he has drawn Cinqbars already for fifty pounds this year, and will have some half of his last remittance, if I don't keep a look-out, the swindling thief!"

And so frightened was Tufthunt at the notion of Brandon's return to power and dishonest use of it, that he was at the time on the point of writing to Lord Ringwood to tell him of his son's doings, only he wanted some money deucedly himself. Of Mr. Tufthunt's *physique* and history it is necessary merely to say, that he was the son of a country attorney who was agent to a lord; he had been sent to a foundation-school, where he distinguished himself for ten years, by fighting and being flogged more than any boy of the five hundred. From the foundation-school he went to college with an exhibition, which was succeeded by a fellowship, which was to end in a living. In his person Mr. Tufthunt was short and bow-legged; he wore a sort of clerico-sporting costume, consisting of a black-straight-cut coat and light drab breeches, with a vast number of buttons at the ankles; a sort of dress much affectioned by sporting gentlemen of the university in the author's time.

Well, Brandon said he had some letters to write, and promised to follow his friend, which he did; but, if the truth must be told, so infatuated was the young man become with his passion, with the resistance he had met with, and so nervous from the various occurrences of the morning, that he passed the half hour during which he was free from Cinqbars' society in kneeling, imploring, weeping at Caroline's little garret-door, which had remained piteously closed to him. He was wild with disappointment, mortification—mad, longing to see her. The cleverest coquette in Europe could not have so inflamed him. His first act on entering the dinner-room was to drink off a large tumbler of champagne; and when Cinqbars, in his elegant way, began to rally him upon his wildness, Mr. Brandon only growled and cursed with frightful vehemency, and applied again to the bottle. His face, which had been quite white, grew a bright red; his tongue, which had been tied, began to chatter vehemently; before the fish was off the table, Mr. Brandon showed strong symptoms of intoxication; before the dessert appeared, Mr. Tufthunt, winking knowingly to Lord Cinqbars, had begun to draw him out; and Brandon, with a number of shrieks and oaths, was narrating the history of his attachment.

"Look you, Tufthunt," said he, wildly; "hang you, I hate you, but I *must* talk! I've been, for two months now, in this cursed hole; in a rickety lodging, with a vulgar family; as vulgar, by Jove, as you are yourself!"

Mr. Tufthunt did not like this style of address half so much as Lord Cinqbars, who was laughing immoderately, and to whom Tufthunt whispered rather sheepishly, "Pooh, pooh, he's drunk!"

"*Drunk!* no, sir," yelled out Brandon; "I'm mad, though, with the prudery of a little devil of fifteen, who has cost me more trouble than it would take me to seduce every one of your sisters—ha, ha! every one of the Miss Tufthunts, by Jove! Miss Suky Tufthunt, Miss Dolly Tufthunt, Miss Anna-Maria Tufthunt, and the whole bunch. Come, sir, don't sit scowling at *me*, or I'll brain you with the decanter." (Tufthunt was down again on the sofa.) "I've borne with the girl's mother, and her father, and her sisters, and a cook in the house, and a scoundrel of a painter, that I'm going to fight about her; and for what?—why, for a letter, which says, 'George, I'll kill myself! George, I'll kill myself!'—ha, ha! a little devil like that *killing* herself——ha, ha! and I—I who—who adore her, who am mad for——"

"Mad, I believe he is," said Tufthunt; and at this moment Mr. Brandon was giving the most unequivocal signs of madness; he plunged his head into the corner of the sofa, and was kicking his feet violently into the cushions.

"You don't understand him, Tufty my boy," said Lord Cinqbars, with a very superior air. "You ain't up to these things, I tell you; and I suspect, by Jove, that you never were in love in your life. *I* know what it is, sir. And as for Brandon, heaven bless you! I've often seen him in that way when we were abroad. When he has an intrigue, he's mad about it. Let me see, there was the Countess Fritzch, at Baden-Baden; there was the woman at Pau; and that girl—at Paris, was it?—no, at Vienna. He went on just so about them all; but I'll tell you what, when *we* do the thing, we do it easier, my boy, hay?"

And so saying, my lord cocked up his little sallow, beardless face into a grin, and then fell to eyeing a glass of execrable claret across a candle. *An intrigue*, as he called it, was the little creature's delight; and until the time should arrive when he could have one himself, he loved to talk of those of his friends.

As for Tufthunt, we may fancy how that gentleman's previous affection for Brandon was increased by the latter's brutal addresses to him. Brandon continued to drink and to talk, though not always in the sentimental way in which he had spoken about his loves and injuries. Growing presently madly jocose as he had before been madly melancholy, he narrated to the two gentlemen the particulars of his quarrel with Fitch, mimicking the little painter's manner in an excessively comic way, and giving the most ludicrous account of his person, kept his companions in a roar of laughter. Cinqbars swore that he would see the fun in the morning, and agreed that if the painter wanted a second, either he or Tufthunt would act for him.

Now my Lord Cinqbars had an excessively clever servant, a merry rogue, whom he had discovered in the humble capacity of scout's assistant at Christchurch, and raised to be his valet. The chief

duties of the valet were to black his lord's beautiful boots, that
we have admired so much, and put his lordship to bed when overtaken with liquor. He heard every word of the young men's talk (it
being his habit, much encouraged by his master, to join occasionally .
in the conversation); and in the course of the night, when at supper
with Monsieur Donnerwetter and Mdlle. Augustine, he related every
word of the talk abovestairs, mimicking Brandon quite as cleverly
as the latter had mimicked Fitch. When then, after making his
company laugh by describing Brandon's love-agonies, Mr. Tom
informed them how that gentleman had a rival, with whom he was
going to fight a duel the next morning—an artist-fellow with an
immense beard, whose name was Fitch, to his surprise Mdlle. Augustine burst into a scream of laughter, and exclaimed, "*Feesh, Feesh!
c'est notre homme;*—it is our man, sare! Saladin, remember you
Mr. Fish?"

Saladin said gravely, " Missa Fis, Missa Fis! know 'um quite well,
Missa Fis! Painter-man, big beard, gib Saladin bit injyrubby,
Missis lub Missa Fis!"

It was too true, the fat lady was the famous MRS. CARRICK-
FERGUS, and she had come all the way from Rome in pursuit of
her adored painter.

CHAPTER IX.

WHICH THREATENS DEATH, BUT CONTAINS A GREAT DEAL OF MARRYING.

As the morrow was to be an eventful day in the lives of all the
heroes and heroines of this history, it will be as well to state how
they passed the night previous. Brandon, like the English before
the battle of Hastings, spent the evening in feasting and carousing;
and Lord Cinqbars, at twelve o'clock, his usual time after his usual
quantity of drink, was carried up to bed by the servant kept by his
lordship for that purpose. Mr. Tufthunt took this as a hint to wish
Brandon good-night, at the same time promising that he and Cinqbars
would not fail him in the morning about the duel.

Shall we confess that Mr. Brandon, whose excitement now began to wear off, and who had a dreadful headache, did not at all relish the idea of the morrow's combat?

"If," said he, "I shoot this crack-brained painter, all the world will cry out, 'Murder!' If he shoot me, all the world will laugh at me! And yet, confound him! he seems so bent upon blood, that there is no escaping a meeting."

"At any rate," Brandon thought, "there will be no harm in a letter to Caroline." So, on arriving at home, he sat down and wrote a very pathetic one; saying that he fought in her cause, and if he died, his last breath should be for her. So having written, he jumped into bed, and did not sleep one single wink all night.

As Brandon passed his night like the English, Fitch went through his like the Normans, in fasting, and mortification, and meditation. The poor fellow likewise indited a letter to Caroline: a very long and strong one, interspersed with pieces of poetry, and containing the words we have just heard him utter out of the window. Then he thought about making his will: but he recollected, and, indeed, it was a bitter thought to the young man, that there was not one single soul in the wide world who cared for him—except, indeed, thought he, after a pause, that poor Mrs. Carrickfergus at Rome, who *did* like me, and was the only person who ever bought my drawings. So he made over all his sketches to her, regulated his little property, found that he had money enough to pay his washer-woman; and so, having disposed of his worldly concerns, Mr. Fitch also jumped into bed, and speedily fell into a deep sleep. Brandon could hear him snoring all night, and did not feel a bit the more comfortable because his antagonist took matters so unconcernedly.

Indeed, our poor painter had no guilty thoughts in his breast, nor any particular revenge against Brandon, now that the first pangs of mortified vanity were over. But, with all his vagaries, he was a man of spirit; and after what had passed in the morning, the treason that had been done him, and the insults heaped upon him, he felt that the duel was irrevocable. He had a misty notion, imbibed somewhere, that it was the part of a gentleman's duty to fight duels, and had long been seeking for an opportunity. "Suppose I do die," said he, "what's the odds? Caroline doesn't care for me. Dr. Wackerbart's boys won't have their drawing-lesson next Wednesday; and no more will be said of poor Andrea."

And now for the garret. Caroline was wrapped up in her own

woes, poor little soul ! and in the arms of the faithful Becky cried herself to sleep.   But the slow hours passed on ; and the tide, which had been out, now came in ; and the lamps waxed fainter and fainter ; and the watchman cried six o'clock ; and the sun arose and ´gilded the minarets of Margate ; and Becky got up and scoured the steps, and the kitchen, and made ready the lodgers' breakfasts ; and at half-past eight there came a thundering rap at the door, and two gentlemen, one with a mahogany case under his arm, asked for Mr. Brandon, and were shown up to his room by the astonished Becky, who was bidden by Mr. Brandon to get breakfast for three.

The thundering rap awakened Mr. Fitch, who rose and dressed himself in his best clothes, gave a twist of the curling-tongs to his beard, and conducted himself throughout with perfect coolness. Nine o'clock struck, and he wrapped his cloak round him, and put under his cloak that pair of foils which we have said he possessed, and did not know in the least how to use.   However, he had heard his *camarades d'atelier*, at Paris and Rome, say that they were the best weapons for duelling ; and so forth he issued.

Becky was in the passage as he passed down ; she was always scrubbing there.   "Becky," said Fitch, in a hollow voice, "here is a letter ; if I should not return in half an hour, give it to Miss Gann, and promise on your honour that she shall not have it sooner." Becky promised.   She thought the painter was at some of his mad tricks.   He went out of the door saluting her gravely.

But he went only a few steps and came back again.   "Becky," said he, "you—you've always been a good girl to me, and here's something for you ; per'aps we shan't—we shan't see each other for some time."   The tears were in his eyes as he spoke, and he handed her over seven shillings and fourpence halfpenny, being every farthing he possessed in the world.

"Well, I'm sure ! " said Becky ; and that was all she said, for she pocketed the money, and fell to scrubbing again.

Presently the three gentlemen upstairs, came clattering down. "Lock bless you, don't be in such a 'urry ! " exclaimed Becky ; "it's full herly yet, and the water's not biling."

"We'll come back to breakfast, my dear," said one, a little gentleman in high-heeled boots ; "and, I thay, mind and have thum thoda-water."   And he walked out, twirling his cane.   His friend with the case followed him.   Mr. Brandon came last.

He too turned back after he had gone a few paces. "Becky," said he, in a grave voice, "if I am not back in half-an-hour, give that to Miss Gann."

Becky was fairly flustered by this; and after turning the letters round and round, and peeping into the sides, and looking at the seals very hard, she like a fool determined that she would not wait half-an-hour, but carry them up to Miss Caroline; and so up she mounted, finding pretty Caroline in the act of lacing her stays.

And the consequences of Becky's conduct was that little Carry left off lacing her stays (a sweet little figure the poor thing looked in them; but that is neither here nor there), took the letters, looked at one which she threw down directly; at the other, which she eagerly opened, and having read a line or two, gave a loud scream, and fell down dead in a fainting fit!

*　　　*　　　*　　　*　　　*

Waft us, O Muse! to Mr. Wright's hotel, and quick narrate what chances there befel. Very early in the morning Mdlle. Augustine made her appearance in the apartment of Miss Runt, and with great glee informed that lady of the event which was about to take place. "Figurez-vous, mademoiselle, que notre homme va se battre—oh, but it will be droll to see him sword in hand!"

"Don't plague me with your ojous servants' quarrels, Augustine; that horrid courier is always quarrelling and tipsy."

"Mon Dieu, qu'elle est bête!" exclaimed Augustine: "but I tell you it is not the courier; it is he, l'objet, le peintre dont madame s'est amourachée, Monsieur Feesh."

"Mr. Fitch!" cried Runt, jumping up in bed. "Mr. Fitch going to fight! Augustine, my stockings—quick, my *robe-de-chambre*—tell me when, how, where?"

And so Augustine told her that the combat was to take place at nine that morning, behind the Windmill, and that the gentleman with whom Mr. Fitch was to go out, had been dining at the hotel the night previous, in company with the little milor, who was to be his second.

Quick as lightning flew Runt to the chamber of her patroness. That lady was in a profound sleep; and I leave you to imagine what were her sensations on awaking and hearing this dreadful tale.

Such is the force of love, that although, for many years, Mrs. Carrickfergus had never left her bed before noon, although in all her wild wanderings after the painter she, nevertheless, would have her tea and cutlet in bed, and her doze likewise, before she set forth on a journey —she now started up in an instant, forgetting her nap, mutton-chops, everything, and began dressing with a promptitude which can only be equalled by Harlequin when disguising himself in a pantomime. She would have had an attack of nerves, only she knew there was no time for it ; and I do believe that twenty minutes were scarcely over her head, as the saying is, when her bonnet and cloak were on, and with her whole suite, and an inn-waiter or two whom she pressed into her service, she was on full trot to the field of action. For twenty years before, and from that day to this, Marianne Carrickfergus never had or has walked so quickly.

*   *   *   *   *

"Hullo, here'th a go !" exclaimed Lord Viscount Cinqbars, as they arrived on the ground behind the Windmill ; "cuth me there'th only one man ! "

This was indeed the case ; Mr. Fitch, in his great cloak, was pacing slowly up and down the grass, his shadow stretching far in the sunshine. Mr. Fitch was alone too ; for the fact is, he had never thought about a second. This he admitted frankly, bowing with much majesty to the company as they came up. "But that, gents," said he, "will make no difference, I hope, nor prevent fair play from being done." And, flinging off his cloak, he produced the foils, from which the buttons had been taken off. He went up to Brandon, and was for offering him one of the weapons, just as they do at the theatre. Brandon stepped back, rather abashed : Cinqbars looked posed ; Tufthunt delighted. "Ecod," said he, "I hope the bearded fellow will give it him."

"Excuse me, sir," said Mr. Brandon; "as the challenged party, I demand pistols."

Mr. Fitch, with great presence of mind and gracefulness, stuck the swords into the grass.

"Oh, pithtolth of courth," lisped my lord; and presently called aside Tufthunt, to whom he whispered something in great glee ; to which Tufthunt objected at first, saying, "No, d—— him, let him fight." "And your fellowship and living, Tufty my boy?" interposed my lord; and then they walked on. After a couple of minutes, during which Mr. Fitch was employed in examining Mr. Brandon from the toe upwards to the crown of his head, or hat,

just as Mr. Widdicombe does Mr. Cartlich, before those two gentlemen proceed to join in combat on the boards of Astley's Amphi-
theatre (indeed poor Fitch had no other standard of chivalry)—when
Fitch had concluded this examination, of which Brandon did not
know what the deuce to make, Lord Cinqbars came back to the
painter, and gave him a nod.

"Sir," said he, "as you have come unprovided with a second, I,
with your leave, will act as one. My name is Cinqbars—Lord Cinqbars ; and though I had come to the ground to act as the friend of
my friend here, Mr. Tufthunt will take that duty upon him ; and as it
appears to me there can be no other end to this unhappy affair, we
will proceed at once."

It is a marvel how Lord Cinqbars ever made such a gentlemanly
speech. When Fitch heard that he was to have a lord for a second,
he laid his hand on his chest, and vowed it was the greatest h-honour
of his life ; and was turning round to walk towards his ground, when
my lord, gracefully thrusting his tongue into his cheek, and bringing
his thumb up to his nose, twiddled about his fingers for a moment,
and said to Brandon, "Gammon !"

Mr. Brandon smiled, and heaved a great, deep, refreshing sigh.
The truth was, a load was taken off his mind, of which he was
very glad to be rid ; for there was something in the coolness of
that crazy painter that our fashionable gentleman did not at all
approve of.

"I think, Mr. Tufthunt," said Lord Cinqbars, very loud, "that
considering the gravity of the case—threatening horsewhipping, you
know, lie on both sides, and lady in the case—I think we must have
the barrier-duel."

"What's that ? " asked Fitch.

"The simplest thing in the world ; and," in a whisper, "let me
add, the best for you. Look here. We shall put you at twenty paces,
and a hat between you. You walk forward and fire when you like.
When you fire, you stop ; and you both have the liberty of walking
up to the hat. Nothing can be more fair than that."

"Very well," said Fitch ; and, with a great deal of preparation,
the pistols were loaded.

"I tell you what," whispered Cinqbars to Fitch, "if I hadn't
chosen this way you were a dead man. If he fires he hits you dead.
You must not let him fire, but have him down first."

" I'll try," said Fitch, who was a little pale, and thanked his noble friend for his counsel. The hat was placed and the men took their places.

" Are you all ready?"

" Ready," said Brandon.

" Advance when I drop my handkerchief." And presently down it fell, Lord Cinqbars crying, " Now ! "

The combatants both advanced, each covering his man. When he had gone about six paces, Fitch stopped, fired, and—missed. He grasped his pistol tightly, for he was very near dropping it; and then stood biting his lips, and looking at Brandon, who grinned savagely, and walked up to the hat.

" Will you retract what you said of me yesterday, you villain?" said Brandon.

" I can't."

" Will you beg for life?"

" No."

" Then take a minute, and make your peace with God, for you are a dead man."

Fitch dropped his pistol to the ground, shut his eyes for a moment, and flinging up his chest and clenching his fists, said, " *Now I'm ready.*"

Brandon *fired*—and strange to say, Andrea Fitch, as he gasped and staggered backwards, saw, or thought he saw, Mr. Brandon's pistol flying up in the air, where it went off, and heard that gentleman yell out an immense oath in a very audible voice. When he came to himself, a thick stick was lying at Brandon's feet ; Mr. Brandon was capering about the ground, and cursing and shaking a maimed elbow, and a whole posse of people were rushing upon them. The first was the great German courier, who rushed upon Brandon, and shook that gentleman, and shouting, " Schelm ! spitzbube ! blagard ! goward ! " in his ear. " If I had not drown my stick and brogen his damt arm, he wod have murdered dat boor young man."

The German's speech contained two unfounded assertions ; in the first place Brandon would not have murdered Fitch ; and, secondly, his arm was not broken—he had merely received a blow on that part which anatomists call the funny-bone : a severe blow, which sent the pistol spinning into the air, and caused the gentleman to scream with pain. Two waiters seized upon the murderer, too ; a baker, who had been brought from his rounds, a bellman, several boys,—were yelling round him, and shouting out, " Pole-e-eace ! "

Next to these came, panting and blowing, some women. Could Fitch believe his eyes ?—that fat woman in red satin !—yes—no—yes —he was, he was in the arms of Mrs. Carrickfergus !

   *   *   *   *   *   *   *

The particulars of this meeting are too delicate to relate. Suffice it that somehow matters were explained, Mr. Brandon was let loose, and a fly was presently seen to drive up, into which Mr. Fitch consented to enter with his new-found friend.

Brandon had some good movements in him. As Fitch was getting into the carriage, he walked up to him and held out his left hand : " I can't offer you my right hand, Mr. Fitch, for that cursed courier's stick has maimed it ; but I hope you will allow me to apologize for my shameful conduct to you, and to say that I never in my life met a more gallant fellow than yourself."

" That he is, by Jove ! " said my Lord Cinqbars.

Fitch blushed as red as a peony, and trembled very much. "And yet," said he, " you would have murdered me just now, Mr. Brandon. I can't take your 'and, sir."

" Why, you great flat," said my lord, wisely, "he couldn't have hurt you, nor you him. There wath no ballth in the pithtolth."

" What," said Fitch, starting back, "do you gents call that *a joke?* Oh, my lord, my lord ! " And here poor Fitch actually burst into tears on the red satin bosom of Mrs. Carrickfergus : she and Miss Runt were crying as hard as they could. And so, amidst much shouting and huzzaing, the fly drove away.

" What a blubbering, abthurd donkey ! " said Cinqbars, with his usual judgment ; " ain't he, Tufthunt ? "

Tufthunt, of course, said yes ; but Brandon was in a virtuous mood. " By heavens ! I think his tears do the man honour. When I came out with him this morning, I intended to act fairly by him. And as for Mr. Tufthunt, who calls a man a coward because he cries—Mr. Tufthunt knows well what a pistol is, and that some men don't care to face it, brave as they are."

Mr. Tufthunt understood the hint, and bit his lips and walked on. And as for that worthy moralist, Mr. Brandon, I am happy to say that there was some good fortune in store for him, which, though similar in kind to that bestowed lately upon Mr. Fitch, was superior in degree.

It was no other than this, that forgetting all maidenly decency and decorum, before Lord Viscount Cinqbars and his friend, that silly little creature, Caroline Gann, rushed out from the parlour into the passage—she had been at the window ever since she was rid of her fainting fit! and ah! what agonies of fear had that little panting heart endured during the half-hour of her lover's absence !—Caroline Gann, I say, rushed into the passage, and leaped upon the neck of Brandon, and kissed him, and called him her dear, dear, dear, darling George, and sobbed, and laughed, until George, taking her round the waist gently, carried her into the little dingy parlour, and closed the door behind him."

"Egad," cried Cinqbars, "this is quite a *thene!* Hullo, Becky, Polly, what's your name ?—bring uth up the breakfatht; and I hope you've remembered the thoda-water. Come along up thtairth, Tufty my boy."

*　　　*　　　*　　　*　　　*

When Brandon came upstairs and joined them, which he did in a minute or two, consigning Caroline to Becky's care, his eyes were full of tears ; and when Cinqbars began to rally him in his usual delicate way, Brandon said gravely, "No laughing, sir, if you please; for I swear that that lady before long shall be my wife."

"Your wife !—and what will your father say, and what will your duns say, and what will Miss Goldmore say, with her hundred thousand pounds ?" cried Cinqbars.

"Miss Goldmore be hanged," said Brandon, "and the duns too; and my father may reconcile it to himself as he can." And here Brandon fell into a reverie.

"It's no use thinking," he cried, after a pause. "You see what a girl it is, Cinqbars. I love her—by heavens, I'm mad with love for her ! She shall be mine, let what will come of it. And besides," he added, in a lower tone of voice, "why need, why need my father know anything about it ?"

"O flames and furies, what a lover it is !" exclaimed his friend. "But, by Jove, I like your spirit; and hang all governors say I. Stop—a bright thought ! If you must marry, why here's Tom Tufthunt, the very man to do your business." Little Lord Cinqbars was delighted with the excitement of the affair, and thought to himself, "By Jove, this *is* an intrigue !"

"What, is Tufthunt in orders ?" said Brandon.

"Yes," replied that reverend gentleman : "don t you see my coat ?   I took orders six weeks ago, on my fellowship.   Cinqbars' governor has promised me a living."

"And you shall marry George here, so you shall."

"What, without a licence ?"

"Hang the licence !—we won't peach, will we, George ?"

"Her family must know nothing of it," said George, "or *they* would."

"Why should they ?   Why shouldn't Tom marry you in this very room, without any church or stuff at all ?"

Tom said : "You'll hold me out, my lord, if anything comes of it ; and, if Brandon likes, why, I *will*.   He's done for if he does," muttered Tufthunt, "and I have had my revenge on him, the bullying, supercilious blackleg."

*   *   *   *   *

And so on that very day, in Brandon's room, without a licence, and by that worthy clergyman the Rev. Thomas Tufthunt, with my Lord Cinqbars for the sole witness, poor Caroline Gann, who knew no better, who never heard of licences, and did not know what banns meant, was married in a manner to the person calling himself George Brandon ; George Brandon not being his real name.

No writings at all were made, and the ceremony merely read through.   Becky, Caroline's sole guardian, when the poor girl kissed her, and, blushing, showed her gold ring, thought all was in order : and the happy couple set off for Dover that day, with fifty pounds which Cinqbars lent the bridegroom.

Becky received a little letter from Caroline, which she promised to carry to her mamma at Swigby's : and it was agreed that she was to give warning, and come and live with her young lady.   Next morning Lord Cinqbars and Tufthunt took the boat for London ; the latter uneasy in mind, the former vowing that "he'd never spent such an exciting day in his life, and loved an intrigue of all things."

Next morning, too, the great travelling-chariot of Mrs. Carrick-fergus rolled away with a bearded gentleman inside.   Poor Fitch had been back to his lodgings to try one more chance with Caroline, and he arrived in time—to see her get into a postchaise alone with Brandon.

Six weeks afterwards *Galignani's Messenger* contained the following announcement :—

"Married, at the British embassy, by Bishop Luscombe, Andrew Fitch, Esq., to Marianne Caroline Matilda, widow of the late Antony Carrickfergus, of Lombard Street and Gloucester Place, Esquire. The happy pair, after a magnificent *déjeûné*, set off for the south in their splendid carriage-and-four. Miss Runt officiated as bride's-maid; and we remarked among the company Earl and Countess Crabs, General Sir Rice Curry, K.C.B., Colonel Wapshot, Sir Charles Swang, the Hon. Algernon Percy Deuceace and his lady, Count Punter, and others of the *élite* of the fashionables now in Paris. The bridegroom was attended by his friend Michael Angelo Titmarsh, Esquire; and the lady was given away by the Right Hon. the Earl of Crabs. On the departure of the bride and bridegroom the festivities were resumed, and many a sparkling bumper of Meurice's champagne was quaffed to the health of the hospitable and interesting couple."

And with one more marriage this chapter shall conclude. About this time the British Auxiliary Legion came home from Spain; and Lieut.-General Swabber, a knight of San Fernando, of the order of Isabella the Catholic, of the Tower and Sword, who, as plain Lieutenant Swabber, had loved Miss Isabella Macarty, as a general now actually married her. I leave you to suppose how glorious Mrs. Gann was, and how Gann got tipsy at the "Bag of Nails;" but as her daughters each insisted upon their 30*l.* a year income, and Mrs. Gann had so only 60*l.* left, she was obliged still to continue the lodging-house at Margate, in which have occurred the most interesting passages of this SHABBY GENTEEL STORY.

Becky never went to her young mistress, who was not heard of after she wrote the letter to her parent, saying that she was married to Mr. Brandon; but, for *particular reasons*, her dear husband wished to keep his marriage secret, and for the present her beloved parents must be content to know she was happy. Gann missed his little Carry at first a good deal, but spent more and more of his time at the alehouse, as his house with only Mrs. Gann in it was too hot for him. Mrs. Gann talked unceasingly of her daughter the squire's lady, and her daughter the general's wife; but never once mentioned Caroline after the first burst of wonder and wrath at her departure.

God bless thee, poor Caroline! Thou art happy now, for some short space at least; and here, therefore, let us leave thee.

THE ADVENTURES OF PHILIP

ON HIS WAY THROUGH THE WORLD;

SHOWING

WHO ROBBED HIM, WHO HELPED HIM, AND WHO
PASSED HIM BY.

VOL. I.   7

TO

M. I. HIGGINS,

IN GRATEFUL REMEMBRANCE OF OLD FRIENDSHIP AND KINDNESS,

Kensington, July, 1862.

THE ADVENTURES OF PHILIP.

CHAPTER I.

DOCTOR FELL.

OT attend her own son when he is ill!" said my mother. "She does not deserve to have a son!" And Mrs. Pendennis looked towards her own only darling whilst uttering this indignant exclamation. As she looked, I know what passed through her mind. She nursed me, she dressed me in little caps and long-clothes, she attired me in my first jacket and trousers. She watched at my bedside through my infantile and juvenile ailments. She tended me

7—2

through all my life, she held me to her heart with infinite prayers and blessings. She is no longer with us to bless and pray ; but from heaven, where she is, I know her love pursues me ; and often and often I think she is here, only invisible.

"Mrs. Firmin would be of no good," growled Dr. Goodenough. "She would have hysterics, and the nurse would have two patients to look after."

"Don't tell *me*," cries my mother, with a flush on her cheeks. "Do you suppose if that child" (meaning, of course, her paragon) "were ill, I would not go to him ?"

"My dear, if that child were hungry, you would chop off your head to make him broth," says the doctor, sipping his tea.

"*Potage à la bonne femme*," says Mr. Pendennis. "Mother, we have it at the club. You would be done with milk, eggs, and a quantity of vegetables. You would be put to simmer for many hours in an earthen pan, and——"

"Don't be horrible, Arthur !" cries a young lady, who was my mother's companion of those happy days.

"And people when they knew you would like you very much."

My uncle looked as if he did not understand the allegory.

"What is this you are talking about ? *potage à la*—what-d'ye-call-'im ?" says he. "I thought we were speaking of Mrs. Firmin, of Old Parr Street. Mrs. Firmin is a doosid delicate woman," interposed the Major. "All the females of that family are. Her mother died early. Her sister, Mrs. Twysden, is very delicate. She would be of no more use in a sick-room than a—than a bull in a china-shop, begad ! and she might catch the fever, too."

"And so might you, Major !" cries the Doctor. "Aren't you talking to me, who have just come from the boy ? Keep your distance, or I shall bite you."

The old gentleman gave a little backward movement with his chair.

"Gad, it's no joking matter," says he ; " I've known fellows catch fevers at—at ever so much past my age. At any rate, the boy is no boy of mine, begad ! I dine at Firmin's house, who has married into a good family, though he is only a doctor, and——"

"And pray what was my husband ?" cried Mrs. Pendennis.

"Only a doctor, indeed !" calls out Goodenough. "My dear creature, I have a great mind to give him the scarlet fever this minute !"

"My father was a surgeon and apothecary, I have heard," says the widow's son.

"And what then? And I should like to know if a man of one of the most ancient families in the kingdom—in the empire, begad! —hasn't a right to pursoo a learned, a useful, an honourable profession. My brother John was——"

"A medical practitioner!" I say, with a sigh.

And my uncle arranges his hair, puts his handkerchief to his teeth, and says—

"Stuff! nonsense—no patience with these personalities, begad! Firmin is a doctor, certainly—so are you—so are others. But Firmin is a university man, and a gentleman.   Firmin has travelled. Firmin is intimate with some of the best people in England, and has married into one of the first families. Gad, sir, do you suppose that a woman bred up in the lap of luxury—in the very lap, sir—at Ringwood and Whipham, and at Ringwood House in Walpole Street, where she was absolute mistress, begad—do you suppose such a woman is fit to be nursetender in a sick-room? She never *was* fit for that, or for anything except—" (here the Major saw smiles on the countenances of some of his audience)—"except, I say, to preside at Ringwood House and—and adorn society, and that sort of thing. And if such a woman chooses to run away with her uncle's doctor, and marry below her rank—why, *I* don't think it's a laughing matter, hang me if I do."

"And so she stops at the Isle of Wight, whilst the poor boy remains at the school," sighs my mother.

"Firmin can't come away. He is in attendance on the Grand Dook. The prince is never easy without Firmin. He has given him his Order of the Swan. They are moving heaven and earth in high quarters; and I bet you even, Goodenough, that that boy whom you have been attending will be a baronet—if you don't kill him off with your confounded potions and pills, begad!"

Dr. Goodenough only gave a humph and contracted his great eyebrows.

My uncle continued—

"I know what you mean. Firmin is a gentlemanly man—a handsome man. I remember his father, Brand Firmin, at Valenciennes with the Dook of York—one of the handsomest men in Europe. Firebrand Firmin they used to call him—a red-headed fellow—a tremendous duellist : shot an Irishman—became serious in after life, and that sort of thing—quarrelled with his son, who was doosid wild in early days. Gentlemanly man, certainly, Firmin. Black hair : his father had red. So much the better for the doctor ; but—but—we understand each other, I think, Goodenough ? and you and I have seen some queer fishes in our time."

And the old gentleman winked and took his snuff graciously, and, as it were, puffed the Firmin subject away.

"Was it to show me a queer fish that you took me to Dr. Firmin's house in Parr Street ?" asked Mr. Pendennis of his uncle. "The house was not very gay, nor the mistress very wise, but they were all as kind as might be ; and I am very fond of the boy."

"So did Lord Ringwood, his mother's uncle, like him," cried Major Pendennis. "That boy brought about a reconciliation between his mother and his uncle, after her runaway match. I suppose you know she ran away with Firmin, my dear ? "

My mother said " she had heard something of the story." And the Major once more asserted that Dr. Firmin was a wild fellow twenty years ago. At the time of which I am writing he was Physician to the Plethoric Hospital, Physician to the Grand Duke of Gröningen, and knight of his order of the Black Swan, member of many learned societies, the husband of a rich wife, and a person of no small consideration.

As for his son, whose name figures at the head of these pages, you may suppose he did not die of the illness about which we had just been talking. A good nurse waited on him, though his mamma was in the country. Though his papa was absent, a very competent physician was found to take charge of the young patient, and preserve his life for the benefit of his family, and the purposes of this history.

We pursued our talk about Philip Firmin and his father, and his grand-uncle the Earl, whom Major Pendennis knew intimately well, until Dr. Goodenough's carriage was announced, and our kind physician took leave of us, and drove back to London. Some who spoke on that summer evening are no longer here to speak or listen. Some who were young then have topped the hill and are descending towards the valley of the shadows. "Ah," says old Major Pendennis, shaking his brown curls, as the Doctor went away ; " did you see, my good soul, when I spoke about his *confrère*, how glum Goodenough looked ? They don't love each other, my dear,

Two of a trade don't agree, and besides I have no doubt the other doctor-fellows are jealous of Firmin, because he lives in the best society. A man of good family, my dear. There has already been a great *rapprochement;* and if Lord Ringwood is quite reconciled to him, there's no knowing what luck that boy of Firmin's may come to."

Although Dr. Goodenough might think but lightly of his *confrère,* a great portion of the public held him in much higher estimation: and especially in the little community of Grey Friars, of which the kind reader has heard in previous works of the present biographer, Dr. Brand Firmin was a very great favourite, and received with much respect and honour. Whenever the boys at that school were afflicted with the common ailments of youth, Mr. Spratt, the school apothecary, provided for them; and by the simple, though disgusting remedies which were in use in those times, generally succeeded in restoring his young patients to health. But if young Lord Egham (the Marquis of Ascot's son, as my respected reader very likely knows) happened to be unwell, as was frequently the case, from his lordship's great command of pocket-money and imprudent fondness for the contents of the pastrycook's shop; or if any very grave case of illness occurred in the school, then, quick, the famous Dr. Firmin, of Old Parr Street, Burlington Gardens, was sent for; and an illness must have been very severe, if *he* could not cure it. Dr. Firmin had been a school-fellow, and remained a special friend, of the head-master. When young Lord Egham, before mentioned, (he was our only lord, and therefore we were a little proud and careful of our darling youth,) got the erysipelas, which swelled his head to the size of a pumpkin, the doctor triumphantly carried him through his illness, and was complimented by the head-boy in his Latin oration on the annual speech-day for his superhuman skill and godlike delight *salutem hominibus dando.* The head-master turned towards Dr. Firmin, and bowed: the governors and bigwigs buzzed to one another, and looked at him: the boys looked at him: the physician held his handsome head down towards his shirt-frill. His modest eyes would not look up from the spotless lining of the broad-brimmed hat on his knees. A murmur of applause hummed through the ancient hall, a scuffling of young feet, a rustling of new cassocks among the masters, and a refreshing blowing of noses ensued, as the orator polished off his period, and then passed to some other theme.

Amidst the general enthusiasm, there was one member of the auditory scornful and dissentient. This gentleman whispered to his comrade at the commencement of the phrase concerning the doctor the, I believe of Eastern derivation, monosyllable "Bosh!" and he added sadly, looking towards the object of all this praise, "He can't construe the Latin—though it is all a parcel of humbug."

"Hush, Phil!" said his friend; and Phil's face flushed red, as Dr. Firmin, lifting up his eyes, looked at him for one moment; for the recipient of all this laudation was no other than Phil's father.

The illness of which we spoke had long since passed away. Philip was a schoolboy no longer, but in his second year at the university, and one of half-a-dozen young men, ex-pupils of the school, who had come up for the annual dinner. The honours of this year's dinner were for Dr. Firmin, even more than for Lord Ascot in his star and ribbon, who walked with his arm in the doctor's into chapel. His lordship faltered when, in his after-dinner speech, he alluded to the inestimable services and skill of his tried old friend, whom he had known as a fellow-pupil in those walls— (loud cheers)—whose friendship had been the delight of his life—a friendship which he prayed might be the inheritance of their children. (Immense applause; after which Dr. Firmin spoke.)

The doctor's speech was perhaps a little commonplace; the Latin quotations which he used were not exactly novel; but Phil need not have been so angry or ill-behaved. He went on sipping sherry, glaring at his father, and muttering observations that were anything but complimentary to his parent. "Now look," says he, "he is going to be overcome by his feelings. He will put his hand-kerchief up to his mouth, and show his diamond ring. I told you so! It's too much. I can't swallow this . . . this sherry. I say, you fellows, let us come out of this, and have a smoke somewhere." And Phil rose up and quitted the dining-room, just as his father was declaring what a joy, and a pride, and a delight it was to him to think that the friendship with which his noble friend honoured him was likely to be transmitted to their children, and that when he had passed away from this earthly scene (cries of "No, no!" "May you live a thousand years!") it would be his joy to think that his son would always find a friend and protector in the noble, the princely house of Ascot.

We found the carriages waiting outside Grey Friars' Gate, and

Philip Firmin, pushing me into his father's, told the footman to drive home, and that the doctor would return in Lord Ascot's carriage. Home then to Old Parr Street we went, where many a time as a boy I had been welcome. And we retired to Phil's private den in the back buildings of the great house: and over our cigars we talked of the Founder's-day Feast, and the speeches delivered; and of the old Cistercians of our time, and how Thompson was married, and Johnson was in the army, and Jackson (not red-haired Jackson, pig-eyed Jackson,) was first in his year, and so forth; and in this twaddle were most happily engaged, when Phil's father flung open the tall door of the study.

"Here's the governor!" growled Phil; and in an undertone, "What does *he* want?"

"The governor," as I looked up, was not a pleasant object to behold. Dr. Firmin had very white false teeth, which perhaps were a little too large for his mouth, and these grinned in the gas-light very fiercely. On his cheeks were black whiskers, and over his glaring eyes fierce black eyebrows, and his bald head glittered like a billiard-ball. You would hardly have known that he was the original of that melancholy philosophic portrait which all the patients admired in the doctor's waiting-room.

"I find, Philip, that you took my carriage," said the father; "and Lord Ascot and I had to walk ever so far for a cab!"

"Hadn't he got his own carriage? I thought, of course, he would have his carriage on a State-day, and that you would come home with the lord," said Philip.

"I had promised to bring *him* home, sir!" said the father.

"Well, sir, I'm very sorry," continued the son, curtly.

"Sorry!" screams the other.

"I can't say any more, sir, and I *am* very sorry," answers Phil; and he knocked the ash of his cigar into the stove.

The stranger within the house hardly knew how to look on its master or his son. There was evidently some dire quarrel between them. The old man glared at the young one, who calmly looked his father in the face. Wicked rage and hate seemed to flash from the doctor's eyes, and anon came a look of wild pitiful supplication towards the guest, which was most painful to bear. In the midst of what dark family mystery was I? What meant this cruel spectacle of the father's terrified anger, and the son's scorn?

" I—I appeal to you, Pendennis," says the doctor, with a choking utterance and a ghastly face.

" Shall we begin *ab ovo*, sir ? " says Phil.   Again the ghastly look of terror comes over the father's face.

" I—I promise to bring one of the first noblemen in England," gasps the doctor, " from a public dinner, in my carriage ; and my son takes it, and leaves me and Lord Ascot to walk !—Is it fair, Pendennis ?   Is it the conduct of a gentleman to a gentleman ; of a son to a father ? "

" No, sir," I said, gravely, " nothing can excuse it."   Indeed I was shocked at the young man's obduracy and undutifulness.

" I told you it was a mistake ! " cries Phil, reddening.   " I heard Lord Ascot order his own carriage ; I made no doubt he would bring my father home.   To ride in a chariot with a footman behind me, is no pleasure to me, and I would far rather have a Hansom and a cigar.   It was a blunder, and I am sorry for it—there !   And if I live to a hundred I can't say more."

" If you are sorry, Philip," groans the father, " it is enough." " You remember, Pendennis, when—when my son and I were not on this—on this footing," and he looked up for a moment at a picture which was hanging over Phil's head—a portrait of Phil's mother ; the lady of whom my own mother spoke, on that evening when we had talked of the boy's illness.   Both the ladies had passed from the world now, and their images were but painted shadows on the wall.

The father had accepted an apology, though the son had made none.   I looked at the elder Firmin's face, and the character written on it.   I remembered such particulars of his early history as had been told to me ; and I perfectly recalled that feeling of doubt and mis-liking which came over my mind when I first saw the doctor's hand-some face some few years previously, when my uncle first took me to the doctor's in Old Parr Street ; little Phil being then a flaxen-headed, pretty child, who had just assumed his first trousers, and I a fifth-form boy at school.

My father and Dr. Firmin were members of the medical pro-fession.   They had been bred up as boys at the same school, whither families used to send their sons from generation to generation, and long before people had ever learned that the place was unwholesome. Grey Friars was smoky, certainly ; I think in the time of the Plague great numbers of people were buried there.   But had the school been situated in the most picturesque swamp in England, the general health of the boys could not have been better. We boys used to hear of epidemics occurring in other schools, and were almost sorry that they did not come to ours, so that we might shut up, and get longer vacations. Even that illness which subsequently befell Phil Firmin himself attacked no one else—the boys all luckily going home for the holidays on the very day of poor Phil's seizure; but of this illness more anon. When it was determined that little Phil Firmin was to go to Grey Friars, Phil's father bethought him that Major Pendennis, whom he met in the world and society, had a nephew at the place, who might protect the little fellow, and the Major took his nephew to see Dr. and Mrs. Firmin one Sunday after church, and we had lunch at Old Parr Street, and there little Phil was presented to me, whom I promised to take under my protection. He was a simple little man; an artless child, who had not the least idea of the dignity of a fifth-form boy. He was quite unabashed in talking to me and other persons, and has remained so ever since. He asked my uncle how he came to have such odd hair. He partook freely of the delicacies on the table. I remember he hit me with his little fist once or twice, which liberty at first struck me with a panic of astonishment, and then with a sense of the ridiculous so exquisitely keen, that I burst out into a fit of laughter. It was, you see, as if a stranger were to hit the Pope in the ribs, and call him "Old boy;" as if Jack were to tweak one of the giants by the nose; or Ensign Jones to ask the Duke of Wellington to take wine. I had a strong sense of humour, even in those early days, and enjoyed this joke accordingly.

"Philip!" cries mamma, "you will hurt Mr. Pendennis."

"I will knock him down!" shouts Phil. Fancy knocking *me* down,—ME, a fifth-form boy!

"The child is a perfect Hercules," remarks the mother.

"He strangled two snakes in his cradle," says the doctor, looking at me. (It was then, as I remember, I felt *Dr. Fell* towards him.)

"La, Dr. Firmin!" cries mamma, "I can't bear snakes. I remember there was one at Rome, when we were walking one day, a great, large snake, and I hated it, and I cried out, and I nearly fainted; and my uncle Ringwood said I ought to like snakes, for one might be an agreeable rattle; and I have read of them being charming in India, and I dare say you have, Mr. Pendennis, for I am told you are very clever; and I am not in the least; I wish I were; but my husband is, very—and so Phil will be. Will you be a very clever boy, dear? He was named after my dear papa, who was killed at Busaco when I was quite, quite a little thing, and we wore mourning, and we went to live with my uncle Ringwood afterwards; but Maria and I had both our own fortunes; and I am sure I little thought I should marry a physician—la, one of uncle Ringwood's grooms, I should. as soon have thought of marrying him!—but, you know, my husband is one of the cleverest men *in the world.* Don't tell me,—you are, dearest, and you know it; and when a man is clever, I don't value his rank in life; no, not if he was that fender; and I always said to uncle Ringwood, 'Talent I will marry, for talent I adore;' and I *did* marry you, Dr. Firmin, you know I did, and this child is your image. And you will be kind to him at school," says the poor lady, turning to me, her eyes filling with tears, "for talent is always kind, except uncle Ringwood, and he was very ——"

"A little more wine, Mr. Pendennis?" said the doctor—*Dr. Fell* still, though he was most kind to me. "I shall put my little man under your care, and I know you will keep him from harm. I hope you will do us the favour to come to Parr Street whenever you are free. In my father's time we used to come home of a Saturday from school, and enjoyed going to the play." And the doctor shook me cordially by the hand, and, I must say, continued his kindness to me as long as ever I knew him. When we went away, my uncle Pendennis told me many stories about the great earl and family of Ringwood, and how Dr. Firmin had made a match—a match of the affections—with this lady, daughter of Philip Ringwood, who was killed at Busaco; and how she had been a great beauty, and was a perfect *grande dame* always; and, if not the cleverest, certainly one of the kindest and most amiable women in the world.

In those days I was accustomed to receive the opinions of my informant with such respect that I at once accepted this statement as authentic. Mrs. Firmin's portrait, indeed, was beautiful: it was painted by young Mr. Harlowe, that year he was at Rome, and when in eighteen days he completed a copy of the "Transfiguration," to the admiration of all the Academy; but I, for my part, only remember a lady weak, and thin, and faded, who never came out of her dressing-room until a late hour in the afternoon, and whose super-annuated smiles and grimaces used to provoke my juvenile sense of humour. She used to kiss Phil's brow; and, as she held the boy's hand in one of her lean ones, would say, " Who would suppose such a great boy as that could be my son?" " Be kind to him when I am gone," she sighed to me, one Sunday evening, when I was taking leave of her, as her eyes filled with tears, and she placed the thin hand in mine for the last time. The doctor, reading by the fire, turned round and scowled at her from under his tall shining forehead. "You are nervous, Louisa, and had better go to your room, I told you you had," he said, abruptly. " Young gentlemen, it is time for you to be off to Grey Friars.   Is the cab at the door, Brice?" And he took out his watch—his great shining watch, by which he had felt the pulses of so many famous personages, whom his prodigious skill had rescued from disease. And at parting, Phil flung his arms round his poor mother, and kissed her under the glossy curls; the borrowed curls! and he looked his father resolutely in the face (whose own glance used to fall before that of the boy), and bade him a gruff good-night, ere we set forth for Grey Friars.

CHAPTER II.

AT SCHOOL AND AT HOME.

I DINED yesterday with three gentlemen, whose time of life may be guessed by their conversation, a great part of which consisted of Eton reminiscences and lively imitations of Dr. Keate. Each one, as he described how he had been flogged, mimicked to the best of his power the manner and the mode of operating of the famous doctor. His little parenthetical remarks during the ceremony were recalled with great facetiousness: the very *hwhish* of the rods was parodied with thrilling fidelity, and after a good hour's conversation, the subject was brought to a climax by a description of that awful night when the doctor called up squad after squad of boys from their beds in their respective boarding-houses, whipped through the whole night, and castigated I don't know how many hundred rebels. All these mature men laughed, prattled, rejoiced, and became young again, as they recounted their stories; and each of them heartily and eagerly bade the stranger to understand how Keate was a thorough gentleman. Having talked about their floggings, I say, for an hour at least, they apologized to me for dwelling upon a subject which after all was strictly local:

but, indeed, their talk greatly amused and diverted me, and I hope, and am quite ready, to hear all their jolly stories over again.

Be not angry, patient reader of former volumes by the author of the present history, if I am garrulous about Grey Friars, and go back to that ancient place of education to find the heroes of our tale. We are but young once. When we remember that time of youth, we are still young. He over whose head eight or nine lustres have passed, if he wishes to write of boys, must recall the time when he himself was a boy. Their habits change; their waists are longer or shorter; their shirt-collars stick up more or less; but the boy is the boy in King George's time as in that of his royal niece—once our maiden queen, now the anxious mother of many boys. And young fellows are honest, and merry, and idle, and mischievous, and timid, and brave, and studious, and selfish, and generous, and mean, and false, and truth-telling, and affectionate, and good, and bad, now as in former days. He with whom we have mainly to do is a gentleman of mature age now walking the street with boys of his own. He is not going to perish in the last chapter of these memoirs—to die of consumption with his love weeping by his bedside, or to blow his brains out in despair, because she has been married to his rival, or killed out of a gig, or otherwise done for in the last chapter but one. No, no; we will have no dismal endings. Philip Firmin is well and hearty at this minute, owes no man a shilling, and can enjoy his glass of port in perfect comfort. So, my dear miss, if you want a pulmonary romance, the present won't suit you. So, young gentleman, if you are for melancholy, despair, and sardonic satire, please to call at some other shop. That Philip shall have his trials is a matter of course—may they be interesting, though they do not end dismally! That he shall fall and trip in his course sometimes is pretty certain. Ah, who does not upon this life-journey of ours? Is not our want the occasion of our brother's charity, and thus does not good come out of that evil? When the traveller (of whom the Master spoke) fell among the thieves, his mishap was contrived to try many a heart beside his own—the Knave's who robbed him, the Levite's and Priest's who passed him by as he lay bleeding, the humble Samaritan's whose hand poured oil into his wound, and held out its pittance to relieve him.

So little Philip Firmin was brought to school by his mamma in her carriage, who entreated the housekeeper to have a special charge of that angelic child; and as soon as the poor lady's back was turned, Mrs. Bunce emptied the contents of the little boy's trunk into one of sixty or seventy little cupboards, wherein reposed other boys' clothes and haberdashery: and then Mrs. Firmin requested to see the Rev. Mr. X., in whose house Philip was to board, and besought him, and explained many things to him, such as the exceeding delicacy of the child's constitution, &c. &c.; and Mr. X., who was very good-natured, patted the boy kindly on the head, and sent for the other Philip, Philip Ringwood, Phil's cousin, who had arrived at Grey Friars an hour or two before; and Mr. X. told Ringwood to take care of the little fellow; and Mrs. Firmin, choking behind her pocket-handkerchief, gurgled out a blessing on the grinning youth, and at one time had an idea of giving Master Ringwood a sovereign, but paused, thinking he was too big a boy, and that she might not take such a liberty, and presently she was gone; and little Phil Firmin was introduced to the long-room and his schoolfellows of Mr. X.'s house; and having plenty of money, and naturally finding his way to the pastrycook's, the next day, after school, he was met by his cousin Ringwood and robbed of half the tarts which he had purchased. A fortnight afterwards, the hospitable doctor and his wife asked their young kinsman to Old Parr Street, Burlington Gardens, and the two boys went; but Phil never mentioned anything to his parents regarding the robbery of tarts, being deterred, perhaps, from speaking by awful threats of punishment which his cousin promised to administer when they got back to school, in case of the little boy's confession. Subsequently, Master Ringwood was asked once in every term to Old Parr Street; but neither Mrs. Firmin, nor the doctor, nor Master Firmin liked the baronet's son, and Mrs. Firmin pronounced him a violent, rude boy.

I, for my part, left school suddenly and early, and my little *protégé* behind me. His poor mother, who had promised herself to come for him every Saturday, did not keep her promise. Smithfield is a long way from Piccadilly; and an angry cow once scratched the panels of her carriage, causing her footman to spring from his board into a pig-pen, and herself to feel such a shock, that no wonder she was afraid of visiting the City afterwards. The circumstances of this accident she often narrated to us. Her anecdotes were not numerous, but she told them repeatedly. In imagination, sometimes, I can hear her ceaseless, simple cackle; see her faint eyes, as she prattles on unconsciously, and watch the dark looks of her handsome, silent husband, scowling from under his eyebrows and smiling behind his teeth. I dare say he ground those teeth with suppressed rage sometimes. I dare say to bear with her endless volubility must have tasked his endurance. He may have treated her ill, but she tried him. She, on her part, may have been a not very wise woman, but she was kind to me. Did not her housekeeper make me the best of tarts, and keep goodies from the company dinners for the young gentlemen when they came home? Did not her husband give me of his fees? I promise you, after I had seen Dr. Fell a few times, that first unpleasing impression produced by his darkling countenance and sinister good looks wore away. He was a gentleman. He had lived in the great world, of which he told anecdotes delightful to boys to hear; and he passed the bottle to me as if I was a man.

I hope and think I remembered the injunction of poor Mrs. Firmin to be kind to her boy. As long as we stayed together at Grey Friars, I was Phil's champion whenever he needed my protection, though of course I could not always be present to guard the little scapegrace from all the blows which were aimed at his young face by pugilists of his own size. There were seven or eight years' difference between us (he says ten, which is absurd, and which I deny); but I was always remarkable for my affability, and, in spite of our disparity of age, would often graciously accept the general invitation I had from his father for any Saturday and Sunday when I would like to accompany Philip home.

Such an invitation is welcome to any schoolboy. To get away from Smithfield, and show our best clothes in Bond Street, was always a privilege. To strut in the Park on Sunday, and nod to the other fellows who were strutting there too, was better than remaining at school, "doing 'Diates aron,'" as the phrase used to be, having that endless roast-beef for dinner, and hearing two sermons in chapel. There may have been more lively streets in London than Old Parr Street; but it was pleasanter to be there than to look at Goswell Street over Grey Friars' wall; and so the present biographer and reader's very humble servant found Dr. Firmin's house an agreeable resort. Mamma was often ailing, or, if well, went out into the world with her husband; in either case, we boys had a good dinner provided for us, with the special dishes which Phil loved; and after dinner we adjourned to the play, not being by any means too proud to sit in the pit with Mr. Brice, the doctor's confidential man. On Sunday we went to church at Lady Whittlesea's, and back to school in the evening; when the doctor almost always *gave us a fee.* If he did not dine at home (and I own his absence did not much damp our pleasure), Brice would lay a small enclosure on the young gentlemen's coats, which we transferred to our pockets. I believe schoolboys disdain fees in the present disinterested times.

Everything in Dr. Firmin's house was as handsome as might be, and yet somehow the place was not cheerful. One's steps fell noiselessly on the faded Turkey carpet; the room was large, and all save the dining-table in a dingy twilight. The picture of Mrs. Firmin looked at us from the wall, and followed us about with wild violet eyes. Philip Firmin had the same violet odd bright eyes, and the same coloured hair of an auburn tinge; in the picture it fell in long wild masses over the lady's back as she leaned with bare arms on a harp. Over the sideboard was the doctor, in a black velvet coat and a fur collar, his hand on a skull, like Hamlet. Skulls of oxen, horned, with wreaths, formed the cheerful ornaments of the cornice. On the side-table glittered a pair of cups, given by grateful patients, looking like receptacles rather for funereal ashes than for festive flowers or wine. Brice, the butler, wore the gravity and costume of an undertaker. The footman stealthily moved hither and thither, bearing the dinner to us; we always spoke under our breath whilst we were eating it. " The room don't look more cheerful of a morning when the patients are sitting here, I can tell you," Phil would say; indeed, we could well fancy that it was dismal. The drawing-room had a rhubarb-coloured flock paper (on account of the governor's attachment to the shop, Master Phil said), a great piano, a harp smothered in a leather bag in the corner, which the languid owner now never touched; and everybody's face seemed scared and pale in the great looking-glasses, which reflected you over and over again into the distance, so that you seemed to twinkle off right through the Albany into Piccadilly.

Old Parr Street has been a habitation for generations of surgeons and physicians. I suppose the noblemen for whose use the street was intended in the time of the early Georges fled, finding the neighbourhood too dismal, and the gentlemen in black coats came and took possession of the gilded, gloomy chambers which the sacred *mode* vacated. These mutations of fashion have always been matters of profound speculation to me. Why shall not one moralize over London, as over Rome, or Baalbec, or Troy town? I like to walk among the Hebrews of Wardour Street, and fancy the place, as it once was, crowded with chairs and gilt chariots, and torches flashing in the hands of the running footmen. I have a grim pleasure in thinking that Golden Square was once the resort of the aristocracy, and Monmouth Street the delight of the genteel world. What shall prevent us Londoners from musing over the decline and fall of city sovereignties, and drawing our cockney morals? As the late Mr. Gibbon meditated his history leaning against a column in the Capitol, why should not I muse over mine, reclining under an arcade of the Pantheon? Not the Pantheon at Rome, in the Cabbage Market by the Piazza Navona, where the immortal gods were worshipped,—the immortal gods who are now dead; but the Pantheon in Oxford Street, ladies, where you purchase feeble pomatums, music, glassware, and baby-linen; and which has its history too. Have not Selwyn, and Walpole, and March, and Carlisle figured there? Has not Prince Florizel flounced through the hall in his rustling domino, and danced there in powdered splendour? and when the ushers refused admission to lovely Sophy Baddeley, did not the young men, her adorers, draw their rapiers and vow to slay the doorkeepers; and, crossing the glittering blades over the enchantress' head, make a warlike triumphal arch for her to pass under, all flushed, and smiling, and perfumed, and painted? The lives of streets are as the lives of men, and shall not the street-preacher if so minded, take for the text of his sermon the stones in the gutter? That you were once the resort of the fashion, O Monmouth Street! by the invocation of blessed St. Giles shall I not improve that sweet thought into a godly discourse, and make the ruin edifying? *O mes frères!* There were splendid thoroughfares, dazzling company, bright illuminations, in *our* streets when our hearts were young: we entertained in them a noble youthful company of chivalrous hopes and lofty ambitions; of blushing thoughts in snowy robes spotless and virginal. See, in the embrasure of the window, where you sat looking to the stars, and nestling by the soft side of your first love, hang Mr. Moses' bargains of turned old clothes, very cheap; of worn old boots, bedraggled in how much and how many people's mud; a great bargain. See! along the street, strewed with flowers once mayhap—a fight of beggars for the refuse of an apple-stall, or a tipsy basket-woman reeling shrieking to the station. O me! O my beloved congregation! I have preached this stale sermon to you for ever so many years. O my jolly companions, I have drunk many a bout with you, and always found *vanitas vanitatum* written on the bottom of the pot!

I choose to moralize now when I pass the place. The garden has run to seed, the walks are mildewed, the statues have broken noses, the gravel is dank with green moss, the roses are withered, and the nightingales have ceased to make love. It *is* a funereal street, Old Parr Street, certainly ; the carriages which drive there ought to have feathers on the roof, and the butlers who open the doors should wear weepers— so the scene strikes you now as you pass along the spacious empty pavement. You are bilious, my good man. Go and pay a guinea to one of the doctors in those houses ; there are still doctors there. He will prescribe taraxacum for you, or pil : hydrarg : Bless you! in *my* time, to us gentlemen of the fifth form, the place was bearable. The yellow fogs didn't damp our spirits—and we never thought them too thick to keep us away from the play : from the chivalrous Charles Kemble, I tell you, my Mirabel, my Mercutio, my princely Falconbridge : from his adorable daughter (O my distracted heart!) : from the classic Young : from the glorious Long Tom Coffin : from the unearthly Vanderdecken—"Return, O my love, and we'll never, never part" (where art thou, sweet singer of that most thrilling ditty of my youth?) : from the sweet, sweet *Victorine* and the *Bottle Imp*. Oh, to see that *Bottle Imp* again, and hear that song about the "Pilgrim of Love!" Once, but—hush ;—this is a secret—we had private boxes, the doctor's grand friends often sending him these ; and finding the opera rather slow, we went to a concert in M–d–n Lane, near Covent Garden, and heard the most celestial glees, over a supper of fizzing sausages and mashed potatoes, such as the world has never seen since. We did no harm ; but I dare say it was very wrong. Brice, the butler, ought not to have taken us. We bullied him, and made him take us where we liked. We had rum-shrub in the housekeeper's room, where we used to be diverted by the society of *other* butlers of the neighbouring nobility and gentry, who would step in. Perhaps it was wrong to leave us so to the company of servants. Dr. Firmin used to go to his grand parties, Mrs. Firmin to bed. "Did we enjoy the performance last night?" our host would ask at breakfast. "Oh, yes, we enjoyed the performance!"

But my poor Mrs. Firmin fancied that we enjoyed *Semiramide* or the *Donna del Lago;* whereas we had been to the pit at the Adelphi (out of our own money), and seen that jolly John Reeve, and laughed—laughed till we were fit to drop—and stayed till the curtain was down. And then we would come home, and, as aforesaid, pass a delightful hour over supper, and hear the anecdotes of Mr. Brice's friends, the other butlers. Ah, that was a time indeed! There never was any liquor so good as rum-shrub, never; and the sausages had a flavour of Elysium. How hushed we were when Dr. Firmin, coming home from his parties, let himself in at the street-door! Shoeless, we crept up to our bedrooms. And we came down to breakfast with innocent young faces—and let Mrs. Firmin, at lunch, prattle about the opera; and there stood Brice and the footman behind us, looking quite grave, the abominable hypocrites!

Then, sir, there was a certain way, out of the study window, or through the kitchen, and over the leads, to a building, gloomy indeed, but where I own to have spent delightful hours of the most flagitious and criminal enjoyment of some delicious little Havannahs, ten to the shilling. In that building there were stables once, doubtless occupied by great Flemish horses and rumbling gold coaches of Walpole's time; but a celebrated surgeon, when he took possession of the house, made a lecture-room of the premises,—"And this door," says Phil, pointing to one leading into the mews, "was very convenient for having *the bodies* in and out"—a cheerful reminiscence. Of this kind of furniture there was now very little in the apartment, except a dilapidated skeleton in a corner, a few dusty casts of heads, and bottles of preparations on the top of an old bureau, and some mildewed harness hanging on the walls. This apartment became Mr. Phil's smoking-room when, as he grew taller, he felt himself too dignified to sit in the kitchen regions : the honest butler and housekeeper themselves pointing out to their young master that his place was elsewhere than among the servants. So there, privately and with great delectation, we smoked many an abominable cigar in that dreary backroom, the gaunt walls and twilight ceilings of which were by no means melancholy to us, who found forbidden pleasures the sweetest, after the absurd fashion of boys. Dr. Firmin was an enemy to smoking, and ever accustomed to speak of the practice with eloquent indignation. "It was a low practice—the habit of cabmen, pot-house frequenters, and Irish apple-women," the doctor would say, as Phil and his friend looked at each other with a stealthy joy. Phil's father was ever scented and neat, the pattern of handsome propriety. Perhaps he had a clearer perception regarding manners than respecting morals; perhaps his conversation was full of platitudes, his talk (concerning people of fashion chiefly) mean and uninstructive, his behaviour to young Lord Egham rather fulsome and lacking of dignity. Perhaps, I say, the idea may have entered into young Mr. Pendennis's mind that his hospitable entertainer and friend, Dr. Firmin, of Old Parr Street, was what at the present day might be denominated an old humbug; but modest young men do not come quickly to such unpleasant conclusions regarding their seniors. Dr. Firmin's manners were so good, his forehead was so high, his frill so fresh, his hands so white and slim, that for some considerable time we ingenuously admired him; and it was not without a pang that we came to view him as he actually was—no, not as he actually was—no man whose early nurture was kindly can judge quite impartially the man who has been kind to him in boyhood.

I quitted school suddenly, leaving my little Phil behind me, a brave little handsome boy, endearing himself to old and young by his good looks, his gaiety, his courage, and his gentlemanly bearing. Once in a way a letter would come from him, full of that artless affection and tenderness which fills boys' hearts, and is so touching in their letters. It was answered with proper dignity and condescension on the senior boy's part. Our modest little country home kept up a friendly intercourse with Dr. Firmin's grand London mansion, of which, in his visits to us, my uncle, Major Pendennis, did not fail to bring news. A correspondence took place between the ladies of each house. We supplied Mrs. Firmin with little country presents, tokens of my mother's good-will and gratitude towards the friends who had been kind to her son. I went my way to the university, having occasional glimpses of Phil at school. I took chambers in the Temple, which he found great delight in visiting; and he liked our homely dinner from Dick's, and a bed on the sofa, better than the splendid entertainments in Old Parr Street and his great gloomy chamber there. He had grown by this time to be ever so much taller than his senior, though he always persists in looking up to me unto the present day.

A very few weeks after my poor mother passed that judgment on Mrs. Firmin, she saw reason to regret and revoke it. Phil's mother, who was afraid, or perhaps was forbidden, to attend her son in his illness at school, was taken ill herself.

Phil returned to Grey Friars in a deep suit of black; the servants on the carriage wore black too; and a certain tyrant of the place, beginning to laugh and jeer because Firmin's eyes filled with tears at some ribald remark, was gruffly rebuked by Sampson major, the cock of the whole school; and with the question, "Don't you see the poor beggar's in mourning, you great brute?" was kicked about his business.

When Philip Firmin and I met again, there was crape on both our hats. I don't think either could see the other's face very well. I went to see him in Parr Street, in the vacant, melancholy house, where the poor mother's picture was yet hanging in her empty drawing-room.

"She was always fond of you, Pendennis," said Phil. "God bless you for being so good to her. You know what it is to lose— to lose what loves you best in the world. I didn't know how— how I loved her, till I had lost her." And many a sob broke his words as he spoke.

Her picture was removed from the drawing-room presently into Phil's own little study—the room in which he sat and defied his father. What had passed between them? The young man was very much changed. The frank looks of old days were gone, and Phil's face was haggard and bold. The doctor would not let me have a word more with his son after he had found us together, but with dubious appealing looks, followed me to the door, and shut it upon me. I felt that it closed upon two unhappy men.

CHAPTER III.

A CONSULTATION.

HOULD I peer into Firmin's privacy, and find the key to that secret? What skeleton was there in the closet? In the *Cornhill Magazine,** you may remember, there were some verses about a portion of a skeleton. Did you remark how the poet and present proprietor of the human skull at once settled the sex of it, and determined off-hand that it must have belonged to a woman? Such skulls are locked up in many gentlemen's hearts and memories. Bluebeard, you know, had a whole museum of them— as that imprudent little last wife of his found out to her cost. And, on the other hand, a lady, we suppose, would select hers of the sort which had carried beards when in the flesh. Given a neat locked skeleton cupboard, belonging to a man of a certain age, to ascertain the sex of the original owner of the bones, you have not much need of a picklock or a blacksmith. There is no use in forcing the hinge, or scratching the pretty panel. *We* know what is inside—we arch rogues and men of the world. Murders, I suppose, are not many— enemies and victims of our hate and anger, destroyed and trampled out of life by us, and locked out of sight: but corpses of our dead loves, my dear sir—my dear madam—have we not got them stowed away in cupboard after cupboard, in bottle after bottle? Oh, fie!

* No. 12 : December 1860.

And young people! What doctrine is this to preach to *them*, who spell your book by papa's and mamma's knee? Yes, and how wrong it is to let them go to church, and see and hear papa and mamma publicly on their knees, calling out, and confessing to the whole congregation, that they are sinners! So, though I had not the key, I could see through the panel and the glimmering of the skeleton inside.

Although the elder Firmin followed me to the door, and his eyes only left me as I turned the corner of the street, I felt sure that Phil ere long would open his mind to me, or give me some clue to that mystery. I should hear from him why his bright cheeks had become hollow, why his fresh voice, which I remember so honest and cheerful, was now harsh and sarcastic, with tones that often grated on the hearer, and laughter that gave pain. It was about Philip himself that my anxieties were. The young fellow had inherited from his poor mother a considerable fortune—some eight or nine hundred a year, we always understood. He was living in a costly, not to say extravagant manner. I thought Mr. Philip's juvenile remorses were locked up in the skeleton closet, and was grieved to think he had fallen in mischief's way. Hence, no doubt, might arise the anger between him and his father. The boy was extravagant and headstrong; and the parent remonstrant and irritated.

I met my old friend Dr. Goodenough at the club one evening; and as we dined together I discoursed with him about his former patient, and recalled to him that day, years back, when the boy was ill at school, and when my poor mother and Phil's own were yet alive.

Goodenough looked very grave.

"Yes," he said, "the boy was very ill; he was nearly gone at that time—at that time—when his mother was in the Isle of Wight, and his father dangling after a prince. We thought one day it was all over with him; but ——"

"But a good doctor interposed between him and *pallida mors*."

"A good doctor? a good nurse! The boy was delirious, and had a fancy to walk out of window, and would have done so, but for one of my nurses. You know her."

"What! the Little Sister?"

"Yes, the Little Sister."

"And it was she who nursed Phil through his fever, and saved his life? I drink her health. She is a good little soul."

"Good!" said the doctor, with his gruffest voice and frown.—

(He was always most fierce when he was most tender-hearted.) "Good, indeed! Will you have some more of this duck?—Do. You have had enough already, and it's very unwholesome. Good, sir? But for women, fire and brimstone ought to come down and consume this world. Your dear mother was one of the good ones. I was attending you when you were ill, at those horrible chambers you had in the Temple, at the same time when young Firmin was ill at Grey Friars. And I suppose I must be answerable for keeping two scapegraces in the world."

"Why didn't Dr. Firmin come to see him?"

"Hm! his nerves were too delicate. Besides, he *did* come. Talk of the * * *"

The personage designated by asterisks was Phil's father, who was also a member of our club, and who entered the dining-room, tall, stately, and pale, with his stereotyped smile, and wave of his pretty hand. By the way, that smile of Firmin's was a very queer contortion of the handsome features. As you came up to him, he would draw his lips over his teeth, causing his jaws to wrinkle (or dimple if you will) on either side. Meanwhile his eyes looked out from his face, quite melancholy and independent of the little transaction in which the mouth was engaged. Lips said, "I am a gentleman of fine manners and fascinating address, and I am supposed to be happy to see you. How do you do?" Dreary, sad, as into a great blank desert, looked the dark eyes. I *do* know one or two, but only one or two faces of men, when oppressed with care, which can yet smile *all over*.

Goodenough nods grimly to the smile of the other doctor, who blandly looks at our table, holding his chin in one of his pretty hands.

"How do?" growls Goodenough. "Young hopeful well?"

"Young hopeful sits smoking cigars till morning with some friends of his," says Firmin, with the sad smile directed towards me this time. "Boys will be boys." And he pensively walks away from us with a friendly nod towards me; examines the dinner-card in an attitude of melancholy grace; points with the jewelled hand to the dishes which he will have served, and is off, and simpering to another acquaintance at a distant table.

"I thought he would take that table," says Firmin's cynical *confrère.*

· "In the draught of the door? Don't you see how the candle flickers? It is the worst place in the room!"

"Yes; but don't you see who is sitting at the next table?"

Now at the next table was a n–blem–n of vast wealth, who was growling at the quality of the mutton cutlets, and the half-pint of sherry which he had ordered for his dinner. But as his lordship has nothing to do with the ensuing history, of course we shall not violate confidence by mentioning his name. We could see Firmin smiling on his neighbour with his blandest melancholy, and the waiters presently bearing up the dishes which the doctor had ordered for his own refection. *He* was no lover of mutton-chops and coarse sherry, as I knew, who had partaken of many a feast at his board. I could see the diamond twinkle on his pretty hand, as it daintily poured out creaming wine from the ice-pail by his side—the liberal hand that had given me many a sovereign when I was a boy.

"I can't help liking him," I said to my companion, whose scornful eyes were now and again directed towards his colleague.

"This port is very sweet. Almost all port is sweet now," remarks the doctor.

"He was very kind to me in my school-days; and Philip was a fine little fellow."

"Handsome a boy as ever I saw. Does he keep his beauty? Father was a handsome man—very. Quite a lady-killer—I mean out of his practice!" adds the grim doctor. "What is the boy doing?"

"He is at the university. He has his mother's fortune. He is wild and unsettled, and I fear he is going to the bad a little."

"Is he? Shouldn't wonder!" grumbles Goodenough.

We had talked very frankly and pleasantly until the appearance of the other doctor, but with Firmin's arrival Goodenough seemed to button up his conversation. He quickly stumped away from the dining-room to the drawing-room, and sat over a novel there until time came when he was to retire to his patients or his home.

That there was no liking between the doctors, that there was a difference between Philip and his father, was clear enough to me: but the causes of these differences I had yet to learn. The story came to me piecemeal; from confessions here, admissions there, deductions of my own. I could not, of course, be present at many of the scenes which I shall have to relate as though I had witnessed them ; and the posture, language, and inward thoughts of Philip and his friends, as here related, no doubt are fancies of the narrator in many cases ; but the story is as authentic as many histories, and the reader need only give such an amount of credence to it as he may judge that its verisimilitude warrants.

Well, then, we must not only revert to that illness which befell when Philip Firmin was a boy at Grey Friars, but go back yet farther in time to a period which I cannot precisely ascertain.

The pupils of old Gandish's painting academy may remember a ridiculous little man, with a great deal of wild talent, about the ultimate success of which his friends were divided. Whether Andrew was a genius, or whether he was a zany, was always a moot question among the frequenters of the Greek Street billiard-rooms, and the noble disciples of the Academy and St. Martin's Lane. He may have been crazy and absurd ; he may have had talent too : such characters are not unknown in art or in literature. He broke the Queen's English ; he was ignorant to a wonder ; he dressed his little person in the most fantastic raiment and queerest cheap finery : he wore a beard, bless my soul ! twenty years before beards were known to wag in Britain. He was the most affected little creature, and, if you looked at him, would *pose* in attitudes of such ludicrous dirty dignity, that if you had had a dun waiting for money in the hall of your lodging-house, or your picture refused at the Academy—if you were suffering under ever so much calamity—you could not help laughing. He was the butt of all his acquaintances, the laughing-stock of high and low, and he had as loving, gentle, faithful, honourable a heart as ever beat in a little bosom. He is gone to his rest now ; his palette and easel are waste timber ; his genius, which made some little flicker of brightness, never shone much, and is extinct. In an old album that dates back for more than a score of years, I sometimes look at poor Andrew's strange wild sketches. He might have done something had he continued to remain poor ; but a rich widow, whom he met at Rome, fell in love with the strange errant painter, pursued him to England, and married him in spite of himself. His genius drooped under the servitude : he lived but a few short years, and died of a consumption, of which the good Goodenough's skill could not cure him.

One day, as he was driving with his wife in her splendid barouche through the Haymarket, he suddenly bade the coachman stop, sprang over the side of the carriage before the steps could be let fall, and his astonished wife saw him shaking the hands of a shabbily dressed little woman who was passing,—shaking both her hands, and weeping, and gesticulating, and twisting his beard and mustachios, as his wont was when agitated. Mrs. Montfitchet (the wealthy Mrs. Carrickfergus she had been, before she married the painter), the owner of a young husband, who had sprung from her side, and out of her carriage, in order to caress a young woman passing in the street, might well be disturbed by this demonstration ; but she was a kind-hearted woman, and when Montfitchet, on reascending into the family coach, told his wife the history of the person of whom he had just taken leave, she cried plentifully too. She bade the coachman drive straightway to her own house : she rushed up to her own apartments, whence she emerged, bearing an immense bag full of wearing apparel, and followed by a panting butler, carrying a bottle-basket and a pie : and she drove off, with her pleased Andrew by her side, to a court in St. Martin's Lane, where dwelt the poor woman with whom he had just been conversing.

It had pleased heaven, in the midst of dreadful calamity, to send her friends and succour. She was suffering under misfortune, poverty, and cowardly desertion. A man who had called himself Brandon when he took lodgings in her father's house, married her, brought her to London, tired of her, and left her. She had reason to think he had given a false name when he lodged with her father : he fled, after a few months, and his real name she never knew. When he deserted her, she went back to her father, a weak man, married to a domineering woman, who pretended to disbelieve the story of her marriage, and drove her from the door. Desperate, and almost mad, she came back to London, where she still had some little relics of property that her fugitive husband left behind him. He promised, when he left her, to remit her money ; but he sent none, or she refused it—or, in her wildness and despair, lost the dreadful paper which announced his desertion, and that he was married before, and that to pursue him would ruin him, and he knew she never would do *that*—no, however much he might have wronged her.

She was penniless then,—deserted by all,—having made away with the last trinket of her brief days of love, having sold the last little remnant of her poor little stock of clothing,—alone in the great-wilderness of London, when it pleased God to send her succour in the person of an old friend who had known her, and even loved her, in happier days. When the Samaritans came to this poor child, they found her sick and shuddering with fever. They brought their doctor to her, who is never so eager as when he runs up a poor man's stair. And, as he watched by the bed where her kind friends came to help her, he heard her sad little story of trust and desertion.

Her father was a humble person who had seen better days ; and poor little Mrs. Brandon had a sweetness and simplicity of manner which exceedingly touched the good doctor. She had little education, except that which silence, long-suffering, seclusion, will sometimes give. When cured of her illness, there was the great and constant evil of poverty to meet and overcome. How was she to live ? He got to be as fond of her as of a child of his own. She was tidy, thrifty, gay at times, with a little simple cheerfulness. The little flowers began to bloom as the sunshine touched them. Her whole life hitherto had been cowering under neglect, and tyranny, and gloom.

Mr. Montfitchet was for coming so often to look after the little outcast whom he had succoured that I am bound to say Mrs. M. became hysterically jealous, and waited for him on the stairs as he came down swathed in his Spanish cloak, pounced on him, and called him a monster. Goodenough was also, I fancy suspicious of Montfitchet, and Montfitchet of Goodenough. Howbeit, the doctor vowed that he never had other than the feeling of a father towards his poor little *protégée*, nor could any father be more tender. He did not try to take her out of her station in life. He found, or she found for herself, a work which she could do. " Papa used to say no one ever nursed him so nice as I did," she said. " I think I could do that better than anything, except my needle, but I like to be useful to poor sick people best. I don't think about myself then, sir." And for this business good Mr. Goodenough had her educated and employed.

The widow died in course of time whom Mrs. Brandon's father had married, and her daughters refused to keep him, speaking very disrespectfully of this old Mr. Gann, who was, indeed, a weak old man. And now Caroline came to the rescue of her old father. She was a shrewd little Caroline. She had saved a little money. Goodenough gave up a country-house, which he did not care to use, and lent Mrs. Brandon the furniture. She thought she could keep a lodging-house and find lodgers. Montfitchet had painted her. There was a sort of beauty about her which the artists admired. When Ridley the Academician had the small-pox, she attended him, and caught the malady. She did not mind; not she. "It won't spoil my beauty," she said. Nor did it. The disease dealt very kindly with her little modest face. I don't know who gave her the nick-name, but she had a good roomy house in Thornhaugh Street, an artist on the first and second floor; and there never was a word of scandal against the Little Sister, for was not her father in permanence sipping gin-and-water in the ground-floor parlour? As we called her "the Little Sister," her father was called "the Captain"—a bragging, lazy, good-natured old man—not a reputable captain—and very cheerful, though the conduct of his children, he said, had repeatedly broken his heart.

I don't know how many years the Little Sister had been on duty when Philip Firmin had his scarlet fever. It befell him at the end of the term, just when all the boys were going home. His tutor and his tutor's wife wanted their holidays, and sent their own children out of the way. As Phil's father was absent, Dr. Goodenough came, and sent his nurse in. The case grew worse, so bad that Dr. Firmin was summoned from the Isle of Wight, and arrived one evening at Grey Friars—Grey Friars so silent now, so noisy at other times with the shouts and crowds of the playground.

Dr. Goodenough's carriage was at the door when Dr. Firmin's carriage drove up.

"How was the boy?"

"He had been very bad. He had been wrong in the head all day, talking and laughing quite wild-like," the servant said.

The father ran up the stairs.

Phil was in a great room, in which were several empty beds of boys gone home for the holidays. The windows were opened into Grey Friars Square. Goodenough heard his colleague's carriage drive up, and rightly divined that Phil's father had arrived. He came out, and met Firmin in the ante-room.

"Head has wandered a little. Better now, and quiet;" and the one doctor murmured to the other the treatment which he had pursued.

Firmin stept in gently towards the patient, near whose side the Little Sister was standing.

"Who is it?" asked Phil.

"It is I, dear. Your father," said Dr. Firmin, with real tenderness in his voice.

The Little Sister turned round once, and fell down like a stone by the bedside.

"You infernal villain!" said Goodenough, with an oath, and a step forward.   "You are the man!"

"Hush!   The patient, if you please, Dr. Goodenough," said the other physician.

CHAPTER IV.

A GENTEEL FAMILY.

AVE you made up your mind on the question of seeming and being in the world? I mean, suppose you *are* poor, is it right for you to *seem* to be well off? Have people an honest right to keep up appearances? Are you justified in starving your dinner-table in order to keep a carriage; to have such an expensive house that you can't by any possibility help a poor relation; to array your daughters in costly milliners' wares because they live with girls whose parents are twice as rich? Sometimes it is hard to say where honest pride ends and hypocrisy begins. To obtrude your poverty is mean and slavish; as it is odious for a beggar to ask compassion by showing his sores. But to simulate prosperity—to be wealthy and lavish thrice a year when you ask your friends, and for the rest of the time to munch a crust and sit by one candle—are the folks who practise this deceit worthy of applause or a whipping? Sometimes it is noble pride, sometimes shabby swindling. When I see Eugenia with her dear children exquisitely neat and cheerful; not showing the slightest semblance of poverty, or uttering the smallest complaint;

persisting that Squanderfield, her husband, treats her well, and is good at heart; and denying that he leaves her and her young ones in want; I admire and reverence that noble falsehood—that beautiful constancy and endurance which disdains to ask compassion. When I sit at poor Jezebella's table, and am treated to her sham bounties and shabby splendour, I only feel anger for the hospitality, and that dinner, and guest, and host, are humbugs together.

Talbot Twysden's dinner-table is large, and the guests most respectable. There is always a bigwig or two present, and a dining dowager who frequents the greatest houses. There is a butler who offers you wine; there's a *menu du diner* before Mrs. Twysden; and to read it you would fancy you were at a good dinner. It tastes of chopped straw. Oh, the dreary sparkle of that feeble champagne; the audacity of that public-house sherry; the swindle of that acrid claret; the fiery twang of that clammy port! I have tried them all, I tell you! It is sham wine, a sham dinner, a sham welcome, a sham cheerfulness among the guests assembled. I feel that that woman eyes and counts the cutlets as they are carried off the tables; perhaps watches that one which you try to swallow. She has counted and grudged each candle by which the cook prepares the meal. Does her big coachman fatten himself on purloined oats and beans, and Thorley's food for cattle? Of the rinsings of those wretched bottles the butler will have to give a reckoning in the morning. Unless you are of the very great *monde*, Twysden and his wife think themselves better than you are, and seriously patronize you. They consider it is a privilege to be invited to those horrible meals to which they gravely ask the greatest folks in the country. I actually met Winton there—the famous Winton—the best dinner-giver in the world (ah, what a position for man!) I watched him, and marked the sort of wonder which came over him as he tasted and sent away dish after dish, glass after glass. "Try that Château Margaux, Winton!" calls out the host. "It is some that Bottleby and I imported." Imported! I see Winton's face as he tastes the wine, and puts it down. He does not like to talk about that dinner. He has lost a day. Twysden will continue to ask him every year; will continue to expect to be asked in return, with Mrs. Twysden and one of his daughters; and will express his surprise loudly at the club, saying, "Hang Winton! Deuce take the fellow! He has sent me no game this year!" When foreign dukes and princes arrive, Twysden

MR. FROG REQUESTS THE HONOUR OF PRINCE OX'S COMPANY AT DINNER.

straightway collars them, and invites them to his house. And sometimes they go once—and then ask, "*Qui donc est ce Monsieur Twisden, qui est si drôle?*" And he elbows his way up to them at the Minister's assemblies, and frankly gives them his hand. And calm Mrs. Twysden wriggles, and works, and slides, and pushes, and tramples if need be, her girls following behind her, until she too has come up under the eyes of the great man, and bestowed on him a smile and a curtsey. Twysden grasps prosperity cordially by the hand. He says to success, "Bravo!" On the contrary, I never saw a man more resolute in not knowing unfortunate people, or more daringly forgetful of those whom he does not care to remember. If this Levite met a wayfarer, going down from Jerusalem, who had fallen among thieves, do you think he would stop to rescue the fallen man? He would neither give wine, nor oil, nor money. He would pass on perfectly satisfied with his own virtue, and leave the other to go, as best he might, to Jericho.

What is this? Am I angry because Twysden has left off asking me to his vinegar and chopped hay? No. I think not. Am I hurt because Mrs. Twysden sometimes patronizes my wife, and sometimes cuts her? Perhaps. Only women thoroughly know the insolence of women towards one another in the world. That is a very stale remark. They receive and deliver stabs, smiling politely. Tom Sayers could not take punishment more gaily than they do. If you could but see *under* the skin, you would find their little hearts scarred all over with little lancet digs. I protest I have seen my own wife enduring the impertinence of this woman, with a face as calm and placid as she wears when old Twysden himself is talking to her, and pouring out one of his maddening long stories. Oh, no! I am not angry at all. I can see *that* by the way in which I am writing of these folks. By the way, whilst I am giving this candid opinion of the Twysdens, do I sometimes pause to consider what they think of *me?* What do I care? Think what you like. Meanwhile we bow to one another at parties. We smile at each other in a sickly way. And as for the dinners in Beaunash Street, I hope those who eat them enjoy their food.

Twysden is one of the chiefs now of the Powder and Pomatum Office, (the Pigtail branch was finally abolished in 1833, after the Reform Bill, with a compensation to the retiring under-secretary), and his son is a clerk in the same office. When they came out, the daughters were very pretty—even my wife allows that.   One of them used to ride in the Park with her father or brother daily; and knowing what his salary and wife's fortune were, and what the rent of his house in Beaunash Street, everybody wondered how the Twysdens could make both ends meet.   They had horses, carriages, and a great house fit for at least five thousand a year; they had not half as much, as everybody knew; and it was supposed that old Ringwood must make his niece an allowance.   She certainly worked hard to get it.   I spoke of stabs anon, and poor little breasts and sides scarred all over.   No nuns, no monks, no fakeers take whippings more kindly than some devotees of the world; and, as the punishment is one for edification, let us hope the world lays smartly on to back and shoulders, and uses the thong well.

When old Ringwood, at the close of his lifetime, used to come to visit his dear niece and her husband and children, he always brought a cat-o'-nine-tails in his pocket, and administered it to the whole household.   He grinned at the poverty, the pretence, the meanness of the people, as they knelt before him and did him homage.   The father and mother trembling brought the girls up for punishment, and, piteously smiling, received their own boxes on the ear in presence of their children.   "Ah!" the little French governess used to say, grinding her white teeth, "I like milor to come.   All day you vip me.   When milor come, he vip you, and you kneel down and kiss de rod."

They certainly knelt and took their whipping with the most exemplary fortitude.   Sometimes the lash fell on papa's back, sometimes on mamma's: now it stung Agnes, and now it lighted on Blanche's pretty shoulders.   But I think it was on the heir of the house, young Ringwood Twysden, that my lord loved best to operate. Ring's vanity was very thin-skinned, his selfishness easily wounded, and his contortions under punishment amused the old tormentor.

As my lord's brougham drives up—the modest little brown brougham, with the noble horse, the lord chancellor of a coachman, and the ineffable footman—the ladies, who know the whirr of the wheels, and may be quarrelling in the drawing-room, call a truce to the fight, and smooth down their ruffled tempers and raiment. Mamma is writing at her table, in that beautiful, clear hand which we all admire; Blanche is at her book; Agnes is rising from the piano quite naturally.   A quarrel between those gentle, smiling, delicate creatures ! Impossible ! About your most common piece of hypocrisy how men will blush and bungle : how easily, how gracefully, how consummately, women will perform it !

"Well," growls my lord, "you are all in such pretty attitudes, I make no doubt you have been sparring. I suspect, Maria, the men must know what devilish bad tempers the girls have got. Who can have seen you fighting? You're quiet enough here, you little monkeys. I tell you what it is. Ladies'-maids get about and talk to the valets in the housekeeper's room, and the men tell their masters. Upon my word I believe it was that business last year at Whipham which frightened Greenwood off. Famous match. Good house in town and country. No mother alive. Agnes might have had it her own way, but for that——"

"We are not all angels in our family, uncle!" cries Miss Agnes, reddening.

"And your mother is too sharp. The men are afraid of you, Maria. I've heard several young men say so. At White's they talk about it quite freely. Pity for the girls. Great pity. Fellows come and tell me. Jack Hall, and fellows who go about everywhere."

"I'm sure I don't care what Captain Hall says about me—odious little wretch!" cries Blanche.

"There you go off in a tantrum ! Hall never has any opinion of his own. He only fetches and carries what other people say. And he says, fellows say they are frightened of your mother. La bless you ! Hall has no opinion. A fellow might commit murder, and Hall would wait at the door. Quite a discreet man. But I told him to ask about you. And that's what I hear. And he says that Agnes is making eyes at the doctor's boy."

"It's a shame," cries Agnes, shedding tears under her martyrdom.

"Older than he is ; but that's no obstacle. Good-looking boy, I suppose you don't object to that? Has his poor mother's money, and his father's : must be well to do. A vulgar fellow, but a clever fellow, and a determined fellow, the doctor—and a fellow who, I suspect, is capable of anything. Shouldn't wonder at that fellow marrying some rich dowager. Those doctors get an immense influence over women ; and unless I'm mistaken in my man, Maria, your poor sister got hold of a——"

"Uncle!" cries Mrs. Twysden, pointing to her daughters, "before these——"

"Before those innocent lambs!　Hem!　Well, I think Firmin is of the wolf sort:" and the old noble laughed, and showed his own fierce fangs as he spoke.

"I grieve to say, my lord, I agree with you," remarks Mr. Twysden.　"I don't think Firmin a man of high principle.　A clever man?　Yes.　An accomplished man?　Yes.　A good physician?　Yes.　A prosperous man?　Yes.　But what's a man without principle?"

"You ought to have been a parson, Twysden."

"Others have said so, my lord.　My poor mother often regretted that I didn't choose the Church.　When I was at Cambridge I used to speak constantly at the Union.　I practised.　I do not disguise from you that my aim was public life.　I am free to confess I think the House of Commons would have been my sphere ; and, had my means permitted, should certainly have come forward."

Lord Ringwood smiled, and winked to his niece—

"He means, my dear, that he would like to wag his jaws at my expense, and that I should put him in for Whipham."

"There are, I think, worse Members of Parliament," remarked Mr. Twysden.

"If there was a box of 'em like you, what a cage it would be!" roared my lord.　"By George, I'm sick of jaw.　And I would like to see a king of spirit in this country, who would shut up the talking-shops and gag the whole chattering crew!"

"I am a partisan of order—but a lover of freedom," continues Twysden.　"I hold that the balance of our constitution——"

I think my lord would have indulged in a few of those oaths with which his old-fashioned conversation was liberally garnished ; but the servant, entering at this moment, announces Mr. Philip Firmin ; and ever so faint a blush flutters up in Agnes' cheek, who feels that the old lord's eye is upon her.

"So, sir, I saw you at the Opera last night," says Lord Ringwood.

"I saw you, too," says downright Phil.

The women looked terrified, and Twysden scared.　The Twysdens had Lord Ringwood's box sometimes.　But there were boxes in which the old man sat, and in which they never *could* see him.

"Why don't you look at the stage, sir, when you go to the Opera, and not at me?　When you go to church you ought to look at the parson, oughtn't you?" growled the old man.　"I'm about as good to look at as the fellow who dances first in the ballet—and very nearly as old. But if I were you, I should think looking at the Ellsler better fun."

And now you may fancy of what old, old times we are writing—times in which those horrible old male dancers yet existed—hideous old creatures, with low dresses and short sleeves, and wreaths of flowers, or hats and feathers round their absurd old wigs—who skipped at the head of the ballet. Let us be thankful that those old apes have almost vanished off the stage, and left it in possession of the beauteous bounders of the other sex. Ah, my dear young friends, time *will* be when these too will cease to appear more than mortally beautiful ! To Philip, at his age, they yet looked as lovely as houris. At this time the simple young fellow, surveying the ballet from his stall at the Opera, mistook carmine for blushes, pearl-powder for native snows, and cotton-wool for natural symmetry; and I dare say when he went into the world was not more clear-sighted about its rouged innocence, its padded pretensions, and its painted candour.

Old Lord Ringwood had a humorous pleasure in petting and coaxing Philip Firmin before Philip's relatives of Beaunash Street. Even the girls felt a little plaintive envy at the partiality which uncle Ringwood exhibited for Phil ; but the elder Twysdens and Ringwood Twysden, their son, writhed with agony at the preference which the old man sometimes showed for the doctor's boy. Phil was much taller, much handsomer, much stronger, much better tempered, and much richer, than young Twysden. He would be the sole inheritor of his father's fortune, and had his mother's thirty thousand pounds. Even when they told him his father would marry again, Phil laughed, and did not seem to care—" I wish him joy of his new wife," was all he could be got to say: " when he gets one, I suppose I shall go into chambers. Old Parr Street is not as gay as Pall Mall." I am not angry with Mrs. Twysden for having a little jealousy of her nephew. Her boy and girls were the fruit of a dutiful marriage ; and Phil was the son of a disobedient child. Her children were always on their best behaviour before their great uncle ; and Phil cared for him no more than for any other man ; and he liked Phil the best. Her boy was as humble and eager to please as any of his lordship's humblest henchmen ; and Lord Ringwood snapped at him, browbeat him, and trampled on the poor darling's tenderest feelings, and treated him scarcely better than a lacquey.   As for poor Mr. Twysden, my lord not only yawned unreservedly in his face—that could not be helped; poor Talbot's talk set many of his acquaintance asleep—but laughed at him, interrupted him, and told him to hold his tongue.   On this day, as the family sat together at the pleasant hour—the before-dinner hour—the fireside and tea-table hour—Lord Ringwood said to Phil—

"Dine with me to-day, sir?"

"Why does he not ask me, with my powers of conversation?" thought old Twysden to himself.

"Hang him, he always asks that beggar," writhed young Twysden, in his corner.

"Very sorry, sir, can't come.   Have asked some fellows to dine at the 'Blue Posts,'" says Phil.

"Confound you, sir, why don't you put 'em off?" cries the old lord.   "*You'd* put 'em off, Twysden, wouldn't you?"

"Oh, sir!" the heart of father and son both beat.

"You know you would; and you quarrel with this boy for not throwing his friends over.   Good-night, Firmin, since you won't come."

And with this my lord was gone.

The two gentlemen of the house glumly looked from the window, and saw my lord's brougham drive swiftly away in the rain.

"I hate your dining at those horrid taverns," whispered a young lady to Philip.

"It is better fun than dining at home," Philip remarks.

"You smoke and drink too much.   You come home late, and you don't live in a proper *monde*, sir!" continues the young lady.

"What would you have me do?"

"Oh, nothing.   You must dine with those horrible men," cries Agnes; "else you might have gone to Lady Pendleton's to-night."

"I can throw over the men easily enough, if you wish," answered the young man.

"I?   I have no wish of the sort.   Have you not already refused uncle Ringwood?"

"*You* are not Lord Ringwood," says Phil, with a tremor in his voice.   "I don't know there is much I would refuse you."

"You silly boy!   What do I ever ask you to do that you ought to refuse?   I want you to live in our world, and not with your dreadful wild Oxford and Temple bachelors. I don't want you to smoke. I want you to go into the world of which you have the *entrée* —and you refuse your uncle on account of some horrid engagement at a tavern!"

"Shall I stop here? Aunt, will you give me some dinner—here?" asks the young man.

"We have dined: my husband and son dine out," said gentle Mrs. Twysden.

There was cold mutton and tea for the ladies; and Mrs. Twysden did not like to seat her nephew, who was accustomed to good fare and high living, to that meagre meal.

"You see I must console myself at the tavern," Philip said. "We shall have a pleasant party there."

"And pray who makes it?" asks the lady.

"There is Ridley the painter."

"My dear Philip! Do you know that his father was actually——"

"In the service of Lord Todmorden? He often tells us so. He is a queer character, the old man."

"Mr. Ridley is a man of genius, certainly. His pictures are delicious, and he goes everywhere—but—but you provoke me, Philip, by your carelessness; indeed you do. Why should you be dining with the sons of footmen, when the first houses in the country might be open to you? You pain me, you foolish boy."

"For dining in company of a man of genius? Come, Agnes!" And the young man's brow grew dark. "Besides," he added, with a tone of sarcasm in his voice, which Miss Agnes did not like at all— "besides, my dear, you know he dines at Lord Pendleton's."

"What is that you are talking of Lady Pendleton, children?" asked watchful mamma from her corner.

"Ridley dines there. He is going to dine with me at a tavern to-day. And Lord Halden is coming—and Mr. Winton is coming— having heard of the famous beefsteaks."

"Winton! Lord Halden! Beefsteaks! Where? By George! I have a mind to go, too! Where do you fellows dine? *au cabaret?* Hang me, I'll be one," shrieked little Twysden, to the terror of Philip, who knew his uncle's awful powers of conversation. But Twysden remembered himself in good time, and to the intense relief of young Firmin. "Hang me, I forgot! Your aunt and I dine with the Bladeses. Stupid old fellow, the admiral, and bad wine—

which is unpardonable; but we must go—*on n'a que sa parole*, hey?
Tell Winton that I had meditated joining him, and that I have still
some of that Château Margaux he liked. Halden's father I know
well. Tell him so. Bring him here. Maria, send a Thursday card
to Lord Halden! You must bring him here to dinner, Philip. *That's*
the best way to make acquaintance, my boy!" And the little man
swaggers off, waving a bed-candle, as if he was going to quaff a
bumper of sparkling spermaceti.

The mention of such great personages as Lord Halden and
Mr. Winton silenced the reproofs of the pensive Agnes.

"You won't care for our quiet fireside whilst you live with those
fine people, Philip," she sighed. There was no talk now of his
throwing himself away on bad company.

So Philip did not dine with his relatives : but Talbot Twysden
took good care to let Lord Ringwood know how young Firmin had
offered to dine with his aunt that day after refusing his lordship.
And everything to Phil's discredit, and every act of extravagance or
wildness which the young man committed, did Phil's uncle, and
Phil's cousin Ringwood Twysden, convey to the old nobleman.
Had not these been the informers, Lord Ringwood would have been
angry : for he exacted obedience and servility from all round about
him. But it was pleasanter to vex the Twysdens than to scold and
browbeat Philip, and so his lordship chose to laugh and be amused
at Phil's insubordination. He saw, too, other things of which he did
not speak. He was a wily old man, who could afford to be blind
upon occasion.

What do you judge from the fact that Philip was ready to make
or break engagements at a young lady's instigation? When you were
twenty years old, had no young ladies an influence over *you?* Were
they not commonly older than yourself? Did your youthful passion
lead to anything, and are you very sorry now that it did not?
Suppose you had had your soul's wish and married her, of what age
would she be now? And now when you go into the world and see
her, *do* you on your conscience very much regret that the little affair
came to an end? Is it that (lean, or fat, or stumpy, or tall) woman
with all those children whom you once chose to break your heart
about; and do you still envy Jones? | Philip was in love with his
cousin, no doubt, but at the university had he not been previously
in love with the Tomkinsian professor's daughter Miss Budd; and

had he not already written verses to Miss Flower, his neighbour's daughter in Old Parr Street? And don't young men always begin by falling in love with ladies older than themselves? Agnes certainly was Philip's senior, as her sister constantly took care to inform him.

And Agnes might have told stories about Blanche, if she chose—as you may about me, and I about you. Not quite true stories, but stories with enough alloy of lies to make them serviceable coin; stories such as we hear daily in the world; stories such as we read in the most learned and conscientious history-books, which are told by the most respectable persons, and perfectly authentic until contradicted. It is only *our* histories that can't be contradicted (unless, to be sure, novelists contradict themselves, as sometimes they will). What *we* say about people's virtues, failings, characters, you may be sure is all true. And I defy any man to assert that my opinion of the Twysden family is malicious, or unkind, or unfounded in any particular. Agnes wrote verses, and set her own and other writers' poems to music. Blanche was scientific, and attended the Albemarle Street lectures sedulously. They are both clever women as times go ; well educated and accomplished, and very well mannered when they choose to be pleasant. If you were a bachelor, say, with a good fortune, or a widower who wanted consolation, or a lady giving very good parties and belonging to the *monde*, you would find them agreeable people. If you were a little Treasury clerk, or a young barrister with no practice, or a lady, old or young, *not* quite of the *monde*, your opinion of them would not be so favourable. I have seen them cut, and scorn, and avoid, and caress, and kneel down and worship the same person. When Mrs. Lovel first gave parties, don't I remember the shocked countenances of the Twysden family? Were ever shoulders colder than yours, dear girls? Now they love her ; they fondle her step-children ; they praise her to her face and behind her handsome back ; they take her hand in public ; they call her by her Christian name ; they fall into ecstasies over her toilettes, and would fetch coals for her dressing-room fire if she but gave them the word. *She* is not changed. She is the same lady who once was a governess, and no colder and no warmer since then. But you see her prosperity has brought virtues into evidence, which people did not perceive when she was poor. Could people see Cinderella's beauty when she was in rags by the fire, or until she stepped out

of her fairy coach in her diamonds?   How *are* you to recognize
a diamond in a dusthole?   Only very clever eyes can do that.
Whereas a lady in a fairy coach and eight naturally creates a sensation; and enraptured princes come and beg to have the honour of
dancing with her.

In the character of infallible historian, then, I declare that if
Miss Twysden at three-and-twenty feels ever so much or little attachment for her cousin who is not yet of age, there is no reason to be angry
with her.   A brave, handsome, blundering, downright young fellow,
with broad shoulders, high spirits, and quite fresh blushes on his face,
with very good talents, (though he has been wofully idle, and requested
to absent himself temporarily from his university,) the possessor of a
competent fortune and the heir of another, may naturally make some
impression on a lady's heart with whom kinsmanship and circumstance
bring him into daily communion.   When had any sound so hearty as
Phil's laugh been heard in Beaunash Street?   His jolly frankness
touched his aunt, a clever woman.   She would smile and say, "My
dear Philip, it is not only what you say, but what you are going to
say next, which keeps me in such a perpetual tremor."   There may
have been a time once when she was frank and cordial herself: ever
so long ago, when she and her sister were two blooming girls, lovingly
clinging together, and just stepping forth into the world.   But if you
succeed in keeping a fine house on a small income; in showing a
cheerful face to the world though oppressed with ever so much care;
in bearing with dutiful reverence an intolerable old bore of a husband
(and I vow it is this quality in Mrs. Twysden for which I most admire
her); in submitting to defeats patiently; to humiliations with smiles,
so as to hold your own in your darling *monde;* you may succeed, but
you must give up being frank and cordial.   The marriage of her
sister to the doctor gave Maria Ringwood a great panic, for Lord
Ringwood was furious when the news came.   Then, perhaps, she
sacrificed a little private passion of her own: then she set her cap
at a noble young neighbour of my lord's, who jilted *her;* then she
took up with Talbot Twysden, Esquire, of the Powder and Pomatum
Office, and made a very faithful wife to him, and was a very careful
mother to his children.   But as for frankness and cordiality, my good
friend, accept from a lady what she can give you—good manners,
pleasant talk, and decent attention.   If you go to her breakfast-table,
don't ask for a roc's egg, but eat that moderately fresh hen's egg

which John brings you. When Mrs. Twysden is in her open carriage in the Park, how prosperous, handsome, and jolly she looks—the girls how smiling and young (that is, you know, considering all things) ; the horses look fat, the coachman and footman wealthy and sleek; they exchange bows with the tenants of other carriages —well-known aristocrats. Jones and Brown, leaning over the railings, and seeing the Twysden equipage pass, have not the slightest doubt that it contains people of the highest wealth and fashion. " I say, Jones my boy, what noble family has the motto, *Wel done Twys done?* and what clipping girls there were in that barouche ! " B. remarks to J. ; " and what a handsome young swell that is riding the bay-mare, and leaning over and talking to the yellow-haired girl ! " And it is evident to one of those gentlemen, at least, that he has been looking at your regular first-rate tiptop people.

As for Phil Firmin on his bay-mare, with his geranium in his button-hole, there is no doubt that Philippus looks as handsome, and as rich, and as brave as any lord. And I think Brown must have felt a little pang when his friend told him, " That a lord ! Bless you, it's only a swell doctor's son." But while J. and B. fancy all the little party very happy, they do not hear Phil whisper to his cousin, " I hope you liked *your partner* last night?" and they do not see how anxious Mrs. Twysden is under her smiles, how she perceives Colonel Shafto's cab coming up (the dancer in question), and how she would rather have Phil anywhere than by that particular wheel of her carriage ; how Lady Braglands has just passed them by without noticing them—Lady Braglands, who has a ball, and is determined *not* to ask that woman and her two endless girls ; and how, though Lady Braglands won't see Mrs. Twysden in her great staring equipage, and the three faces which have been beaming smiles at her, she instantly perceives Lady Lovel, who is passing ensconced in her little brougham, and kisses her fingers twenty times over. How should poor J. and B., who are not, *vous comprenez, du monde,* understand these mysteries?

" That's young Firmin, is it, that handsome young fellow ? " says Brown to Jones.

" Doctor married the Earl of Ringwood's niece—ran away with her, you know."

" Good practice ? "

" Capital. First-rate. All the tiptop people. Great ladies' doctor.

Can't do without him.   Makes a fortune, besides what he had with his wife."

"We've seen his name—the old man's—on some very queer paper," says B. with a wink to J.   By which I conclude they are City gentlemen.   And they look very hard at friend Philip, as he comes to talk and shake hands with some pedestrians who are gazing over the railings at the busy and pleasant Park scene.

CHAPTER V.

THE NOBLE KINSMAN.

AVING had occasion to mention a noble earl once or twice, I am sure no polite reader will consent that his lordship should push through this history along with the crowd of commoner characters, and without a special word regarding himself. If you are in the least familiar with Burke or Debrett, you know that the ancient family of Ringwood has long been famous for its great possessions, and its loyalty to the British crown.

In the troubles which unhappily agitated this kingdom after the deposition of the late reigning house, the Ringwoods were implicated with many other families, but on the accession of his Majesty George III. these differences happily ended, nor had the monarch any subject more loyal and devoted than Sir John Ringwood, Baronet, of Wingate and Whipham Market. Sir John's influence sent three Members to Parliament ; and during the dangerous and vexatious period of the American war, this influence was exerted so cordially and consistently in the cause of order and the crown, that his Majesty thought fit to advance Sir John to the dignity of Baron Ringwood. Sir John's brother, Sir Francis Ringwood, of Appleshaw, who followed the

profession of the law, also was promoted to be a Baron of his
Majesty's Court of Exchequer. ·The first baron, dying A. D. 1786,
was succeeded by the eldest of his two sons—John, second Baron
and first Earl of Ringwood.   His lordship's brother, the Honourable
Colonel Philip Ringwood, died gloriously, at the head of his regiment
and in the defence of his country, in the battle of Busaco, 1810,
leaving two daughters, Louisa and Maria, who henceforth lived with
the earl their uncle.

The Earl of Ringwood had but one son, Charles Viscount Cinqbars,
who, unhappily, died of a decline, in his twenty-second year.   And
thus the descendants of Sir Francis Ringwood became heirs to the
earl's great estates of Wingate and Whipham Market, though not of
the peerages which had been conferred on the earl and his father.

Lord Ringwood had, living with him, two nieces, daughters of his
late brother, Colonel Philip Ringwood, who fell in the Peninsular
War.   Of these ladies, the youngest, Louisa, was his lordship's
favourite; and though both the ladies had considerable fortunes of
their own, it was supposed their uncle would further provide for
them, especially as he was on no very good terms with his cousin,
Sir John of the Shaw, who took the Whig side in politics, whilst his
lordship was a chief of the Tory party.

Of these two nieces, the eldest, Maria, never any great favourite
with her uncle, married, 1824, Talbot Twysden, Esq., a Commissioner of Powder and Pomatum Tax; but the youngest, Louisa,
incurred my lord's most serious anger by eloping with George Brand
Firmin, Esq., M.D., a young gentleman ·of Cambridge University,
who had been with Lord Cinqbars when he died at Naples, and had
brought home his body to Wingate Castle.

The quarrel with the youngest niece, and the indifference with
which he generally regarded the elder (whom his lordship was in the
habit of calling an old schemer), occasioned at first a little *rapprochement* between Lord Ringwood and his heir, Sir John of Appleshaw;
but both gentlemen were very firm, not to say obstinate in their
natures.   They had a quarrel with respect to the cutting off of a
small entailed property, of which the earl wished to dispose; and
they parted with much rancour and bad language on his lordship's
part, who was an especially free-spoken nobleman, and apt to call a
spade a spade, as the saying is.

After this difference, and to spite his heir, it was supposed that the Earl of Ringwood would marry. He was little more than seventy years of age, and had once been of a very robust constitution. And though his temper was violent and his person not at all agreeable (for even in Sir Thomas Lawrence's picture his countenance is very ill-favoured), there is little doubt he could have found a wife for the asking among the young beauties of his own county, or the fairest of May Fair.

But he was a cynical nobleman, and perhaps morbidly conscious of his own ungainly appearance. " Of course I can buy a wife " (his lordship would say). " Do you suppose people won't sell their daughters to a man of my rank and means ? Now look at me, my good sir, and say whether any woman alive could fall in love with me ? I have been married, and once was enough. I hate ugly women, and your virtuous women, who tremble and cry in private, and preach at a man, bore me. Sir John Ringwood of Appleshaw is an ass, and I hate him ; but I don't hate him enough to make myself miserable for the rest of my days, in order to spite him. When I drop, I drop. Do you suppose I care what comes after me ? " And with much sardonical humour this old lord used to play off one good dowager after another who would bring her girl in his way. He would send pearls to Emily, diamonds to Fanny, opera-boxes to lively Kate, books of devotion to pious Selinda, and, at the season's end, drive back to his lonely great castle in the west. They were all the same, such was his lordship's opinion. I fear, a wicked and corrupt old gentleman, my dears. But ah, would not a woman submit to some sacrifices to reclaim that unhappy man ; to lead that gifted but lost being into the ways of right ; to convert to a belief in woman's purity that erring soul ? They tried him with high-church altar-cloths for his chapel at Wingate ; they tried him with low-church tracts ; they danced before him ; they jumped fences on horseback ; they wore bandeaux or ringlets, according as his taste dictated ; they were always at home when he called, and poor you and I were gruffly told they were engaged ; they gushed in gratitude over his bouquets ; they sang for him, and their mothers, concealing their sobs, mur-mured, " What an angel that Cecilia of mine is ! " Every variety of delicious chaff they flung to that old bird. But he was uncaught at the end of the season : he winged his way back to his western hills. And if you dared to say that Mrs. Netley had tried to take him, or Lady Trapboys had set a snare for him, you know you were a wicked, gross calumniator, and notorious everywhere for your dull and vulgar abuse of women.

Now, in the year 1830, it happened that this great nobleman was seized with a fit of the gout, which had very nearly consigned his estates to his kinsman the Baronet of Appleshaw. A revolution took place in a neighbouring State. An illustrious reigning family was expelled from its country, and projects of reform (which would pretty certainly end in revolution) were rife in ours. The events in France, and those pending at home, so agitated Lord Ringwood's mind, that he was attacked by one of the severest fits of gout under which he ever suffered. His shrieks, as he was brought out of his yacht at Ryde to a house taken for him in the town, were dreadful; his language to all persons about him was frightfully expressive, as Lady Quamley and her daughter, who had sailed with him several times, can vouch. An ill return that rude old man made for all their kindness and attention to him. They had danced on board his yacht; they had dined on board his yacht; they had been out sailing with him, and cheerfully braved the inconveniences of the deep in his company. And when they ran to the side of his chair—as what would they not do to soothe an old gentleman in illness and distress? —when they ran up to his chair as it was wheeled along the pier, he called mother and daughter by the most vulgar and opprobrious names, and roared out to them to go to a place which I certainly shall not more particularly mention.

Now it happened, at this period, that Dr. and Mrs. Firmin were at Ryde with their little boy, then some three years of age. The doctor was already taking his place as one of the most fashionable physicians then in London, and had begun to be celebrated for the treatment of this especial malady. (Firmin on " Gout and Rheumatism" was, you remember, dedicated to his Majesty George IV.) Lord Ringwood's valet bethought him of calling the doctor in, and mentioned how he was present in the town. Now Lord Ringwood was a nobleman who never would allow his angry feelings to stand in the way of his present comforts or ease. He instantly desired Mr. Firmin's attendance, and submitted to his treatment; a part of which was a *hauteur* to the full as great as that which the sick man exhibited. Firmin's appearance was so tall and grand, that he looked vastly more noble than a great many noblemen. Six feet, a high manner, a polished forehead, a flashing eye, a snowy shirt-frill, a rolling velvet collar, a beautiful hand appearing under a velvet cuff—all these advantages he possessed and used. He did not make the slightest allusion to bygones, but treated his patient with a perfect courtesy and an impenetrable self-possession.

This defiant and darkling politeness did not always displease the old man. He was so accustomed to slavish compliance and eager obedience from all people round about him, that he sometimes wearied of their servility, and relished a little independence. Was it from calculation, or because he was a man of high spirit, that Firmin determined to maintain an independent course with his lordship? From the first day of their meeting he never departed from it, and had the satisfaction of meeting with only civil behaviour from his noble relative and patient, who was notorious for his rudeness and brutality to almost every person who came in his way.

From hints which his lordship gave in conversation, he showed the doctor that he was acquainted with some particulars of the latter's early career. It had been wild and stormy. Firmin had incurred debts; had quarrelled with his father; had left the university and gone abroad; had lived in a wild society, which used dice and cards every night, and pistols sometimes in the morning; and had shown a fearful dexterity in the use of the latter instrument, which he employed against the person of a famous Italian adventurer, who fell under his hand at Naples. When this century was five-and-twenty years younger, the crack of the pistol-shot might still occasionally be heard in the suburbs of London in the very early morning; and the dice-box went round in many a haunt of pleasure. The knights of the Four Kings travelled from capital to capital, and engaged each other or made prey of the unwary. Now, the times are changed. The cards are coffined in their boxes. Only *sous-officiers*, brawling in their provincial cafés over their dominos, fight duels. "Ah, dear me," I heard a veteran punter sigh the other day at Bays's, "isn't it a melancholy thing to think, that if I wanted to amuse myself with a fifty-pound note, I don't know the place in London where I could go and lose it?" And he fondly recounted the names of twenty places where he could have cheerfully staked and lost his money in his young time.

After a somewhat prolonged absence abroad, Mr. Firmin came back to this country, was permitted to return to the university, and left it with the degree of Bachelor of Medicine. We have told how

'he ran away with Lord Ringwood's niece, and incurred the anger of
that nobleman.   Beyond abuse and anger his lordship was powerless.
The young lady was free to marry whom she liked, and her uncle to
disown or receive him ; and accordingly she was, as we have seen,
disowned by his lordship, until he found it convenient to forgive her.
What were Lord Ringwood's intentions regarding his property, what
were his accumulations, and who his heirs would be, no one knew.
Meanwhile, of course, there were those who felt a very great interest
on the point.   Mrs. Twysden and her husband and children were
hungry and poor.   If uncle Ringwood had money to leave, it would
be very welcome to those three darlings, whose father had not a
great income like Dr. Firmin.   Philip was a dear, good, frank,
amiable, wild fellow, and they all loved him.   But he had his faults
—that could not be concealed—and so poor Phil's faults were pretty
constantly canvassed before uncle Ringwood, by dear relatives who
knew them only too well.   The dear relatives !   How kind they
are !   I don't think Phil's aunt abused him to my lord.   That quiet
woman calmly and gently put forward the claims of her own darlings,
and affectionately dilated on the young man's present prosperity,
and magnificent future prospects.   The interest of thirty thousand
pounds now, and the inheritance of his father's great accumulations !
What young man could want for more ?   Perhaps he had too much
already.   Perhaps he was too rich to work.   The sly old peer
acquiesced in his niece's statements, and perfectly understood the
point towards which they tended.   "A thousand a year !   What's a
thousand a year ?" growled the old lord.   "Not enough to make a
gentleman, more than enough to make a fellow idle."

   "Ah, indeed, it was but a small income," sighed Mrs. Twysden.
"With a large house, a good establishment, and Mr. Twysden's
salary from his office—it was but a pittance."

   "Pittance ! Starvation," growls my lord, with his usual frankness.
"Don't I know what housekeeping costs ; and see how you screw ?
Butlers and footmen, carriages and job-horses, rent and dinners—
though yours, Maria, are not famous."

   "Very bad—I know they are very bad," says the contrite lady.
"I wish we could afford any better."

   "Afford any better ?   Of course you can't.   You are the crockery
pots, and you swim down-stream with the brass pots.   I saw Twysden
the other day walking down St. James's Street with Rhodes—that tall

fellow." (Here my lord laughed, and showed many fangs, the exhibition of which gave a peculiarly fierce air to his lordship when in good-humour.) "If Twysden walks with a big fellow, he always tries to keep step with him. *You* know that." Poor Maria naturally knew her husband's peculiarities; but she did not say that she had no need to be reminded of them.

"He was so blown he could hardly speak," continued uncle Ringwood; "but he would stretch his little legs, and try and keep up. He has a little body, *le cher mari*, but a good pluck. Those little fellows often have. I've seen him half dead out shooting, and plunging over the ploughed fields after fellows with twice his stride. Why don't men sink in the world, I want to know? Instead of a fine house, and a parcel of idle servants, why don't you have a maid and a leg of mutton, Maria? You go half crazy in trying to make both ends meet. You know you do. It keeps you awake of nights; *I* know that very well. You've got a house fit for people with four times your money. I lend you my cook and so forth; but I can't come and dine with you unless I send the wine in. Why don't you have a pot of porter, and a joint, or some tripe?—tripe's a famous good thing. The miseries which people entail on themselves in trying to live beyond their means are perfectly ridiculous, by George! Look at that fellow who opened the door to me; he's as tall as one of my own men. Go and live in a quiet little street in Belgravia somewhere, and have a neat little maid. Nobody will think a penny the worse of you—and you will be just as well off as if you lived here with an extra couple of thousand a year. The advice I am giving you is worth half that, every shilling of it."

"It is very good advice; but I think, sir, I should prefer the thousand pounds," said the lady.

"Of course you would. That is the consequence of your false position. One of the good points about that doctor is, that he is as proud as Lucifer, and so is his boy. They are not always hungering after money. They keep their independence; though he'll have his own too, the fellow will. Why, when I first called him in, I thought, as he was a relation, he'd doctor me for nothing; but he wouldn't. He would have his fee, by George! and wouldn't come without it. Confounded independent fellow Firmin 'is. And so is the young one."

But when Twysden and his son (perhaps inspirited by Mrs.

Twysden) tried once or twice to be independent in the presence of this lion, he roared, and he rushed at them, and he rent them, so that they fled from him howling. And this reminds me of an old story I have heard—quite an old, old story, such as kind old fellows at clubs love to remember—of my lord, when he was only Lord Cinqbars, insulting a half-pay lieutenant, in his own county, who horsewhipped his lordship in the most private and ferocious manner. It was said Lord Cinqbars had had a rencontre with poachers; but it was my lord who was poaching and the lieutenant who was defending his own dovecot. I do not say that this was a model nobleman; but that, when his own passions or interests did not mislead him, he was a nobleman of very considerable acuteness, humour, and good sense; and could give quite good advice on occasion. If men would kneel down and kiss his boots, well and good. There was the blacking, and you were welcome to embrace toe and heel. But those who would not, were free to leave the operation alone. The Pope himself does not demand the ceremony from Protestants; and if they object to the slipper, no one thinks of forcing it into their mouths. Phil and his father probably declined to tremble before the old man, not because they knew he was a bully who might be put down, but because they were men of spirit, who cared not whether a man was bully or no.

I have told you I like Philip Firmin, though it must be confessed that the young fellow had many faults, and that his career, especially his early career, was by no means exemplary. Have I ever excused his conduct to his father, or said a word in apology of his brief and inglorious university career? I acknowledge his shortcomings with that candour which my friends exhibit in speaking of mine. Who does not see a friend's weaknesses, and is so blind that he cannot perceive that enormous beam in his neighbour's eye? Only a woman or two, from time to time. And even they are undeceived some day. A man of the world, I write about my friends as mundane fellow-creatures. Do you suppose there are many angels here? I say again, perhaps a woman or two. But as for you and me, my good sir, are there any signs of wings sprouting from *our* shoulder-blades? Be quiet. Don't pursue your snarling, cynical remarks, but go on with your story.

As you go through life, stumbling, and slipping, and staggering to your feet again, ruefully aware of your own wretched weakness, and praying, with a contrite heart, let us trust, that you may not be led into temptation, have you not often looked at other fellow-sinners, and speculated with an awful interest on their career? Some there are on whom, quite in their early lives, dark Ahrimanes has seemed to lay his dread mark: children, yet corrupt, and wicked of tongue; tender of age, yet cruel; who should be truth-telling and generous yet (they were at their mothers' bosoms yesterday), but are false and cold and greedy before their time. Infants almost, they practise the art and selfishness of old men. Behind their candid faces are wiles and wickedness, and a hideous precocity of artifice. I can recall such, and in the vista of far-off, unforgotten boyhood, can see marching that sad little procession of *enfans perdus.* May they be saved, pray heaven! Then there is the doubtful class, those who are still on trial; those who fall and rise again; those who are often worsted in life's battle; beaten down, wounded, imprisoned; but escape and conquer sometimes. And then there is the happy class about whom there seems no doubt at all: the spotless and white-robed ones, to whom virtue is easy; in whose pure bosoms faith nestles, and cold doubt finds no entrance; who are children, and good; young men, and good; husbands and fathers, and yet good. Why could the captain of our school write his Greek iambics without an effort, and without an error? Others of us blistered the page with unavailing tears and blots, and might toil ever so and come in lag last at the bottom of the form. Our friend Philip belongs to the middle-class, in which you and I probably are, my dear sir—not yet, I hope, irredeemably consigned to that awful third class, whereof mention has been made.

But, being *homo,* and liable to err, there is no doubt Mr. Philip exercised his privilege, and there was even no little fear at one time that he should overdraw his account. He went from school to the university, and there distinguished himself certainly, but in a way in which very few parents would choose that their sons should excel. That he should hunt, that he should give parties, that he should pull a good oar in one of the best boats on the river, that he should speak at the Union—all these were very well. But why should he speak such awful radicalism and republicanism—he with noble blood in his veins, and the son of a parent whose interest at least it was to keep well with people of high station?

"Why, Pendennis," said Dr. Firmin to me with tears in his eyes, and much genuine grief exhibited on his handsome pale face—"why should it be said that Philip Firmin—both of whose grandfathers fought nobly for their king—should be forgetting the principles of his family, and—and, I haven't words to tell you how deeply he disappoints me. Why, I actually heard of him at that horrible Union advocating the death of Charles the First! I was wild enough myself when I was at the university, but I was a gentleman."

"Boys, sir, are boys," I urged. "They will advocate anything for an argument; and Philip would have taken the other side quite as readily."

"Lord Axminster and Lord St. Dennis told me of it at the club. I can tell you it has made a most painful impression," cried the father. "That my son should be a radical and a republican, is a cruel thought for a father; and I, who had hoped for Lord Ringwood's borough for him—who had hoped—who had hoped very much better things for him and from him. He is not a comfort to me. You saw how he treated me one night? A man might live on different terms, I think, with his only son!" And with a breaking voice, a pallid cheek, and a real grief at his heart, the unhappy physician moved away.

How had the doctor bred his son, that the young man should be thus unruly? Was the revolt the boy's fault, or the father's? Dr. Firmin's horror seemed to be because his noble friends were horrified by Phil's radical doctrine. At that time of my life, being young and very green, I had a little mischievous pleasure in infuriating Squaretoes, and causing him to pronounce that I was "a dangerous man." Now, I am ready to say that Nero was a monarch with many elegant accomplishments, and considerable natural amiability of disposition. I praise and admire success wherever I meet it. I make allowance for faults and shortcomings, especially in my superiors; and feel that, did we know all, we should judge them very differently. People don't believe me, perhaps, quite so much as formerly. But I don't offend: I trust I don't offend. Have I said anything painful? Plague on my blunders! I recall the expression. I regret it. I contradict it flat.

As I am ready to find excuses for everybody, let poor Philip come in for the benefit of this mild amnesty; and if he vexed his father, as he certainly did, let us trust—let us be thankfully sure—he was not so black as the old gentleman depicted him. Nay, if I have painted the Old Gentleman himself as rather black, who knows but that this was an error, not of his complexion, but of my vision? Phil was unruly because he was bold, and wild, and young. His father was hurt, naturally hurt, because of the boy's extravagances and follies. They will come together again, as father and son should. These little differences of temper will be smoothed and equalized anon. The boy *has* led a wild life. He has been obliged to leave college. He has given his father hours of anxiety and nights of painful watching. But stay, father, what of you? Have you shown to the boy the practice of confidence, the example of love and honour? Did you accustom him to virtue, and teach truth to the child at your knee? "Honour your father and mother." Amen. May his days be long who fulfils the command: but implied, though unwritten on the table, is there not the order, "Honour your son and daughter?" Pray heaven that we, whose days are already not few in the land, may keep this ordinance too.

What had made Philip wild, extravagant, and insubordinate? Cured of that illness in which we saw him, he rose up, and from school went his way to the university, and there entered on a life such as wild young men will lead. From that day of illness his manner towards his father changed, and regarding the change the elder Firmin seemed afraid to question his son. He used the house as if his own, came and absented himself at will, ruled the servants, and was spoiled by them; spent the income which was settled on his mother and her children, and gave of it liberally to poor acquaintances. To the remonstrances of old friends he replied that he had a right to do as he chose with his own; that other men who were poor might work, but that he had enough to live on, without grinding over classics and mathematics. He was implicated in more rows than one; his tutors saw him not, but he and the proctors became a great deal too well acquainted. If I were to give a history of Mr. Philip Firmin at the university, it would be the story of an Idle Apprentice, of whom his pastors and masters were justified in prophesying evil. He was seen on lawless London excursions, when his father and tutor supposed him unwell in his rooms in college. He made acquaintance with jolly companions, with whom his father grieved that he should be intimate. He cut the astonished uncle Twysden in London Street, and blandly told him that he must be mistaken— he one Frenchman, he no speak English. He stared the master of his own college out of countenance, dashed back to college with a Turpin-like celerity, and was in rooms with a ready-proved alibi when inquiries were made. I am afraid there is no doubt that Phil screwed up his tutor's door; Mr. Okes discovered him in the act. He had to go down, the young prodigal. I wish I could say he was repentant. But he appeared before his father with the utmost non-chalance; said that he was doing no good at the university, and should be much better away, and then went abroad on a dashing tour to France and Italy, whither it is by no means our business to follow him. Something had poisoned the generous blood. The once kindly honest lad was wild and reckless. He had money in sufficiency, his own horses and equipage, and free quarters in his father's house. But father and son scarce met, and seldom took a meal together. " I know his haunts, but I don't know his friends, Pendennis," the elder man said. " I don't think they are vicious, so much as low. I do not charge him with vice, mind you ; but with idleness, and a fatal love of low company, and a frantic, suicidal determination to fling his chances in life away. Ah, think where he might be, and where he is !"

Where he was ? Do not be alarmed. Philip was only idling. Philip might have been much more industriously, more profitably, and a great deal more wickedly employed. What is now called Bohemia had no name in Philip's young days, though many of us knew the country very well. A pleasant land, not fenced with drab stucco, like Tyburnia or Belgravia ; not guarded by a huge standing army of footmen ; not echoing with noble chariots ; not replete with polite chintz drawing-rooms and neat tea-tables ; a land over which hangs an endless fog, occasioned by much tobacco ; a land of chambers, billiard-rooms, supper-rooms, oysters ; a land of song ; a land where soda-water flows freely in the morning ; a land of tin-dish covers from taverns, and frothing porter ; a land of lotos-eating (with lots of cayenne pepper), of pulls on the river, of delicious reading of novels, magazines, and saunterings in many studios ; a land where men call each other by their Christian names ; where most are poor, where almost all are young, and where, if a few oldsters do enter, it is because they have preserved more tenderly and carefully than other folks their youthful spirits, and the delightful capacity to be idle. I have lost my way to Bohemia now, but it is certain that Prague is the most picturesque city in the world.

Having long lived there, and indeed only lately quitted the

Bohemian land at the time whereof I am writing, I could not quite participate in Dr. Firmin's indignation at his son persisting in his bad courses and wild associates. When Firmin had been wild himself, he had fought, intrigued, and gambled in good company. Phil chose his friends amongst a banditti never heard of in fashionable quarters. Perhaps he liked to play the prince in the midst of these associates, and was not averse to the flattery which a full purse brought him among men most of whose pockets had a meagre lining. He had not emigrated to Bohemia, and settled there altogether. At school and in his brief university career he had made some friends who lived in the world, and with whom he was still familiar. " These come and knock at my front door, my father's door," he would say, with one of his old laughs ; " the Bandits, who have the signal, enter only by the dissecting-room. I know which are the most honest, and that it is not always the poor Freebooters who best deserve to be hanged."

Like many a young gentleman who has no intention of pursuing legal studies seriously, Philip entered at an inn of court, and kept his terms duly, though he vowed that his conscience would not allow him to practise (I am not defending the opinions of this squeamish moralist—only stating them). His acquaintance here lay amongst the Temple Bohemians. He had part of a set of chambers in Parchment Buildings, to be sure, and you might read on a door, " Mr. Cassidy, Mr. P. Firmin, Mr. Vanjohn ;" but were these gentlemen likely to advance Philip in life ? Cassidy was a newspaper reporter, and young Vanjohn a betting-man who was always attending races. Dr. Firmin had a horror of newspaper-men, and considered they belonged to the dangerous classes, and treated them with a distant affability.

" Look at the governor, Pen," Philip would say to the present chronicler. " He always watches you with a secret suspicion, and has never got over his wonder at your being a gentleman. I like him when he does the Lord Chatham business, and condescends towards you, and gives you his hand to kiss. He considers he is your better, don't you see ? Oh, he is a paragon of a père noble, the governor is ! and I ought to be a young Sir Charles Grandison." And the young scapegrace would imitate his father's smile, and the doctor's manner of laying his hand to his breast and putting out his neat right leg, all of which movements or postures were, I own, rather pompous and affected.

Whatever the paternal faults were, you will say that Philip was not the man to criticize them; nor in this matter shall I attempt to defend him. My wife has a little pensioner whom she found wandering in the street, and singing a little artless song. The child could not speak yet—only warble its little song; and had thus strayed away from home, and never once knew of her danger. We kept her for a while, until the police found her parents. Our servants bathed her, and dressed her, and sent her home in such neat clothes as the poor little wretch had never seen until fortune sent her in the way of those good-natured folks. She pays them frequent visits. When she goes away from us, she is always neat and clean; when she comes to us, she is in rags and dirty: a wicked little slattern! And pray, whose duty is it to keep her clean? and has not the parent in this case forgotten to honour her daughter? Suppose there is some reason which prevents Philip from loving his father—that the doctor has neglected to cleanse the boy's heart, and by carelessness and indifference has sent him erring into the world. If so, woe be to that doctor! If I take my little son to the tavern to dinner, shall I not assuredly pay? If I suffer him in tender youth to go astray, and harm comes to him, whose is the fault?

Perhaps the very outrages and irregularities of which Phil's father complained, were in some degree occasioned by the elder's own faults. He was so laboriously obsequious to great men, that the son in a rage defied and avoided them. He was so grave, so polite, so complimentary, so artificial, that Phil, in revolt at such hypocrisy, chose to be frank, cynical, and familiar. The grave old bigwigs whom the doctor loved to assemble, bland and solemn men of the ancient school, who dined solemnly with each other at their solemn old houses —such men as old Lord Botley, Baron Bumpsher, Cricklade, (who published "Travels in Asia Minor," 4to, 1804,) the Bishop of St. Bees, and the like—wagged their old heads sadly when they collogued in clubs, and talked of poor Firmin's scapegrace of a son. He would come to no good; he was giving his good father much pain; he had been in all sorts of rows and disturbances at the university, and the Master of Boniface reported most unfavourably of him. And at the solemn dinners in Old Parr Street—the admirable, costly, silent dinners—he treated these old gentlemen with a familiarity which caused the old heads to shake with surprise and choking indignation. Lord Botley and Baron Bumpsher had proposed and seconded Firmin's boy at the Megatherium club. The pallid old boys toddled away in alarm when he made his appearance there. He brought a smell of tobacco-smoke with him. He was capable of smoking in the drawing-room itself. They trembled before Philip, who, for his part, used to relish their senile anger ; and loved, as he called it, to tie all their pigtails together.

In no place was Philip seen or heard to so little advantage as in his father's house. " I feel like a humbug myself amongst those old humbugs," he would say to me. " Their old jokes, and their old compliments, and their virtuous old conversation sicken me. Are all old men humbugs, I wonder?" It is not pleasant to hear misan-thropy from young lips, and to find eyes that are scarce twenty years old already looking out with distrust on the world.

In other houses than his own I am bound to say Philip was much more amiable, and he carried with him a splendour of gaiety and cheerfulness which brought sunshine and welcome into many a room which he frequented. I have said that many of his companions were artists and journalists, and their clubs and haunts were his own. Ridley the Academician had Mrs. Brandon's rooms in Thornhaugh Street, and Philip was often in J. J.'s studio, or in the widow's little room below. He had a very great tenderness and affection for her ; her presence seemed to purify him ; and in her company the boiste-rous, reckless young man was invariably gentle and respectful. Her eyes used to fill with tears when she spoke about him ; and when he was present, followed and watched him with sweet motherly devotion. It was pleasant to see him at her homely little fireside, and hear his jokes and prattle, with a fatuous old father, who was one of Mrs. Brandon's lodgers. Philip would play cribbage for hours with this old man, frisk about him with a hundred harmless jokes, and walk out by his invalid chair, when the old captain went to sun himself in the New Road. He was an idle fellow, Philip, that's the truth. He had an agreeable perseverance in doing nothing, and would pass half a day in perfect contentment over his pipe, watching Ridley at his easel. J. J. painted that charming head of Philip which hangs in Mrs. Brandon's little room—with the fair hair, the tawny beard and whiskers, and the bold blue eyes.

Phil had a certain after-supper song of "Garryowen na Gloria," which it did you good to hear, and which, when sung at his full pitch, you might hear for a mile round. One night I had been to dine in Russell Square, and was brought home in his carriage by Dr. Firmin, who was of the party. As we came through Soho, the windows of a certain club-room called the "Haunt" were open, and we could hear Philip's song booming through the night, and especially a certain wild-Irish war-whoop with which it concluded, amidst universal applause and enthusiastic battering of glasses.

The poor father sank back in the carriage as though a blow had struck him. "Do you hear his voice?" he groaned out. "Those are his haunts. My son, who might go anywhere, prefers to be captain in a pothouse, and sing songs in a taproom!"

I tried to make the best of the case. I knew there was no harm in the place; that clever men of considerable note frequented it. But the wounded father was not to be consoled by such commonplaces; and a deep and natural grief oppressed him in consequence of the faults of his son.

What ensued by no means surprised me. Among Dr. Firmin's patients was a maiden lady of suitable age and large fortune, who looked upon the accomplished doctor with favourable eyes. That he should take a companion to cheer him in his solitude was natural enough, and all his friends concurred in thinking that he should marry. Every one had cognizance of the quiet little courtship, except the doctor's son, between whom and his father there were only too many secrets.

Some man in a club asked Philip whether he should condole with him or congratulate him on his father's approaching marriage? His what? The younger Firmin exhibited the greatest surprise and agitation on hearing of this match. He ran home: he awaited his father's return. When Dr. Firmin came home and betook himself to his study, Philip confronted him there. "This must be a lie, sir, which I have heard to-day," the young man said, fiercely.

"A lie! what lie, Philip?" asked the father. They were both very resolute and courageous men.

"That you are going to marry Miss Benson."

"Do you make my house so happy, that I don't need any other companion?" asked the father.

"That's not the question," said Philip, hotly. "You can't and mustn't marry that lady, sir."

"And why not, sir?"

"Because in the eyes of God and Heaven you are married already,—

sir.   And I swear I will tell Miss Benson the story to-morrow, if you persist in your plan."

"So you know that story?" groaned the father.

"Yes.   God forgive you," said the son.

"It was a fault of my youth that has been bitterly repented."

"A fault!—a crime!" said Philip.

"Enough, sir!   Whatever my fault, it is not for you to charge me with it."

"If you won't guard your own honour, I must.   I shall go to Miss Benson now."

"If you go out of this house you don't pretend to return to it."

"Be it so.   Let us settle our accounts, and part, sir."

"Philip, Philip! you break my heart," cried the father.

"You don't suppose mine is very light, sir," said the son.

Philip never had Miss Benson for a mother-in-law.   But father and son loved each other no better after their dispute.

CHAPTER VI.

BRANDON'S.

HORNHAUGH STREET is but a poor place now, and the houses look as if they had seen better days: but that house with the cut centre drawing-room window, which has the name of Brandon on the door, is as neat as any house in the quarter, and the brass plate always shines like burnished gold. About Easter time many fine carriages stop at that door, and splendid people walk in, introduced by a tidy little maid, or else by an athletic Italian, with a glossy black beard and gold earrings, who conducts them to the drawing-room floor, where Mr. Ridley, the painter, lives, and where his pictures are privately exhibited before they go to the Royal Academy.

As the carriages drive up, you will often see a red-faced man, in an olive-green wig, smiling blandly over the blinds of the parlour, on the ground-floor. That is Captain Gann, the father of the lady who keeps the house. I don't know how he came by the rank of captain, but he has borne it so long and gallantly that there is no use in any longer questioning the title. He does not claim it, neither does he deny it. But the wags who call upon Mrs. Brandon can always, as the phrase is, "draw" her father, by speaking of Prussia, France, Waterloo, or battles in general, until the Little Sister says, "Now, never mind about the battle of Waterloo, papa" (she says Pa—her *h*'s are irregular—I can't help it)—"Never mind about Waterloo, papa; you've told them all about it. And don't go on, Mr. Beans, don't, *please*, go on in that way."

Young Beans has already drawn "Captain Gann (assisted by Shaw, the Life-Guardsman) killing twenty-four French cuirassiers at Waterloo." "Captain Gann defending Hougoumont." "Captain Gann, called upon by Napoleon Buonaparte to lay down his arms, saying, ' A captain of militia dies, but never surrenders.'" "The Duke of Wellington pointing to the advancing Old Guard, and saying, ' Up, Gann, and at them.'" And these sketches are so droll, that even the Little Sister, Gann's own daughter, can't help laughing at them. To be sure, she loves fun, the Little Sister ; laughs over droll books; laughs to herself, in her little quiet corner at work; laughs over pictures; and, at the right place, laughs and sympathizes too. Ridley says, he knows few better critics of pictures than Mrs. Brandon. She has a sweet temper, a merry sense of humour, that makes the cheeks dimple and the eyes shine ; and a kind heart, that has been sorely tried and wounded, but is still soft and gentle. Fortunate are they whose hearts, so tried by suffering, yet recover their health. Some have illnesses from which there is no recovery, and drag through life afterwards, maimed and invalided.

But this Little Sister, having been subjected in youth to a dreadful trial and sorrow, was saved out of them by a kind Providence, and is now so thoroughly restored as to own that she is happy, and to thank God that she can be grateful and useful. When poor Mont-fitchet died, she nursed him through his illness as tenderly as his good wife herself. In the days of her own chief grief and misfortune, her father, who was under the domination of his wife, a cruel and blundering woman, thrust out poor little Caroline from his door, when she returned to it the broken-hearted victim of a scoundrel's seduction ; and when the old captain was himself in want and houseless, she had found him, sheltered and fed him. And it was from that day her wounds had begun to heal, and, from gratitude for this immense piece of good fortune vouchsafed to her, that her happiness and cheerfulness returned. Returned? There was an old servant of the family, who could not stay in the house because she was so abominably disrespectful to the captain, and this woman said she had never known Miss Caroline so cheerful, nor so happy, nor so good-looking, as she was now.

So Captain Gann came to live with his daughter, and patronized her with much dignity. He had a very few yearly pounds, which served to pay his club expenses, and a portion of his clothes. His club, I need not say, was at the "Admiral Byng," Tottenham Court Road, and here the captain met frequently a pleasant little society, and bragged unceasingly about his former prosperity.

I have heard that the country-house in Kent, of which he boasted, was a shabby little lodging-house at Margate, of which the furniture was sold in execution; but if it had been a palace the captain would not have been out of place there, one or two people still rather fondly thought. His daughter, amongst others, had tried to fancy all sorts of good of her father, and especially that he was a man of remarkably good manners. But she had seen one or two gentlemen since she knew the poor old father—gentlemen with rough coats and good hearts, like Dr. Goodenough; gentlemen with superfine coats and superfine double-milled manners, like Dr. Firmin, and hearts—well, never mind about that point; gentlemen of no *h*'s, like the good, dear, faithful benefactor who had rescued her at the brink of despair; men of genius, like Ridley; great hearty, generous, honest gentlemen, like Philip;—and this illusion about Pa, I suppose, had vanished along with some other fancies of her poor little maiden youth. The truth is, she had an understanding with the "Admiral Byng:" the landlady was instructed as to the supplies to be furnished to the captain; and as for his stories, poor Caroline knew them a great deal too well to believe in them any more.

I would not be understood to accuse the captain of habitual inebriety. He was a generous officer, and his delight was, when in cash, to order "glasses round" for the company at the club, to whom he narrated the history of his brilliant early days, when he lived in some of the tiptop society of this city, sir—a society in which, we need not say, the custom always is for gentlemen to treat other gentlemen to rum-and-water. Never mind—I wish we were all as happy as the captain. I see his jolly face now before me as it blooms through the window in Thornhaugh Street, and the wave of the somewhat dingy hand which sweeps me a gracious recognition.

The clergyman of the neighbouring chapel was a very good friend of the Little Sister, and has taken tea in her parlour; to which circumstance the captain frequently alluded, pointing out the very chair on which the divine sat. Mr. Gann attended his ministrations regularly every Sunday, and brought a rich, though somewhat worn, bass voice to bear upon the anthems and hymns at the chapel. His style was more florid than is general now among church singers, and, indeed, had been acquired in a former age and in the performance of rich Bacchanalian chants, such as delighted the contemporaries of our Incledons and Brahams. With a very little entreaty, the captain could be induced to sing at the club ; and I must own that Phil Firmin would draw the captain out, and extract from him a song of ancient days ; but this must be in the absence of his daughter, whose little face wore an air of such extreme terror and disturbance when her father sang, that he presently ceased from exercising his musical talents in her hearing. He hung up his lyre, whereof it must be owned that time had broken many of the once resounding chords.

With a sketch or two contributed by her lodgers—with a few gim-cracks from the neighbouring Wardour Street presented by others of her friends—with the chairs, tables, and bureaux as bright as bees'-wax and rubbing could make them—the Little Sister's room was a cheery little place, and received not a little company. She allowed Pa's pipe. "It's company to him," she said. "A man can't be doing much harm when he is smoking his pipe." And she allowed Phil's cigar. Anything was allowed to Phil, the other lodgers declared, who professed to be quite jealous of Philip Firmin. She had a very few books. "When I was a girl I used to be always reading novels," she said ; "but, la, they're mostly nonsense. There's Mr. Pendennis, who comes to see Mr. Ridley. I wonder how a married man can go on writing about love, and all that stuff !" And, indeed, it is rather absurd for elderly fingers to be still twanging Dan Cupid's toy bow and arrows. Yesterday is gone—yes, but very well remembered ; and we think of it the more now we know that To-morrow is not going to bring us much.

Into Mrs. Brandon's parlour Mr. Ridley's old father would some-times enter of evenings, and share the bit of bread and cheese, or the modest supper of Mrs. Brandon and the captain. The homely little meal has almost vanished out of our life now, but in former days it assembled many a family round its kindly board. A little modest supper-tray—a little quiet prattle—a little kindly glass that cheered and never inebriated. I can see friendly faces smiling round such a meal, at a period not far gone, but how distant ! I wonder whether there are any old folks now, in old quarters of old country towns, who come to each other's houses in sedan-chairs, at six o'clock, and play at quadrille until supper-tray time ? Of evenings

Ridley and the captain, I say, would have a solemn game at cribbage, and the Little Sister would make up a jug of something good for the two oldsters. She liked Mr. Ridley to come, for he always treated her father so respectful, and was quite the gentleman. And as for Mrs. Ridley, Mr. R.'s "good lady,"—was she not also grateful to the Little Sister for having nursed her son during his malady? Through their connection they were enabled to procure Mrs. Brandon many valuable friends; and always were pleased to pass an evening with the captain, and were as civil to him as they could have been had he been at the very height of his prosperity and splendour. My private opinion of the old captain, you see, is that he was a worthless old captain, but most fortunate in his early ruin, after which he had lived very much admired and comfortable, sufficient whisky being almost always provided for him.

Old Mr. Ridley's respect for her father afforded a most precious consolation to the Little Sister. Ridley liked to have the paper read to him. He was never quite easy with print, and to his last days, many words to be met with in newspapers and elsewhere used to occasion the good butler much intellectual trouble. The Little Sister made his lodgers' bills out for him (Mr. R., as well as the captain's daughter, strove to increase a small income by the letting of furnished apartments), or the captain himself would take these documents in charge; he wrote a noble mercantile hand, rendered now somewhat shaky by time, but still very fine in flourishes and capitals, and very much at worthy Mr. Ridley's service. Time was, when his son was a boy, that J. J. himself had prepared these accounts, which neither his father nor his mother were very competent to arrange. "We were not, in our young time, Mr. Gann," Ridley remarked to his friend, "brought up to much scholarship; and very little book-learning was given to persons in *my* rank of life. It was necessary and proper for you gentlemen, of course, sir." "Of course, Mr. Ridley," winks the other veteran over his pipe. "But I can't go and ask my son John James to keep his old father's books now as he used to do—which to do so is, on the part of you and Mrs. Brandon, the part of true friendship, and I value it, sir, and so do my son John James reckonize and value it, sir." Mr. Ridley had served gentlemen of the *bonne école.* No nobleman could be more courtly and grave than he was. In Mr. Gann's manner there was more humorous playfulness, which in no way, however, diminished

THE OLD FOGIES.

the captain's high breeding. As he continued to be intimate with Mr. Ridley, he became loftier and more majestic. I think each of these elders acted on the other, and for good ; and I hope Ridley's opinion was correct, that Mr. Gann was ever the gentleman. To see these two good fogies together was a spectacle for edification. Their tumblers kissed each other on the table. Their elderly friendship brought comfort to themselves and their families. A little matter of money once created a coolness between the two old gentlemen. But the Little Sister paid the outstanding account between her father and Mr. Ridley : there never was any further talk of pecuniary loans between them ; and when they went to the " Admiral Byng," each paid for himself.

Phil often heard of that nightly meeting at the " Admiral's Head," and longed to be of the company. But even when he saw the old gentlemen in the Little Sister's parlour, they felt dimly that he was making fun of them. The captain would not have been able to brag so at ease had Phil been continually watching him. " I have 'ad the honour of waiting on your worthy father at my Lord Todmorden's table. Our little club ain't no place for you, Mr. Philip, nor for my son, though he's a good son, and proud me and his mother is of him, which he have never gave us a moment's pain, except when he was ill, since he have came to man's estate, most thankful am I, and with my hand on my heart, for to be able to say so. But what is good for me and Mr. Gann, won't suit you young gentlemen. *You* ain't a tradesman, sir, else I'm mistaken in the family, which I thought the Ringwoods one of the best in England, and the Firmins, a good one likewise." Mr. Ridley loved the sound of his own voice. At the festive meetings of the club, seldom a night passed in which he did not compliment his brother Byngs and air his own oratory. Under this reproof Phil blushed, and hung his conscious head with shame. " Mr. Ridley," says he, " you shall find I won't come where I am not welcome ; and if I come to annoy you at the 'Admiral Byng,' may I be taken out on the quarterdeck and shot." On which Mr. Ridley pronounced Philip to be a " most sing'lar, astrornary, and ascentric young man. A good heart, sir. Most generous to relieve distress. Fine talent, sir ; but I fear—I fear they won't come to much good, Mr. Gann—saving your presence, Mrs. Brandon, m'm, which, of course, you *always* stand up for him."

When Philip Firmin had had his pipe and his talk with the Little

Sister in her parlour, he would ascend and smoke his second, third, tenth pipe in J. J. Ridley's studio. He would pass hours before J. J.'s easel, pouring out talk about politics, about religion, about poetry, about women, about the dreadful slavishness and meanness of the world; unwearied in talk and idleness, as placid J. J. was in listening and labour. The painter had been too busy in life over his easel to read many books. His ignorance of literature smote him with a frequent shame. He admired book-writers, and young men of the university who quoted their Greek and their Horace glibly. He listened with deference to their talk on such matters; no doubt got good hints from some of them; was always secretly pained and surprised when the university gentlemen were beaten in argument, or loud and coarse in conversation, as sometimes they would be. " J. J. is a very clever fellow of course," Mr. Jarman would say of him, " and the luckiest man in Europe. He loves painting, and he is at work all day. He loves toadying fine people, and he goes to a tea-party every night." You all knew Jarman of Charlotte Street, the miniature-painter? He was one of the kings of the " Haunt." His tongue spared no one. He envied all success, and the sight of prosperity made him furious : but to the unsuccessful he was kind ; to the poor eager with help and prodigal of compassion ; and that old talk about nature's noblemen and the glory of labour was very fiercely and eloquently waged by him. His friends admired him : he was the soul of independence, and thought most men sneaks who wore clean linen and frequented gentlemen's society : but it must be owned his landlords had a bad opinion of him, and I have heard of one or two of his pecuniary transactions which certainly were not to Mr. Jarman's credit. Jarman was a man of remarkable humour. He was fond of the widow, and would speak of her goodness, usefulness, and honesty with tears in his eyes. She was poor and struggling yet. Had she been wealthy and prosperous, Mr. Jarman would not have been so alive to her merit.

We ascend to the room on the first-floor, where the centre window has been heightened, so as to afford an upper light, and under that stream of radiance we behold the head of an old friend, Mr. J. J. Ridley, the R. Academician. Time has somewhat thinned his own copious locks, and prematurely streaked the head with silver. His face is rather wan ; the eager, sensitive hand which poises brush and palette, and quivers over the picture, is very thin : round his eyes

are many lines of ill health and, perhaps, care, but the eyes are as
bright as ever, and, when they look at the canvas or the model
which he transfers to it, clear, and keen, and happy. He has a very
sweet singing voice, and warbles at his work, or whistles at it, smiling.
He sets his hand little feats of skill to perform, and smiles with a
boyish pleasure at his own matchless dexterity. I have seen him,
with an old pewter mustard-pot for a model, fashion a splendid
silver flagon in one of his pictures; paint the hair of an animal, the
folds and flowers of a bit of brocade, and so forth, with a perfect
delight in the work he was performing: a delight lasting from
morning till sundown, during which time he was too busy to touch
the biscuit and glass of water which was prepared for his frugal
luncheon. He is greedy of the last minute of light, and never can
be got from his darling pictures without a regret. To be a painter,
and to have your hand in perfect command, I hold to be one of life's
summa bona. The happy mixture of hand and head work must
render the occupation supremely pleasant. In the day's work must
occur endless delightful difficulties and occasions for skill. Over
the details of that armour, that drapery, or what not, the sparkle of
that eye, the downy blush of that cheek, the jewel on that neck,
there are battles to be fought and victories to be won. Each day
there must occur critical moments of supreme struggle and triumph,
when struggle and victory must be both invigorating and exquisitely
pleasing—as a burst across country is to a fine rider perfectly
mounted, who knows that his courage and his horse will never fail
him. There is the excitement of the game, and the gallant delight
in winning it. Of this sort of admirable reward for their labour, no
men, I think, have a greater share than painters (perhaps a violin-
player perfectly and triumphantly performing his own beautiful composition may be equally happy). Here is occupation: here is
excitement: here is struggle and victory: and here is profit. Can
man ask more from fortune? Dukes and Rothschilds may be envious
of such a man.

Though Ridley has had his trials and troubles, as we shall
presently learn, his art has mastered them all. Black care may have
sat in crupper on that Pegasus, but has never unhorsed the rider.
In certain minds, art is, dominant and superior to all beside—
stronger than love, stronger than hate, or care, or penury. As
soon as the fever leaves the hand free, it is seizing and fondling the

pencil. Love may frown and be false, but the other mistress never will. She is always true: always new: always the friend, companion, inestimable consoler. So John James Ridley sat at his easel from breakfast till sundown, and never left his work quite willingly. I wonder are men of other trades so enamoured of theirs; whether lawyers cling to the last to their darling reports; or writers prefer their desks and inkstands to society, to friendship, to dear idleness? I have seen no men in life loving their profession so much as painters, except, perhaps, actors, who, when not engaged themselves, always go to the play.

Before this busy easel Phil would sit for hours, and pour out endless talk and tobacco-smoke. His presence was a delight to Ridley's soul; his face a sunshine; his voice a cordial. Weakly himself, and almost infirm of body, with sensibilities tremulously keen, the painter most admired amongst men strength, health, good spirits, good breeding. Of these, in his youth, Philip had a wealth of endowment; and I hope these precious gifts of fortune have not left him in his maturer age. I do not say that with all men Philip was so popular. There are some who never can pardon good fortune, and in the company of gentlemen are on the watch for offence; and, no doubt, in his course through life, poor downright Phil trampled upon corns enough of those who met him in his way. "Do you know why Ridley is so fond of Firmin?" asked Jarman. "Because Firmin's father hangs on to the nobility by the pulse, whilst Ridley, you know, is connected with them through the sideboard." So Jarman had the double horn for his adversary: he could despise a man for not being a gentleman, and insult him for being one. I have met with people in the world with whom the latter offence is an unpardonable crime—a cause of ceaseless doubt, division, and suspicion. What more common or natural, Bufo, than to hate another for being what you are not? The story is as old as frogs, bulls, and men.

Then, to be sure, besides your enviers in life, there are your admirers. Beyond wit, which he understood—beyond genius, which he had—Ridley admired good looks and manners, and always kept some simple hero whom he loved secretly to cherish and worship. He loved to be amongst beautiful women and aristocratical men. Philip Firmin, with his republican notions and downright bluntness of behaviour to all men of rank superior to him, had a grand high manner of his own; and if he had scarce twopence in his pocket, would have put his hands in them with as much independence as the greatest dandy who ever sauntered on Pall Mall pavement. What a coolness the fellow had! Some men may, not unreasonably, have thought it impudence. It fascinated Ridley. To be such a man; to have such a figure and manner; to be able to look society in the face, slap it on the shoulder, if you were so minded, and hold it by the button—what would not Ridley give for such powers and accomplishments? You will please to bear in mind, I am not saying that J. J. was right, only that he was as he was. I hope we shall have nobody in this story without his little faults and peculiarities. Jarman was quite right when he said Ridley loved fine company. I believe his pedigree gave him secret anguishes. He would rather have been gentleman than genius ever so great; but let you and me, who have no weaknesses of our own, try and look charitably on this confessed foible of my friend.

J. J. never thought of rebuking Philip for being idle. Phil was as the lilies of the field, in the painter's opinion. He was not called upon to toil or spin; but to take his ease, and grow and bask in sunshine, and be arrayed in glory. The little clique of painters knew what Firmin's means were. Thirty thousand pounds of his own. Thirty thousand pounds down, sir; and the inheritance of his father's immense fortune! A splendour emanated from this gifted young man. His opinions, his jokes, his laughter, his song, had the weight of thirty thousand down, sir; and &c. &c. What call had *he* to work? Would you set a young nobleman to be an apprentice? Philip was free to be as idle as any lord, if he liked. He ought to wear fine clothes, ride fine horses, dine off plate, and drink champagne every day. J. J. would work quite cheerfully till sunset, and have an eightpenny plate of meat in Wardour Street and a glass of porter for his humble dinner. At the "Haunt," and similar places of Bohemian resort, a snug place near the fire was always found for Firmin. Fierce republican as he was, Jarman had a smile for his lordship, and used to adopt particularly dandified airs when he had been invited to Old Parr Street to dinner. I dare say Philip liked flattery. I own that he was a little weak in this respect, and that you and I, my dear sir, are, of course, far his superiors. J. J., who loved him, would have had him follow his aunt's and cousin's advice, and live in better company; but I think the painter would not have liked his pet to soil his hands with too much work, and rather admired Mr. Phil for being idle.

The Little Sister gave him advice, to be sure, both as to the company he should keep and the occupation which was wholesome for him. But when others of his acquaintance hinted that his idleness would do him harm, she would not hear of their censure. "Why should he work if he don't choose?" she asked. "He has no call to be scribbling and scrabbling. You wouldn't have *him* sitting all day painting little dolls' heads on canvas, and working like a slave. A pretty idea, indeed! His uncle will get him an appointment. That's the thing *he* should have. He should be secretary to an ambassador abroad, and he *will* be!" In fact Phil, at this period, used to announce his wish to enter the diplomatic service, and his hope that Lord Ringwood would further his views in that respect. Meanwhile he was the king of Thornhaugh Street. He might be as idle as he chose, and Mrs. Brandon had always a smile for him. He might smoke a great deal too much, but she worked dainty little cigar-cases for him. She hemmed his fine cambric pocket-handkerchiefs, and embroidered his crest at the corners. She worked him a waistcoat so splendid that he almost blushed to wear it, gorgeous as he was in apparel at this period, and sumptuous in chains, studs, and haberdashery. I fear Dr. Firmin, sighing out his disappointed hopes in respect of his son, has rather good cause for his dissatisfaction. But of these remonstrances the Little Sister would not hear. "Idle, why not? Why should he work? Boys will be boys. I dare say his grumbling old Pa was not better than Philip when *he* was young!" And this she spoke with a heightened colour in her little face, and a defiant toss of her head, of which I did not understand all the significance then; but attributed her eager partisanship to that admirable injustice which belongs to all good women, and for which let us be daily thankful. I know, dear ladies, you are angry at this statement. But, even at the risk of displeasing *you*, we must tell the truth. You would wish to represent yourselves as equitable, logical, and strictly just. So, I dare say Dr. Johnson would have liked Mrs. Thrale to say to him, "Sir, your manners are graceful; your person elegant, cleanly, and eminently pleasing; your appetite small (especially for tea), and your dancing equal to the Violetta's;" which, you perceive, is merely ironical. Women equitable, logical, and strictly just! Mercy upon us! If they were, population would cease, the world would be a howling wilderness. Well, in a word, this Little Sister petted and coaxed Philip Firmin in such an absurd way that every one remarked it—those who had no friends, no sweethearts, no mothers, no daughters, no wives, and those who were petted, and coaxed, and spoiled at home themselves; as I trust, dearly beloved, is your case.

Now, again, let us admit that Philip's father had reason to be angry with the boy, and deplore his son's taste for low company; but excuse the young man, on the other hand, somewhat for his fierce revolt and profound distaste at much in his home circle which annoyed him. "By heaven!" he would roar out, pulling his hair and whiskers, and with many fierce ejaculations, according to his wont, "the solemnity of those humbugs sickens me so, that I should like to crown the old bishop with the soup-tureen, and box Baron Bumpsher's ears with the saddle of mutton. At my aunt's, the humbug is just the same. It's better done, perhaps; but oh, Pendennis! if you could but know the pangs which tore into my heart, sir, the vulture which gnawed at this confounded liver, when I saw women—women who ought to be pure—women who ought to be like angels—women who ought to know no art but that of coaxing our griefs away and soothing our sorrows—fawning, and cringeing, and scheming; cold to this person, humble to that, flattering to the rich, and indifferent to the humble in station. I tell you I have seen all this, Mrs. Pendennis! I won't mention names, but I have met with those who have made me old before my time—a hundred years old! The zest of life is passed from me" (here Mr. Phil would gulp a bumper from the nearest decanter at hand). "But if I like what your husband is pleased to call low society, it is because I have seen the other. I have dangled about at fine parties, and danced at fashionable balls. I have seen mothers bring their virgin daughters up to battered old rakes, and ready to sacrifice their innocence for fortune or a title. The atmosphere of those polite drawing-rooms stifles me. I can't bow the knee to the horrible old Mammon. I walk about in the crowds as lonely as if I was in a wilderness; and don't begin to breathe freely until I get some honest tobacco to clear the air. As for your husband" (meaning the writer of this memoir), "he cannot help himself; he is a worldling, of the earth, earthy. If a duke were to ask him to dinner to-morrow, the parasite owns that he would go. Allow me, my friends, my freedom, my rough com-

panions, in their work-day clothes.   I don't hear such lies and
flatteries come from behind pipes, as used to pass from above white
chokers when I was in the world."   And he would tear at his cravat,
as though the mere thought of the world's conventionality well nigh
strangled him.

This, to be sure, was in a late stage of his career, but I take up
the biography here and there, so as to give the best idea I may of
my friend's character.   At this time—he is out of the country just
now, and besides, if he saw his own likeness staring him in the face,
I am confident he would not know it—Mr. Philip, in some things,
was as obstinate as a mule, and in others as weak as a woman.   He
had a childish sensibility for what was tender, helpless, pretty, or
pathetic ; and a mighty scorn of imposture, wherever he found it.
He had many good purposes, which were often very vacillating, and
were but seldom performed.   He had a vast number of evil habits,
whereof, you know, idleness is said to be the root.   Many of these
evil propensities he coaxed and cuddled with much care ; and though
he roared out *peccavi* most frankly when charged with his sins, this
criminal would fall to peccation very soon after promising amend-
ment.   What he liked he would have.   What he disliked he could
with the greatest difficulty be found to do.   He liked good dinners,
good wine, good horses, good clothes, and late hours ; and in all
these comforts of life (or any others which he fancied, or which were
within his means) he indulged himself with perfect freedom.   He
hated hypocrisy on his own part, and hypocrites in general.   He said
everything that came into his mind about things and people ; and, of
course, was often wrong and often prejudiced, and often occasioned
howls of indignation or malignant whispers of hatred by his free
speaking.   He believed everything that was .said to him until his
informant had misled him once or twice, after which he would believe
nothing.   And here you will see that his impetuous credulity was as
absurd as the subsequent obstinacy of his unbelief.   My dear young
friend, the profitable way in life is the middle way.   Don't quite
believe anybody, for he may mislead you ; neither disbelieve him,
for that is uncomplimentary to your friend.   Black is not so very
black ; and as for white, *bon Dieu !* in our climate what paint will
remain white long ?   If Philip was self-indulgent, I suppose other
people are self-indulgent likewise : and besides, you know, your faultless heroes have ever so long gone out of fashion.   To be young, to

be good-looking, to be healthy, to be hungry three times a day, to have plenty of money, a great alacrity of sleeping, and nothing to do —all these, I dare say, are very dangerous temptations to a man, but I think I know some who would like to undergo the dangers of the trial. Suppose there be holidays, is there not work-time too? Suppose to-day is feast-day; may not tears and repentance come to-morrow? Such times are in store for Master Phil, and so please to let him have rest and comfort for a chapter or two.

CHAPTER VII.

IMPLETUR VETERIS BACCHI.

THAT time, that merry time, of Brandon's, of Bohemia, of oysters, of idleness, of smoking, of song at night and profuse soda-water in the morning, of a pillow, lonely and bachelor it is true, but with few cares for bedfellows, of plenteous pocket-money, of ease for to-day and little heed for to-morrow, was often remembered by Philip in after days. Mr. Phil's views of life were not very exalted, were they? The fruits of this world, which he devoured with such gusto, I must own were of the common kitchen-garden sort; and the lazy rogue's ambition went no farther than to stroll along the sunshiny wall, eat his fill, and then repose comfortably in the arbour under the arched vine. Why did Phil's mother's parents leave her thirty thousand pounds? I dare say some misguided people would be glad to do as much for their sons; but, if I have ten, I am determined they shall either have a hundred thousand a piece, or else bare bread and cheese. "Man was made to labour, and to be lazy," Phil would affirm with his usual energy of expression. "When the Indian warrior goes on the hunting path, he is sober, active, indomitable.

No dangers fright him, and no labours tire. He endures the cold of the winter; he couches on the forest leaves; he subsists on frugal roots or the casual spoil of his bow. When he returns to his village, he gorges to repletion; he sleeps, perhaps, to excess. When the game is devoured, and the fire-water exhausted, again he sallies forth into the wilderness; he outclimbs the 'possum and he throttles the bear. I am the Indian: and this 'Haunt' is my wigwam! Barbara my squaw, bring me oysters; bring me a jug of the frothing black beer of the pale-faces, or I will hang up thy scalp on my tent-pole?" And old Barbara, the good old attendant of this " Haunt" of Bandits, would say, "Law, Mr. Philip, how you do go on, to be sure!" Where is the " Haunt" now? and where are the merry men all who there assembled? The sign is down; the song is silent; the sand is swept from the floor; the pipes are broken, and the ashes are scattered.

A little more gossip about his merry days, and we have done. He, Philip, was called to the bar in due course, and at his call-supper we assembled a dozen of his elderly and youthful friends. The chambers in Parchment Buildings were given up to him for this day. Mr. Van John, I think, was away attending a steeple-chase; but Mr. Cassidy was with us, and several of Philip's acquaintances of school, college, and the world. There was Philip's father, and Philip's uncle Twysden, and I, Phil's revered and respectable school senior, and others of our ancient seminary. There was Burroughs, the second wrangler of his year, great in metaphysics, greater with the knife and fork. There was Stackpole, Eblana's favourite child— the glutton of all learning, the master of many languages, who stuttered and blushed when he spoke his own. There was Pinker-ton, who, albeit an ignoramus at the university, was already winning prodigious triumphs at the Parliamentary bar, and investing in Consols to the admiration of all his contemporaries. There was Rosebury the beautiful, the May-Fair pet and delight of Almack's, the cards on whose mantelpiece made all men open the eyes of wonder, and some of us dart the scowl of envy. There was my Lord Egham, Lord Ascot's noble son. There was Tom Dale, who, having carried on his university career too splendidly, had come to grief in the midst of it, and was now meekly earning his bread in the reporters' gallery, alongside of Cassidy. There was Macbride, who, having thrown up his fellowship and married his cousin, was now doing a brave battle with poverty, and making literature feed him until law should reward him more splendidly. There was Haythorn, the country gentleman, who ever remembered his old college chums, and kept the memory of that friendship up by constant reminders of pheasants and game in the season. There were Raby and Maynard from the Guards' Club (Maynard sleeps now under Crimean snows), who preferred arms to the toga ; but carried into their military life the love of their old books, the affection of their old friends. Most of these must be mute personages in our little drama. Could any chronicler remember the talk of all of them ?

Several of the guests present were members of the Inn of Court (the Upper Temple), which had conferred on Philip the degree of Barrister-at-Law. He had dined in his wig and gown (Blackmore's wig and gown) in the inn-hall that day, in company with other members of his inn ; and, dinner over, we adjourned to Phil's chambers in Parchment Buildings, where a dessert was served, to which Mr. Firmin's friends were convoked.

The wines came from Dr. Firmin's cellar. His servants were in attendance to wait upon the company. Father and son both loved splendid hospitalities, and, so far as creature comforts went, Philip's feast was richly provided. "A supper, I love a supper of all things ! And in order that I might enjoy yours, I only took a single mutton-chop for dinner !" cried Mr. Twysden, as he greeted Philip. Indeed, we found him, as we arrived from Hall, already in the chambers, and eating the young barrister's dessert. "He's been here ever so long," says Mr. Brice, who officiated as butler, "pegging away at the olives and maccaroons. Shouldn't wonder if he has pocketed some." There was small respect on the part of Brice for Mr. Twysden, whom the worthy butler frankly pronounced to be a stingy 'umbug. Meanwhile, Talbot believed that the old man respected him, and always conversed with Brice, and treated him with a cheerful cordiality.

The outer Philistines quickly arrived, and but that the wine and men were older, one might have fancied oneself at a college wine-party. Mr. Twysden talked for the whole company. He was radiant. He felt himself in high spirits. He did the honours of Philip's table. Indeed, no man was more hospitable with other folks' wine. Philip himself was silent and nervous. I asked him if the awful ceremony, which he had just undergone, was weighing on his mind?

He was looking rather anxiously towards the door; and, knowing somewhat of the state of affairs at home, I thought that probably he and his father had had one of the disputes which of late days had become so frequent between them.

The company were nearly all assembled and busy with their talk, and drinking the doctor's excellent claret, when Brice entering, announced Dr. Firmin and Mr. Tufton Hunt.

"Hang Mr. Tufton Hunt," Philip was going to say; but he started up, went forward to his father, and greeted him very respectfully. He then gave a bow to the gentleman introduced as Mr. Hunt, and they found places at the table, the doctor taking his with his usual handsome grace.

The conversation, which had been pretty brisk until Dr. Firmin came, drooped a little after his appearance. "We had an awful row two days ago," Philip whispered to me. "We shook hands and are reconciled, as you see. He won't stay long. He will be sent for in half an hour or so. He will say he has been sent for by a duchess, and go and have tea at the club."

Dr. Firmin bowed, and smiled sadly at me, as Philip was speaking. I dare say I blushed somewhat, and felt as if the doctor knew what his son was saying to me. He presently engaged in conversation with Lord Egham; he hoped his good father was well?

"You keep him so, doctor. You don't give a fellow a chance," says the young lord.

"Pass the bottle, you young men! Hey! We intend to see you all out!" cries Talbot Twysden, on pleasure bent and of the frugal mind.

"Well said, sir," says the stranger introduced as Mr. Hunt; "and right good wine. Ha, Firmin! I think I know the tap!" and he smacked his lips over the claret. "It's your twenty-five, and no mistake."

"The red-nosed individual seems a connoisseur," whispered Rosebury at my side.

The stranger's nose, indeed, was somewhat rosy. And to this I may add that his clothes were black, his face pale, and not well shorn, his white neckcloth dingy, and his eyes bloodshot.

"He looks as if he had gone to bed in his clothes, and carries a plentiful flue about his person. Who *is* your father's esteemed friend ?" continues the wag, in an under voice.

"You heard his name, Rosebury," says the young barrister, gloomily.

"I should suggest that your father is in difficulties, and attended by an officer of the sheriff of London, or perhaps subject to mental aberration, and placed under the control of a keeper."

"Leave me alone, do !" groaned Philip. And here Twysden, who was longing for an opportunity to make a speech, bounced up from his chair, and stopped the facetious barrister's further remarks by his own eloquence. His discourse was in praise of Philip, the new-made barrister. "What! if no one else will give that toast, your uncle will, and many a heartfelt blessing go with you too, my boy !" cried the little man. He was prodigal of benedictions. He dashed aside the tear-drop of emotion. He spoke with perfect fluency, and for a considerable period. He really made a good speech, and was greeted with deserved cheers when at length he sat down.

Phil stammered a few words in reply to his uncle's voluble com- pliments; and then Lord Ascot, a young nobleman of much familiar humour, proposed Phil's father, his health, and song. The physician made a neat speech from behind his ruffled shirt. He was agitated by the tender feelings of a paternal heart, he said, glancing benignly at Phil, who was cracking filberts. To see his son happy; to see him surrounded by such friends ; to know him embarked this day in a profession which gave the greatest scope for talents, the noblest reward for industry, was a proud and happy moment to him, Dr. Firmin. What had the poet observed ? "*Ingenuas didicisse fideliter artes*" (hear, hear !) "*emollit mores,*"—yes, "*emollit mores.*" He drank a bumper to the young barrister (he waved his ring, with a thimbleful of wine in his glass). He pledged the young friends whom he saw assembled to cheer his son on his onward path. He thanked them with a father's heart ! He passed his emerald ring across his eyes for a moment, and lifted them to the ceiling, from which quarter he requested a blessing on his boy. As though "spirits" approved of his invocation, immense thumps came from above, along with the plaudits which saluted the doctor's speech from the gentlemen round the table. But the upper thumps were derisory, and came from Mr. Buffers, of the third floor, who chose this method of mocking our harmless little festivities.

I think these cheers from the facetious Buffers, though meant in scorn of our party, served to enliven it and make us laugh. Spite of all the talking, we were dull ; and I could not but allow the force of my neighbour's remark, that we were sat upon and smothered by the old men. One or two of the younger gentlemen chafed at the licence for tobacco-smoking not being yet accorded. But Philip interdicted this amusement as yet.

"Don't," he said; "my father don't like it. He has to see patients to-night; and they can't bear the smell of tobacco by their bedsides." '

The impatient youths waited with their cigar-cases by their sides. They longed for the withdrawal of the obstacle to their happiness.

"He won't go, I tell you. He'll be sent for," growled Philip to me.

The doctor was engaged in conversation to the right and left of him, and seemed not to think of a move. But, sure enough, at a few minutes after ten o'clock, Dr. Firmin's footman entered the room with a note, which Firmin opened and read, as Philip looked at me with a grim humour in his face. I think Phil's father knew that we knew he was acting. However, he went through the comedy quite gravely.

"A physician's time is not his own," he said, shaking his handsome, melancholy head. "Good-by, my dear lord! Pray remember me at home! Good night, Philip, my boy, and good speed to you in your career! Pray, pray don't move."

And he is gone, waving the fair hand and the broad-brimmed hat, with the beautiful white lining. Phil conducted him to the door, and heaved a sigh as it closed upon his father—a sigh of relief, I think, that he was gone.

"Exit Governor. What's the Latin for Governor?" says Lord Egham, who possessed much native humour, but not very profound scholarship. "A most venerable old parent, Firmin. That hat and appearance would command any sum of money."

"Excuse me," lisps Rosebury, "but why didn't he take his elderly friend with him—the dilapidated clerical gentleman who is drinking claret so freely? And also, why did he not remove your avuncular orator? Mr. Twysden, your interesting young neophyte has provided us with an excellent specimen of the cheerful produce of the Gascon grape."

"Well, then, now the old gentleman is gone, let us pass the bottle and make a night of it. Hey, my lord?" cries Twysden. "Philip, your claret is good! I say, do you remember some Château Margaux I had, which Winton liked so? It must be good if *he* praised it, I can tell you. I imported it myself, and gave him the address of the Bordeaux merchant; and he said he had seldom tasted any like it. Those were his very words. I must get you fellows to come and taste it some day."

"Some day! What day? Name it, generous Amphitryon!" cries Rosebury.

"Some day at seven o'clock. With a plain, quiet dinner—a clear soup, a bit of fish, a couple of little entrées, and a nice little roast. That's my kind of dinner. And we'll taste that claret, young men. It is not a heavy wine. It is not a first-class wine. I don't mean even to say it is a dear wine, but it has a bouquet and a pureness. What, you *will* smoke, you fellows?"

"We *will* do it, Mr. Twysden. Better do as the rest of us do. Try one of these."

The little man accepts the proffered cigar from the young nobleman's box, lights it, hems and hawks, and lapses into silence.

"I thought that would do for him," murmurs the facetious Egham. "It is strong enough to blow his old head off, and I wish it would. That cigar," he continues, "was given to my father by the Duke of Medina Sidonia, who had it out of the Queen of Spain's own box. She smokes a good deal, but naturally likes 'em mild. I can give you a stronger one."

"Oh, no. I dare say this is very fine. Thank you!" says poor Talbot.

"Leave him alone, can't you!" says Philip. "Don't make a fool of him before the young men, Egham."

Philip still looked very dismal in the midst of the festivity. He was thinking of his differences with his absent parent.

We might all have been easily consoled, if the doctor had taken away with him the elderly companion whom he had introduced to Phil's feast. He could not have been very welcome to our host, for Phil scowled at his guest, and whispered, "Hang Hunt!" to his neighbour.

"Hang Hunt"—the Reverend Tufton Hunt was his name—was in nowise disconcerted by the coolness of his reception. He drank his wine very freely; addressed himself to his neighbours affably; and called out a loud "Hear, hear!" to Twysden, when that gentleman announced his intention of making a night of it. As Mr. Hunt warmed with wine he spoke to the table. He talked a great deal about the Ringwood family, had been very intimate at Wingate, in old days, as he told Mr. Twysden, and an intimate friend of poor Cinqbars, Lord Ringwood's only son. Now, the memory of the late Lord Cinqbars was not an agreeable recollection to the relatives of the house of Ringwood. He was in life a dissipated and disreputable young lord. His name was seldom mentioned in his family; never by his father, with whom he had had many quarrels.

"You know I introduced Cinqbars to your father, Philip?" calls out the dingy clergyman.

"I have heard you mention the fact," says Philip.

"They met at a wine in my rooms in Corpus. Brummell Firmin we used to call your father in those days. He was the greatest buck in the university—always a dressy man, kept hunters, gave the best dinners in Cambridge. We were a wild set. There was Cinqbars, Brand Firmin, Beryl, Toplady, about a dozen of us, almost all noblemen or fellow-commoners—fellows who all kept their horses and had their private servants."

This speech was addressed to the company, who yet did not seem much edified by the college recollections of the dingy elderly man.

"Almost all Trinity men, sir! We dined with each other week about. Many of them had their tandems. Desperate fellow across country your father was. And—but we won't tell tales out of school, hey?"

"No; please don't, sir," said Philip, clenching his fists, and biting his lips. The shabby, ill-bred, swaggering man was eating Philip's salt; Phil's lordly ideas of hospitality did not allow him to quarrel with the guest under his tent.

"When he went out in medicine, we were all of us astonished. Why, sir, Brand Firmin, at one time, was the greatest swell in the university," continued Mr. Hunt, "and such a plucky fellow! So was poor Cinqbars, though he had no stamina. He, I, and Firmin, fought for twenty minutes before Caius' Gate with about twenty bargemen, and you should have seen your father hit out! I was a handy one in those days, too, with my fingers. We learned the noble art of self-defence in my time, young gentlemen! We used to have Glover, the boxer, down from London who gave us lessons. Cinqbars was a pretty sparrer—but no stamina. Brandy killed him, sir—brandy killed him! Why, this is some of your governor's wine! He and I have been drinking it to-night in Parr Street, and talking over old times."

"I am glad, sir, you found the wine to your taste," says Philip, gravely.

"I did, Philip my boy! And when your father said he was coming to your wine, I said I'd come too."

"I wish somebody would fling him out of window," groaned Philip.

"A most potent, grave, and reverend senior," whispered Rosebury to me. "I read billiards, Boulogne, gambling-houses, in his noble lineaments. Has he long adorned your family circle, Firmin?"

"I found him at home about a month ago, in my father's ante-room, in the same clothes, with a pair of mangy moustaches on his face; and he has been at our house every day since."

"*Echappé de Toulon*," says Rosebury, blandly, looking towards the stranger. "*Cela se voit. Homme parfaitement distingué.* You are quite right, sir. I was speaking of you; and asking our friend Philip where it was I had the honour of meeting you abroad last year? This courtesy," he gently added, "will disarm tigers."

"I *was* abroad, sir, last year," said the other, nodding his head.

"Three to one he was in Boulogne gaol, or perhaps officiating chaplain at a gambling-house. Stop, I have it! Baden Baden, sir?"

"I was there, safe enough," says the clergyman. "It is a very pretty place; but the air of the *Après* kills you. Ha! ha! Your father used to shake his elbow when he was a youngster too, Philip! I can't help calling you Philip. I have known your father these thirty years. We were college chums, you know."

"Ah! what would I give," sighs Rosebury, "if that venerable being would but address me by my Christian name! Philip do something to make your party go. The old gentlemen are throttling it. Sing something, somebody! or let us drown our melancholy in wine. You expressed your approbation of this claret, sir, and claimed a previous acquaintance with it?"

"I've drunk two dozen of it in the last month," says Mr. Hunt, with a grin.

"Two dozen and four, sir," remarks Mr. Brice, putting a fresh bottle on the table.

"Well said, Brice! I make the Firmin Arms my head-quarters; and honour the landlord with a good deal of my company," remarks Mr. Hunt.

"The Firmin Arms is honoured by having such supporters!" says Phil, glaring, and with a heaving chest. At each moment he was growing more and more angry with that parson.

At a certain stage of conviviality Phil was fond of talking of his pedigree; and, though a professor of very liberal opinions, was not a little proud of some of his ancestors.

"Oh, come, I say! Sink the heraldry!" cries Lord Egham.

"I am very sorry! I would do anything to oblige you, but I can't help being a gentleman!" growls Philip.

"Oh, I say! if you intend to come King Richard III. over us—" breaks out my lord.

"Egham! your ancestors were sweeping counters when mine stood by King Richard in that righteous fight!" shouts Philip.

That monarch had conferred lands upon the Ringwood family. Richard III. was Philip's battle-horse; when he trotted it after dinner he was splendid in his chivalry.

"Oh, I say! If you are to saddle White Surrey, fight Bosworth Field, and murder the kids in the Tower!" continues Lord Egham.

"Serve the little brutes right!" roars Phil. "They were no more heirs of the blood royal of England than——"

"I dare say! Only I'd rather have a song now the old boy is gone. I say, you fellows, chant something, do now! Bar all this row about Bosworth Field and Richard the Third! Always does it when he's beer on board—always does it, give you my honour!" whispers the young nobleman to his neighbour.

"I am a fool! I am a fool!" cries Phil, smacking his forehead. "There are moments when the wrongs of my race *will* intervene. It's not your fault, Mr. What-d'ye-call-'im, that you alluded to my arms in a derisive manner. I bear you no malice! Nay, I ask your pardon! Nay! I pledge you in this claret, which is good, though it's my governor's. In our house everything isn't, hum——— .Bosh! it's twenty-five claret, sir! Egham's father gave him a pipe of it for saving a life which might be better spent; and I believe the apothecary would have pulled you through, Egham, just as well as my governor. But the wine's good! Good! Brice, some more claret! A song! Who spoke of a song? Warble us something, Tom Dale! A song, a song, a song!"

Whereupon the exquisite ditty of "Moonlight on the Tiles" was given by Tom Dale with all his accustomed humour. Then politeness demanded that our host should sing one of his songs, and as 'I have heard him perform it many times, I have the privilege of here reprinting it: premising that the tune and chorus were taken from a German song-book, which used to delight us melodious youth in bygone days. Philip accordingly lifted up his great voice and sang :—

Doctor Luther.

"For the souls' edification
Of this decent congregation,
Worthy people! by your grant,
I will sing a holy chant,
  I will sing a holy chant.
If the ditty sound but oddly,
'Twas a father wise and godly,
Sang it so long ago.
    Then sing as Doctor Luther sang,
    As Doctor Luther sang,
    Who loves not wine, woman, and song,
    He is a fool his whole life long.

"He by custom patriarchal,
Loved to see the beaker sparkle,
And he thought the wine improved,
Tasted by the wife he loved,
  By the kindly lips he loved.
Friends! I wish this custom pious
Duly were adopted by us,
To combine love, song, wine;
    And sing as Doctor Luther sang,
    As Doctor Luther sang,
    Who loves not wine, woman, and song,
    He is a fool his whole life long.

> "Who refuses this our credo,
> And demurs to drink as we do,
> Were he holy as John Knox,
> I'd pronounce him heterodox.
>   I'd pronounce him heterodox.
> And from out this congregation,
> With a solemn commination,
> Banish quick the heretic,
>   Who would not sing as Luther sang,
>   As Doctor Luther sang,
>   Who loves not wine, woman, and song,
>   He is a fool his whole life long."

The reader's humble servant was older than most of the party assembled at this symposium, which may have taken place some score of years back ; but as I listened to the noise, the fresh laughter, the songs remembered out of old university days, the talk and cant phrases of the old school of which most of us had been disciples, dear me, I felt quite young again, and when certain knocks came to the door about midnight, enjoyed quite a refreshing pang of anxious interest for a moment, deeming the proctors were rapping, having heard our shouts in the court below. The late comer, however, was only a tavern waiter, bearing a supper-tray ; and we were free to speechify, shout, quarrel, and be as young as we liked, with nobody to find fault, except, perchance, the bencher below, who, I dare say, was kept awake with our noise.

When that supper arrived, poor Talbot Twysden, who had come so far to enjoy it, was not in a state to partake of it. Lord Egham's cigar had proved too much for him ; and the worthy gentleman had been lying on a sofa, in a neighbouring room, for some time past, in a state of hopeless collapse. He had told us, whilst yet capable of speech, what a love and regard he had for Philip ; but between him and Philip's father there was but little love. They had had that worst and most irremediable of quarrels, a difference about twopence-halfpenny in the division of the property of their late father-in-law. Firmin still thought Twysden a shabby curmudgeon ; and Twysden considered Firmin an unprincipled man. When Mrs. Firmin was alive, the two poor sisters had had to regulate their affections by the marital orders, and to be warm, cool, moderate, freezing, according to their husbands' state for the time being. I wonder are there many real reconciliations ? Dear Tomkins and I are reconciled, I know. We have met and dined at Jones's. And ah! how fond we are of each other! Oh, very! So with Firmin and Twysden. They met, and shook hands with perfect animosity. So did Twysden junior and Firmin junior. Young Twysden was the elder, and thrashed and bullied Phil as a boy, until the latter arose and pitched his cousin downstairs. Mentally, they were always kicking each other downstairs. Well, poor Talbot could not partake of the supper when it came, and lay in a piteous state on the neighbouring sofa of the absent Mr. Van John.

Who would go home with him, where his wife must be anxious about him? I agreed to convoy him, and the parson said he was going our way, and would accompany us. We supported this senior through the Temple, and put him on the front seat of a cab. The cigar had disgracefully overcome him; and any lecturer on the evils of smoking might have pointed his moral on the helpless person of this wretched gentleman.

The evening's feasting had only imparted animation to Mr. Hunt, and occasioned an agreeable *abandon* in his talk. I had seen the man before in Dr. Firmin's house, and own that his society was almost as odious to me as to the doctor's son Philip. On all subjects and persons, Phil was accustomed to speak his mind out a great deal too openly; and Mr. Hunt had been an object of special dislike to him ever since he had known Hunt. I tried to make the best of the matter. Few men of kindly feeling and good station are without a dependant or two. Men start together in the race of life; and Jack wins, and Tom falls by his side. The successful man succours and reaches a friendly hand to the unfortunate competitor. Remembrance of early times gives the latter a sort of right to call on his luckier comrade; and a man finds himself pitying, then enduring, then embracing a companion for whom, in old days, perhaps, he never had had any regard or esteem. A prosperous man ought to have followers: if he has none, he has a hard heart.

This philosophizing was all very well. It was good for a man not to desert the friends of his boyhood. But to live with such a cad as that—with that creature, low, servile, swaggering, besotted—"How could his father, who had fine tastes, and loved grand company, put up with such a fellow?" asked Phil. "I don't know when the man is the more odious: when he is familiar, or when he is respectful; when he is paying compliments to my father's guests in

Parr Street, or telling hideous old stale stories, as he did at my call-supper."

The wine of which Mr. Hunt freely partook on that occasion made him, as I have said, communicative. "Not a bad fellow, our host," he remarked, on his part, when we came away together. "Bumptious, good-looking, speaks his mind, hates me, and I don't care. He must be well to do in the world, Master Philip."

I said I hoped and thought so.

"Brummell Firmin must make four or five thousand a year. He was a wild fellow in my time, I can tell you—in the days of the wild Prince and 'Poins—stuck at nothing, spent his own money, ruined himself, fell on his legs somehow, and married a fortune. Some of us have not been so lucky. I had nobody to pay *my* debts. I missed my fellowship by idling and dissipating with those confounded hats and silver-laced gowns. I liked good company in those days—always did when I could get it. If you were to write my adventures, now, you would have to tell some queer stories. I've been every-where; I've seen high and low—'specially low. I've tried school-mastering, bear-leading, newspapering, America, West Indies. I've been in every city in Europe. I haven't been as lucky as Brummell Firmin. He rolls in his coach, he does, and I walk in my highlows. Guineas drop into his palm every day, and are uncommonly scarce in mine, I can tell you; and poor old Tufton Hunt is not much better off at fifty odd than he was when he was an undergraduate at eighteen. How do you do, old gentleman? Air do you good? Here we are at Beaunash Street; hope you've got the key, and missis won't see you." A large butler, too well bred to express astonishment at any event which occurred out of doors, opened Mr. Twysden's, and let in that lamentable gentleman. He was very pale and solemn. He gasped out a few words, intimating his intention to fix a day to ask us to come and dine soon, and taste that wine that Winton liked so. He waved an· unsteady hand to us. If Mrs. Twysden was on the stairs to see the condition of her lord, I hope she took possession of the candle. Hunt grumbled as we came out : " He might have offered us some refreshment after bringing him all that way home. It's only half-past one. There's no good in going to bed so soon as that. Let us go and have a drink somewhere. I know a very good crib close by. No, you won't? I say" (here he burst into a laugh which startled the sleeping street), " I know what you've been thinking all the time in the cab. You are a swell,—you are, too! You have been thinking, 'This dreary old parson will try and borrow money from me.' But I won't, my boy. I've got a banker. Look here! Fee, faw, fum. You understand. I can get the sovereigns out of my medical swell in Old Parr Street. I prescribe bleeding for him— I drew him to-night. He is a very kind fellow, Brummell Firmin is. He can't deny such a dear old friend anything. Bless him!" And as he turned away to some midnight haunt of his own, he tossed up his hand in the air. I heard him laughing through the silent street, and Policeman X, tramping on his beat, turned round and suspiciously eyed him.

Then I thought of Dr. Firmin's dark melancholy face and eyes. Was a benevolent remembrance of old times the bond of union between these men? All my house had long been asleep, when I opened and gently closed my house-door. By the twinkling night-lamp I could dimly see child and mother softly breathing. Oh, blessed they on whose pillow no remorse sits! Happy you who have escaped temptation!

I may have been encouraged in my supicions of the dingy clergyman by Philip's own surmises regarding him, which were expressed with the speaker's usual candour. "The fellow calls for what he likes at the 'Firmin Arms,'" said poor Phil; "and when my father's big-wigs assemble, I hope the reverend gentleman dines with them. I should like to see him hobnobbing with old Bumpsher, or slapping the bishop on the back. He lives in Sligo Street, round the corner, so as to be close to our house and yet preserve his own elegant independence. Otherwise, I wonder he has not installed himself in Old Parr Street, where my poor mother's bedroom is vacant. The doctor does not care to use that room. I remember now how silent they were when together, and how terrified she always seemed before him. What has he done? I know of one affair in his early life. Does this Hunt know of any more? They have been accomplices in some conspiracy, sir; I dare say with that young Cinqbars, of whom Hunt is for ever bragging: the worthy son of the worthy Ringwood. I say, does wickedness run in the blood? My grandfathers, I have heard, were honest men. Perhaps they were only not found out; and the family taint will show in me some day. There are times when I feel the devil so strong within me, that I think some day he must have the mastery. I'm not quite bad yet: but I tremble lest I should go. Suppose I were to drown, and go down? It's not a jolly thing, Pendennis, to have such a father as mine. Don't humbug *me* with your charitable palliations and soothing surmises. You put me in mind of the world then, by Jove, you do! I laugh, and I drink, and I make merry, and sing, and smoke endless tobacco ; and I tell you, I always feel as if a little sword was dangling over my skull which will fall some day and split it. Old Parr Street is mined, sir,—mined! And some morning we shall be blown into blazes—into blazes, sir ; mark my words! That's why I'm so careless and so idle, for which you fellows are always bothering and scolding me. There's no use in settling down until the explosion is over, don't you see? *Incedo per ignes suppositos*, and, by George! sir, I feel my bootsoles already scorching. Poor thing! poor mother" (he apostrophized his mother's picture which hung in the room where we were talking,) "were you aware of the secret, and was it the knowledge of that which made your poor eyes always look so frightened? She was always fond of you, Pen. Do you remember how pretty and graceful she used to look as she lay on her sofa upstairs, or smiled out of her carriage as she kissed her hand to us boys? I say, what if a woman marries, and is coaxed and wheedled by a soft tongue, and runs off, and afterwards finds her husband has a cloven foot?"

"Ah, Philip!"

"What is to be the lot of the son of such a man? Is my hoof cloven, too?" It was on the stove, as he talked, extended in American fashion. "Suppose there's no escape for me, and I inherit my doom, as another man does gout or consumption? Knowing this fate, what is the use, then, of doing anything in particular? I tell you, sir, the whole edifice of our present life will crumble in and smash." (Here he flings his pipe to the ground with an awful shatter.) "And until the catastrophe comes, what on earth is the use of setting to work, as you call it? You might as well have told a fellow, at Pompeii, to select a profession the day before the eruption."

"If you know that Vesuvius is going to burst over Pompeii," I said, somewhat alarmed, "why not go to Naples, or farther if you will?"

"Were there not men in the sentry-boxes at the city gates,"

asked Philip, "who might have run, and yet remained to be burned there? Suppose, after all, the doom isn't hanging over us,—and the fear of it is only a nervous terror of mine? Suppose it comes, and I survive it? The risk of the game gives a zest to it, old boy. Besides, there is Honour: and some One Else is in the case, from whom a man *could* not part in an hour of danger." And here he blushed a fine red, heaved a great sigh, and emptied a bumper of claret.

CHAPTER VIII.

WILL BE PRONOUNCED TO BE CYNICAL BY THE BENEVOLENT.

ENTLE readers will not, I trust, think the worse of their most obedient humble servant for the confession that I talked to my wife on my return home regarding Philip and his affairs. When I choose to be frank, I hope no man can be more open than myself: when I have a mind to be quiet, no fish can be more mute. I have kept secrets so ineffably, that I have utterly forgotten them, until my memory was refreshed by people who also knew them. But what was the use of hiding this one from the being to whom I open all, or almost all—say all, excepting just one or two of the closets of this heart? So I say to her, "My love; it is as I suspected. Philip and his cousin Agnes are carrying on together."

"Is Agnes the pale one, or the *very* pale one?" asks the joy of my existence.

"No, the elder is Blanche. They are both older than Mr. Firmin : but Blanche is the elder of the two."

"Well, I am not saying anything malicious, or contrary to the fact, am I, sir?"

No. Only I know by her looks, when another lady's name is mentioned, whether my wife likes her or not. And I am bound to say, though this statement may meet with a denial, that her countenance does not vouchsafe smiles at the mention of all ladies' names.

"You don't go to the house? You and Mrs. Twysden have called on each other, and there the matter has stopped? Oh, I know! It is because poor Talbot brags so about his wine, and gives such abominable stuff, that you have such an un-Christian feeling for him!"

"That is the reason, I dare say," says the lady.

"No. It is no such thing. Though you *do* know sherry from port, I believe upon my conscience you do not avoid the Twysdens because they give bad wine. Many others sin in that way, and you forgive them. You like your fellow-creatures better than wine—some fellow-creatures—and you dislike some fellow-creatures worse than medicine. You swallow them, madam. You say nothing, but your looks are dreadful. You make wry faces: and when you have taken them, you want a piece of sweetmeat to take the taste out of your mouth."

The lady, thus wittily addressed, shrugs her lovely shoulders. My wife exasperates me in many things; in getting up at insane hours to go to early church, for instance; in looking at me in a particular way at dinner, when I am about to eat one of those *entrées* which Dr. Goodenough declares disagree with me; in nothing more than in that obstinate silence, which she persists in maintaining sometimes when I am abusing people, whom I do not like, whom she does not like, and who abuse me. This reticence makes me wild. What confidence can there be between a man and his wife, if he can't say to her, "Confound So-and-so, I hate him;" or, "What a prig What-d'ye-call-'im is!" or, "What a bloated aristocrat Thingamy has become, since he got his place!" or what you will?

"No," I continue, "I know why you hate the Twysdens, Mrs. Pendennis. You hate them because they move in a world which you can only occasionally visit. You envy them because they are hand-in-glove with the great; because they possess an easy grace, and a frank and noble elegance with which common country-people and apothecaries' sons are not endowed."

"My dear Arthur, I do think you are ashamed of being an apothecary's son; you talk about it so often," says the lady. Which was all very well: but you see she was not answering my remarks about the Twysdens.

"You are right, my dear," I say then. "I ought not to be censorious, being myself no more virtuous than my neighbour."

"I know people abuse you, Arthur ; but I think you are a very good sort of man," says the lady, over her little tea-tray.

"And so are the Twysdens very good people—very nice, artless, unselfish, simple, generous, well-bred people. Mr. Twysden is all heart : Twysden's conversational powers are remarkable and pleasing : and Philip is eminently fortunate in getting one of those charming girls for a wife."

"I've no patience with them," cries my wife, losing that quality to my great satisfaction : for then I knew I had found the crack in Madam Pendennis's armour of steel, and had smitten her in a vulnerable little place.

"No patience with them ? Quiet, lady-like young women !" I cry.

"Ah," sighs my wife, "what have they got to give Philip in return for——"

"In return for his thirty thousand ? They will have ten thousand pounds apiece when their mother dies."

"Oh ! I wouldn't have our boy marry a woman like one of those, not if she had a million. I wouldn't, my child and my blessing !" (This is addressed to a little darling who happens to be eating sweet cakes, in a high chair, off the little table by his mother's side, and who, though he certainly used to cry a good deal at that period, shall be a mute personage in this history.)

"You are alluding to Blanche's little affair with——"

"No, I am not, sir !"

"How do you know which one I meant, then ?——Or that notorious disappointment of Agnes, when Lord Farintosh became a widower ? If he wouldn't, she couldn't, you know, my dear. And I am sure she tried her best : at least, everybody said so."

"Ah ! I have no patience with the way in which you people of the world treat the most sacred of subjects—the most sacred, sir. Do you hear me ? Is a woman's love to be pledged, and withdrawn every day ? Is her faith and purity only to be a matter of barter, and rank, and social consideration ? I am sorry, because I don't wish to see Philip, who is good, and honest, and generous, and true as yet— however great his faults may be—because I don't wish to see him given up to——Oh ! its shocking, shocking !"

Given up to what ? to anything dreadful in this world, or the next ? Don't imagine that Philip's relations thought they were doing

Phil any harm by condescending to marry him, or themselves any injury. A doctor's son, indeed! Why, the Twysdens were far better placed in the world than their kinsmen of Old Parr Street; and went to better houses. The year's levée and drawing-room would have been incomplete without Mr. and Mrs. Twysden. There might be families with higher titles, more wealth, higher positions; but the world did not contain more respectable folks than the Twysdens: of this every one of the family was convinced, from Talbot himself down to his heir. If somebody or some Body of savans would write the history of the harm that has been done in the world by people who believe themselves to be virtuous, what a queer, edifying book it would be, and how poor oppressed rogues might look up! Who burn the Protestants?—the virtuous Catholics, to be sure. Who roast the Catholics?—the virtuous Reformers. Who thinks I am a dangerous character, and avoids me at the club?—the virtuous Squaretoes. Who scorns? who persecutes? who doesn't forgive?— the virtuous Mrs. Grundy. She remembers her neighbour's peccadilloes to the third and fourth generation; and if she finds a certain man fallen in her path, gathers up her affrighted garments with a shriek, for fear the muddy, bleeding wretch should contaminate her, and passes on.

I do not seek to create even surprises in this modest history, or condescend to keep candid readers in suspense about many matters which might possibly interest them. For instance, the matter of love has interested novel-readers for hundreds of years past, and doubtless will continue so to interest them. Almost all young people read love-books and histories with eagerness, as oldsters read books of medicine, and whatever it is—heart-complaint, gout, liver, palsy—cry, "Exactly so, precisely my case!" Phil's first love-affair, to which we are now coming, was a false start. I own it at once. And in this commencement of his career I believe he was not more or less fortunate than many and many a man and woman in this world. Suppose the course of true love always did run 'smooth, and everybody married his or her first love. Ah! what would marriage be?

A generous young fellow comes to market with a heart ready to leap out of his waistcoat, for ever thumping and throbbing, and so wild that he can't have any rest till he has disposed of it. What wonder if he falls upon a wily merchant in Vanity Fair, and barters his all for a stale bauble not worth sixpence? Phil chose to fall in love with his cousin ; and I warn you that nothing will come of that passion, except the influence which it had upon the young man's character. Though my wife did not love the Twysdens, she loves sentiment, she loves love-affairs—all women do. Poor Phil used to bore *me* after dinner with endless rodomontades about his passion and his charmer ; but my wife was never tired of listening. " You are a selfish, heartless, *blasé* man of the world, you are," he would say. " Your own immense and undeserved good fortune in the matrimonial lottery has rendered you hard, cold, crass, indifferent. You have been asleep, sir, twice to-night, whilst I was talking. I will go up and tell madam everything. *She* has a heart." And presently, engaged with my book or my after-dinner doze, I would hear Phil striding and creaking overhead, and plunging energetic pokers in the drawing-room fire.

Thirty thousand pounds to begin with ; a third part of that sum coming to the lady from her mother ; all the doctor's savings and property ;—here certainly was enough in possession and expectation to satisfy many young couples ; and as Phil is twenty-two, and Agnes (must I own it ?) twenty-five, and as she has consented to listen to the warm outpourings of the eloquent and passionate youth, and exchange for his fresh, new-minted, golden sovereign heart, that used little threepenny-piece, her own—why should they not marry at once, and so let us have an end of them and this history ? They have plenty of money to pay the parson and the postchaise ; they may drive off to the country, and live on their means, and lead an existence so humdrum and tolerably happy that Phil may grow quite too fat, lazy, and unfit for his present post of hero of a novel. But stay —there are obstacles ; coy, reluctant, amorous delays. After all, Philip is a dear, brave, handsome, wild, reckless, blundering boy, treading upon everybody's dress-skirts, smashing the little Dresden ornaments and the pretty little decorous gimcracks of society, life, conversation ;—but there is time yet. Are you so very sure about that money of his mother's ? and how is it that his father, the doctor, has not settled accounts with him yet ? *C'est louche.* A family of high position and principle must look to have the money matters in perfect order, before they consign a darling accustomed to every luxury to the guardianship of a confessedly wild and eccentric, though generous and amiable young man. Besides—ah ! besides—besides !

" . . . . It's horrible, Arthur ! It's cruel, Arthur ! It's a shame to judge a woman, or Christian people so! Oh ! my loves ! my blessings ! would I sell *you ?* " says this young mother, clutching a little belaced, befurbelowed being to her heart, infantine, squalling, with blue shoulder-ribbons, a mottled little arm that has just been vaccinated, and the sweetest red shoes. " Would I sell *you ?* " says mamma. Little Arty, I say, squalls ; and little Nelly looks up from her bricks with a wondering, whimpering expression.

Well, I am ashamed to say what the " besides " is ; but the fact is, that young Woolcomb of the Life Guards Green, who has inherited immense West India property, and, we will say, just a teaspoonful of that dark blood which makes a man naturally partial to blonde beauties, has cast his opal eyes very warmly upon the golden-haired Agnes of late ; has danced with her not a little ; and when Mrs. Twysden's barouche appears by the Serpentine, you may not unfrequently see a pair of the neatest little yellow kid gloves just playing with the reins, a pair of the prettiest little boots just touching the stirrup, a magnificent horse dancing, and tittupping, and tossing, and performing the most graceful caracoles and gambadoes, and on the magnificent horse a neat little man with a blazing red flower in his bosom, and glancing opal eyes, and a dark complexion, and hair so *very* black and curly, that I really almost think in some of the Southern States of America he would be likely to meet with rudeness in a railway-car.

But in England we know better. In England Grenville Woolcomb is a man and a brother. Half of Arrowroot Island, they say, belongs to him ; besides Mangrove Hall, in Hertfordshire ; ever so much property in other counties, and that fine house in Berkeley Square. He is called the Black Prince behind the scenes of many theatres : ladies nod at him from those broughams which, you understand, need not be particularized. The idea of his immense riches is confirmed by the known fact that he is a stingy Black Prince, and most averse to parting with his money except for his own adornment or amusement. When he receives at his country-house, his entertainments are, however, splendid. He has been flattered, followed, caressed all his life, and allowed by a fond mother to have his own way; and as this has never led him to learning, it must be owned that his literary acquirements are small, and his writing defective. But in the management of his pecuniary affairs he is very keen and clever. His horses cost him less than any young man's in England

LAURA'S FIRESIDE.

who is so well mounted. No dealer has ever been known to get the better of him ; and, though he is certainly close about money, when his wishes have very keenly prompted him, no sum has been known to stand in his way.

Witness the purchase of the ——. But never mind scandal. Let bygones be bygones. A young doctor's son, with a thousand a year for a fortune, may be considered a catch in some circles, but not, *vous concevez*, in the upper regions of society. And dear woman —dear, angelic, highly accomplished, respectable woman—does she not know how to pardon many failings in our sex? Age? psha ! She will crown my bare old poll with the roses of her youth. Complexion? What contrast is sweeter and more touching than Desdemona's golden ringlets on swart Othello's shoulder? A past life of selfishness and bad company? Come out from among the swine, my prodigal, and I will purify thee !

This is what is called cynicism, you know. Then I suppose my wife is a cynic, who clutches her children to her pure heart, and prays gracious heaven to guard them from selfishness, from worldliness, from heartlessness, from wicked greed.

CHAPTER IX.

CONTAINS ONE RIDDLE WHICH IS SOLVED, AND PERHAPS SOME MORE.

INE is a modest muse, and as the period of the story arrives when a description of love-making is justly due, my Mnemosyne turns away from the young couple, drops a little curtain over the embrazure where they are whispering, heaves a sigh from her elderly bosom, and lays a finger on her lip. Ah, Mnemosyne dear! we will not be spies on the young people. We will not scold them. We won't talk about their doings much. When we were young, we too, perhaps, were taken in under Love's tent; we have eaten of his salt: and partaken of his bitter, his delicious bread. Now we are padding the hoof lonely in the wilderness, we will not abuse our host, will we? We will couch under the stars, and think fondly of old times, and to-morrow resume the staff and the journey.

And yet, if a novelist may chronicle any passion, its flames, its raptures, its whispers, its assignations, its sonnets, its quarrels, sulks, reconciliations, and so on, the history of such a love as this first of Phil's may be excusable in print, because I don't believe it was a real love at all, only a little brief delusion of the senses, from which I give you warning that our hero will recover before many chapters are over. What! my brave boy, shall we give your heart away for good and all, for better or for worse, till death do you part? What! my Corydon and sighing swain, shall we irrevocably bestow you upon Phyllis, who, all the time you are piping and paying court to her, has Melibœus in the cupboard, and ready to be produced should he prove to be a more eligible shepherd than t'other? I am not such a savage towards my readers or hero, as to make them undergo the misery of such a marriage.

Philip was very little of a club or society man. He seldom or ever entered the "Megatherium," or when there stared and scowled round him savagely, and laughed strangely at the ways of the inhabitants. He made but a clumsy figure in the world, though in person, handsome, active, and proper enough; but he would for ever put his great foot through the World's flounced skirts, and she would stare, and cry out, and hate him. He was the last man who was aware of the Woolcomb flirtation, when hundreds of people, I dare say, were simpering over it.

"Who is that little man who comes to your house, and whom I sometimes see in the Park, aunt—that little man with the very white gloves and the very tawny complexion?" asks Philip.

"That is Mr. Woolcomb, of the Life Guards Green," aunt remembers.

"An officer is he?" says Philip, turning round to the girls. "I should have thought he would have done better for the turban and cymbals." And he laughs and thinks he has said a very clever thing. Oh, those good things about people and against people! Never, my dear young friend, say them to anybody—not to a stranger, for he will go away and tell; not to the mistress of your affections, for you may quarrel with her, and then *she* will tell; not to your son, for the artless child will return to his schoolfellows and say: "Papa says Mr. Blenkinsop is a muff." My child, or what not, praise everybody: smile on everybody: and everybody will smile on you in return, a sham smile, and hold you out a sham hand; and, in a word, esteem you as you deserve. No. I think

—you and I will take the ups and the downs, the roughs and the smooths of this daily existence and conversation. We will praise those whom we like, though nobody repeat our kind sayings ; and say our say about those whom we dislike, though we are pretty sure our words will be carried by tale-bearers, and increased and multiplied, and remembered long after we have forgotten them. We drop a little stone—a little stone that is swallowed up and disappears, but the whole pond is set in commotion, and ripples in continually widening circles long after the original little stone has popped down and is out of sight. Don't your speeches of ten years ago—maimed, distorted, bloated it may be out of all recognition—come strangely back to their author?

Phil, five minutes after he had made the joke, so entirely forgot his saying about the Black Prince and the cymbals, that, when Captain Woolcomb scowled at him with his fiercest eyes, young Firmin thought that this was the natural expression of the captain's swarthy countenance, and gave himself no further trouble regarding it. "By George! sir," said Phil afterwards, speaking of this officer, "I remarked that he grinned, and chattered, and showed his teeth; and remembering it was the nature of such baboons to chatter and grin, had no idea that this chimpanzee was more angry with me than with any other gentleman. You see, Pen, I am a white-skinned man ; I am pronounced even red-whiskered by the ill-natured. It is not the prettiest colour. But I had no idea that I was to have a mulatto for a rival. I am not so rich, certainly, but I have enough. I can read and spell correctly, and write with tolerable fluency. I could not, you know, could I, reasonably suppose that I need fear competition, and that the black horse would beat the bay one ? Shall I tell you what she used to say to me ? There is no kissing and telling, mind you. No, by George. Virtue and prudence were for ever on her lips ! She warbled little sermons to me ; hinted gently that I should see to safe investments of my property, and that no man, not even a father, should be the sole and uncontrolled guardian of it. She asked me, sir, scores and scores of little sweet, timid, innocent questions about the doctor's property, and how much did I think it was, and how had he laid it out ? What virtuous parents that angel had ! How they brought her up, and educated her dear blue eyes to the main chance ! She knows the price of housekeeping, and the value of railway shares ; she invests capital—

for herself in this world and the next. She mayn't do right always, but wrong? O fie, never! I say, Pen, an undeveloped angel with wings folded under her dress; not perhaps your mighty, snow-white, flashing pinions that spread out and soar up to the highest stars, but a pair of good serviceable drab dove-coloured wings, that will support her gently and equably just over our heads, and help to drop her softly when she condescends upon us. When I think, sir, that I might have been married to a genteel angel and am single still,—oh! it's despair, it's despair!"

But Philip's little story of disappointed hopes and bootless passion must be told in terms less acrimonious and unfair than the gentle-man would use, naturally of a sanguine, swaggering talk, prone to exaggerate his own disappointments, and call out, roar—I dare say swear—if his own corn was trodden upon, as loudly as some men who may have a leg taken off.

This I can vouch for Miss Twysden, Mrs. Twysden, and all the rest of the family :—that if they, what you call, jilted Philip, they did so without the slightest hesitation or notion that they were doing a dirty action. Their actions never *were* dirty or mean ; they were necessary, I tell you, and calmly proper. They ate cheese-parings with graceful silence; they cribbed from board-wages ; they turned hungry servants out of doors; they remitted no chance in their own favour; they slept gracefully under scanty coverlids; they lighted niggard fires ; they locked the caddy with the closest lock, and served the teapot with the smallest and least frequent spoon. But you don't suppose they thought they were mean, or that they did wrong? Ah ! it is admirable to think of many, many, ever so many respectable families of your acquaintance and mine, my dear friend, and how they meet together and humbug each other ! " My dear, I have cribbed half an inch of plush out of James's small-clothes." " My love, I have saved a halfpenny out of Mary's beer. Isn't it time to dress for the duchess's; and don't you think John might wear that livery of Thomas's, who only had it a year, and died of the small-pox? It's a little tight for him, to be sure, but," &c. What is this ? —I profess to be an impartial chronicler of poor Phil's fortunes, misfor-tunes, friendships, and what-nots, and am getting almost as angry with these Twysdens as Philip ever was himself.

Well, I am not mortally angry with poor Traviata tramping the pavement, with the gas-lamp flaring on her poor painted smile, else

my indignant virtue and squeamish modesty would never walk Piccadilly or get the air. But Lais, quite moral, and very neatly, primly,
and straitly laced;—Phryne, not the least dishevelled, but with a
fixature for her hair, and the best stays, fastened by mamma;—your
High Church or Evangelical Aspasia, the model of all proprieties,
and owner of all virgin-purity blooms, ready to sell her cheek to the
oldest old fogey who has money and a title;—*these* are the Unfor-
tunates, my dear brother and sister sinners, whom I should like to see
repentant and specially trounced first. Why, some of these are put
into reformatories in Grosvenor Square. They wear a prison dress of
diamonds and Chantilly lace. Their parents cry, and thank heaven
as they sell them; and all sorts of revered bishops, clergy, relations,
dowagers, sign the book, and ratify the ceremony. Come! let us
call a midnight meeting of those who have been sold in marriage, I
say, and what a respectable, what a genteel, what a fashionable,
what a brilliant, what an imposing, what a multitudinous assembly
we will have; and where's the room in all Babylon big enough to
hold them?

Look into that grave, solemn, dingy, somewhat naked, but elegant
drawing-room, in Beaunash Street, and with a little fanciful opera-
glass you may see a pretty little group or two engaged at different
periods of the day. It is after lunch, and before Rotten Row ride
time (this story, you know, relates to a period ever so remote, and
long before folks thought of riding in the Park in the forenoon).
After lunch, and before Rotten Row time, saunters into the drawing-
room a fair-haired young fellow with large feet and chest, careless of
gloves, with auburn whiskers blowing over a loose collar, and—must
I confess it?—a most undeniable odour of cigars about his person.
He breaks out regarding the debate of the previous night, or the
pamphlet of yesterday, or the poem of the day previous, or the
scandal of the week before, or upon the street-sweeper at the corner,
or the Italian and monkey before the Park—upon whatever, in a
word, moves his mind for the moment. If Philip has had a bad
dinner yesterday (and happens to remember it), he growls, grumbles,
nay, I dare say, uses the most blasphemous language against the
cook, against the waiters, against the steward, against the committee,
against the whole society of the club where he has been dining. If
Philip has met an organ-girl with pretty eyes and a monkey in the
street, he has grinned and wondered over the monkey; he has wagged

his head, and sung all the organ's tunes; he has discovered that the little girl is the most ravishing beauty eyes ever looked on, and that her scoundrelly Savoyard father is most likely an Alpine miscreant who has bartered away his child to a pedlar of the beggarly cheesy valleys, who has sold her to a friend *qui fait la traite des hurdigurdies*, and has disposed of her in England. If he has to discourse on the poem, pamphlet, magazine article—it is written by the greatest genius, or the greatest numskull, that the world now exhibits. *He* write! A man who makes fire rhyme with Marire! This vale of tears and world which we inhabit does not contain such an idiot. Or have you seen Dobbins's poem? Agnes, mark my words for it, there is a genius in Dobbins which some day will show what I have always surmised, what I have always imagined possible, what I have always felt to be more than probable, what, by George! I feel to be perfectly certain, and any man is a humbug who contradicts it, and a malignant miscreant, and the world is full of fellows who will never give another man credit; and I swear that to recognize and feel merit in poetry, painting, music, rope-dancing, anything, is the greatest delight and joy of my existence. I say—what was I saying?

"You were saying, Philip, that you love to recognize the merits of all men whom you see," says gentle Agnes, "and I believe you do."

"Yes!" cries Phil, tossing about the fair locks. "I think I do. Thank heaven, I do. I know fellows who can do many things better than I do—everything better than I do."

"Oh, Philip!" sighs the lady.

"But I don't hate 'em for it."

"You never hated any one, sir. You are too brave! Can you fancy Philip hating any one, mamma?"

Mamma is writing: "Mr. and Mrs. Talbot Twysden request the honour of Admiral and Mrs. Davis Locker's company at dinner on Thursday the so-and-so." "Philip what?" says mamma, looking up from her card. "Philip hating any one! Philip eating any one! Philip! we have a little dinner on the 24th. We shall ask your father to dine. We must not have too many of the family. Come in afterwards, please."

"Yes, aunt," says downright Phil, "I'll come, if you and the girls wish. You know tea is not my line; and I don't care about dinners, except in my own way, and with——"

"And with your own horrid set, sir !"

"Well," says Sultan Philip, flinging himself out on the sofa, and lording on the ottoman, " I like mine ease and mine inn."

"Ah, Philip ! you grow more selfish every day. I mean men do," sighed Agnes.

You will suppose mamma leaves the room at this juncture. She has that confidence in dear Philip and the dear girls, that she sometimes *does* leave the room when Agnes and Phil are together. She will leave REUBEN, the eldest born, with her daughters : but my poor dear little younger son of a Joseph, if you suppose she will leave the room and *you* alone in it—O my dear Joseph, you may just jump down the well at once ! Mamma, I say, has left the room at last, bowing with a perfect sweetness and calm grace and gravity ; and she has slipped down the stairs, scarce more noisy than the shadow that slants over the faded carpet (oh ! the faded shadow, the faded sunshine !)—mamma is gone, I say, to the lower regions, and with perfect good breeding is torturing the butler on his bottle-rack—is squeezing the housekeeper in her jam-closet—is watching the three cold cutlets shuddering in the larder behind the wires—is blandly glancing at the kitchen-maid until the poor wench fancies the piece of bacon is discovered which she gave to the crossing-sweeper—and calmly penetrating John until he feels sure his inmost heart is revealed to her, as it throbs within his worsted-laced waistcoat, and she knows about that pawning of master's old boots, (beastly old highlows !) and —and, in fact, all the most intimate circumstances of his existence. A wretched maid, who has been ironing collars, or what not, gives her mistress a shuddering curtsey, and slinks away with her laces ; and meanwhile our girl and boy are prattling in the drawing-room.

About what ? About everything on which Philip chooses to talk. There is nobody to contradict him but himself, and then his pretty hearer vows and declares he has not been so very contradictory. He spouts his favourite poems. "Delightful! Do, Philip, read us some Walter Scott ! He is, as you say, the most fresh, the most manly, the most kindly of poetic writers—not of the first class, certainly. In fact, he has written most dreadful bosh, as you call it so drolly ; and so has Wordsworth, though he is one of the greatest of men, and has reached sometimes to the very greatest height and sublimity of poetry ; but now you put it, I must confess he is often an old bore, and I certainly should have gone to sleep during the ' Excursion,' only you read it so nicely. You don't think the new composers as good as the old ones, and love mamma's old-fashioned playing? Well, Philip, it is delightful, so ladylike, so feminine!" Or, perhaps, Philip has just come from Hyde Park, and says, "As I passed by Apsley House, I saw the Duke come out, with his old blue frock and white trousers and clear face. I have seen a picture of him in an old *European Magazine*, which I think I like better than all—gives me the idea of one of the brightest men in the world. The brave eyes gleam at you out of the picture; and there's a smile on the resolute lips, which seems to ensure triumph. Agnes, Assaye must have been glorious!"

"Glorious, Philip!" says Agnes, who had never heard of Assaye before in her life. Arbela, perhaps; Salamis, Marathon, Agincourt, Blenheim, Busaco—where dear grandpapa was killed—Waterloo, Armageddon; but Assaye? Que voulez-vous?

"Think of that ordinarily prudent man, and how greatly he knew how to dare when occasion came! I should like to have died after winning such a game. He has never done anything so exciting since."

"A game? I thought it was a battle just now," murmurs Agnes in her mind; but there may be some misunderstanding. "Ah, Philip," she says, "I fear excitement is too much the life of all young men now. When will you be quiet and steady, sir?"

"And go to an office every day, like my uncle and cousin; and read the newspaper for three hours, and trot back and see you."

"Well, sir! that ought not to be such very bad amusement," says one of the ladies.

"What a clumsy wretch I am! my foot is always trampling on something or somebody!" groans Phil.

"You must come to us, and we will teach you to dance, Bruin!" says gentle Agnes, smiling on him. I think when very much agitated, her pulse must have gone up to forty. Her blood must have been a light pink. The heart that beat under that pretty white chest, which she exposed so liberally, may have throbbed pretty quickly once or twice with waltzing, but otherwise never rose or fell beyond its natural gentle undulation. It may have had throbs of grief at a disappointment occasioned by the milliner not bringing a dress home; or have felt some little fluttering impulse of youthful passion when it was in short frocks, and Master Grimsby at the dancing-school showed some preference for another young pupil out of the nursery. But feelings, and hopes, and blushes, and passions now? Psha! They pass away like nursery dreams. Now there are only proprieties. What is love, young heart? · It is two thousand a year, — at the very lowest computation; and, with the present rise in wages and house-rent, that calculation can't last very long. Love? Attachment? Look at Frank Maythorn, with his vernal blushes, his leafy whiskers, his sunshiny, laughing face, and all the birds of spring carolling in his jolly voice; and old General Pinwood hobbling in on his cork leg, with his stars and orders, and leering round the room from under his painted eyebrows. Will my modest nymph go to Maythorn, or to yonder leering Satyr, who totters towards her in his white and rouge? Nonsense. She gives her garland to the old man, to be sure. He is ten times as rich as the young one. And so they went on in Arcadia itself, *really*. Not in that namby-pamby ballet and idyll world, where they tripped up to each other in rhythm, and talked hexameters; but in the real downright, no-mistake country—Arcadia—where Tityrus, fluting to Amaryllis in the shade, had his pipe very soon put out when Melibœus (the great grazier) performed on his melodious, exquisite, irresistible cowhorn; and where Daphne's mother dressed her up with ribbons and drove her to market, and sold her, and swapped her, and bartered her like any other lamb in the fair. This one has been trotted to the market so long now that she knows the way herself. Her baa has been heard for—do not let us count how many seasons. She has nibbled out of countless hands; frisked in many thousand dances; come · quite harmless away from goodness knows how many wolves. Ah! ye lambs and raddled innocents of our Arcadia! Ah, old *Ewe!* Is it of your ladyship this fable is narrated? I say it is as old as Cadmus, and man- and mutton- kind.

So, when Philip comes to Beaunash Street, Agnes listens to him most kindly, sweetly, gently, and affectionately. Her pulse goes up very nearly half a beat when the echo of his horse's heels is heard in the quiet street. It undergoes a corresponding depression when the daily grief of parting is encountered and overcome. Blanche and Agnes don't love each other very passionately. If I may say as much regarding those two lambkins, they butt at each other—they quarrel with each other—but they have secret understandings. During Phil's visits the girls remain together, you understand, or mamma is with the young people. Female friends may come in to call on Mrs. Twysden, and the matrons whisper together, and glance at the cousins, and look knowing. "Poor orphan boy !" mamma says to a sister matron. "I am like a mother to him since my dear sister died. His own home is so blank, and ours so merry, so affectionate ! There may be intimacy, tender regard, the utmost confidence between cousins—there may be future and even closer ties between them—but you understand, dear Mrs. Matcham, no engagement between them. He is eager, hot-headed, impetuous, and imprudent, as we all know. She has not seen the world enough— is not sure of herself, poor dear child ! Therefore every circumspection, every caution is necessary. There must be no engagement, no letters between them. My darling Agnes does not write to ask him to dinner without showing the note to me or her father. My dearest girls respect themselves." "Of course, my dear Mrs. Twysden, they are admirable, both of them. Bless you, darlings ! Agnes, you look radiant ! Ah, Rosa, my child, I wish you had dear Blanche's complexion !"

"And isn't it monstrous keeping that poor boy hanging on until Mr. Woolcomb has made up his mind about coming forward ? " says dear Mrs. Matcham to her own daughter, as her brougham-door closes on the pair. "Here he comes ! Here is his cab. Maria Twysden is one of the smartest women in England—that she is."

"How odd it is, mamma, that the *beau cousin* and Captain Woolcomb are always calling, and never call together!" remarks the *ingénue*.

"They might quarrel if they met. They say young Mr. Firmin is very quarrelsome and impetuous ! " says mamma.

"But how are they kept apart ? "

"Chance, my dear ! mere chance ! " says mamma. And they agree to say it is chance—and they agree to pretend to believe one another. And the girl and the mother know everything about Woolcomb's property, everything about Philip's property and expectations, everything about all the young men in London, and those coming on. And Mrs. Matcham's girl fished for Captain Woolcomb last year in Scotland, at Loch-hookey ; and stalked him to Paris ; and they went down on their knees to Lady Banbury when they heard of the theatricals at the Cross ; and pursued that man about until he is forced to say, " Confound me! hang me ! it's too bad of that woman and her daughter, it is now, I give you my honour it is ! And all the fellows chaff me ! And she took a house in Regent's Park, opposite our barracks, and asked for her daughter to learn to ride in our school—I'm blest if she didn't, Mrs. Twysden ! and I thought my black mare would have kicked her off one day—I mean the daughter—but she stuck on like grim death ; and the fellows call them Mrs. Grim Death and her daughter. Our surgeon called them so, and a doosid rum fellow—and they chaff me about it, you know—ever so many of the fellows do—and *I'm* not going to be had in that way by Mrs. Grim Death and her daughter ! No, not as I knows, if you please ! "

" You are a dreadful man, and you gave her a dreadful name, Captain Woolcomb !" says mamma.

" It wasn't me. It was the surgeon, you know, Miss Agnes : a doosid funny and witty fellow, Nixon is—and sent a thing once to *Punch*, Nixon did. I heard him make the riddle in Albany Barracks and it riled Foker so ! You've no idea how it riled Foker, for he's in it ! "

· " In it ? " asks Agnes, with the gentle smile, the candid blue eyes —the same eyes, expression, lips, that smile and sparkle at Philip.

" Here it is ! Capital ! Took it down. Wrote it into my pocket-book at once as Nixon made it. ' *All doctors like my first, that's clear !*' Doctor Firmin does that. Old Parr Street party ! Don't you see, Miss Agnes ? FEE ! Don't you see ?"

" Fee ! Oh, you droll thing !" cries Agnes, smiling, radiant, very · much puzzled.

" ' My second,'" goes on the young officer—" ' *My second gives us Foker's beer !*'"

" ' *My whole's the shortest month in all the year !*' Don't you see, Mrs. Twysden ? FEE-BREWERY, DON'T YOU SEE ? February ! A doosid good one, isn't it now ? and I wonder *Punch* never put it in. And upon my word, I used to spell it Febuary before, I did ; and I dare say ever so many fellows do still. And I know the right way now, and all from that riddle which Nixon made."

The ladies declare he is a droll man, and full of fun. He rattles on, artlessly telling his little stories of sport, drink, adventure, in which the dusky little man himself is a prominent figure. Not honey-mouthed Plato would be listened to more kindly by those three ladies. A bland, frank smile shines over Talbot Twysden's noble face, as he comes in from his office, and finds the creole prattling. "What ! *you* here, Woolcomb? Hay ! Glad to see you !" And the gallant hand goes out and meets and grasps Woolcomb's tiny kid glove.

"He has been so amusing, papa ! He has been making us die with laughing ! Tell papa that riddle you made, Captain Woolcomb ?"

"That riddle I made ? That riddle Nixon, our surgeon, made. ' All doctors like my first, that's clear,' " &c.

And *da capo*. And the family, as he expounds this admirable rebus, gather round the young officer in a group, and the curtain drops.

As in a theatre booth at a fair there are two or three performances in a day, so in Beaunash Street a little genteel comedy is played twice :—at four o'clock with Mr. Firmin, at five o'clock with Mr. Woolcomb ; and for both young gentlemen, same smiles, same eyes, same voice, same welcome. Ah, bravo ! ah, encore !

CHAPTER X.

IN WHICH WE VISIT "ADMIRAL BYNG."

ROM long residence in Bohemia, and fatal love of bachelor ease and habits, Master Philip's pure tastes were so destroyed, and his manners so perverted that, you will hardly believe it, he was actually indifferent to the pleasures of the refined home we have just been describing ; and, when Agnes was away, sometimes even when she was at home, was quite relieved to get out of Beaunash Street. He is hardly twenty yards from the door, when out of his pocket there comes a case; out of the case there jumps an aromatic cigar, which is scattering fragrance around as he is marching briskly northwards to his next house of call. The pace is even more lively now than when he is hastening on what you call the wings of love to Beaunash Street. At the house whither he is now going, he and the cigar are always welcome. There is no need of munching orange chips, or chewing scented pills, or flinging your weed away half a mile before you reach Thornhaugh Street—the low, vulgar place. I promise you Phil may smoke at Brandon's, and find others doing the same. He may set the house on fire, if so minded, such a favourite is he there ; and the Little Sister, with her kind, beaming smile, will be there to bid him welcome. How that woman loved Phil, and how he loved her, is quite a curiosity; and both of them used to be twitted with this attachment by their mutual friends, and blush as they acknowledged it. Ever since the little nurse had saved his life as a schoolboy, it was *à la vie à la mort* between them. Phil's father's chariot used to come to Thornhaugh Street sometimes —at rare times—and the doctor descend thence and have colloquies with the Little Sister. She attended a patient or two of his. She was certainly very much better off in her money matters in these late years, since she had known Dr. Firmin. Do you think she took money from him? As a novelist, who knows everything about his people, I am constrained to say, Yes. She took enough to pay some little bills of her weak-minded old father, and send the bailiff's hand from his old collar. But no more. " I think you owe him as much as that," she said to the doctor. But as for compliments between them—" Dr. Firmin, I would die rather than be beholden to you for anything," she said, with her little limbs all in a tremor, and her eyes flashing anger. " How dare you, sir, after old days, be a coward and pay compliments to me; I will tell your son of you, sir!" and the little woman looked as if she could have stabbed the elderly libertine there as he stood. And he shrugged his handsome shoulders : blushed a little too, perhaps : gave her one of his darkling looks, and departed. She had believed him once. She had married him, as she fancied. He had tired of her ; forsaken her ; left her—left her even without a name. She had not known his for long years after her trust and his deceit. " No, sir, I wouldn't have your name now, not if it were a lord's, I wouldn't, and a coronet on your carriage. You are beneath me now, Mr. Brand Firmin!" she had said.

How came she to love the boy so? Years back, in her own horrible extremity of misery, she could remember a week or two of a brief, strange, exquisite happiness, which came to her in the midst of her degradation and desertion, and for a few days a baby in her arms, with eyes like Philip's. It was taken from her, after a few days —only sixteen days. Insanity came upon her, as her dead infant was carried away:—insanity, and fever, and struggle—ah! who knows how dreadful? She never does. There is a gap in her life which she never can recall quite. But George Brand Firmin, Esq., M.D., knows how very frequent are such cases of mania, and that women who don't speak about them often will cherish them for years after they appear to have passed away. The Little Sister says, quite gravely, sometimes, "They are allowed to come back. They do come back. Else what's the good of little cherubs bein' born, and smilin', and happy, and beautiful—say, for sixteen days, and then an end? I've talked about it to many ladies in grief sim'lar to mine was, and it comforts them. And when I saw that child on his sick-bed, and he lifted his eyes, *I knew him*, I tell you, Mrs. Ridley.   I don't speak about it ; but I knew him, ma'am ; my angel came back again. I know him by the eyes. Look at 'em. Did you ever see such eyes? They look as if they had seen heaven. His father's don't." Mrs. Ridley believes this theory solemnly, and I think I know a lady, nearly connected with myself, who can't be got quite to disown it. And this secret opinion to women in grief and sorrow over their new-born lost infants Mrs. Brandon persists in imparting. "*I* know a case," the nurse murmurs, " of a poor mother who lost her child at sixteen days old ; and sixteen years after, on the very day, she saw him again."

Philip knows so far of the Little Sister's story, that he is the object of this delusion, and, indeed, it very strangely and tenderly affects him. He remembers fitfully the illness through which the Little Sister tended him, the wild paroxysms of his fever, his head throbbing on her shoulders—cool tamarind drinks which she applied to his lips—great gusty night shadows flickering through the bare school dormitory—the little figure of the nurse gliding in and out of the dark.   He must be aware of the recognition, which we know of, and which took place at his bedside, though he has never mentioned it—not to his father, not to Caroline. But he clings to the woman, and shrinks from the man. Is it instinctive love and antipathy? The special reason for his quarrel with his father the junior Firmin has never explicitly told me then or since. I have known sons much more confidential, and who, when their fathers tripped and stumbled, would bring their acquaintances to jeer at the patriarch in his fall.

One day, as Philip enters Thornhaugh Street, and the Sister's little parlour there, fancy his astonishment on finding his father's dingy friend, the Rev. Tufton Hunt, at his ease by the fireside. "Surprised to see *me* here, eh?" says the dingy gentleman, with a sneer at Philip's lordly face of wonder and disgust.   " Mrs. Brandon and I turn out to be very old friends."

" Yes, sir, old acquaintances," says the Little Sister, very gravely.

"The Captain brought me home from the club at the ' Byng.'

Jolly fellows the Byngs. My service to you, Mr. Gann and Mrs. Brandon." And the two persons addressed by the gentleman, who is "taking some refreshment," as the phrase is, made a bow in acknowledgment of this salutation.

"You should have been at Mr. Philip's call-supper, Captain Gann," the divine resumes. "That *was* a night! Tiptop swells—noblemen—first-rate claret. That claret of your father's, Philip, is pretty nearly drunk down. And your song was famous. Did you ever hear him sing, Mrs. Brandon?"

"Who do you mean by *him?*" says Philip, who always boiled with rage before this man.

Caroline divines the antipathy. She lays a little hand on Philip's arm. "Mr. Hunt has been having too much, I think," she says. "I *did* know him ever so long ago, Philip!"

"What does he mean by Him?" again says Philip, snorting at Tufton Hunt.

"Him?—Dr. Luther's Hymn! 'Wein, Weber, und Gesang,' to be sure!" cries the clergyman, humming the tune. "I learned it in Germany myself—passed a good deal of time in Germany, Captain Gann—six months in a specially shady place—*Quod* Strasse, in Frankfort-on-the-Maine—being persecuted by some wicked Jews there. And there was another poor English chap in the place, too, who used to chirp that song behind the bars, and died there, and disappointed the Philistines. I've seen a deal of life, I have; and met with a precious deal of misfortune; and borne it pretty stoutly, too, since your father and I were at college together, Philip. You don't do anything in this way? Not so early, eh? It's good rum, Gann, and no mistake." And again the chaplain drinks to the Captain, who waves the dingy hand of hospitality towards his dark guest.

For several months past Hunt had now been a resident in London, and a pretty constant visitor at Dr. Firmin's house. He came and went at his will. He made the place his house of call; and in the doctor's trim, silent, orderly mansion, was perfectly free, talkative, dirty, and familiar. Philip's loathing for the man increased till it reached a pitch of frantic hatred. Mr. Phil, theoretically a Radical, and almost a Republican (in opposition, perhaps, to his father, who, of course, held the highly respectable line of politics)—Mr. Sansculotte Phil was personally one of the most aristocratic and overbearing of young gentlemen ; and had a contempt and hatred for mean people, for base people, for servile people, and especially for too familiar people, which was not a little amusing sometimes, which was provoking often, but which he never was at the least pains of disguising. His uncle and cousin Twysden, for example, he treated not half so civilly as their footmen. Little Talbot humbled himself before Phil, and felt not always easy in his company. Young Twysden hated him, and did not disguise his sentiments at the club, or to their mutual acquaintance behind Phil's broad back. And Phil, for his part, adopted towards his cousin a kick-me-downstairs manner, which I own must have been provoking to that gentleman, who was Phil's senior by three years, a clerk in a public office, a member of several good clubs, and altogether a genteel member of society. Phil would often forget Ringwood Twysden's presence, and pursue his own conversation entirely regardless of Ringwood's observations. He *was* very rude, I own. *Que voulez-vous ?* We have all of us our little failings, and one of Philip's was an ignorant impatience of bores, parasites, and pretenders.

So no wonder my young gentleman was not very fond of his father's friend, the dingy gaol chaplain. I, who am the most tolerant man in the world, as all my friends know, liked Hunt little better than Phil did. The man's presence made me uneasy. His dress, his complexion, his teeth, his leer at women—*Que sçais-je ?*—everything was unpleasant about this Mr. Hunt, and his gaiety and familiarity more specially disgusting than even his hostility. The wonder was that battle had not taken place between Philip and the gaol clergyman, who, I suppose, was accustomed to be disliked, and laughed with cynical good-humour at the other's disgust.

Hunt was a visitor of many tavern parlours ; and one day, strolling out of the " Admiral Byng," he saw his friend Dr. Firmin's well-known equipage stopping at a door in Thornhaugh Street, out of which the doctor presently came ; " Brandon " was on the door. Brandon, Brandon ? Hunt remembered a dark transaction of more than twenty years ago—of a woman deceived by this Firmin, who then chose to go by the name of Brandon. " He lives with her still, the old hypocrite, or he has gone back to her," thought the parson. Oh, you old sinner ! And the next time he called in Old Parr Street on his dear old college friend, Mr. Hunt was specially jocular, and frightfully unpleasant and familiar.

"Saw your trap Tottenham Court Road way," says the slang parson, nodding to the physician.

"Have some patients there. People are ill in Tottenham Court Road," remarks the doctor.

"*Pallida mors æquo pede*—hay, doctor? What used Flaccus to say, when we were undergrads?"

"*Æquo pede,*" sighs the doctor, casting up his fine eyes to the ceiling.

"Sly old fox! Not a word will he say about her!" thinks the clergyman. "Yes, yes, I remember. And, by Jove! Gann was the name."

Gann was also the name of that queer old man who frequented the "Admiral Byng," where the ale was so good—the old boy whom they called the Captain. Yes; it was clear now. That ugly business was patched up. The astute Hunt saw it all. The doctor still kept up a connection with the—the party. And that is her old father, sure enough. "The old fox, the old fox! I've earthed him, have I? This is a good game. I wanted a little something to do, and this will excite me," thinks the clergyman.

I am describing what I never could have seen or heard, and can guarantee only verisimilitude, not truth, in my report of the private conversation of these worthies. The end of scores and scores of Hunt's conversations with his friend was the same—an application for money. If it rained when Hunt parted from his college chum, it was, " I say, doctor, I shall spoil my new hat, and I'm blest if I have any money to take a cab. Thank you, old boy. Au revoir." If the day was fine, it was, " My old blacks show the white seams so, that you must out of your charity rig me out with a new pair. Not your tailor. He is too expensive. Thank you—a couple of sovereigns will do." And the doctor takes two from the mantelpiece, and the divine retires, jingling the gold in his greasy pocket.

The doctor is going after the few words about *pallida mors*, and has taken up that well-brushed broad hat, with that ever-fresh lining, which we all admire in him—"Oh, I say, Firmin!" breaks out the clergyman. "Before you go out, you must lend me a few sov's, please. They've cleaned me out in Air Street. That confounded roulette! It's a madness with me."

"By George!" cries the other, with a strong execration, "you are too bad, Hunt. Every week of my life you come to me for money. You have had plenty. Go elsewhere. I won't give it you."

"Yes, you will, old boy," says the other, looking at him a terrible look; "for——"

"For what?" says the doctor, the veins of his tall forehead growing very full.

"For old times' sake," says the clergyman. "There's seven of 'em on the table in bits of paper—that'll do nicely. And he sweeps the fees with a dirty hand into a dirty pouch. "Halloa! Swearin' and cursin' before a clergyman. Don't cut up rough, old fellow! Go and take the air. It'll cool you."

"I don't think I would like that fellow to attend me, if I was sick," says Hunt, shuffling away, rolling the plunder in his greasy hand. "I don't think I'd like to meet him by moonlight alone, in a *very* quiet lane. He's a determined chap. And his eyes mean *miching malecho*, his eyes do. Phew!" And he laughs, and makes a rude observation about Dr. Firmin's eyes.

That afternoon, the gents who used the "Admiral Byng" remarked the reappearance of the party who looked in last evening, and who now stood glasses round, and made himself uncommon agreeable to be sure. Old Mr. Ridley says he is quite the gentleman. "Hevident have been in foring parts a great deal, and speaks the languages. Probbly have 'ad misfortunes, which many 'ave 'ad them. Drinks rum-and-water tremenjous. 'Ave scarce no heppytite. Many get into this way from misfortunes. A plesn man, most well informed on almost every subjeck. Think he's a clergyman. He and Mr. Gann have made quite a friendship together, he and Mr. Gann 'ave. Which they talked of Watloo, and Gann is very fond of that, Gann is, most certny." I imagine Ridley delivering these sentences, and alternate little volleys of smoke, as he sits behind his sober calumet and prattles in the tavern parlour.

After Dr. Firmin has careered through the town, standing by sick-beds with his sweet sad smile, fondled and blessed by tender mothers who hail him as the saviour of their children, touching ladies' pulses with a hand as delicate as their own, patting little fresh cheeks with courtly kindness—little cheeks that owe their roses to his marvellous skill; after he has soothed and comforted my lady, shaken hands with my lord, looked in at the club, and exchanged courtly salutations with brother bigwigs, and driven away in the handsome carriage with the noble horses—admired, respecting, respectful, saluted, saluting—so that every man says, "Excellent man, Firmin. Excellent doctor, excellent man. Safe man. Sound man. Man of good family. Married a rich wife. Lucky man." And so on. After the day's triumphant career, I fancy I see the doctor driving homeward, with those sad, sad eyes, that haggard smile.

He comes whirling up Old Parr Street just as Phil saunters in from Regent Street, as usual, cigar in mouth. He flings away the cigar as he sees his father, and they enter the house together.

" Do you dine at home, Philip ? " the father asks.

" Do you, sir ? I will if you do," says the son, "and if you are alone."

" Alone. Yes. That is, there'll be Hunt, I suppose, whom you don't like. But the poor fellow has few places to dine at. What? D—— Hunt? That's a strong expression about a poor fellow in misfortune, and your father's old friend."

I am afraid Philip had used that wicked monosyllable whilst his father was speaking, and at the mention of the clergyman's detested name. " I beg your pardon, father. It slipped out in spite of me. I can't help it. I hate the fellow."

" You don't disguise your likes or dislikes, Philip," says, or rather groans, the safe man, the sound man, the prosperous man, the lucky man, the miserable man. For years and years he has known that his boy's heart has revolted from him, and detected him, and gone from him ; and with shame and remorse, and sickening feeling, he lies awake in the night-watches, and thinks how he is alone—alone in the world. Ah ! Love your parents, young ones ! O Father Beneficent ! strengthen our hearts : strengthen and purify them so that we may not have to blush before our children !

" You don't disguise your likes and dislikes, Philip," says the father then, with a tone that smites strangely and keenly on the young man.

There is a great tremor in Philip's voice, as he says, " No, father, I can't bear that man, and I can't disguise my feelings. I have just parted from the man. I have just met him."

" Where ? "

" At—at Mrs. Brandon's, father." He blushes like a girl as he speaks.

At the next moment he is scared by the execration which hisses from his father's lips, and the awful look of hate which the elder's face assumes—that fatal, forlorn, fallen, lost look which, man and—

boy, has often frightened poor Phil. Philip did not like that look, nor indeed that other one, which his father cast at Hunt, who presently swaggered in.

"What! *you* dine here? We rarely do papa the honour of dining with him," says the parson, with his knowing leer. "I suppose, doctor, it is to be fatted-calf day now the prodigal has come home. There's worse things than a good fillet of veal; eh?"

Whatever the meal might be, the greasy chaplain leered and winked over it as he gave it his sinister blessing. The two elder guests tried to be lively and gay, as Philip thought, who took such little trouble to disguise his own moods of gloom or merriment. Nothing was said regarding the occurrences of the morning when my young gentleman had been rather rude to Mr. Hunt; and Philip did not need his father's caution to make no mention of his previous meeting with their guest. Hunt, as usual, talked to the butler, made sidelong remarks to the footman, and garnished his conversation with slippery double-entendre and dirty old-world slang. Betting-houses, gambling-houses, Tattersall's fights, and their frequenters, were his cheerful themes, and on these he descanted as usual. The doctor swallowed this dose, which his friend poured out, without the least expression of disgust. On the contrary, he was cheerful: he was for an extra bottle of claret—it never could be in better order than it was now.

The bottle was scarce put on the table, and tasted and pronounced perfect, when—oh! disappointment!—the butler reappears with a note for the doctor. One of his patients. He must go. She has little the matter with her. She lives hard by, in May Fair. "You and Hunt finish this bottle, unless I am back before it is done; and if it is done, we'll have another," says Dr. Firmin, jovially. "Don't stir, Hunt"—and Dr. Firmin is gone, leaving Philip alone with the guest to whom he had certainly been rude in the morning.

"The doctor's patients often grow very unwell about claret time," growls Mr. Hunt, some few minutes after. "Never mind. The drink's good—good! as somebody said at your famous call-supper, *Mr.* Philip—won't call you Philip, as you don't like it. You were uncommon crusty to me in the morning, to be sure. In my time there would have been bottles broke, or worse, for that sort of treatment."

"I have asked your pardon," Philip said. "I was annoyed about

—no matter what—and had no right to be rude to Mrs. Brandon's guest."

"I say, did you tell the governor that you saw me in Thornhaugh Street?" asks Hunt.

"I was very rude and ill-tempered, and again I confess I was wrong," said Phil, boggling and stuttering, and turning very red. He remembered his father's injunction.

"I say again, sir, did you tell your father of our meeting this morning?" demands the clergyman.

"And pray, sir, what right have you to ask me about my private conversation with my father?" asks Philip, with towering dignity.

"You won't tell me? Then you *have* told him. He's a nice man, your father is, for a moral man."

"I am not anxious for your opinion about my father's morality, Mr. Hunt," says Philip, gasping in a bewildered manner, and drumming the table. "I am here to replace him in his absence, and treat his guest with civility."

"Civility! Pretty civility!" says the other, glaring at him.

"Such as it is, sir, it is my best, and—I—I have no other," groans the young man.

"Old friend of your father's, a university man, a Master of Arts, a gentleman born, by Jove! a clergyman—though I sink that——"

"Yes, sir, you do sink that," says Philip.

"Am I a dog," shrieks out the clergyman, "to be treated by you in this way? Who are you? Do you know who you are?"

"Sir, I am striving with all my strength to remember," says Philip.

"Come! I say! don't try any of your confounded airs on *me!*" shrieks Hunt, with a profusion of oaths, and swallowing glass after glass from the various decanters before him. "Hang me, when I was a young man, I would have sent one—two at your nob, though you were twice as tall! Who are you, to patronize your senior, your father's old pal—a university man :—you confounded, super-cilious——"

"I am here to pay every attention to my father's guest," says Phil ; "but, if you have finished your wine, I shall be happy to break up the meeting, as early as you please."

"You shall pay me ; I swear you shall," said Hunt.

"Oh, Mr. Hunt!" cried Philip, jumping up, and clenching his great fists, "I should desire nothing better."

The man shrank back, thinking Philip was going to strike him (as Philip told me in describing the scene), and made for the bell. But when the butler came, Philip only asked for coffee ; and Hunt, uttering a mad oath or two, staggered out of the room after the servant. Brice said he had been drinking before he came. He was often so. And Phil blessed his stars that he had not assaulted his father's guest then and there, under his own roof-tree.

He went out into the air. He gasped and cooled himself under the stars. He soothed his feelings by his customary consolation of tobacco. He remembered that Ridley in Thornhaugh Street held a divan that night ; and jumped into a cab, and drove to his old friend.

The maid of the house, who came to the door as the cab was driving away, stopped it ; and as Phil entered the passage, he found the Little Sister and his father talking together in the hall. The doctor's broad hat shaded his face from the hall-lamp, which was burning with an extra brightness, but Mrs. Brandon's was very pale, and she had been crying.

She gave a little scream when she saw Phil. "Ah ! is it you, dear ?" she said. She ran up to him : seized both his hands : clung to him, and sobbed a thousand hot tears on his hand. "I never—will. Oh, never, never, never !" she murmured.

The doctor's broad chest heaved as with a great·sigh of relief. He looked at the woman and at his son with a strange smile ;—not a sweet smile.

"God bless you, Caroline," he said, in his pompous, rather theatrical way.

"Good night, sir," said Mrs. Brandon, still clinging to Philip's hand, and making the doctor a little humble curtsey. And when he was gone, again she kissed Philip's hand, and dropped her tears on it, and said, " Never, my dear ; no, never, never ! "

CHAPTER XI.

IN WHICH PHILIP IS VERY ILL TEMPERED.

HILIP had long divined a part of his dear little friend's history. An uneducated young girl had been found, cajoled, deserted by a gentleman of the world. And poor Caroline was the victim, and Philip's own father the seducer. He easily guessed as much as this of the sad little story. Dr. Firmin's part in it was enough to shock his son with a thrill of disgust, and to increase the mistrust, doubt, alienation, with which the father had long inspired the son. What would Philip feel, when all the pages of that dark book were opened to him, and he came to hear of a false marriage, and a ruined and outcast woman, deserted for years by the man to whom he himself was most bound? In a word, Philip had considered this as a mere case of early libertinism, and no more; and it was as such, in the very few words which he may have uttered to me respecting this matter, that he had chosen to regard it. I knew no more than my friend had told me of the story as yet; it was only by degrees that I learned it, and as events, now subsequent, served to develop and explain it.

The elder Firmin, when questioned by his old acquaintance, and, as it appeared, accomplice of former days, regarding the end of a certain intrigue at Margate, which had occurred some four or five and twenty years back, and when Firmin, having reason to avoid his college creditors, chose to live away and bear a false name, had told the clergyman a number of falsehoods which appeared to satisfy him. What had become of that poor litttle thing about whom he had made such a fool of himself? Oh, she was dead, dead ever so many years before. He had pensioned her off. She had married, and died in Canada—yes, in Canada. Poor little thing! Yes, she was a good little thing, and, at one time, he had been very soft about her. I am sorry to have to state of a respectable gentleman that he told lies, and told lies habitually and easily. But, you see, if you commit a crime, and break a seventh commandment let us say, or an eighth, or choose any number you will—you will probably have to back the lie of action by the lie of the tongue, and so you are fairly warned, and I have no help for you. If I murder a man, and the policeman inquires, " Pray, sir, did you cut this here gentleman's throat?" I must bear false witness, you see, out of self-defence, though I may be naturally a most reliable, truth-telling man. And so with regard to many crimes which gentlemen commit—it is painful to have to say respecting gentlemen, but they become neither more nor less than habitual liars, and have to go lying on through life to you, to me, to the servants, to their wives, to their children, to —— oh, awful name! I bow and humble myself. May we kneel, may we kneel, nor strive to speak our falsehoods before Thee!

And so, my dear sir, seeing that after committing any infraction of the moral laws, you must tell lies in order to back yourself out of your scrape, let me ask you, as a man of honour and a gentleman, whether you had not better forego the crime, so as to avoid the un-avoidable, and unpleasant, and daily recurring necessity of the sub-sequent perjury? A poor young girl of the lower orders, cajoled, or ruined, more or less, is of course no great matter. The little baggage is turned out of doors—worse luck for her!—or she gets a place, or she marries one of her own class, who has not the exquisite delicacy belonging to " gentle blood"—and there is an end of her. But if you marry her privately and irregularly yourself, and then throw her off, and then marry somebody else, you are brought to book in all sorts of unpleasant ways. I am writing of quite an old story, be pleased to remember. The first part of the history I myself printed some twenty years ago ; and if you fancy I allude to any more modern period, madam, you are entirely out in your conjecture.

It must have been a most unpleasant duty for a man of fashion, honour, and good family, to lie to a poor tipsy, disreputable bankrupt merchant's daughter, such as Caroline Gann, but George Brand Firmin, Esq., M.D., had no other choice, and when he lied—as in severe cases, when he administered calomel—he thought it best to give the drug freely. Thus he lied to Hunt, saying that Mrs. Brandon was long since dead in Canada; and he lied to Caroline, prescribing for her the very same pill, as it were, and saying that Hunt was long since dead in Canada too. And I can fancy few more painful and humiliating positions for a man of rank and fashion and reputation, than to have to demean himself so far as to tell lies to a little low-bred person, who gets her bread as a nurse of the sick, and has not the proper use of her *h*'s.

"Oh, yes, Hunt!" Firmin had said to the Little Sister, in one of those sad little colloquies which sometimes took place between him and his victim, his wife of old days. "A wild, bad man, Hunt was —in days when I own I was little better! I have deeply repented since, Caroline; of nothing more than of my conduct to you; for you were worthy of a better fate, and you loved me truly—madly."

"Yes," says Caroline.

"I was wild then! I was desperate! I had ruined my fortunes, estranged my father from me, was hiding from my creditors under an assumed name—that under which I saw you. Ah, why did I ever come to your house, my poor child? The mark of the demon was upon me. I did not dare to speak of marriage before my father. You have yours, and tend him with your ever constant goodness. Do you know that my father would not see me when he died? Oh, it's a cruel thing to think of!" And the suffering creature slaps his tall forehead with his trembling hand; and some of his grief about his own father, I dare say, is sincere, for he feels the shame and remorse of being alienated from his own son.

As for the marriage—that it was a most wicked and unjustifiable deceit, he owned; but he was wild when it took place, wild with debt and with despair at his father's estrangement from him—but the fact was, it was no marriage.

"I am glad of that!" sighed the poor Little Sister.

"Why?" asked the other eagerly. His love was dead, but his vanity was still hale and well. "Did you care for somebody else, Caroline? Did you forget your George, whom you used to——"

"No!" said the little woman, bravely. "But I couldn't live with a man who behaved to any woman so dishonest as you behaved

to me.   I liked you because I thought you was a gentleman.   My
poor painter was whom you used to despise and trample to hearth—
and my dear dear Philip is, Mr. Firmin.   But gentlemen tell the
truth!   Gentlemen don't deceive poor innocent girls, and desert 'em
without a penny!"

"Caroline! I was driven by my creditors.   I——"

"Never mind.   It's over now.   I bear you no malice, Mr. Firmin, but I would not marry you, no, not to be doctor's wife to the
Queen!"

This had been the Little Sister's language when there was no
thought of the existence of Hunt, the clergyman who had celebrated
their marriage; and I don't know whether Firmin was most piqued
or pleased at the divorce which the little woman pronounced of her
own decree.   But when the ill-omened Hunt made his appearance,
doubts and terrors filled the physician's mind.   Hunt was needy,
greedy, treacherous, unscrupulous, desperate.   He could hold this
marriage over the doctor.   He could threaten, extort, expose, perhaps
invalidate Philip's legitimacy.-   The first marriage, almost certainly,
was null, but the scandal would be fatal to Firmin's reputation and
practice.   And the quarrel with his son entailed consequences not
pleasant to think of.   You see George Firmin, Esq., M.D., was a man
with a great development of the back head; when he willed a thing,
he willed it so fiercely that he *must* have it, never mind the consequences.   And so he had willed to make himself master of poor
little Caroline : and so he had willed, as a young man, to have horses,
splendid entertainments, roulette and écarté, and so forth; and the
bill came at its natural season, and George Firmin, Esq., did not
always like to pay.   But for a grand, prosperous, highly bred gentleman in the best society—with a polished forehead and manners, and
universally looked up to—to have to tell lies to a poor, little, timid,
uncomplaining, sick-room nurse, it *was* humiliating, wasn't it?   And
I can feel for Firmin.

To have to lie to Hunt was disgusting : but somehow not so
exquisitely mean and degrading as to have to cheat a little trusting,
humble, houseless creature, over the bloom of whose gentle young
life his accursed foot had already trampled.   But then this Hunt
was such a cad and ruffian that there need be no scruple about
humbugging *him;* and if Firmin had had any humour he might
have had a grim sort of pleasure in leading the dirty clergyman

a dance thoro' bush thoro' briar. So, perhaps (of course I have no means of ascertaining the fact), the doctor did not altogether dislike the duty which now devolved on him of hoodwinking his old acquaintance and accomplice. I don't like to use such a vulgar phrase regarding a man in Doctor Firmin's high social position, as to say of him and the gaol-chaplain that it was "thief catch thief;" but at any rate Hunt is such a low, graceless, friendless vagabond, that if he comes in for a few kicks, or is mystified, we need not be very sorry. When Mr. Thurtell is hung we don't put on mourning. His is a painful position for the moment; but, after all, he has murdered Mr. William Weare.

Firmin was a bold and courageous man, hot in pursuit, fierce in desire, but cool in danger, and rapid in action. Some of his great successes as a physician arose from his daring and successful practice in sudden emergency. While Hunt was only lurching about the town an aimless miscreant, living from dirty hand to dirty mouth, and as long as he could get drink, cards, and shelter, tolerably content, or at least pretty easily appeased by a guinea-dose or two— Firmin could adopt the palliative system; soothe his patient with an occasional bounty; set him to sleep with a composing draught of claret or brandy; and let the day take care of itself. He might die; he might have a fancy to go abroad again; he might be transported for forgery or some other rascaldom, Dr. Firmin would console himself; and he trusted to the chapter of accidents to get rid of his friend. But Hunt, aware that the woman was alive whom he had actually, though unlawfully married to Firmin, became an enemy whom it was necessary to subdue, to cajole, or to bribe, and the sooner the doctor put himself on his defence the better. What should the defence be? Perhaps the most effectual was a fierce attack on the enemy; perhaps it would be better to bribe him. The course to be taken would be best ascertained after a little previous reconnoitring.

"He will try and inflame Caroline," the doctor thought, "by representing her wrongs and her rights to her. He will show her that, as my wife, she has a right to my name and a share of my income. A less mercenary woman never lived than this poor little creature. She disdains money, and, except for her father's sake, would have taken none of mine. But to punish me for certainly rather shabby behaviour; to claim and take her own right and position in the world as an honest woman, may she not be induced to declare war against me, and stand by her marriage? After she left home, her two Irish half-sisters deserted her and spat upon her; and when she would have returned, the heartless women drove her from the door. Oh, the vixens! And now to drive by them in her carriage, to claim a maintenance from me, and to have a right to my honourable name, would she not have her dearest revenge over her sisters by so declaring her marriage?"

Firmin's noble mind misgave him very considerably on this point. He knew women, and how those had treated their little sister. Was it in human nature not to be revenged? These thoughts rose straightway in Firmin's mind, when he heard that the much dreaded meeting between Caroline and the chaplain had come to pass.

As he ate his dinner with his guest, his enemy, opposite to him, he was determining on his plan of action. The screen was up, and he was laying his guns behind it, so to speak. Of course he was as civil to Hunt as the tenant to his landlord when he comes with no rent. So the doctor laughed, joked, bragged, talked his best, and was thinking the while what was to be done against the danger.

He had a plan which might succeed. He must see Caroline immediately. He knew the weak point of her heart, and where she was most likely to be vulnerable. And he would act against her as barbarians of old acted against their enemies, when they brought the captive wives and children in front of the battle, and bade the foe strike through them. He knew how Caroline loved his boy. It was through that love he would work upon her. As he washes his pretty hands for dinner, and bathes his noble brow, he arranges his little plan. He orders himself to be sent for soon after the second bottle of claret—and it appears the doctor's servants were accustomed to the delivery of these messages from their master to himself. The plan arranged, now let us take our dinner and our wine, and make ourselves comfortable until the moment of action. In his wild-oats days, when travelling abroad with wild and noble companions, Firmin had fought a duel or two, and was always remarkable for his gaiety of conversation and the fine appetite which he showed at breakfast before going on to the field. So, perhaps, Hunt, had he not been stupefied by previous drink, might have taken the alarm by remarking Firmin's extra courtesy and gaiety, as they dined together. It was *nunc vinum, cras æquor*.

NURSE AND DOCTOR.

When the second bottle of claret was engaged, Dr. Firmin starts. He has an advance of half-an-hour at least on his adversary, or on the man who may be his adversary. If the Little Sister is at home, he will see her—he will lay bare his candid heart to her, and make a clean breast of it. The Little Sister was at home.

" I want to speak to you very particularly about that case of poor Lady Humandhaw," says he, dropping his voice.

" I will step out, my dear, and take a little fresh air," says Captain Gann ; meaning that he will be off to the "Admiral Byng ;" and the two are together.

" I have had something on my conscience. I have deceived you, Caroline," says the doctor, with the beautiful shining forehead and hat.

" Ah, Mr. Firmin," says she, bending over her work; "you've used me to that."

" A man whom you knew once, and who tempted me for his own selfish ends to do a very wrong thing by you—a man whom I thought dead is alive :—Tufton Hunt, who performed that—that illegal cere- mony at Margate, of which so often and often on my knees I have repented, Caroline !"

The beautiful hands are clasped, the beautiful deep voice thrills lowly through the room ; and if a tear or two can be squeezed out of the beautiful eyes, I dare say the doctor will not be sorry.

" He has been here to-day. Him and Mr. Philip was here and quarrelled. Philip has told you, I suppose, sir ?"

" Before heaven, ' on the word of a gentleman,' when I said he was dead, Caroline, I thought he was dead ! Yes, I declare, at our college, Maxwell—Dr. Maxwell—who had been at Cambridge with us, told me that our old friend Hunt had died in Canada." (This, my beloved friends and readers, may not have been the precise long bow which George Firmin, Esq., M.D., pulled ; but that he twanged a famous lie out, whenever there was occasion for the weapon, I assure you is an undoubted fact.) " Yes, Dr. Maxwell told me our old friend was dead—our old friend ? My worst enemy and yours ! But let that pass. It was he, Caroline, who led me into crimes which I have never ceased to deplore."

" Ah, Mr. Firmin," sighs the Little Sister, " since I've known you, you was big enough to take care of yourself in that way."

" I have not come to excuse myself, Caroline," says the deep sweet voice. "I have done you enough wrong, and I feel it here—at this heart. I have not come to speak about myself, but of some one I love the best of all the world—the only being I *do* love—some one you love, you good and generous soul—about Philip."

"What is it about Philip?" asks Mrs. Brandon, very quickly.

"Do you want harm to happen to him?"

"Oh, my darling boy, no!" cries the Little Sister, clasping her little hands.

"Would you keep him from harm?"

"Ah, sir, you know I would. When he had the scarlet fever, didn't I pour the drink down his poor throat, and nurse him, and tend him, as if, as if—as a mother would her own child?"

"You did, you did, you noble, noble woman; and heaven bless you for it! A father does. I am not all heartless, Caroline, as you deem me, perhaps."

"I don't think it's much merit, your loving *him*," says Caroline, resuming her sewing. And, perhaps, she thinks within herself, "What is he a-coming to?" You see she was a shrewd little person, when her passions and partialities did not overcome her reason; and she had come to the conclusion that this elegant Dr. Firmin, whom she had admired so once, was a—not altogether veracious gentleman. In fact, I heard her myself say afterwards, "La! he used to talk so fine, and slap his hand on his heart, you know; but I usedn't to believe him, no more than a man in a play." "It's not much merit your loving that boy," says Caroline, then. "But what about him, sir?"

Then Firmin explained. This man Hunt was capable of any crime for money or revenge. Seeing Caroline was alive . . .

"I s'pose you told him I was dead too, sir," says she, looking up from the work.

"Spare me, spare me! Years ago, perhaps, when I had lost sight of you, I may, perhaps, have thought . . ."

"And it's not to you, George Brandon—it's not to you," cries Caroline, starting up, and speaking with her sweet, innocent, ringing voice; "it's to kind, dear friends,—it's to my good God that I owe my life, which you had flung it away. And I paid you back by guarding your boy's dear life, I did, under—under Him who giveth and taketh. And bless His name!"

"You are a good woman, and I am a bad, sinful man, Caroline," says the other. "You saved my Philip's—our Philip's life, at the risk of your own. Now I tell you that another immense danger menaces him, and may come upon him any day as long as yonder scoundrel is alive. Suppose his character is assailed; suppose, thinking you dead, I married another?"

"Ah, George, you never thought me dead; though, perhaps, you wished it, sir. And many would have died," added the poor Little Sister.

"Look, Caroline! If I was married to you, my wife—Philip's mother—was not my wife, and he is her natural son. The property he inherits does not belong to him. The children of his grandfather's other daughter claim it, and Philip is a beggar. Philip, bred as he has been—Philip, the heir to a mother's large fortune."

"And—and his father's, too?" asks Caroline, anxiously.

"I daren't tell you—though, no, by heavens! I can trust you with everything. My own great gains have been swallowed up in speculations which have been almost all fatal. There has been a fate hanging over me, Caroline—a righteous punishment for having deserted you. I sleep with a sword over my head, which may fall and destroy me. I walk with a volcano under my feet, which may burst any day and annihilate me. And people speak of the famous Dr. Firmin, the rich Dr. Firmin, the prosperous Dr. Firmin! I shall have a title soon, I believe. I am believed to be happy, and I am alone, and the wretchedest man alive."

"Alone, are you?" said Caroline. "There was a woman once would have kept by you, only you—you flung her away. Look here, George Brandon. It's over with us. Years and years ago it lies where a little cherub was buried. But I love my Philip; and I won't hurt him, no, never, never, never!"

And as the doctor turned to go away, Caroline followed him wistfully into the hall, and it was there that Philip found them.

Caroline's tender "never, never," rang in Philip's memory as he sat at Ridley's party, amidst the artists and authors there assembled. Phil was thoughtful and silent. He did not laugh very loud. He did not praise or abuse anybody outrageously, as was the wont of that most emphatic young gentleman. He scarcely contradicted a single person; and perhaps, when Larkins said Scumble's last picture was beautiful, or Bunch, the critic of the *Connoisseur*, praised Bowman's last novel, contented himself with a scornful "Ho!" and a pull at his whiskers, by way of protest and denial. Had he been in his usual fine spirits, and enjoying his ordinary flow of talk, he would have informed Larkins and the assembled company not only that Scumble was an impostor, but that he, Larkins, was an idiot for admiring him. He would have informed Bunch that he was infatuated about that jackass Bowman, that cockney, that wretched ignoramus, who didn't know his own or any other language. He would have taken down one of Bowman's stories from the shelf, and proved the folly, imbecility, and crass ignorance of that author. (Ridley has a simple little stock of novels and poems in an old cabinet in his studio, and reads them still with much artless wonder and respect.) Or, to be sure, Phil would have asserted propositions the exact contrary of those here maintained, and declared that Bowman was a genius, and Scumble a most accomplished artist. But then, you know, somebody else must have commenced by taking the other side. Certainly a more paradoxical, and provoking, and obstinate, and contradictory disputant than Mr. Phil I never knew. I never met Dr. Johnson, who died before I came up to town ; but I do believe Phil Firmin would have stood up and argued even with *him.*

At these Thursday divans the host provided the modest and kindly refreshment, and Betsy the maid, or Virgilio the model, travelled to and fro with glasses and water. Each guest brought his own smoke, and I promise you there were such liberal contributions of the article, that the studio was full of it ; and newcomers used to be saluted by a roar of laughter as you heard, rather than saw, them entering, and choking in the fog. It was, " Holloa, Prodgers ! is that you, old boy?" and the beard of Prodgers (that famous sculptor) would presently loom through the cloud. It was, " Newcome, how goes ? " and Mr. Clive Newcome (a mediocre artist, I must own, but a famous good fellow, with an uncommonly pretty villa and pretty and rich wife at Wimbledon) would make his appearance, and be warmly greeted by our little host.   It was " Is that you, F. B. ? would you like a link, old boy, to see you through the fog ? " And the deep voice of Frederick Bayham, Esquire (the eminent critic on Art), would boom out of the tobacco-mist, and would exclaim, " A link ? I would like a drink." Ah, ghosts of youth, again ye draw near ! Old figures glimmer through the cloud. Old songs echo out of the distance. What were you saying anon about Dr. Johnson, boys? I am sure some of us must remember him. As for me, I am so old, that I might have been at Edial school—the other pupil along with little Davy Garrick and his brother.

We had a bachelor's supper in the Temple so lately that I think we must pay but a very brief visit to a smoking party in Thornhaugh Street, or the ladies will say that we are too fond of bachelor habits, and keep our friends away from their charming and amiable society. A novel must not smell of cigars much, nor should its refined and genteel page be stained with too frequent brandy-and-water. Please to imagine, then, the prattle of the artists, authors, and amateurs assembled at Ridley's divan. Fancy Jarman, the miniature painter, drinking more liquor than any man present, asking his neighbour (*sub voce*) why Ridley does not give his father (the old butler) five shillings to wait; suggesting that perhaps the old man is gone out, and is getting seven-and-sixpence elsewhere; praising Ridley's picture aloud, and sneering at it in an undertone; and when a man of rank happens to enter the room, shambling up to him and fawning on him, and cringing to him with fulsome praise and flattery. When the gentleman's back is turned, Jarman can spit epigrams at it. I hope he will never forgive Ridley, and always continue to hate him : for hate him Jarman will, as long as he is prosperous, and curse him as long as the world esteems him. Look at Pym, the incumbent of Saint Bronze hard by, coming in to join the literary and artistic assembly, and choking in his white neckcloth to the diversion of all the company who can see him ! Sixteen, eighteen, twenty men are assembled. Open the windows, or sure they will all be stifled with the smoke ! Why, it fills the whole house so, that the Little Sister has to open her parlour window on the ground-floor, and gasp for fresh air.

Phil's head and cigar are thrust out from a window above, and he lolls there, musing about his own affairs, as his smoke ascends to the skies. Young Mr. Philip Firmin is known to be wealthy, and his father gives very good parties in Old Parr Street, so Jarman sidles up to Phil and wants a little fresh air too. He enters into conversation by abusing Ridley's picture that is on the easel.

"Everybody is praising it; what do *you* think of it, Mr. Firmin ? Very queer drawing about those eyes, isn't there ?"

"Is there ?" growls Phil.

"Very loud colour."

"Oh !" says Phil.

" The composition is so clearly prigged from Raphael."

" Indeed ! "

" I beg your pardon.   I don't think you know who I am," continues the other, with a simper.

" Yes, I do," says Phil, glaring at him.   " You're a painter and your name is Mr. Envy."

" Sir ! " shrieks the painter; but he is addressing himself to the tails of Phil's coat, the superior half of Mr. Firmin's body is stretching out of the window.   Now, you may speak of a man behind his back, but not to him.   So Mr. Jarman withdraws, and addresses himself, face to face, to somebody else in the company.   I daresay he abuses that upstart, impudent, bumptious young doctor's son. Have I not owned that Philip was often very rude? and to-night he is in a specially bad humour.

As he continues to stare into the street, who is that who has just reeled up to the railings below, and is talking in at Mrs. Brandon's window?   Whose blackguard voice and laugh are those which Phil recognizes with a shudder ?   It is the voice and laugh of our friend Mr. Hunt, whom Philip left not very long since, near his father's house in Old Parr Street; and both of those familiar sounds are more vinous, more odious, more impudent than they were even two hours ago.

" Holloa ! I say ! " he calls out with a laugh and a curse.   " Pst ! Mrs. What-d'you-call-em !   Hang it !   don't shut the window.   Let a fellow in ! " and as he looks towards the upper window, where Philip's head and bust appear dark before the light, Hunt cries out, " Holloa ! what game's up now, I wonder?   Supper and ball.   Shouldn't be surprised."   And he hiccups a waltz tune, and clatters time to it with his dirty boots.

" Mrs. What-d'you-call ! Mrs. B— ! " the sot then recommences to shriek out.   " Must see you—most particular business.   Private and confidential.   Hear of something to your advantage."   And rap, rap, rap, he is now thundering at the door.   In the clatter of twenty voices few hear Hunt's noise except Philip; or, if they do, only imagine that another of Ridley's guests is arriving.

At the hall-door there is talk and altercation, and the high shriek of a well-known odious voice.   Philip moves quickly from his window, shoulders friend Jarman at the studio door, and hustling past him obtains, no doubt, more good wishes from that ingenious

artist. Philip is so rude and overbearing that I really have a mind to
depose him from his place of hero—only, you see, we are committed.
His name is on the page overhead, and we can't take it down and
put up another. The Little Sister is standing in her hall by the just
opened door, and remonstrating with Mr. Hunt, who appears to wish
to force his way in.

"Pooh! shtuff, my dear! If he's here I musht see him—particular business—get out of that!" and he reels forward and against
little Caroline's shoulder.

"Get away, you brute, you!" cries the little lady. "Go home,
Mr. Hunt; you are worse than you were this morning." She is a
resolute little woman, and puts out a firm little arm against this
odious invader. She has seen patients in hospital raging in fever:
she is not frightened by a tipsy man. "La! is it you, Mr. Philip?
Who ever will take this horrid man? He ain't fit to go upstairs
among the gentlemen; indeed he ain't."

"You said Firmin was here—and it isn't the father. It's the
cub! I want the doctor. Where's the doctor?" hiccups the
chaplain, lurching against the wall; and then he looks at Philip
with bloodshot eyes, that twinkle hate. "Who wantsh you, I shlike
to know? Had enough of you already to-day. Conceited brute.
Don't look at *me* in that sortaway! I ain't afraid of you—ain't
afraid anybody. Time was when I was a young man fight you as
soon as look at you. I say, Philip!"

"Go home, now. Do go home, there's a good man," says the
landlady.

"I say! Look here—hic—hi! Philip! On your word as a
gentleman, your father's not here? He's a sly old boots, Brummell
Firmin is—Trinity man—I'm not a Trinity man—Corpus man. I
say, Philip, give us your hand. Bear no malice. Look here—something very particular. After dinner—went into Air Street—you
know—*rouge gagne, et couleur*—cleaned out. Cleaned out, on the
honour of a gentleman and master of arts of the University of
Cambridge. So was your father—no, he went out in medicine.
I say, Philip, hand us out five sovereigns, and let's try the luck
again! What, you won't! It's mean, I say. Don't be mean."

"Oh, here's five shillings! Go and have a cab. Fetch a cab for
him, Virgilio, do!" cries the mistress of the house.

"That's not enough, my dear!" cries the chaplain, advancing

towards Mrs. Brandon, with such a leer and air, that Philip, half choked with passion, runs forward, grips Hunt by the collar, and crying out, "You filthy scoundrel! as this is not my house, I may kick you out of it!"—in another instant has run Hunt through the passage, hurled him down the steps, and sent him sprawling into the kennel.

"Row down below," says Rosebury, placidly, looking from above. "Personal conflict. Intoxicated individual—in gutter. Our impetuous friend has floored him."

Hunt, after a moment, sits up and glares at Philip. He is not hurt. Perhaps the shock has sobered him. He thinks, perhaps, Philip is going to strike again. "Hands off, BASTARD!" shrieks out the prostrate wretch.

"O Philip, Philip! He's mad, he's tipsy!" cries out the Little Sister, running into the street. She puts her arms round Philip. "Don't mind him, dear—he's mad! Policeman! The gentleman has had too much. Come in, Philip; come in!"

She took him into her little room. She was pleased with the gallantry of the boy. She liked to see him just now, standing over her enemy, courageous, victorious, her champion. "La! how savage he did look; and how brave and strong you are! But the little wretch ain't fit to stand before such as you!" And she passed her little hand down his arm, of which the muscles were all in a quiver from the recent skirmish.

"What did the scoundrel mean by calling me bastard?" said Philip, the wild blue eyes glaring round about with more than ordinary fierceness.

"Nonsense, dear! Who minds anything he says, that beast? His language is always horrid; he's not a gentleman. He had had too much this morning when he was here. What matters what he says? He won't know anything about it to-morrow. But it was kind of my Philip to rescue his poor little nurse, wasn't it? Like a novel. Come in, and let me make you some tea. Don't go to no more smoking: you have had enough. Come in and talk to me."

And, as a mother, with sweet pious face, yearns to her little children from her seat, she fondles him, she watches him; she fills her teapot from her singing kettle. She talks—talks in her homely way, and on this subject and that. It is a wonder how she prattles on, who is generally rather silent. She won't see Phil's eyes, which are following her about very strangely and fiercely. And when again he mutters, "What did he mean by . . ." "La, my dear, how cross you are!" she breaks out. "It's always so; you won't be happy without your cigar. Here's a cheroot, a beauty! Pa brought it home from the club. A China captain gave him some. You must light it at the little end. There!" And if I could draw the picture which my mind sees of her lighting Phil's cheroot for him, and smiling the while, the little innocent Delilah coaxing and wheedling this young Samson, I know it would be a pretty picture. I wish Ridley would sketch it for me.

CHAPTER XII.

DAMOCLES.

N the next morning, at an hour so early that Old Parr Street was scarce awake, and even the maids who wash the broad steps of the houses of the tailors and medical gentlemen who inhabit that region had not yet gone down on their knees before their respective doors, a ring was heard at Dr. Firmin's night-bell, and when the door was opened by the yawning attendant, a little person in a grey gown and a black bonnet made her appearance, handed a note to the servant, and said the case was most urgent and the doctor must come at once. Was not Lady Humandhaw the noble person whom we last mentioned, as the invalid about whom the doctor and the nurse had spoken a few words on the previous evening? The Little Sister, for it was she, used the very same name to the servant, who retired grumbling to waken up his master and deliver the note.

Nurse Brandon sat awhile in the great gaunt dining-room where hung the portrait of the doctor in his splendid black collar and cuffs, and contemplated this masterpiece until an invasion of housemaids drove her from the apartment, when she took refuge in that other little room to which Mrs. Firmin's portrait had been consigned.

"That's like him ever so many years and years ago," she thinks. " It is a little handsomer ; but it has his wicked look that I used to think so killing, and so did my sisters, both of them—they were ready to tear out each other's eyes for jealousy. And that's Mrs. Firmin !

Well, I suppose the painter haven't flattered her. If he have she could have been no great things, Mrs. F. couldn't." And the doctor, entering softly by the opened door and over the thick Turkey carpet, comes up to her noiselessly, and finds the Little Sister gazing at the portrait of the departed lady.

"Oh, it's you, is it? I wonder whether you treated her no better than you treated me, Dr. F. I've a notion she's not the only one. She don't look happy, poor thing," says the little lady.

"What is it, Caroline?" asks the deep-voiced doctor; "and what brings you so early?"

The Little Sister then explains to him. "Last night after he went away Hunt came, sure enough. He had been drinking. He was very rude, and Philip wouldn't bear it. Philip had a good courage of his own and a hot blood. And Philip thought Hunt was insulting her, the Little Sister. So he up with his hand and down goes Mr. Hunt on the pavement. Well, when he was down he was in a dreadful way, and he called Philip a dreadful name:"

"A name? what name?" Then Caroline told the doctor the name Mr. Hunt had used; and if Firmin's face usually looked wicked, I dare say it did not seem very angelical when he heard how this odious name had been applied to his son. "Can he do Philip a mischief?" Caroline continued. "I thought I was bound to tell his father. Look here, Dr. F., I don't want to do my dear boy a harm. But suppose what you told me last night isn't true—as I don't think you much mind!—mind—saying things as are incorrect you know, when us women are in the case. But suppose when you played the villain, thinking only to take in a poor innocent girl of sixteen, it was you who were took in, and that I was your real wife after all? There would be a punishment!"

"I should have an honest and good wife, Caroline," said the doctor, with a groan.

"This would be a punishment, not for you, but for my poor Philip," the woman goes on. "What has he done, that his honest name should be took from him—and his fortune perhaps? I have been lying broad awake all night thinking of him. Ah, George Brandon! Why, why did you come to my poor old father's house, and bring this misery down on me, and on your child unborn?"

"On myself, the worst of all," says the doctor.

"You deserve it. But it's us innocent that has had, or will have, to suffer most. O George Brandon! Think of a poor child, flung away, and left to starve and die, without even so much as knowing your real name! Think of your boy, perhaps brought to shame and poverty through your fault!"

"Do you suppose I don't often think of my wrong?" says the doctor. "That it does not cause me sleepless nights, and hours of anguish? Ah! Caroline!" and he looks in the glass; "I am not shaved, and it's very unbecoming," he thinks; that is, if I may dare to read his thoughts, as I do to report his unheard words.

"You think of your wrong now it may be found out, I dare say!" says Caroline. "Suppose this Hunt turns against you? He is desperate; mad for drink and money; has been in gaol—as he said this very night to me and my papa. He'll do or say anything. If you treat him hard, and Philip *have* treated him hard—not harder than served him right though—he'll pull the house down and himself under it; but he'll be revenged. Perhaps he drank so much last night that he may have forgot. But I fear he means mischief, and I came here to say so, and hoping that you might be kep' on your guard, Doctor F., and if you have to quarrel with him, I don't know what you ever will do, I am sure—no more than if you had to fight a chimney-sweep in the street. I have been awake all night thinking, and as soon as ever I saw the daylight, I determined I would run and tell you."

"When he called Philip that name, did the boy seem much disturbed?" asked the doctor.

"Yes; he referred to it again and again—though I tried to coax him out of it. But it was on his mind last night, and I am sure he will think of it the first thing this morning. Ah, yes, doctor! conscience will sometimes let a gentleman doze; but after discovery has come, and opened your curtains, and said, ' You desired to be called early!' there's little use in trying to sleep much. You look very much frightened, Doctor F.," the nurse continues. "You haven't such a courage as Philip has; or as you had when you were a young man, and came a leading poor girls astray. You used to be afraid of nothing then. Do you remember that fellow on board the steamboat in Scotland in our wedding-trip, and, la! I thought you was going to kill him. That poor little Lord Cinqbars told me ever so many stories then about your courage and shooting people. It wasn't very courageous, leaving a poor girl without even a name, and scarce a guinea, was it? But I ain't come to call up old stories—only to warn you. Even in old times, when he married us, and I thought he was doing a kindness, I never could abide this horrible man. In Scotland, when you was away shooting with your poor little lord, the things Hunt used to say and *look* was dreadful. I wonder how ever you, who were gentlemen, could put up with such a fellow! Ah, that was a sad honeymoon of ours! I wonder why I'm a thinking of it now? I suppose it's from having seen the picture of the other one —poor lady!"

"I have told you, Caroline, that I was so wild and desperate at that unhappy time, I was scarcely accountable for my actions. If I left you, it was because I had no other resource but flight. I was a ruined, penniless man, but for my marriage with Ellen Ringwood. You don't suppose the marriage was happy? Happy! when have I ever been happy? My lot is to be wretched, and bring wretched-ness down on those I love! On you, on my father, on my wife, on my boy—I am a doomed man. Ah, that the innocent should suffer for me!" And our friend looks askance in the glass, at the blue chin, and hollow eyes which make his guilt look the more haggard.

"I never had my lines," the Little Sister continued, "I never knew there were papers, or writings, or anything but a ring and a clergyman, when you married me. But I've heard tell that people in Scotland don't want a clergyman at all; and if they call them-selves man and wife, they are man and wife. Now, sir, Mr. and Mrs. Brandon certainly did travel together in Scotland—witness that man whom you were going to throw into the lake for being rude to your wife—and . . . . La! Don't fly out so! It wasn't me, a poor girl of sixteen, who did wrong. It was you, a man of the world, who was years and years older."

When Brandon carried off his poor little victim and wife, there had been a journey to Scotland, where Lord Cinqbars, then alive, had sporting quarters. His lordship's chaplain, Mr. Hunt, had been of the party, which fate very soon afterwards separated. Death seized on Cinqbars at Naples. Debt caused Firmin—Brandon, as he called himself then—to fly the country. The chaplain wandered from gaol to gaol. And as for poor little Caroline Brandon, I sup-pose the husband who had married her under a false name thought that to escape her, leave her, and disown her altogether was an easier and less dangerous plan than to continue relations with her. So one day, four months after their marriage, the young couple being then at Dover, Caroline's husband happened to go out for a walk. But he sent away a portmanteau by the back-door when he went out for the walk, and as Caroline was waiting for her little dinner some hours after, the porter who carried the luggage came with a little note from her dearest G. B. : and it was full of little fond expressions of regard and affection, such as gentlemen put into little notes; but dearest G. B. said the bailiffs were upon him, and one of them had arrived that morning, and he must fly : and he took half the money he had, and left half for his little Carry. And he would be back soon, and arrange matters; or tell her where to write and follow him. And she was to take care of her little health, and to write a great deal to her Georgy. And she did not know how to write very well then; but she did her best, and improved a great deal; for, indeed, she wrote a great deal, poor thing. Sheets and sheets of paper she blotted with ink and tears. And then the money was spent; and the next money; and no more came, and no more letters. And she was alone at sea, sinking, sinking, when it pleased heaven to send that friend who rescued her. It is such a sad, sad little story, that in fact I don't like dwelling on it; not caring to look upon poor innocent, trusting creatures in pain.

. . Well, then, when Caroline exclaimed, " La ! don't fly out so, Dr. Firmin !" I suppose the doctor had been crying out, and swearing fiercely, at the recollections of his friend Mr. Brandon, and at the danger which possibly hung over that gentleman. Marriage ceremonies are dangerous risks in jest or in earnest. You can't pretend to marry even a poor old bankrupt lodging-house-keeper's daughter without some risk of being brought subsequently to book. If you have a vulgar wife alive, and afterwards choose to leave her and marry an earl's niece, you will come to trouble, however well connected you are and highly placed in society. If you have had thirty thousand pounds with wife No. 2, and have to pay it back on a sudden, the payment may be inconvenient. You may be tried for bigamy, and sentenced, goodness knows to what punishment. At any rate, if the matter is made public, and you are a most respectable man, moving in the highest scientific and social circles, those circles may be disposed to request you to walk out of their circumference. —A novelist, I know, ought to have no likes, dislikes, pity, partiality

for his characters ; but I declare I cannot help feeling a respectful
compassion for a gentleman who, in consequence of a youthful, and,
I am sure, sincerely regretted folly, may be liable to lose his fortune,
his place in society, and his considerable practice. Punishment
hasn't a right to come with such a *pede claudo.* There ought to be
limitations ; and it is shabby and revengeful of Justice to present her
little bill when it has been more than twenty years owing. . . .
Having had his talk out with the Little Sister, having a long-past
crime suddenly taken down from the shelf; having a remorse long
since supposed to be dead and buried, suddenly starting up in the
most blustering, boisterous, inconvenient manner ; having a rage and
terror tearing him within ; I can fancy this most respectable physician
going about his day's work, and most sincerely sympathize with him.
Who is to heal the physician ? Is he not more sick at heart than most
of his patients that day ? He has to listen to Lady Megrim cackling
for half an hour at least, and describing her little ailments. He
has to listen, and never once to dare to say, " Confound you, old
chatterbox ! What are you prating about your ailments to me, who
am suffering real torture whilst I am smirking in your face ? " He
has to wear the inspiriting smile, to breathe the gentle joke, to
console, to whisper hope, to administer remedy ; and all day, perhaps,
he sees no one so utterly sick, so sad, so despairing, as himself.

The first person on whom he had to practise hypocrisy that day
was his own son, who chose to come to breakfast—a meal of which
son and father seldom now partook in company. " What does he
know, and what does he suspect ? " are the father's thoughts ; but a
louring gloom is on Philip's face, and the father's eyes look into the
son's, but cannot penetrate their darkness.

" Did you stay late last night, Philip ? " says papa.

" Yes, sir, rather late," answers the son.

" Pleasant party ? "

" No, sir, stupid. Your friend Mr. Hunt wanted to come in. He
was drunk, and rude to Mrs. Brandon, and I was obliged to put him
out of the door. He was dreadfully violent and abusive."

" Swore a good deal, I suppose ? "

" Fiercely, sir, and called names."

I dare say Philip's heart beat so when he said these last words,
that they were inaudible : at all events, Philip's father did not appear
to pay much attention to the words, for he was busy reading the

Morning Post, and behind that sheet of fashionable news hid whatever expression of agony there might be on his face. Philip afterwards told his present biographer of this breakfast meeting and dreary *tête-à-tête.* " I burned to ask what was the meaning of that scoundrel's words of the past night," Philip said to his biographer; " but I did. not dare, somehow. You see, Pendennis, it is not pleasant to say point-blank to your father, ' Sir, are you a confirmed scoundrel, or are you not? Is it possible that you have made a double marriage, as yonder other rascal hinted; and that my own legitimacy and my mother's fair fame, as well as poor, harmless Caroline's honour and happiness, have been destroyed by your crime?' But I had lain awake all night thinking about that scoundrel Hunt's words, and whether there was any meaning beyond drunken malice in what he said." So we find that three people had passed a bad night in consequence of Mr. Firmin's evil behaviour of five-and-twenty years back, which surely was a most unreasonable punishment for a sin of such old date. I wish dearly beloved brother sinners, we could take all the punishment for our individual crimes on our individual shoulders : but we drag them all down with us—that is the fact; and when Macheath is condemned to hang, it is Polly and Lucy who have to weep and suffer and wear piteous mourning in their hearts long after the dare-devil rogue has jumped off the Tyburn ladder.

" Well, sir, he did not say a word," said Philip, recounting the meeting to his friend; " not a word, at least, regarding the matter both of us had on our hearts. But about fashion, parties, politics, he discoursed much more freely than was usual with him. He said I might have had Lord Ringwood's seat for Whipham but for my unfortunate politics. What made a Radical of me, he asked, who was naturally one of the most haughty of men? (" and that, I think, perhaps I am," says Phil, " and a good many liberal fellows are.") I should calm down, he was sure—I should calm down, and be of the politics *des hommes du monde.*"

Philip could not say to his father, " Sir, it is seeing you cringe before great ones that has set my own back up." There were countless points about which father and son could not speak; and an invisible, unexpressed, perfectly unintelligible mistrust, always was present when those two were *tête-à-tête.*

Their meal was scarce ended when entered to them Mr. Hunt, with his hat on. I was not present at the time, and cannot speak as a certainty ; but I should think at his ominous appearance Philip may have turned red and his father pale.   " Now is the time," both, I daresay, thought ; and the doctor remembered his stormy young days of foreign gambling, intrigue, and duel, when he was put on his ground before his adversary, and bidden, at a given signal, to fire. One, two, three ! Each man's hand was armed with malice and murder.   Philip had plenty of pluck for his part, but I should think on such an occasion might be a little nervous and fluttered, whereas his father's eye was keen, and his aim rapid and steady.

" You and Philip had a difference last night, Philip tells me," said the doctor.

" Yes, and I promised he should pay me," said the clergyman.

" And I said I should desire no better," says Mr. Phil.

" He struck his senior, his father's friend—a sick man, a clergyman," gasped Hunt.

" Were you to repeat what you did last night, I should repeat what I did," said Phil.   " You insulted a good woman."

" It's a lie, sir," cries the other.

" You insulted a good woman, a lady in her own house, and I turned you out of it," said Phil.

" I say again, it is a lie, sir !" screams Hunt, with a stamp on the table.

" That you should give me the lie, or otherwise, is perfectly immaterial to me.   But whenever you insult Mrs. Brandon, or any harmless woman in my presence, I shall do my best to chastise you," cries Philip of the red moustaches, curling them with much dignity.

" You hear him, Firmin ?" says the parson.

" Faith, I do, Hunt !" says the physician ; " and I think he means what he says, too."

" Oh ! *you* take that line, do you ?" cries Hunt of the dirty hands, the dirty teeth, the dirty neckcloth.

" I take what you call that line ; and whenever a rudeness is offered to that admirable woman in my son's hearing, I shall be astonished if he does not resent it," says the doctor.   " Thank you, Philip !"

The father's resolute speech and behaviour gave Philip great momentary comfort.   Hunt's words of the night before had been occupying the young man's thoughts.   Had Firmin been criminal, he could not be so bold.

16—2

"You talk this way in presence of your son? You have been talking over the matter together before?" asks Hunt.

"We have been talking over the matter before—yes. We were engaged on it when you came into breakfast," says the doctor. "Shall we go on with the conversation where we left it off?"

"Well, do—that is, if you dare," said the clergyman, somewhat astonished.

"Philip, my dear, it is ill for a man to hide his head before his own son; but if I am to speak—and speak I must one day or the other—why not now?"

"Why at all, Firmin?" asks the clergyman, astonished at the other's rather sudden resolve.

"Why? Because I am sick and tired of you, Mr. Tufton Hunt," cries the physician, in his most lofty manner, "of you and your presence in my house; your blackguard behaviour and your rascal extortions—because you will force me to speak one day or the other—and now, Philip, if you like, shall be the day."

"Hang it, I say! Stop a bit!" cries the clergyman.

"I understand you want some more money from me."

"I did promise Jacobs I would pay him to-day, and that was what made me so sulky last night; and, perhaps, I took a little too much. You see my mind was out of order; and what's the use of telling a story that is no good to any one, Firmin—least of all to you," cries the parson, darkly.

"Because, you ruffian, I'll bear with you no, more," cries the doctor, the veins of his forehead swelling as he looks fiercely at his · dirty adversary. "In the last nine months, Philip, this man has had nine hundred pounds from me."

"The luck has been so very bad, so bad, upon my honour, now," grumbles the parson.

"To-morrow he will want more; and the next day more; and the next day more; and, in fine, I won't live with this accursed man of the sea round my neck. You shall have the story; and Mr. Hunt shall sit by and witness against his own crime and mine. I had been very wild at Cambridge, when I was a young man. I had quarrelled with my father, lived with a dissipated set, and beyond my means; and had had my debts paid so often by your grandfather, that I was afraid to ask for more. He was stern to me; I was not dutiful to him. I own my fault. Mr. Hunt can bear witness to what I say.

"I was in hiding at Margate, under a false name. You know the name."

"Yes, sir, I think I know the name," Philip said, thinking he liked his father better now than he had ever liked him in his life, and sighing, "Ah, if he had always been frank and true with me!"

"I took humble lodgings with an obscure family." [If Dr. Firmin had a prodigious idea of his own grandeur and importance, you see I cannot help it—and he was long held to be such a respectable man.] "And there I found a young girl—one of the most innocent beings that ever a man played with and betrayed. Betrayed, I own it, heaven forgive me! The crime has been the shame of my life,— and darkened my whole career with misery. I got a man worse than myself, if that could be. I got Hunt for a few pounds, which he owed me, to make a sham marriage between me and poor Caroline. My money was soon gone. My creditors were after me. I fled the country, and I left her."

"A sham marriage! a sham marriage!" cries the clergyman. "Didn't you make me perform it by holding a pistol to my throat? A fellow won't risk transportation for nothing. But I owed him money for cards, and he had my bill, and he said he would let me off, and that's why I helped him. Never mind. I am out of the business now, Mr. Brummell Firmin, and you are in it. I have read the Act, sir. The clergyman who performs the marriage is liable to punishment, if informed against within three years, and it's twenty years or more. But you, Mr. Brummell Firmin,—your case is different; and you, my young gentleman, with the fiery whiskers, who strike down old men of a night,—you may find some of us know how to revenge ourselves, though we are down." And with this, Hunt rushed to his greasy hat, and quitted the house, discharging imprecations at his hosts as he passed through the hall.

Son and father sat awhile silent, after the departure of their common enemy. At last the father spoke.

"This is the sword that has always been hanging over my head, and it is now falling, Philip."

"What can the man do? Is the first marriage a good marriage?" asked Philip, with alarmed face.

"It is no marriage. It is void to all intents and purposes. You may suppose I have taken care to learn the law about that. Your legitimacy is safe, sure enough. But that man can ruin me, or nearly so. He will try to-morrow, if not to-day. As long as you or I can give him a guinea, he will take it to the gambling-house. I had the mania on me myself once. My poor father quarrelled with me in consequence, and died without seeing me. I married your mother—heaven help her, poor soul ! and forgive me for being but a harsh husband to her—with a view of mending my shattered fortunes. I wished she had been more happy, poor thing. But do not blame me utterly, Philip. I was desperate, and she wished for the marriage so much ! I had good looks and high spirits in those days. People said so." [And here he glances obliquely at his own handsome portrait.] "Now I am a wreck, a wreck ! "

"I conceive, sir, that this will annoy you ; but how can it ruin you ? " asked Philip.

"What becomes of my practice as a family physician ? The practice is not now what it was, between ourselves, Philip, and the expenses greater than you imagine. I have made unlucky speculations. If you count upon much increase of wealth from me, my boy, you will be disappointed ; though you were never mercenary, no, never. But the story bruited about by this rascal, of a physician of eminence engaged in two marriages, do you suppose my rivals won't hear it, and take advantage of it—my patients hear it, and avoid me ? "

" Make terms with the man at once, then, sir, and silence him."

"To make terms with a gambler is impossible. My purse is always there open for him to thrust his hand into when he loses. No man can withstand such a temptation. I am glad you have never fallen into it. I have quarrelled with you sometimes for living with people below your rank : perhaps you were right, and I was wrong. I have liked, always did, I don't disguise it, to live with persons of station. And these, when I was at the University, taught me play and extravagance ; and in the world haven't helped me much. Who would ? Who would ? " and the doctor relapsed into meditation.

A little catastrophe presently occurred, after which Mr. Philip Firmin told me the substance of this story. He described his father's long acquiescence in Hunt's demands, and sudden resistance to them, and was at a loss to account for the change. I did not tell my friend in express terms, but I fancied I could account for the change of behaviour. Dr. Firmin, in his interviews with Caroline, had had his mind set at rest about one part of his danger. The doctor need no longer fear the charge of a double marriage. The Little Sister resigned her claims past, present, future.

If a gentleman is sentenced to be hung, I wonder is it a matter of comfort to him or not to know beforehand the day of the operation? Hunt would take his revenge. When and how? Dr. Firmin asked himself. Nay, possibly, you will have to learn that this eminent practitioner walked about with more than danger hanging imminent over him. Perhaps it was a rope: perhaps it was a sword: some weapon of execution, at any rate, as we frequently may see. A day passes: no assassin darts at the doctor as he threads the dim opera-colonnade passage on his way to his club. A week goes by: no stiletto is plunged into his well-wadded breast as he steps from his carriage at some noble patient's door. Philip says he never knew his father more pleasant, easy, good-humoured, and affable than during this period, when he must have felt that a danger was hanging over him of which his son at this time had no idea. I dined in Old Parr Street once in this memorable period (memorable it seemed to me from immediately subsequent events). Never was the dinner better served: the wine more excellent: the guests and conversation more gravely respectable than at this entertainment; and my neighbour remarked with pleasure how the father and son seemed to be on much better terms than ordinary. The doctor addressed Philip pointedly once or twice; alluded to his foreign travels, spoke of his mother's family—it was most gratifying to see the pair together. Day after day passes so. The enemy has disappeared. At least, the lining of his dirty hat is no longer visible on the broad marble table of Dr. Firmin's hall.

But one day—it may be ten days after the quarrel—a little messenger comes to Philip, and says, " Philip dear, I am sure there is something wrong; that horrible Hunt has been here with a very quiet, soft-spoken old gentleman, and they have been going on with my poor pa about my wrongs and his—his, indeed!—and they have worked him up to believe that somebody has cheated his daughter out of a great fortune; and who can that somebody be but your father? And whenever they see me coming, papa and that horrid Hunt go off to the ' Admiral Byng:' and one night when pa came home he said, ' Bless you, bless you, my poor, innocent, injured child; and blessed you *will* be, mark a fond father's words!' They are scheming something against Philip and Philip's father. Mr. Bond

the soft-spoken old gentleman's name is : and twice there has been a
Mr. Walls to inquire if Mr. Hunt was at our house."

"Mr. Bond?—Mr. Walls?—A gentleman of the name of Bond
was uncle Twysden's attorney.   An old gentleman, with a bald head,
and one eye bigger than the other?"

"Well, this old man has one smaller than the other, I do think,"
says Caroline.   "First man who came was Mr. Walls—a rattling
young fashionable chap, always laughing, talking about theatres,
operas, every thing—came home from the 'Byng' along with pa
and his new friend—oh! I do hate him, that man, that Hunt!—
then he brought the old man, this Mr. Bond.   What are they
scheming against you, Philip?   I tell you this matter is all about
you and your father."

Years and years ago, in the poor mother's lifetime, Philip
remembered an outbreak of wrath on his father's part, who called
uncle Twysden a swindling miser, and this very Mr. Bond a scoundrel
who deserved to be hung, for interfering in some way in the management of a part of the property which Mrs. Twysden and her sister
inherited from their own mother.   That quarrel had been made up,
as such quarrels are.   The brothers-in-law had continued to mistrust
each other ; but there was no reason why the feud should descend to
the children ; and Philip and his aunt, and one of her daughters at
least, were on good terms together.   Philip's uncle's lawyers engaged
with his father's debtor and enemy against Dr. Firmin : the alliance
boded no good.

"I won't tell you what I think, Philip," said the father.   "You
are fond of your cousin?"

"Oh! for ev——"

"For ever, of course!   At least until we change our mind, or
one of us grows tired, or finds a better mate."

"Ah, sir!" cries Philip, but suddenly stops in his remonstrance.

"What were you going to say, Philip, and why do you pause?"

"I was going to say, father, if I might without offending, that I
think you judge hardly of women.   I know two who have been very
faithful to you."

"And I a traitor to both of them.   Yes ; and my remorse, Philip,
my remorse!" says his father in his deepest tragedy voice, clutching
his hand over a heart that I believe beat very coolly.   But, psha!
why am I, Philip's biographer, going out of the way to abuse Philip's

papa? Is not the threat of bigamy and exposure enough to disturb any man's equanimity? I say again, suppose there is another sword —a rope, if you will so call it—hanging over the head of our Damocles of Old Parr Street? . . . . Howbeit, the father and the son met and parted in these days with unusual gentleness and cordiality. And these were the last days in which they were to meet together. Nor could Philip recall without satisfaction, afterwards, that the hand which he took was pressed and given with a real kindness and cordiality.

Why were these the last days son and father were to pass together? Dr. Firmin is still alive. Philip is a very tolerably prosperous gentleman. He and his father parted good friends, and it is the biographer's business to narrate how and wherefore. When Philip told his father that Messrs. Bond and Selby, his uncle Twysden's attorneys, were suddenly interested about Mr. Brandon and his affairs, the father instantly guessed, though the son was too simple as yet to understand, how it was that these gentlemen interfered. If Mr. Brandon-Firmin's marriage with Miss Ringwood was null, her son was illegitimate, and her fortune went to her sister. Painful as such a duty might be to such tender-hearted people as our Twysden acquaintances to deprive a dear nephew of his fortune, yet, after all, duty is duty, and a parent must sacrifice everything for justice and his own children. "Had I been in such a case," Talbot Twysden subsequently and repeatedly declared, "I should never have been easy a moment if I thought I possessed wrongfully a beloved nephew's property. I could not have slept in peace ; I could not have shown my face at my own club, or to my own conscience, had I the weight of such an injustice on my mind." In a word, when he found that there was a chance of annexing Philip's share of the property to his own, Twysden saw clearly that his duty was to stand by his own wife and children.

The information upon which Talbot Twysden, Esq., acted, was brought to him at his office by a gentleman in dingy black, who, after a long interview with him, accompanied him to his lawyer, Mr. Bond, before mentioned. Here, in South Square, Gray's Inn, the three gentlemen held a consultation, of which the results began quickly to show themselves. Messrs. Bond and Selby had an exceedingly lively, cheerful, jovial, and intelligent confidential clerk, who combined business and pleasure with the utmost affability, and was acquainted with a thousand queer things, and queer histories about queer people in this town ; who lent money ; who wanted money ; who was in debt : and who was outrunning the constable ; whose diamonds were in pawn ; whose estates were over-mortgaged ; who was over-building himself ; who was casting eyes of longing at what pretty opera dancer—about races, fights, bill brokers, *quicquid agunt homines.* This Tom Walls had a deal of information, and imparted it so as to make you die of laughing.

The Reverend Tufton Hunt brought this jolly fellow first to the "Admiral Byng," where his amiability won all hearts at the club. At the "Byng" it was not very difficult to gain Captain Gann's easy confidence. And this old man was, in the course of a very trifling consumption of rum-and-water, brought to see that his daughter had been the object of a wicked conspiracy, and was the rightful and most injured wife of a man who ought to declare her fair fame before the world, and put her in possession of a portion of his great fortune.

A great fortune ? How great a fortune ? Was it three hundred thousand, say ? Those doctors, many of them, had fifteen thousand a-year. Mr. Walls (who perhaps knew better) was not at liberty to say what the fortune was : but it was a shame that Mrs. Brandon was kept out of her rights, that was clear.

Old Gann's excitement, when this matter was first broached to him (under vows of profound secrecy) was so intense that his old reason tottered on its rickety old throne. He well nigh burst with longing to speak upon this mystery. Mr. and Mrs. Oves, the esteemed landlord and lady of the "Byng," never saw him so excited. He had a great opinion of the judgment of his friend, Mr. Ridley ; in fact, he must have gone to Bedlam, unless he had talked to somebody on this most nefarious transaction, which might make the blood of every Briton curdle with horror—as he was free to say.

Old Mr. Ridley was of a much cooler temperament, and altogether a more cautious person. The doctor rich ? He wished to tell no secrets, nor to meddle in no gentleman's affairs : but he have heard very different statements regarding Dr. Firmin's affairs.

When dark hints about treason, wicked desertion, rights denied, "and a great fortune which you are kep' out of, my poor Caroline, by a rascally wolf in sheep's clothing, you are ; and I always mistrusted him, from the moment I saw him, and said to your mother,

‛Emily, that Brandon is a bad fellow, Brandon is;' and bitterly, bitterly I've rued ever receiving him under my roof." When speeches of this nature were made to Mrs. Caroline, strange to say, the little lady made light of them. "Oh, nonsense, Pa! Don't be bringing that sad old story up again. I have suffered enough from it already. If Mr. F. left me, he wasn't the only one who flung me away; and I have been able to live, thank mercy, through it all."

This was a hard hit, and not to be parried. The truth is, that when poor Caroline, deserted by her husband, had come back, in wretchedness, to her father's door, the man, and the wife who then ruled him, had thought fit to thrust her away. And she had forgiven them: and had been enabled to heap a rare quantity of coals on that old gentleman's head.

When the Captain remarked his daughter's indifference and unwillingness to reopen this painful question of her sham marriage with Firmin, his wrath was moved, and his suspicion excited. ". Ha!" says he, "have this man been a tampering with you again?"

"Nonsense, Pa!" once more says Caroline. "I tell you, it is this fine-talking lawyers' clerk has been tampering with *you*. You're made a tool of, Pa! and you've been made a tool of all your life!"

"Well, now, upon my honour, my good madam," interposes Mr. Walls.

"Don't talk to me, sir! I don't want any lawyers' clerks to meddle in my business!" cries Mrs. Brandon, very briskly. "I don't know what you're come about. I don't want to know, and I'm most certain it is for no good."

I suppose it was the ill success of his ambassador that brought Mr. Bond himself to Thornhaugh Street; and a more kind, fatherly, little man never looked than Mr. Bond, although he may have had one eye smaller than the other. "What is this, my dear madam, I hear from my confidential clerk, Mr. Walls?" he asked of the Little Sister. "You refuse to give him your confidence because he is only a clerk? I wonder whether you will accord it to me as a principal?"

"She may, sir, she may—every confidence!" says the Captain, laying his hand on that snuffy satin waistcoat which all his friends so long admired on him. "She *might* have spoken to Mr. Walls."

"Mr. Walls is not a family man. I am. I have children at

home, Mrs. Brandon, as old as you are," says the benevolent Bond.
" I would have justice done them, and for you too."

" You're very good to take so much trouble about me all of a
sudden, to be sure," says Mrs. Brandon, demurely.   " I suppose you
don't do it for nothing."

" I should not require much fee to help a good woman to her
rights ; and a lady I don't think needs much persuasion to be helped
to her advantage," remarks Mr. Bond.

" That depends who the helper is."

" Well, if I can do you no harm, and help you possibly to a name,
to a fortune, to a high place in the world, I don't think you need be
frightened.   I don't look very wicked or very artful, do I ? "

" Many is that don't look so.   I've learned as much as that about
you gentlemen," remarks Mrs. Brandon.

" You have been wronged by one man, and doubt all."

" Not all.   Some, sir ! "

" Doubt about me if I can by any possibility injure you.   But
how and why should I ?   Your good father knows what has brought
me here.   I have no secret from him.   Have I, Mr. Gann, or Captain
Gann, as I have heard you addressed ? "

" Mr., sir—plain Mr.—No, sir ; your conduct have been most
open, honourable, and like a gentleman.   Neither would you, sir, do
aught to disparage Mrs. Brandon ; neither would I, her father.   No
ways, I think, would a parent do harm to his own child.   May I offer
you any refreshment, sir ? " and a shaky, a dingy, but a hospitable
hand, is laid upon the glossy cupboard, in which Mrs. Brandon keeps
her modest little store of strong waters.

" Not one drop, thank you !   You trust me, I think, more than
Mrs. Firm — I   beg   your   pardon — Mrs.   Brandon,   is   disposed
to do."

At the utterance of that monosyllable *Firm* Caroline became so
white, and trembled so, that her interlocutor stopped, rather alarmed
at the effect of his word—his word !—his syllable of a word.

The old lawyer recovered himself with much grace.

" Pardon me, madam," he said ; " I know your wrongs ; I know
your most melancholy history ; I know your name, and was going to
use it, but it seemed to renew painful recollections to you, which I
would not needlessly recall."

Captain Gann took out a snuffy pocket-handkerchief, wiped two red eyes and a shirt-front, and winked at the attorney, and gasped in a pathetic manner.

"You know my story and name, sir, who are a stranger to me. Have you told this old gentleman all about me and my affairs, pa?" asks Caroline, with some asperity. "Have you told him that my ma never gave me a word of kindness—that I toiled for you and her like a servant—and when I came back to you, after being deceived and deserted, that you and ma shut the door in my face? You did! you did! I forgive you; but a hundred thousand billion years can't mend that injury, father, while you broke a poor child's heart with it that day! My pa has told you all this, Mr. What's-your-name? I'm s'prized he didn't find something pleasanter to talk about, I'm sure!"

"My love!" interposed the captain.

"Pretty love! to go and tell a stranger in a public-house, and ever so many there besides, I suppose, your daughter's misfortunes, pa. Pretty love! That's what I've had from you!"

"Not a soul, on the honour of a gentleman, except me and Mr. Walls."

"Then what do you come to talk about me at all for? and what scheme on *hearth* are you driving at? and what brings this old man here?" cries the landlady of Thornhaugh Street, stamping her foot.

"Shall I tell you frankly, my good lady? I called you Mrs. Firmin now, because, on my honour and word, I believe such to be your rightful name—because you are the lawful wife of George Brand Firmin. If such be your lawful name, others bear it who have no right to bear it—and inherit property to which they can lay no just claim. In the year 1827, you, Caroline Gann, a child of sixteen, were married by a clergyman whom you know, to George Brand Firmin, calling himself George Brandon. He was guilty of deceiving you; but you were guilty of no deceit. He was a hardened and wily man; but you were an innocent child out of a schoolroom. And though he thought the marriage was not binding upon him, binding it is by Act of Parliament and judges' decision; and you are as assuredly George Firmin's wife, madam, as Mrs. Bond is mine!"

"You have been cruelly injured, Caroline," says the Captain, wagging his old nose over his handkerchief.

Caroline seemed to be very well versed in the law of the transaction. " You mean, sir," she said slowly, " that if me and. Mr. Brandon was married to each other, he knowing that he was only playing at marriage, and me believing that it was all for good, we are really married."

" Undoubtedly you are, madam—my client has—that is, I have had advice on the point."

" But if we both knew that it was—was only a sort of a marriage —an irregular marriage, you know ? "

" Then the Act says that to all intents and purposes the marriage is null and void."

" But you didn't know, my poor innocent child !" cries Mr. Gann. " How should you ? How old was you ? She was a child in the nursery, Mr. Bond, when the villain inveigled her away from her poor old father. *She* knew nothing of irregular marriages."

"Of course she didn't, the poor creature," cries the old gentle. man, rubbing his hands together with perfect good-humour. " Poor young thing, poor young thing ! "

As he was speaking, Caroline, very pale and still, was sitting looking at Ridley's sketch of Philip, which hung in her little room. Presently she turned round on the attorney, folding her little hands over her work.

" Mr. Bond," she said, " girls, though they may be ever so young, know more than some folks fancy. I was more than sixteen when that—that business happened. I wasn't happy at home, and eager to get away. I knew that a gentleman of his rank wouldn't be likely really to marry a poor Cinderella out of a lodging-house, like me. If the truth must be told, I—I knew it was no marriage—never thought it was a marriage—not for good, you know."

And she folds her little hands together as she utters the words, and I dare say once more looks at Philip's portrait.

" Gracious goodness, madam, you must be under some error !" cries the attorney. " How should a child like you know that the marriage was irregular ? "

" Because I had no lines !" cries Caroline quickly. " Never asked for none ! And our maid we had then said to me, ' Miss Carry, where's your lines ? And it's no good without.' And I knew it wasn't ! And I'm ready to go before the Lord Chancellor to-morrow and say so!" cries Caroline, to the bewilderment of her father and her cross-examinant.

"Pause, pause! my good madam!" exclaims the meek old gentleman, rising from his chair.

"Go and tell this to them as sent you, sir!" cries Caroline, very imperiously, leaving the lawyer amazed, and her father's face in a bewilderment, over which we will fling his snuffy old pocket-hand-kerchief.

"If such is unfortunately the case—if you actually mean to abide by this astonishing confession—which deprives you of a high place in society—and—and casts down the hope we had formed of redressing your injured reputation—I have nothing for it! I take my leave, madam! Good morning, Mr. Hum!—Mr. Gann!" And the old lawyer walks out of the Little Sister's room.

"She won't own to the marriage! She is fond of some one else —the little suicide!" thinks the old lawyer, as he clatters down the street to a neighbouring house, where his anxious principal was in waiting. "She's fond of some one else!"

Yes. But the some one else whom Caroline loved was Brand Firmin's son: and it was to save Philip from ruin that the poor Little Sister chose to forget her marriage to his father.

CHAPTER XIII.

LOVE ME LOVE MY DOG.

HILST the battle is raging, the old folks and ladies peep over the battlements, to watch the turns of the combat, and the behaviour of the knights. To princesses in old days, whose lovely hands were to be bestowed upon the conqueror, it must have been a matter of no small interest to know whether the slim young champion with the lovely eyes on the milk-white steed should vanquish, or the dumpy, elderly, square-shouldered, squinting, carroty whiskerando of a warrior who was laying about him so savagely ; and so in this battle, on the issue of which depended the keeping or losing of poor Philip's inheritance, there were several non-combatants deeply interested. [Or suppose we withdraw the chivalrous simile (as in fact the conduct and views of certain parties engaged in the matter were anything but what we call chivalrous), and imagine a wily old monkey who engages a cat to take certain chesnuts out of the fire, and pussy putting her paw through the bars, seizing the nut and then dropping it? Jacko is disappointed and angry, shows his sharp teeth, and bites if he dares. When the attorney went down to do battle for Philip's patrimony, some of those who wanted it were spectators of the fight, and lurking up a tree hard by. When Mr. Bond came forward to try and seize Phil's chesnuts, there was a wily old monkey who thrust the cat's paw out, and proposed to gobble up the smoking prize.

If you have ever been at the "Admiral Byng," you know, my dear madam, that the parlour where the club meets is just behind Mrs. Oves's bar, so that by lifting up the sash of the window which communicates between the two apartments, that good-natured woman may put her face into the club-room, and actually be one of the society. Sometimes for company, old Mr. Ridley goes and sits with Mrs. O—— in her bar, and reads the paper there. He is slow at his reading. The long words puzzle the worthy gentleman. As he has plenty of time to spare, he does not grudge it to the study of his paper.

On the day when Mr. Bond went to persuade Mrs. Brandon in Thornhaugh Street to claim Dr. Firmin for her husband, and to disinherit poor Philip, a little gentleman wrapt most solemnly and mysteriously in a great cloak appeared at the bar of the "Admiral Byng," and said in an aristocratic manner, "You have a parlour, show me to it." And being introduced to the parlour, (where there are fine pictures of Oves, Mrs. O——, and "Spotty-nose," their favourite defunct bull-dog,) sat down and called for a glass of sherry and a newspaper.

The civil and intelligent potboy of the "Byng" took the party *The Advertiser* of yesterday (which to-day's paper was in 'and) and when the gentleman began to swear over the old paper, Frederic gave it as his opinion to his mistress that the new comer was a harbitrary gent,—as, indeed, he was, with the omission, perhaps, of a single letter ; a man who bullied everybody who would submit to be bullied. In fact, it was our friend Talbot Twysden, Esq., Commissioner of the Powder and Pomatum Office ; and I leave those who know him to say whether *he* is arbitrary or not.

To him presently came that bland old gentleman, Mr. Bond, who also asked for a parlour and some sherry and water ; and this is how Philip and his veracious and astute biographer came to know for a certainty that dear uncle Talbot was the person who wished to—to have Philip's chesnuts.

Mr. Bond and Mr. Twysden had been scarcely a minute together, when such a storm of imprecations came clattering through the glass-window which communicates with Mrs. Oves's bar, that I dare say they made the jugs and tumblers clatter on the shelves, and Mr. Ridley, a very modest-spoken man, reading his paper, lay it down with a scared face, and say—"Well, I never." Nor did he often, I dare to say.

This volley was fired by Talbot Twysden, in consequence of his rage at the news which Mr. Bond brought him.

"Well, Mr. Bond; well, Mr. Bond!   What does she say?" he asked of his emissary.

"She will have nothing to do with the business, Mr. Twysden. We can't touch it; and I don't see how we can move her.   She denies the marriage as much as Firmin does : says she knew it was a mere sham when the ceremony was performed."

"Sir, you didn't bribe her enough," shrieked Mr. Twysden. "You have bungled this business; by George you have, sir."

"Go and do it yourself, sir, if you are not ashamed to appear in it," says the lawyer.   "You don't suppose I did it because I liked it; or want to take that poor young fellow's inheritance from him, as you do."

"I wish justice and the law, sir.   If I were wrongfully detaining his property I would give it up.   I would be the first to give it up. I desire justice and law, and employ you because you are a law agent.   Are you not?"

"And I have been on your errand, and shall send in my bill in due time ; and there will be an end of my connection with you as your law agent, Mr. Twysden," cried the old lawyer.

"You know, sir, how badly Firmin acted to me in the last matter."

"Faith, sir, if you ask my opinion as a law agent, I don't think there was much to choose between you.   How much is the sherry-and-water?—keep the change.   Sorry I'd no better news to bring you, Mr. T., and as you are dissatisfied, again recommend you to employ another law agent."

"My good sir, I——"

"My good sir, I have had other dealings with your family, and am no more going to put up with your highti-tightiness than I would with Lord Ringwood's when I was one of *his* law agents.   I am not going to tell Mr. Philip Firmin that his uncle and aunt propose to ease him of his property; but if anybody else does—that good little Mrs. Brandon—or that old goose Mr. What-d'ye-call-um, her father—I don't suppose he will be over well pleased.   I am speaking as a gentleman now, not as a law agent.   You and your nephew had each a half share of Mr. Philip Firmin's grandfather's property, and you wanted it all, that's the truth, and set a law agent to get it for you ; and swore at him because he could not get it from its right owner. And so, sir, I wish you a good morning, and recommend you to take your papers to some other agent, Mr. Twysden." And with this, *exit* Mr. Bond. And now, I ask you, if that secret could be kept which was known through a trembling glass-door to Mrs. Oves of the "Admiral Byng," and to Mr. Ridley the father of J. J., and the obsequious husband of Mrs. Ridley? On that very afternoon, at tea-time, Mrs. Ridley was made acquainted by her husband (in his noble and circumlocutory manner) with the conversation which he had overheard. It was agreed that an embassy should be sent to J. J. on the business, and his advice taken regarding it; and J. J.'s opinion was that the conversation certainly should be reported to Mr. Philip Firmin, who might afterwards act upon it as he should think best.

What? His own aunt, cousins, and uncle agreed in a scheme to overthrow his legitimacy, and deprive him of his grandfather's inheritance? It seemed impossible. Big with the tremendous news, Philip came to his adviser, Mr. Pendennis, of the Temple, and told him what had occurred on the part of father, uncle, and Little Sister. Her abnegation had been so noble, that you may be sure Philip appreciated it; and a tie of friendship was formed between the young man and the little lady even more close and tender than that which had bound them previously. But the Twysdens, his kinsfolk, to employ a lawyer in order to rob him of his inheritance!—Oh, it was dastardly! Philip bawled, and stamped, and thumped his sense of the wrong in his usual energetic manner. As for his cousin Ringwood Twysden, Phil had often entertained a strong desire to wring his neck and pitch him downstairs. "As for Uncle Talbot: that he is an old pump, that he is a pompous old humbug, and the queerest old sycophant, I grant you; but I couldn't have believed him guilty of this. And as for the girls—oh, Mrs. Pendennis, you who are good, you who are kind, although you hate them, I know you do—you can't say, you won't say, that they were in the conspiracy?"

"But suppose Twysden was asking only for what he conceives to be his rights?" asked Mr. Pendennis. "Had your father been married to Mrs. Brandon, you would not have been Dr. Firmin's legitimate son. Had you not been his legitimate son, you had no right to a half-share of your grandfather's property. Uncle Talbot acts only the part of honour and justice in the transaction. He is Brutus, and he orders you off to death, with a bleeding heart."

"And he orders his family out of the way," roars Phil, "so that they mayn't be pained by seeing the execution! I see it all now. I wish somebody would send a knife through me at once, and put an end to me. I see it all now. Do you know that for the last week I have been to Beaunash Street, and found nobody? Agnes had the bronchitis, and her mother was attending to her; Blanche came for a minute or two, and was as cool—as cool as I have seen Lady Iceberg be cool to her. Then they must go away for change of air. They have been gone these three days: whilst Uncle Talbot and that viper of a Ringwood have been closeted with their nice new friend, Mr. Hunt. Oh, conf——! I beg your pardon, ma'am; but I know you always allow for the energy of my language."

" I should like to see that Little Sister, Mr. Firmin. She has not been selfish, or had any scheme but for your good," remarks my wife.

"A little angel who drops her h's—a little heart, so good and tender that I melt as I think of it," says Philip, drawing his big hand over his eyes. "What have men done to get the love of some women? We don't earn it ; we don't deserve it, perhaps. We don't return it. They bestow it on us. I have given nothing back for all this love and kindness, but I look a little like my father of old days, for whom—for whom she had an attachment. And see now how she would die to serve me ! You are wonderful, women are ! your fidelities and your ficklenesses alike marvellous. What can any woman have found to adore in the doctor? Do you think my father could ever have been adorable, Mrs. Pendennis? And yet I have heard my poor mother say she was obliged to marry him. She knew it was a bad match, but she couldn't resist it. In what was my father so irresistible? He is not to *my* taste. Between ourselves, I think he is a——well, never mind what."

" I think we had best not mind what? " says my wife with a smile.

" Quite right—quite right ; only I blurt out everything that is on my mind. Can't keep it in," cries Phil, gnawing his mustachios. " If my fortune depended on my silence I should be a beggar, that's the fact. And, you see, if you had such a father as mine, you yourself would find it rather difficult to hold your tongue about him. But now, tell me: this ordering away of the girls and Aunt Twysden, whilst the little attack upon my property is being carried on—isn't it queer? "

" The question is at an end," said Mr. Pendennis. " You are restored to your *atavis regibus* and ancestral honours. Now that Uncle Twysden can't get the property without you ; have courage, my boy—he may take it, along with the encumbrance."

Poor Phil had not known—but some of us, who are pretty clear-sighted when our noble selves are not concerned, had perceived that Philip's dear aunt was playing fast and loose with the lad, and when his back was turned was encouraging a richer suitor for her daughter.

Hand on heart I can say of my wife, that she meddles with her neighbours as little as any person I ever knew ; but when treacheries in love affairs are in question, she fires up at once, and would persecute to death almost the heartless male or female criminal who would break love's sacred laws. The idea of a man or woman trifling with that holy compact awakens in her a flame of indignation. In curtain confidences (of which let me not vulgarise the arcana) she had given me her mind about some of Miss Twysden's behaviour with that odious blackamoor, as she chose to call Captain Woolcomb, who, I own, had a very slight tinge of complexion ; and when, quoting the words of Hamlet regarding his father and mother, I asked, " Could she on this fair mountain leave to feed, and batten on this Moor ? " Mrs. Pendennis cried out that this matter was all too serious for jest, and wondered how her husband could make word plays about it. Perhaps she has not the exquisite sense of humour possessed by some folks ; or is it that she has more reverence ? In her creed, if not in her church, marriage is a sacrament, and the fond believer never speaks of it without awe.

Now, as she expects both parties to the marriage engagement to keep that compact holy, she no more understands trifling with it than she could comprehend laughing and joking in a church. She has no patience with flirtations as they are called. " Don't tell me, sir," says the enthusiast, " a light word between a man and a married woman ought not to be permitted." And this is why she is harder on the woman than the man, in cases where such dismal matters happen to fall under discussion. A look, a word from a woman, she says, will check a libertine thought or word in a man ; and these cases might be stopped at once if the woman but showed the slightest resolution. She is thus more angry (I am only mentioning the peculiarities, not defending the ethics of this individual moralist)—

she is, I say, more angrily disposed towards the woman than the man in such delicate cases; and, I am afraid, considers that women are for the most part only victims because they choose to be so.

Now, we had happened during this season to be at several entertainments, routs, and so forth, where poor Phil, owing to his unhappy Bohemian preferences and love of tobacco, &c., was not present—and where we saw Miss Agnes Twysden carrying on such a game with the tawny Woolcomb as set Mrs. Laura in a tremor of indignation. What though Agnes's blue-eyed mamma sat near her blue-eyed daughter and kept her keen clear orbs perfectly wide open and cognizant of all that happened? So much the worse for her, the worse for both. It was a shame and a sin that a Christian English mother should suffer her daughter to deal lightly with the most holy, the most awful of human contracts; should be preparing her child who knows for what after misery of mind and soul. Three months ago, you saw how she encouraged poor Philip, and now see her with this mulatto!

"Is he not a man, and a brother, my dear?" perhaps at this Mr. Pendennis interposes.

"Oh, for shame, Pen, no levity on this—no sneers and laughter on this the most sacred subject of all." And here, I dare say the woman falls to caressing her own children and hugging them to her heart as her manner was when moved. *Que voulez vous?* There are some women in the world to whom love and truth are all in all here below. Other ladies there are who see the benefit of a good jointure, a town and country house, and so forth, and who are not so very particular as to the character, intellect, or complexion of gentlemen who are in a position to offer their dear girls these benefits. In fine, I say, that regarding this blue-eyed mother and daughter, Mrs. Laura Pendennis was in such a state of mind that she was ready to tear their blue eyes out.

Nay, it was with no little difficulty that Mrs. Laura could be induced to hold her tongue upon the matter and not give Philip her opinion. "What?" she would ask, "the poor young man is to be deceived and cajoled; to be taken or left as it suits these people; to be made miserable for life certainly if she marries him; and his friends are not to dare to warn him? The cowards! The cowardice of you men, Pen, upon matters of opinion, of you masters and lords of creation, is really despicable, sir! You dare not have opinions, or holding them you dare not declare them and act by them. You compromise with crime every day because you think it would be officious to declare yourself and interfere. You are not afraid of outraging morals, but of inflicting *ennui* upon society, and losing your popularity. You are as cynical as—as, what was the name of the horrid old man who lived in the tub—Demosthenes? —well, Diogenes, then, and the name does not matter a pin, sir. You are as cynical, only you wear fine ruffled shirts and wristbands, and you carry your lantern dark. It is not right to 'put your oar in' as you say in your jargon (and even your slang is a sort of cowardice, sir, for you are afraid to speak the feelings of your heart :—) it is not right to meddle and speak the truth, not right to rescue a poor soul who is drowning—of course not. What call have you fine gentlemen of the world to put your oar in? Let him perish! What did he in that galley? That is the language of the world, baby, darling. And, my poor poor child, when you are sinking, nobody is to stretch out a hand to save you!" As for that wife of mine, when she sets forth the maternal plea, and appeals to the exuberant school of philosophers, I know there is no reasoning with her. I retire to my books, and leave her to kiss out the rest of the argument over the children.

Philip did not know the extent of the obligation which he owed to his little friend and guardian, Caroline; but he was aware that he had no better friend than herself in the world ; and, I dare say, returned to her, as the wont is in such bargains between man and woman— woman and man, at least—a sixpence for that pure gold treasure, her sovereign affection. I suppose Caroline thought her sacrifice gave her a little authority to counsel Philip ; for she it was who, I believe, first bid him to inquire whether that engagement which he had virtually contracted with his cousin was likely to lead to good, and was to be binding upon him but not on her? She brought Ridley to add his doubts to her remonstrances. She showed Philip that not only his uncle's conduct, but his cousin's, was interested, and set him to inquire into it further.

That peculiar form of bronchitis under which poor dear Agnes was suffering was relieved by absence from London. The smoke, the crowded parties and assemblies, the late hours, and, perhaps, the gloom of the house in Beaunash Street, distressed the poor dear child ; and her cough was very much soothed by that fine, cutting east wind, which blows so liberally along the Brighton cliffs, and which is so good for coughs, as we all know. But there was one fault in Brighton which could not be helped in her bad case : it is too near London. The air, that chartered libertine, can blow down from London quite easily ; or people can come from London to Brighton, bringing, I dare say, the insidious London fog along with them. At any rate, Agnes, if she wished for quiet, poor thing, might have gone farther and fared better. Why, if you owe a tailor a bill, he can run down and present it in a few hours. Vulgar, inconvenient acquaintances thrust themselves upon you at every moment and corner. Was ever such a *tohubohu* of people as there assembles? You can't be tranquil, if you will. Organs pipe and scream without cease at your windows. Your name is put down in the papers when you arrive ; and everybody meets everybody ever so many times a day.

On finding that his uncle had set lawyers to work, with the charitable purpose of ascertaining whether Philip's property was legitimately his own, Philip was a good deal disturbed in mind. He could not appreciate that high sense of moral obligation by which Mr. Twysden was actuated. At least, he thought that these inquiries should not have been secretly set a-foot; and as he himself was perfectly open—a great deal too open, perhaps—in his words and his actions, he was hard with those who attempted to hoodwink or deceive him.

It could not be ; ah ! no, it never could be, that Agnes the pure and gentle was privy to this conspiracy. But then, how very—very often of late she had been from home ; how very, very cold Aunt Twysden's shoulder had somehow become. Once, when he reached the door, a fishmonger's boy was leaving a fine salmon at the kitchen,—a salmon and a tub of ice. Once, twice, at five o'clock, when he called, a smell of cooking pervaded the hall,—that hall which culinary odours very seldom visited. Some of those noble Twysden dinners were on the *tapis*, and Philip was not asked. Not to be asked was no great deprivation ; but who were the guests? To be sure, these were trifles light as air; but Philip smelt mischief in the steam of those Twysden dinners. He chewed that salmon with a bitter sauce as he saw it sink down the area steps and disappear with its attendant lobster in the dark kitchen regions.

Yes ; eyes were somehow averted that used to look into his very frankly ; a glove somehow had grown over a little hand which once used to lie very comfortably in his broad palm. Was anybody· else going to seize it, and was it going to paddle in that blackamoor's unblest fingers ? Ah ! fiends and tortures ! a gentleman may cease to love, but does he like a woman to cease to love him ? People carry on ever so long for fear of that declaration that all is over. No confession is more dismal to make. The sun of love has set. We sit in the dark. I mean you, dear madam, and Corydon, or I and Amaryllis ; uncomfortably, with nothing more to say to one another ; with the night dew falling, and a risk of catching cold, drearily contemplating the fading west, with " the cold remains of lustre gone, of fire long past away." Sink, fire of love ! Rise, gentle moon, and mists of chilly evening. And, my good Madam Amaryllis, let us go home to some tea and a fire.

So Philip determined to go and seek his cousin. Arrived at his hotel, (and if it were the * * I can't conceive Philip in much better quarters), he had the opportunity of inspecting those delightful newspaper arrivals, a perusal of which has so often edified us at Brighton. Mr. and Mrs. Penfold, he was informed, continued their residence, No. 96, Horizontal Place ; and it was with those guardians he knew his Agnes was staying. · He speeds to Horizontal Place. Miss Twysden is out. He heaves a sigh, and leaves a card. Has it ever happened to you to leave a card at *that* house—that house which was once THE house—almost your own ; where you were ever welcome ; where the kindest hand was ready to grasp yours, the brightest eye to greet you ? And now your friendship has dwindled away to a little bit of pasteboard, shed once a year, and· poor dear Mrs. Jones (it is with J. you have quarrelled) still calls on the ladies of your family and slips her husband's ticket upon the hall table. Oh, life and time, that it should have come to this ! Oh, gracious powers ! Do you recall the time when Arabella Briggs was Arabella Thompson ? You call and talk *fadaises* to her (at first she is rather nervous, and has the children in) ; you talk rain and fine weather ; the last novel ; the next party ; Thompson in the City ? Yes, Mr. Thompson is in the City. He's pretty well, thank you. Ah ! Daggers, ropes, and poisons, has it come to this ? You are talking about the weather, and another man's health, and another man's children, of which she is mother, to *her ?* Time was the weather was

all a burning sunshine, in which you and she basked; or if clouds
gathered, and a storm fell, such a glorious rainbow haloed round you,
such delicious tears fell and refreshed you, that the storm was more
ravishing than the calm.   And now another man's children are sitting
on her knee—their mother's knee; and once a year Mr. and Mrs. John
Thompson request the honour of Mr. Brown's company at dinner;
and once a year you read in *The Times*, " In Nursery Street, the wife
of J. Thompson, Esq., of a Son."   To come to the once-beloved
one's door, and find the knocker tied up with a white kid glove, is
humiliating—say what you will, it is humiliating.

Philip leaves his card, and walks on to the Cliff, and of course, in
three minutes, meets Clinker.   Indeed, who ever went to Brighton
for half an hour without meeting Clinker?   ·

" Father pretty well?   His old patient, Lady Geminy, is down
here with the children; what a number of them there are, to be sure!
Come to make any stay?   See your cousin, Miss Twysden, is here
with the Penfolds.   Little party at the Grigsons' last night; she
looked uncommonly well; danced ever so many times with the Black
Prince, Woolcomb of the Greens.   Suppose I may congratulate you.
Six thousand five hundred a year now, and thirteen thousand when
his grandmother dies; but those negresses live for ever.   I suppose
the thing is settled.   I saw them on the pier just now, and Mrs. Penfold was reading a book in the arbour.   Book of sermons it was—
pious woman, Mrs. Penfold.   I dare say they are on the pier still."
Striding with hurried steps Philip Firmin makes for the pier.   The
breathless Clinker cannot keep alongside of his face.   I should like
to have seen it when Clinker said that " the thing" was settled
between Miss Twysden and the cavalry gentleman.

There were a few nursery governesses, maids, and children,
paddling about at the end of the pier; and there was a fat woman
reading a book in one of the arbours—but no Agnes, no Woolcomb.
Where can they be?   Can they be weighing each other? or buying
those mad pebbles, which people are known to purchase? or having
their *silhouettes* done in black?   Ha! ha!   Woolcomb would
hardly have *his* face done in black.   The idea would provoke
odious comparisons.   I see Philip is in a dreadfully bad sarcastic
humour.

Up there comes from one of those trap-doors which lead down
from the pier-head to the green sea-waves ever restlessly jumping

HAND AND GLOVE.

below—up there comes a little Skye-terrier dog with a red collar, who as soon as she sees Philip, sings, squeaks, whines, runs, jumps, *flumps* up on him, if I may use the expression, kisses his hands, and with eyes, tongue, paws, and tail shows him a thousand marks of welcome and affection. "What, Brownie, Brownie!" Philip is glad to see the dog, an old friend who has many a time licked his hand and bounced upon his knee.

The greeting over, Brownie, wagging her tail with prodigious activity, trots before Philip—trots down an opening, down the steps under which the waves shimmer greenly, and into quite a quiet remote corner just over the water, whence you may command a most beautiful view of the sea, the shore, the Marine Parade, and the "Albion Hotel," and where, were I five-and-twenty say, with nothing else to do, I would gladly pass a quarter of an hour talking about "Glaucus, or the Wonders of the Deep" with the object of my affections.

Here, amongst the labyrinth of piles, Brownie goes flouncing along till she comes to a young couple who are looking at the view just described. In order to view it better, the young man has laid his hand, a pretty little hand most delicately gloved, on the lady's hand; and Brownie comes up and nuzzles against her, and whines and talks as much as to say, "Here's somebody," and the lady says, "Down Brownie, miss."

"It's no good, Agnes, that dog," says the gentleman (he has very curly, not to say woolly hair, under his natty little hat). "I'll give you a pug with a nose you can hang your hat on. I do know of one now. My man Rummins knows of one. Do you like pugs?"

"I adore them," says the lady.

"I'll give you one, if I have to pay fifty pounds for it. And they fetch a good figure, the real pugs do, I can tell you. Once in London there was an exhibition of 'em, and——"

"Brownie, Brownie, down!" cries Agnes. The dog was jumping at a gentleman, a tall gentleman with a red moustache and beard, who advances through the chequered shade, under the ponderous beams, over the translucent sea.

"Pray don't mind, Brownie won't hurt me," says a perfectly well-known voice, the sound of which sends all the colour shuddering out of Miss Agnes' pink cheeks.

"You see I gave my cousin this dog, Captain Woolcomb," says

the gentleman ; "and the little slut remembers me.   Perhaps Miss Twysden prefers the pug better."

"Sir !"

"If it has a nose you can hang your hat on, it must be a very pretty dog, and I suppose you intend to hang your hat on it a good deal."

"Oh, Philip !" says the lady; but an attack of that dreadful coughing stops further utterance.

CHAPTER XIV.

CONTAINS TWO OF PHILIP'S MISHAPS.

OU know that, in some parts of India, infanticide is the common custom. It is part of the religion of the land, as, in other districts, widow-burning used to be. I can't imagine that ladies like to destroy either themselves or their children, though they submit with bravery, and even cheerfulness, to the decrees of that religion which orders them to make away with their own or their young ones' lives. Now, suppose you and I, as Europeans, happened to drive up where a young creature was just about to roast herself, under the advice of her family and the highest dignitaries of her church; what could we do? Rescue her? No such thing. We know better than to interfere with her, and the laws and usages of her country. We turn away with a sigh from the mournful scene; we pull out our pocket-handkerchiefs, tell coachman to drive on, and leave her to her sad fate.

Now about poor Agnes Twysden: how, in the name of goodness, can we help her? You see she is a well-brought-up and religious young woman of the Brahminical sect. If she is to be sacrificed, that old Brahmin, her father, that good and devout mother, that most special Brahmin her brother, and that admirable girl her strait-laced sister, all insist upon her undergoing the ceremony, and deck her with flowers ere they lead her to that dismal altar flame. Suppose, I say, she has made up her mind to throw over poor Philip, and take on with some one else? What sentiment ought our virtuous bosoms to entertain towards her? Anger? I have just been holding a conversation with a young fellow in rags and without shoes, whose bed is commonly a dry arch, who has been repeatedly in prison, whose father and mother were thieves, and whose grand-fathers were thieves;—are we to be angry with him for following the paternal profession? With one eye brimming with pity, the other steadily keeping watch over the family spoons, I listen to his artless tale. I have no anger against that child; nor towards thee, Agnes, daughter of Talbot the Brahmin.

For though duty is duty, when it comes to the pinch, it is often hard to do. Though dear papa and mamma say that here is a gen-tleman with ever so many thousands a year, an undoubted part in So-and-So-shire, and whole islands in the western main, who is wildly in love with your fair skin and blue eyes, and is ready to fling all his treasures at your feet; yet, after all, when you consider that he is very ignorant, though very cunning; very stingy, though very rich; very ill-tempered, probably, if faces and eyes and mouths can tell truth : and as for Philip Firmin—though actually his legitimacy is dubious, as we have lately heard, in which case his maternal fortune is ours—and as for his paternal inheritance, we don't know whether the doctor is worth thirty thousand pounds or a shilling;—yet, after all—as for Philip—he is a man ; he is a gentleman ; he has brains in his head, and a great honest heart of which he has offered to give the best feelings to his cousin :—I say, when a poor girl has to be off with that old love, that honest and fair love, and be on with the new one, the dark one, I feel for her; and though the Brahmins are, as we know, the most genteel sect in Hindostan, I rather wish the poor child could have belonged to some lower and less rigid sect. Poor Agnes ! to think that he has sat for hours, with mamma and Blanche or the governess, of course, in the room (for, you know, when she and Philip were quite wee wee things dear mamma had little amiable plans in view) ; has sat for hours by Miss Twysden's side pouring out his heart to her; has had, mayhap, little precious moments of con-fidential talk—little hasty whispers in corridors, on stairs, behind window-curtains, and—and so forth in fact. She must remember all this past; and can't, without some pang, listen on the same sofa, behind the same window-curtains, to her dark suitor pouring out his artless tales of barracks, boxing, horseflesh, and the tender passion. He is dull, he is mean, he is ill-tempered, he is ignorant, and the other was   .   .   .   .   ; but she will do her duty : oh, yes ! she will do her duty ! Poor Agnes ! *C'est à fendre le cœur.* I declare I quite feel for her.

When Philip's temper was roused, I have been compelled, as his biographer, to own how very rude and disagreeable he could be ; and you must acknowledge that a young man has some reason to be displeased, when he finds the girl of his heart hand-in-hand with another young gentleman in an occult and shady recess of the wood-work of Brighton Pier. The green waves are softly murmuring : so is the officer of the Life-Guards Green. The waves are kissing the beach. Ah, agonizing thought ! I will not pursue the simile, which may be but a jealous man's mad fantasy. Of this I am sure, no pebble on that beach is cooler than polished Agnes. But, then, Philip drunk with jealousy is not a reasonable being like Philip sober. " He had a dreadful temper," Philip's dear aunt said of him afterwards,—" I trembled for my dear gentle child, united for ever to a man of that violence. Never, in my secret mind, could I think that their union could be a happy one. Besides, you know, the nearness of their relationship. My scruples on that score, dear Mrs. Candour, never, never could be quite got over." And these scruples came to weigh whole tons, when Mangrove Hall, the house in Berkeley Square, and Mr. Woolcomb's West India island were put into the scale along with them.

Of course there was no good in remaining amongst those damp, reeking timbers, now that the pretty little *tête-à-tête* was over. Little Brownie hung fondling and whining round Philip's ankles, as the party ascended to the upper air. " My child, how pale you look ! " cries Mrs. Penfold, putting down her volume. Out of the Captain's opal eyeballs shot lurid flames, and hot blood burned behind his yellow cheeks. In a quarrel, Mr. Philip Firmin could be particularly cool and self-possessed. When Miss Agnes rather piteously intro-duced him to Mrs. Penfold, he made a bow as polite and gracious as any performed by his royal father. " My little dog knew me," he said, caressing the animal. " She is a faithful little thing, and she led me down to my cousin ; and—Captain Woolcomb, I think, is your name, sir ? "

As Philip curls his moustache and smiles blandly, Captain Wool-comb pulls his and scowls fiercely. " Yes, sir," he mutters, " my name is Woolcomb." Another bow and a touch of the hat from

Mr. Firmin.   A touch?—a gracious wave of the hat; acknowledged by no means so gracefully by Captain Woolcomb.

To these remarks Mrs. Penfold says, "Oh!"   In fact, "Oh!" is about the best thing that could be said under the circumstances.

"My cousin, Miss Twysden, looks so pale because she was out very late dancing last night.   I hear it was a very pretty ball.   But ought she to keep such late hours, Mrs. Penfold, with her delicate health?   Indeed, you ought not, Agnes!   Ought she to keep late hours, Brownie?   There—don't, you little foolish thing!   I gave my cousin the dog: and she's very fond of me—the dog is—still.   You were saying, Captain Woolcomb, when I came up, that you would give Miss Twysden a dog on whose nose you could hang your . . . . I beg pardon?"

Mr. Woolcomb, as Philip made this second allusion to the peculiar nasal formation of the pug, ground his little white teeth together, and let slip a most improper monosyllable.   More acute bronchial suffering was manifested on the part of Miss Twysden.   Mrs. Penfold said, "The day is clouding over.   I think, Agnes, I will have my chair, and go home."

"May I be allowed to walk with you as far as your house?" says Philip, twiddling a little locket which he wore at his watch-chain.   It was a little gold locket, with a little pale hair inside. Whose hair could it have been that was so pale and fine?   As for the pretty, hieroglyphical A. T. at the back, those letters might indicate Alfred Tennyson, or Anthony Trollope, who might have given a lock of *their* golden hair to Philip, for I know he is an admirer of their works.

Agnes looked guiltily at the little locket.   Captain Woolcomb pulled his moustache so, that you would have thought he would have pulled it off; and his opal eyes glared with fearful confusion and wrath.

"Will you please to fall back and let me speak to you, Agnes? Pardon me, Captain Woolcomb, I have a private message for my cousin; and I came from London expressly to deliver it."

"If Miss Twysden desires me to withdraw, I fall back in one moment," says the Captain, clenching the little lemon-coloured gloves.

"My cousin and I have lived together all our lives, and I bring her a family message.   Have you any particular claim to hear it, Captain Woolcomb?"

"Not if Miss Twysden don't want me to hear it. . . . . D— the little brute."

"Don't kick poor little harmless Brownie! He shan't kick you, shall he, Brownie?"

"If the brute comes between my shins, I'll kick her!" shrieks the Captain. "Hang her, I'll throw her into the sea!"

"Whatever you do to my dog, I swear I will do to you!" whispers Philip to the Captain.

"Where are you staying?" shrieks the Captain. "Hang you, you shall hear from me."

"Quiet—'Bedford Hotel.' Easy, or I shall think you want the ladies to overhear."

"Your conduct is horrible, sir," says Agnes, rapidly, in the French language. "Mr. does not comprehend it."

"—— it! If you have any secrets to talk, I'll withdraw fast enough, Miss Agnes," says Othello.

"Oh, Grenville! can I have any secrets from you? Mr. Firmin is my first-cousin. We have lived together all our lives. Philip, I—I don't know whether mamma announced to you—my—my engagement with Captain Grenville Woolcomb." The agitation has brought on another severe bronchial attack. Poor, poor little Agnes! What it is to have a delicate throat!

The pier tosses up to the skies, as though it had left its moorings —the houses on the cliff dance and reel, as though an earthquake was driving them—the sea walks up into the lodging-houses—and Philip's legs are failing from under him : it is only for a moment. When you have a large, tough double tooth out, doesn't the chair go up to the ceiling, and your head come off too? But, in the next instant, there is a grave gentleman before you, making you a bow, and concealing something in his right sleeve. The crash is over. You are a man again. Philip clutches hold of the chain-pier for a minute : it does not sink under him. The houses, after reeling for a second or two, reassume the perpendicular, and bulge their bow-windows towards the main. He can see the people looking from the windows, the carriages passing, Professor Spurrier riding on the cliff with eighteen young ladies, his pupils. In long after-days he remembers those absurd little incidents with a curious tenacity.

"This news," Philip says, "was not—not altogether unexpected I congratulate my cousin, I am sure. Captain Woolcomb, had I known this for certain, I am sure I should not have interrupted you. You were going, perhaps, to ask me to your hospitable house, Mrs. Penfold ? "

"Was she though ? " cries the Captain.

"I have asked a friend to dine with me at the ' Bedford,' and shall go to town, I hope, in the morning. Can I take anything for you, Agnes? Good-by : " and he kisses his hand in quite a *dégagé* manner, as Mrs. Penfold's chair turns eastward and he goes to the west. Silently the tall Agnes sweeps along, a fair hand laid upon her friend's chair.

It's over! it's over! She has done it. He was bound, and kept his honour, but she did not : it was she who forsook him. And I fear very much Mr. Philip's heart leaps with pleasure and an immense sensation of relief at thinking he is free. He meets half a dozen acquaintances on the cliff. He laughs, jokes, shakes hands, invites two or three to dinner in the gayest manner. He sits down on that green, not very far from his inn, and is laughing to himself, when he suddenly feels something nestling at his knee,—rubbing, and nestling, and whining plaintively. "What, is that you ? " It is little Brownie, who has followed him. Poor little rogue !

Then Philip bent down his head over the dog, and as it jumped on him, with little bleats, and whines, and innocent caresses, he broke out into a sob, and a great refreshing rain of tears fell from his eyes. Such a little illness ! Such a mild fever ! Such a speedy cure ! Some people have the complaint so mildly that they are scarcely ever kept to their beds. Some bear its scars for ever.

Philip sat resolutely at the hotel all night, having given special orders to the porter to say that he was at home, in case any gentleman should call. He had a faint hope, he afterwards owned, that some friend of Captain Woolcomb might wait on him on that officer's part. He had a faint hope that a letter might come explaining that treason,—as people will have a sick, gnawing, yearning, foolish desire for letters—letters which contain nothing, which never did contain anything—letters which, nevertheless, you———. You know, in fact, about those letters, and there is no earthly use in asking to read Philip's. Have we not all read those love-letters which, after love-quarrels, come into court sometimes? We have all read them ; and how many have written them ? Nine o'clock. Ten o'clock. Eleven o'clock. No challenge from the Captain ; no explanation

from Agnes. Philip declares he slept perfectly well. But poor little
Brownie the dog made a piteous howling all night in the stables.
She was not a well-bred dog. You could not have hung the least hat
on her nose.

We compared anon our dear Agnes to a Brahmin lady, meekly
offering herself up to sacrifice according to the practice used in her
highly respectable caste. Did we speak in anger or in sorrow ?—
surely in terms of respectful grief and sympathy. And if we pity
her, ought we not likewise to pity her highly respectable parents ?
When the notorious Brutus ordered his sons to execution, you can't
suppose he was such a brute as to be pleased ? All three parties
suffered by the transaction : the sons, probably, even more than their
austere father; but it stands to reason that the whole trio were very
melancholy. At least, were I a poet or musical composer depicting
that business, I certainly should make them so. The sons, piping in
a very minor key indeed ; the father's manly basso, accompanied by
deep wind instruments, and interrupted by appropriate sobs. Though
pretty fair Agnes is being led to execution, I don't suppose she likes
it, or that her parents are happy, who are compelled to order the
tragedy.

That the rich young proprietor of Mangrove Hall should be fond
of her was merely a coincidence, Mrs. Twysden afterwards· always
averred. Not for mere wealth—ah, no ! not for mines of gold—
would they sacrifice their darling child. But when that sad Firmin
affair happened, you see it also happened that Captain Woolcomb
was much struck by dear Agnes, whom he met everywhere. Her
scapegrace of a cousin would go nowhere. He preferred his bachelor
associates, and horrible smoking and drinking habits, to the amuse-
ments and pleasures of more refined society. He neglected Agnes.
There is not the slightest doubt he neglected and mortified her, and
his wilful and frequent absence showed how little he cared for her.
Would you blame the dear girl for coldness to a man who himself
showed such indifference to her ? "No, my good Mrs. Candour.
Had Mr. Firmin been ten times as rich as Mr. Woolcomb, I should
have counselled my child to refuse him. *I* take the responsibility of
the measure entirely on myself—I, and her father, and her brother."
So Mrs. Twysden afterwards spoke, in circles where an absurd and
odious rumour ran, that the Twysdens had forced their daughter to
jilt young Mr. Firmin in order to marry a wealthy quadroon. People

will talk, you know, *de me, de te.* If Woolcomb's dinners had not gone off so after his marriage, I have little doubt the scandal would have died away, and he and his wife might have been pretty generally respected and visited.

Nor must you suppose, as we have said, that dear Agnes gave up her first love without a pang. That bronchitis showed how acutely the poor thing felt her position. It broke out very soon after Mr. Woolcomb's attentions became a little particular; and she actually left London in consequence. It is true that he could follow her without difficulty, but so, for the matter of that, could Philip, as we have seen when he came down and behaved so rudely to Captain Woolcomb. And before Philip came, poor Agnes could plead, " My father pressed me sair," as in the case of the notorious Mrs. Robin Gray.

Father and mother both pressed her sair. Mrs. Twysden, I think I have mentioned, wrote an admirable letter, and was aware of her accomplishment. She used to write reams of gossip regularly every week to dear uncle Ringwood when he was in the country : and when her daughter Blanche married, she is said to have written several of her new son's sermons. As a Christian mother, was she not to give her daughter her advice at this momentous period of her life ? That advice went against poor Philip's chances with his cousin, who was kept acquainted with all the circumstances of the controversy of which we have just seen the issue. I do not mean to say that Mrs. Twysden gave an impartial statement of the case. What parties in a lawsuit do speak impartially on their own side or their adversaries'? Mrs. Twysden's view, as I have learned subsequently, and as imparted to her daughter, was this :—That most unprincipled man, Dr. Firmin, who had already attempted, and unjustly, to deprive the Twysdens of a part of their property, had commenced in quite early life his career of outrage and wickedness against the Ringwood family. He had led dear Lord Ringwood's son, poor dear Lord Cinqbars, into a career of vice and extravagance which caused the premature death of that unfortunate young nobleman. Mr. Firmin had then made a marriage, in spite of the tears and entreaties of Mrs. Twysden, with her late unhappy sister, whose whole life had been made wretched by the doctor's conduct. But the climax of outrage and wickedness was, that when he—he, a low, penniless adventurer—married Colonel Ringwood's daughter, he was married already, as could be sworn by the repentant clergyman who had been forced, by threats of punishment which Dr. Firmin held over him, to perform the rite ! " The mind "—Mrs. Talbot Twysden's fine mind—" shuddered at the thought of such wickedness." But most of all (for to think ill of any one whom she had once loved gave her pain) there was reason to believe that the unhappy Philip Firmin was his *father's accomplice,* and that he knew of his *own illegitimacy,* which he was determined to set aside by any *fraud or artifice*—(she trembled, she wept to have to say this : O heaven ! that there should be such perversity in thy creatures !) And so little store did Philip set by *his mother's honour,* that he actually visited the abandoned woman who acquiesced in her own infamy, and had brought such unspeakable disgrace on the Ringwood family ! The thought of this crime had caused Mrs. Twysden and her dear husband nights of sleepless anguish—had made them *years and years* older—had stricken their hearts with a grief which must endure to the *end of their days.* With people so unscrupulous, so grasping, so artful as Dr. Firmin and (must she say ?) his son, they were bound to be *on their guard;* and though they had *avoided* Philip, she had deemed it right, on the rare occasions when she and the young man whom she must now call her *illegitimate* nephew met, to behave as though she knew nothing of this most dreadful controversy.

"And now, dearest child " . . . Surely the moral is obvious? The dearest child " must see at once that any foolish plans which were formed in childish days and under *former delusions* must be cast aside for ever as impossible, as unworthy of a Twysden—of a Ringwood. Be not concerned for the young man himself," wrote Mrs. Twysden—" I blush that he should bear that dear father's name who was slain in honour on Busaco's glorious field. P. F. has *associates* amongst whom he has ever been much more at home than in our refined circle, and habits which will cause him to forget you only too easily. And if near you is one whose ardour shows itself in his every word and action, whose wealth and property may raise you to a place worthy of my child, need I say, a mother's, a father's blessing go with you." This letter was brought to Miss Twysden, at Brighton, by a special messenger ; and the superscription announced that it was " honoured by Captain Grenville Woolcomb."

Now when Miss Agnes has had a letter to this effect (I may at some time tell you how I came to be acquainted with its contents) ;

when she remembers all the abuse her brother lavishes against Philip as, heaven bless some of them ! dear relatives can best do ; when she thinks how cold he has of late been—how he *will* come smelling of cigars—how he won't conform to the usages *du monde*, and has neglected all the decencies of society—how she often can't understand his strange rhapsodies about poetry, painting, and the like, nor how he can live with such associates as those who seem to delight him—and now how he is showing himself actually *unprincipled* and abetting his horrid father ; when we consider mither pressing sair, and all these points in mither's favour, I don't think we can order Agnes to instant execution for the resolution to which she is coming. She will give him up—she will give him up. Good-by, Philip. Good-by the past. Be forgotten, be forgotten, fond words spoken in not unwilling ears ! Be still and breathe not, eager lips, that have trembled so near to one another ! Unlock, hands, and part for ever, that seemed to be formed for life's long journey ! Ah, to part for ever is hard ; but harder and more humiliating still to part without regret !

That papa and mamma had influenced Miss Twysden in her behaviour my wife and I could easily imagine, when Philip, in his wrath and grief, came to us and poured out the feelings of his heart. My wife is a repository of men's secrets, an untiring consoler and comforter ; and she knows many a sad story which we are not at liberty to tell, like this one of which this person, Mr. Firmin, has given us possession.

"Father and mother's orders," shouts Philip, "I dare say, Mrs. Pendennis ; but the wish was father to the thought of parting, and it was for the blackamoor's parks and acres that the girl jilted me. Look here. I told you just now that I slept perfectly well on that infernal night after I had said farewell to her. Well, I didn't. It was a lie. I walked ever so many times the whole length of the cliff, from Hove to Rottingdean almost, and then went to bed afterwards, and slept a little out of sheer fatigue. And as I was passing by Horizontal Terrace (—I happened to pass by there two or three times in the moonlight, like a great jackass—) you know those verses of mine which I have hummed here sometimes ?" (hummed ! he used to *roar* them !) "' When the locks of burnished gold, lady, shall to silver turn !' Never mind the rest. You know the verses about fidelity and old age ? She was singing them on that night, to that negro. And I heard the beggar's voice say, 'Bravo !' through the open windows."

"Ah, Philip! it was cruel," says my wife, heartily pitying our friend's anguish and misfortune. "It was cruel indeed. I am sure we can feel for you. But think what certain misery a marriage with such a person would have been ! Think of your warm heart given away for ever to that heartless creature."

"Laura, Laura, have you not often warned me not to speak ill of people ?" says Laura's husband.

"I can't help it sometimes," cries Laura in a transport. "I try and do my best not to speak ill of my neighbours; but the worldliness of those people shocks me so that I can't bear to be near them. They are so utterly tied and bound by conventionalities, so perfectly convinced of their own excessive high-breeding, that they seem to me more odious and more vulgar than quite low people; and I'm sure Mr. Philip's friend, the Little Sister, is infinitely more ladylike than his dreary aunt or either of his supercilious cousins!" Upon my word, when this lady did speak her mind, there was no mistaking her meaning.

I believe Mr. Firmin took a considerable number of people into his confidence regarding this love affair. He is one of those individuals who can't keep their secrets ; and when hurt he roars so loudly that all his friends can hear. It has been remarked that the sorrows of such persons do not endure very long ; nor surely was there any great need in this instance that Philip's heart should wear a lengthened mourning. Ere long he smoked his pipes, he played his billiards, he shouted his songs; he rode in the Park for the pleasure of severely cutting his aunt and cousins when their open carriage passed, or of riding down Captain Woolcomb or his cousin Ringwood, should either of those worthies come in his way.

One day, when the old Lord Ringwood came to town for his accustomed spring visit, Philip condescended to wait upon him, and was announced to his lordship just as Talbot Twysden and Ringwood his son were taking leave of their noble kinsman. Philip looked at them with a flashing eye and a distended nostril, according to his swaggering wont. I dare say they on their part bore a very mean and hangdog appearance ; for my lord laughed at their discomfiture, and seemed immensely amused as they slunk out of the door when Philip came hectoring in.

"So, sir, there has been a family row. Heard all about it: at least, their side. Your father did me the favour to marry my niece, having another wife already?"

"Having no other wife already, sir—though my dear relations were anxious to show that he had."

"Wanted your money; thirty thousand pound is not a trifle. Ten thousand apiece for those children. And no more need of any confounded pinching and scraping, as they have to do at Beaunash Street. Affair off between you and Agnes? Absurd affair. So much the better."

"Yes, sir, so much the better."

"Have ten thousand apiece. Would have twenty thousand if they got yours. Quite natural to want it."

"Quite."

"Woolcomb a sort of negro, I understand. Fine property here: besides the West India rubbish. Violent man—so people tell me. Luckily Agnes seems a cool, easy-going woman, and must put up with the rough as well as the smooth in marrying a property like that. Very lucky for you that that woman persists there was no marriage with your father. Twysden says the doctor bribed her. Take it he's not got much money to bribe, unless you gave some of yours."

"I don't bribe people to bear false witness, my lord—and if——"

"Don't be in a huff; I didn't say so. Twysden says so—perhaps thinks so. When people are at law they believe anything of one another."

"I don't know what other people may do, sir. If I had another man's money, I should not be easy until I had paid him back. Had my share of my grandfather's property not been lawfully mine—and for a few hours I thought it was not—please God, I would have given it up to its rightful owners—at least, my father would."

"Why, hang it all, man, you don't mean to say your father has not settled with you?"

Philip blushed a little. He had been rather surprised that there had been no settlement between him and his father.

"I am only of age a few months, sir. I am not under any apprehension. I get my dividends regularly enough. One of my grandfather's trustees, General Baynes, is in India. He is to return almost immediately, or we should have sent a power of attorney out to him. There's no hurry about the business."

Philip's maternal grandfather, and Lord Ringwood's brother, the late Colonel Philip Ringwood, had died possessed of but trifling property of his own; but his wife had brought him a fortune of sixty thousand pounds, which was settled on their children, and in the names of trustees—Mr. Briggs, a lawyer, and Colonel Baynes, an East India officer, and friend of Mrs. Philip Ringwood's family. Colonel Baynes had been in England some eight years before; and Philip remembered a kind old gentleman coming to see him at school, and leaving tokens of his bounty behind. The other trustee, Mr. Briggs, a lawyer of considerable county reputation, was dead long since, having left his affairs in an involved condition. During the trustee's absence and the son's minority, Philip's father received the dividends on his son's property, and liberally spent them on the boy. Indeed, I believe that for some little time at college, and during his first journeys abroad, Mr. Philip spent rather more than the income of his maternal inheritance, being freely supplied by his father, who told him not to stint himself. He was a sumptuous man, Dr. Firmin—open-handed—subscribing to many charities—a lover of solemn good cheer. The doctor's dinners and the doctor's equipages were models in their way; and I remember the sincere respect with which my uncle the Major (the family guide in such matters) used to speak of Dr. Firmin's taste. "No duchess in London, sir," he would say, "drove better horses than Mrs. Firmin. Sir George Warrender, sir, could not give a better dinner, sir, than that to which we sat down yesterday." And for the exercise of these civic virtues the doctor had the hearty respect of the good Major.

"Don't tell me, sir," on the other hand, Lord Ringwood would say; "I dined with the fellow once—a swaggering fellow, sir; but a servile fellow. The way he bowed and flattered was perfectly absurd. Those fellows think we like it—and we may. Even at my age, I like flattery—any quantity of it; and not what you call delicate, but strong, sir. I like a man to kneel down and kiss my shoe-strings. I have my own opinion of him afterwards, but that is what I like— what all men like; and that is what Firmin gave in quantities. But you could see that his house was monstrously expensive. His dinner was excellent, and you saw it was good every day—not like your dinners, my good Maria ; not like your wines, Twysden, which, hang it, I can't swallow, unless I send 'em in myself. Even at my own house, I don't give that kind of wine on common occasions which Firmin used to give. I drink the best myself, of course, and give it to some who know ; but I don't give it to common fellows, who come to hunting dinners, or to girls and boys who are dancing at my balls."

"Yes ; Mr. Firmin's dinners were very handsome—and a pretty end came of the handsome dinners !" sighed Mrs. Twysden.

" That's not the question ; I am only speaking about the fellow's meat and drink, and they were both good. And it's my opinion, that fellow will have a good dinner wherever he goes."

I had the fortune to be present at one of these feasts, which Lord Ringwood attended, and at which I met Philip's trustee, General Baynes, who had just arrived from India. I remember now the smallest details of the little dinner,—the brightness of the old plate, on which the doctor prided himself, and the quiet comfort, not to say splendour, of the entertainment. The General seemed to take a great liking to Philip, whose grandfather had been his special friend and comrade in arms. He thought he saw something of Philip Ringwood in Philip Firmin's face.

"Ah, indeed !" growls Lord Ringwood.

"You ain't a bit like him," says the downright General. "Never saw a handsomer or more open-looking fellow than Philip Ringwood."

"Oh ! I dare say I looked pretty open myself forty years ago," said my lord ; "now I'm shut, I suppose. I don't see the least likeness in this young man to my brother."

"That is some sherry as old as the century," whispers the host ; "it is the same the Prince Regent liked so at a Mansion House dinner, five-and-twenty years ago."

"Never knew anything about wine ; was always tippling liqueurs and punch. What do you give for this sherry, doctor ?"

The doctor sighed, and looked up to the chandelier. "Drink it while it lasts, my good lord ; but don't ask me the price. The fact is, I don't like to say what I gave for it."

"You need not stint yourself in the price of sherry, doctor," cries the General gaily ; "you have but one son, and he has a fortune of his own, as I happen to know. You haven't dipped it, Master Philip ?"

"I fear, sir, I may have exceeded my income sometimes, in the last three years ; but my father has helped me."

"Exceeded nine hundred a year ! Upon my word ! When I was a sub, my friends gave me fifty pounds a year, and I never was a shilling in debt ! What are men coming to now ?"

"If doctors drink Prince Regent's sherry at ten guineas a dozen, what can you expect of their sons, General Baynes ?" grumbles my lord.

"My father gives you his best, my lord," says Philip gaily ; "if you know of any better, he will get it for you. *Si non his utere mecum !* Please to pass me that decanter, Pen !"

I thought the old lord did not seem ill pleased at the young man's freedom ; and now, as I recall it, think I can remember that a peculiar silence and anxiety seemed to weigh upon our host—upon him whose face was commonly so anxious and sad.

The famous sherry, which had made many voyages to Indian climes before it acquired its exquisite flavour, had travelled some three or four times round the docter's polished table, when Brice, his man, entered with a letter on his silver tray. Perhaps Philip's eyes and mine exchanged glances in which ever so small a scintilla of mischief might sparkle. The doctor often had letters when he was entertaining his friends ; and his patients had a knack of falling ill at awkward times.

"Gracious heavens !" cries the doctor, when he read the despatch —it was a telegraphic message. "The poor Grand Duke !"

"What Grand Duke ?" asks the surly lord of Ringwood.

"My earliest patron and friend—the Grand Duke of Gröningen ! Seized this morning at eleven at Potzendorff ! Has sent for me. I promised to go to him if ever he had need of me. I must go ! I can save the night-train yet. General ! our visit to the City must be deferred till my return. Get a portmanteau, Brice ; and call a cab at once. Philip will entertain my friends for the evening. My dear lord, you won't mind an old doctor leaving you to attend an old patient? I will write from Gröningen. I shall be there on Friday morning. Farewell, gentlemen ! Brice, another bottle of that sherry ! I pray, don't let anybody stir ! God bless you, Philip, my boy !" And with this the doctor went up, took his son by the hand, and laid the other very kindly on the young man's shoulder. Then he made a bow round the table to his guests—one of his graceful bows, for which he was famous. I can see the sad smile on his face now, and the light from the chandelier over the dining-table glancing from his shining forehead, and casting deep shadows on to his cheek from his heavy brows.

The departure was a little abrupt, and of course cast somewhat of a gloom upon the company.

"My carriage ain't ordered till ten—must go on sitting here, I suppose. Confounded life doctor's must be! Called up any hour in the night! Get their fees! Must go!" growled the great man of the party.

"People are glad enough to have them when they are ill, my lord. I think I have heard that once when you were at Ryde . . ."

The great man started back as if a little shock of cold water had fallen on him; and then looked at Philip with not unfriendly glances. "Treated for gout—so he did. Very well, too!" said my lord; and whispered, not inaudibly, "Cool hand, that boy!" And then his lordship fell to talk with General Baynes about his campaigning, and his early acquaintance with his own brother, Philip's grandfather.

The General did not care to brag about his own feats of arms, but was loud in praises of his old comrade. Philip was pleased to hear his grandsire so well spoken of. The General had known Dr. Firmin's father also, who likewise had been a colonel in the famous old Peninsular army. "A Tartar that fellow was, and no mistake!" said the good officer. "Your father has a strong look of him; and you have a glance of him at times. But you remind me of Philip Ringwood not a little; and you could not belong to a better man."

"Ha!" says my lord. There had been differences between him and his brother. He may have been thinking of days when they were friends. Lord Ringwood now graciously asked if General Baynes was staying in London? But the General had only come to do this piece of business, which must now be delayed. He was too poor to live in London. He must look out for a country place, where he and his six children could live cheaply. "Three boys at school, and one at college, Mr. Philip—you know what that must cost; though, thank my stars, my college boy does not spend nine hundred a year. Nine hundred! Where should we be if he did?" In fact, the days of nabobs are long over, and the General had come back to his native country with only very small means for the support of a great family.

When my lord's carriage came, he departed, and the other guests presently took their leave. The General, who was a bachelor for the nonce, remained awhile, and we three prattled over cheroots in Philip's smoking-room. It was a night like a hundred I have spent there, and yet how well I remember it! We talked about Philip's future prospects, and he communicated his intentions to us in his lordly way. As for practising at the bar: "No, sir," he said, in reply to General Baynes' queries, "he should not make much hand of that; shouldn't if he were ever so poor. He had his own money, and his father's;" and he condescended to say that "he might, perhaps, try for Parliament should an eligible opportunity offer." "Here's a fellow born with a silver spoon in his mouth," says the General, as we walked away together. "A fortune to begin with; a fortune to inherit. My fortune was two thousand pounds, and the price of my two first commissions; and when I die my children will not be quite so well off as their father was when he began!"

Having parted with the old officer at his modest sleeping quarters near his club, I walked to my own home, little thinking that yonder cigar, of which I had shaken some of the ashes in Philip's smoking-room, was to be the last tobacco I ever should smoke there. The pipe was smoked out. The wine was drunk. When that door closed on me, it closed for the last time—at least was never more to admit me as Philip's, as Dr. Firmin's, guest and friend. I pass the place often now. My youth comes back to me as I gaze at those blank, shining windows. I see myself a boy and Philip a child; and his fair mother; and his father, the hospitable, the melancholy, the magnificent. I wish I could have helped him. I wish somehow he had borrowed money. He never did. He gave me his often. I have never seen him since that night when his own door closed upon him.

On the second day after the doctor's departure, as I was at breakfast with my family, I received the following letter:—

"MY DEAR PENDENNIS,—Could I have seen you in private on Tuesday night, I might have warned you of the calamity which was hanging over my house. But to what good end? That you should know a few weeks, hours, before what all the world will ring with to-morrow? Neither you nor I, nor one whom we both love, would have been the happier for knowing my misfortunes a few hours sooner. In four-and-twenty hours every club in London will be busy with talk of the departure of the celebrated Dr. Firmin—the wealthy Dr. Firmin; a few months more and (I have strict and *confidential* reason to believe) hereditary rank would have been mine, but Sir George Firmin would have been an insolvent man, and his son Sir Philip a beggar. Perhaps the thought of this honour has been one of the reasons which has determined me on expatriating myself sooner than I otherwise needed to have done.

"George Firmin, the honoured, the wealthy physician, and his son a beggar? I see you are startled at the news! You wonder how, with a great practice, and no great ostensible expenses, such ruin should have come upon me—upon him. It has seemed as if for years past Fate has been determined to make war upon George Brand Firmin; and who can battle against Fate? A man universally admitted to be of good judgment, I have embarked in mercantile speculations the most promising. Everything upon which I laid my hand has crumbled to ruin; but I can say with the Roman bard, '*Impavidum ferient ruinæ.*' And, almost penniless, almost aged, an exile driven from my country, I seek another where I do not despair—*I even have a firm belief* that I shall be enabled to repair my shattered fortunes! My race has never been deficient in courage, and Philip and *Philip's father* must use all theirs, so as to be enabled to face the dark times which menace them. *Si celeres quatit pennas Fortuna*, we must resign what she gave us, and bear our calamity with unshaken hearts!

"There is a man, I own to you, whom I cannot, I must not face. General Baynes has just come from India, with but very small savings, I fear; and these are jeopardized by his imprudence and my most cruel and unexpected misfortune. I need not tell you that *my all* would have been my boy's. My will, made long since, will be found in the tortoiseshell secretaire standing in my consulting-room under the picture of Abraham offering up Isaac. In it you will see that everything, except annuities to old and deserving servants and a legacy to one excellent and faithful woman whom I own I have wronged—my all, which once was considerable, *is left to my boy*.

"I am now worth less than nothing, and have compromised Philip's property along with my own. As a man of business, General Baynes, Colonel Ringwood's old companion in arms, was culpably careless, and I—alas! that I must own it—deceived him. Being the only surviving trustee (Mrs. Philip Ringwood's other trustee was an unprincipled attorney who has been long dead), General B. signed a paper authorizing, as he imagined, my bankers to receive Philip's dividends, but, in fact, giving me the power to dispose of the capital sum. On my honour, as a man, as a gentleman, as a father, Pendennis, I hoped to replace it! I took it; I embarked it in speculations in which it sank down with ten times the amount of my own private property. Half-year after half-year, with straitened means and with the *greatest difficulty to myself*, my poor boy has had his dividend; and *he* at least has never known what was want or anxiety until now. Want? Anxiety? Pray Heaven he never may suffer the sleepless anguish, the racking care which has pursued me! '*Post equitem sedet atra cura*,' our favourite poet says. Ah! how truly, too, does he remark, '*Patriæ quis exul se quoque fugit?*' Think you where I go grief and remorse will not follow me? They will never leave me until I shall return to this country—for that I *shall* return, my heart tells me—until I can reimburse General Baynes, who stands indebted to Philip through his incautiousness and my overpowering necessity; and my heart—an erring but fond *father's* heart—tells me that my boy will not eventually lose a penny by my misfortune.

"I own, between ourselves, that this illness of the Grand Duke of Gröningen was a pretext which I put forward. You will hear of me ere long from the place whither for some time past I have determined on bending my steps. I placed 100*l.* on Saturday, to Philip's credit, at his banker's. I take little more than that sum with me ; depressed, yet *full of hope;* having done wrong, yet *determined* to retrieve it, and *vowing* that ere I die my poor boy shall not have to blush at bearing the name of " George Brand Firmin.

"Good-by, dear Philip! Your old friend will tell you of my misfortunes. When I write again, it will be to tell you where to address me ; and wherever I am, or whatever misfortunes oppress me, think of me always as your fond " Father."

I had scarce read this awful letter when Philip Firmin himself came into our breakfast-room looking very much disturbed.

CHAPTER XV.

SAMARITANS.

HE children trotted up to their friend with outstretched hands and their usual smiles of welcome. Philip patted their heads, and sat down with very wobegone aspect at the family table. " Ah, friends," said he, " do you know all ? "

" Yes, we do," said Laura, sadly, who has ever compassion for other's misfortunes.

" What ! is it all over the town already ? " asked poor Philip.

" We have a letter from your father this morning." And we brought the letter to him, and showed him the affectionate special . message for himself.

" His last thought was for you, Philip ! " cries Laura. " See here, those last kind words ! "

Philip shook his head. " It is not untrue, what is written here : but it is not all the truth." And Philip Firmin dismayed us by the intelligence which he proceeded to give. There was an execution in the house in Old Parr Street. A hundred clamorous creditors had already appeared there. Before going away, the doctor had taken considerable sums from those dangerous financiers to whom he had been of late resorting. They were in possession of numberless lately signed bills, upon which the desperate man had raised money. He had professed to share with Philip, but he had taken the great share, and left Philip two hundred pounds of his own money. All the rest was gone. All Philip's stock had been sold out. The father's fraud had made him master of the trustee's signature : and Philip Firmin, reputed to be so wealthy, was a beggar, in my room. Luckily he had few, or very trifling, debts. Mr. Philip had a lordly impatience of indebtedness, and, with a good bachelor-income, had paid for all his pleasures as he enjoyed them.

Well! He must work. A young man ruined at two-and-twenty, with a couple of hundred pounds yet in his pocket, hardly knows that he is ruined. He will sell his horses—live in chambers—has enough to go on for a year. "When I am very hard put to it," says Philip, "I will come and dine with the children at one. I dare say you haven't dined much at Williams's in the Old Bailey? You can get a famous dinner there for a shilling—beef, bread, potatoes, beer, and a penny for the waiter." Yes, Philip seemed actually to enjoy his discomfiture. It was long since we had seen him in such spirits. "The weight is off my mind now. It has been throttling me for some time past. Without understanding why or wherefore, I have always been looking out for this. My poor father had ruin written in his face : and when those bailiffs made their appearance in Old Parr Street yesterday, I felt as if I had known them before. I had seen their hooked beaks in my dreams."

"That unlucky General Baynes, when he accepted your mother's trust, took it with its consequences. If the sentry falls asleep on his post, he must pay the penalty," says Mr. Pendennis, very severely.

"Great powers, you would not have me come down on an old man with a large family, and ruin them all?" cries Philip.

"No: I don't think Philip will do that," says my wife, looking exceedingly pleased.

"If men accept trusts they must fulfil them, my dear," cries the master of the house.

"And I must make that old gentleman suffer for my father's wrong? If I do, may I starve! there!" cries Philip.

"And so that poor Little Sister has made her sacrifice in vain!" sighed my wife. "As for the father—oh, Arthur! I can't tell you how odious that man was to me. There was something dreadful about him. And in his manner to women—oh!——"

"If he had been a black draught, my dear, you could not have shuddered more naturally."

" Well, he was horrible ; and I know Philip will be better now he is gone."

Women often make light of ruin. Give them but the beloved objects, and poverty is a trifling sorrow to bear. As for Philip, he, as we have said, is gayer than he has been for years past. The doctor's flight occasions not a little club talk : but, now he is gone, many people see quite well that they were aware of his insolvency, and always knew it must end so. The case is told, is canvassed, is exaggerated as such cases will be. I dare say it forms a week's talk. But people know that poor Philip is his father's largest creditor, and eye the young man with no unfriendly looks when he comes to his club after his mishap,—with burning cheeks, and a tingling sense of shame, imagining that all the world will point at and avoid him as the guilty fugitive's son.

No : the world takes very little heed of his misfortune. One or two old acquaintances are kinder to him than before. A few say his ruin, and his obligation to work, will do him good. Only a very very few avoid him, and look unconscious as he passes them by. Amongst these cold countenances, you, of course, will recognise the faces of the whole Twysden family. Three statues, with marble eyes, could not look more stony-calm than Aunt Twysden and her two daughters, as they pass in the stately barouche. The gentlemen turn red when they see Philip. It is rather late times for Uncle Twysden to begin blushing, to be sure. " Hang the fellow ! he will, of course, be coming for money. Dawkins, I am not at home, mind, when young Mr. Firmin calls." So says Lord Ringwood, regarding Philip fallen among thieves. Ah, thanks to Heaven, travellers find Samaritans as well as Levites on life's hard way ! Philip told us with much humour of a rencontre which he had had with his cousin, Ringwood Twysden, in a public place. Twysden was enjoying himself with some young clerks of his office ; but as Philip advanced upon him, assuming his fiercest scowl and most hectoring manner, the other lost heart, and fled. And no wonder. " Do you suppose," says Twysden, " I will willingly sit in the same room with that cad, after the manner in which he has treated my family ! No, sir !" And so the tall door in Beaunash Street is to open for Philip Firmin no more.

The tall door in Beaunash Street flies open readily enough for another gentleman. A splendid cab-horse reins up before it every day. A pair of varnished boots leap out of the cab, and spring up the broad stairs, where somebody is waiting with a smile of genteel welcome—the same smile—on the same sofa—the same mamma at her table writing her letters. And beautiful bouquets from Covent Garden decorate the room. And after half an hour mamma goes out to speak to the housekeeper, *vous comprenez.* And there is nothing particularly new under the sun. It will shine to-morrow upon pretty much the same flowers, sports, pastimes, &c., which it illuminated yesterday. And when your love-making days are over, miss, and you are married, and advantageously established, shall not your little sisters, now in the nursery, trot down and play their little games? Would you, on your conscience, now—you who are rather inclined to consider Miss Agnes Twysden's conduct as heartless—would you, I say, have her cry her pretty eyes out about a young man who does not care much for her, for whom she never did care much herself, and who is now, moreover, a beggar, with a ruined and disgraced father and a doubtful legitimacy? Absurd! That dear girl is like a beautiful fragrant bower-room at the "Star and Garter" at Richmond, with honeysuckles mayhap trailing round the windows, from which you behold one of the most lovely and pleasant of wood and river scenes. The tables are decorated with flowers, rich wine-cups sparkle on the board, and Captain Jones's party have everything they can desire. Their dinner over, and that company gone, the same waiters, the same flowers, the same cups and crystals, array themselves for Mr. Brown and *his* party. Or, if you won't have Agnes Twysden compared to the "Star and Garter Tavern," which must admit mixed company, liken her to the chaste moon who shines on shepherds of all complexions, swarthy or fair.

When oppressed by superior odds, a commander is forced to retreat, we like him to show his skill by carrying off his guns, treasure, and camp equipages. Doctor Firmin, beaten by fortune and compelled to fly, showed quite a splendid skill and coolness in his manner of decamping, and left the very smallest amount of spoils in the hands of the victorious enemy. His wines had been famous amongst the grave epicures with whom he dined : he used to boast, like a worthy *bon vivant* who knows the value of wine-conversation after dinner, of the quantities which he possessed, and the rare bins which he had in store; but when the executioners came to arrange his sale, there was found only a beggarly account of empty bottles, and I fear some of the unprincipled creditors put in a great quantity of bad liquor which they endeavoured to foist off on the public as the genuine and carefully selected stock of a well-known connoisseur. News of this dishonest proceeding reached Dr. Firmin presently in his retreat; and he showed by his letter a generous and manly indignation at the manner in which his creditors had tampered with his honest name and reputation as a *bon vivant.* *He* have bad wine! For shame! He had the best from the best wine-merchant, and paid, or rather owed, the best prices for it; for of late years the doctor had paid no bills at all: and the wine-merchant appeared in quite a handsome group of figures in his schedule. In like manner his books were pawned to a book auctioneer; and Brice, the butler, had a bill of sale for the furniture. Firmin retreated, we will not say with the honours of war, but as little harmed as possible by defeat. Did the enemy want the plunder of his city? He had smuggled almost all his valuable goods over the wall. Did they desire his ships? He had sunk them: and when at length the conquerors poured into his stronghold, he was far beyond the reach of their shot. Don't we often hear still that Nana Sahib is alive and exceedingly comfortable? We do not love him; but we can't help having a kind of admiration for that slippery fugitive who has escaped from the dreadful jaws of the lion. In a word, when Firmin's furniture came to be sold, it was a marvel how little his creditors benefited by the sale. Contemptuous brokers declared there never was such a shabby lot of goods. A friend of the house and poor Philip bought in his mother's picture for a few guineas; and as for the doctor's own state portrait, I am afraid it went for a few shillings only, and in the midst of a roar of Hebrew laughter. I saw in Wardour Street, not long after, the doctor's sideboard, and what dealers cheerfully call the sarcophagus cellaret. Poor doctor! his wine was all drunken; his meat was eaten up; but his own body had slipped out of the reach of the hook-beaked birds of prey.

We had spoken rapidly in under tones, innocently believing that the young people round about us were taking no heed of our talk. But in a lull of the conversation, Mr. Pendennis junior, who had always been a friend to Philip, broke out with—" Philip! if you are so *very* poor, you'll be hungry, you know, and you may have my piece of bread and jam. And I don't want it, mamma," he added; " and you know Philip has often and often given me things."

"GOOD SAMARITANS."

Philip stooped down and kissed this good little Samaritan. "I'm not hungry, Arty, my boy," he said; "and I'm not so poor but I have got—look here—a fine new shilling for Arty!"

"Oh, Philip, Philip!" cried mamma.

"Don't take the money, Arthur," cried papa.

And the boy, with a rueful face but a manly heart, prepared to give back the coin. "It's quite a new one; and it's a very pretty one: but I won't have it, Philip, thank you," he said, turning very red.

"If he won't, I vow I will give it to the cabman," said Philip.

"Keeping a cab all this while? Oh, Philip, Philip!" again cries mamma the economist.

"Loss of time is loss of money, my dear lady," says Philip, very gravely. "I have ever so many places to go to. When I am set in for being ruined, you shall see what a screw I will become! I must go to Mrs. Brandon, who will be very uneasy, poor dear, until she knows the worst."

"Oh, Philip, I should like so to go with you!" cries Laura. "Pray, give her our very best regards and respects."

"*Merci!*" said the young man, and squeezed Mrs. Pendennis's hand in his own big one. "I will take your message to her, Laura. *J'aime qu'on l'aime, savez-vous?*"

"That means, I love those who love her," cries little Laura; "but, I don't know," remarked this little person afterwards to her paternal confidant, "that I like *all* people to love my mamma. That is, I don't like *her* to like them, papa—only you may, papa, and Ethel may, and Arthur may, and, I think, Philip may, now he is poor and quite, quite alone—and we will take care of him, won't we? And, I think, I'll buy him something with my money which Aunt Ethel gave me."

"And I'll give him my money," cries a boy.

"And I'll div him my—my——" Psha! what matters what the little sweet lips prattled in their artless kindness? But the soft words of love and pity smote the mother's heart with an exquisite pang of gratitude and joy; and I know where her thanks were paid for those tender words and thoughts of her little ones.

Mrs. Pendennis made Philip promise to come to dinner, and also to remember not to take a cab—which promise Mr. Firmin had not much difficulty in executing, for he had but a few hundred yards to walk across the Park from his club; and I must say that my wife took a special care of our dinner that day, preparing for Philip certain dishes which she knew he liked, and enjoining the butler of the establishment (who also happened to be the owner of the house) to fetch from his cellar the very choicest wine in his possession.

I have previously described our friend and his boisterous, impetuous, generous nature. When Philip was moved, he called to all the world to witness his emotion. When he was angry, his enemies were all the rogues and scoundrels in the world. He vowed he would have no mercy on them, and desired all his acquaintances to participate in his anger. How could such an open-mouthed son have had such a close-spoken father? I dare say you have seen very well-bred young people, the children of vulgar and ill-bred parents; the swaggering father have a silent son; the loud mother a modest daughter. Our friend is not Amadis or Sir Charles Grandison; and I don't set him up for a moment as a person to be revered or imitated; but try to draw him faithfully, and as nature made him. As nature made him, so he was. I don't think he tried to improve himself much. Perhaps few people do. They suppose they do: and you read, in apologetic memoirs, and fond biographies, how this man cured his bad temper, and t'other worked and strove until he grew to be almost faultless. Very well and good, my good people. You can learn a language; you can master a science; I have heard of an old square-toes of sixty who learned, by study and intense application, very satisfactorily to dance; but can you, by taking thought, add to your moral stature? Ah me! the doctor who preaches is only taller than most of us by the height of the pulpit: and when he steps down, I dare say he cringes to the duchess, growls at his children, scolds his wife about the dinner. All is vanity, look you: and so the preacher is vanity, too.

Well, then, I must again say that Philip roared his griefs: he shouted his laughter: he bellowed his applause: he was extravagant in his humility as in his pride, in his admiration of his friends and contempt for his enemies: I dare say not a just man, but I have met juster men not half so honest; and certainly not a faultless man, though I know better men not near so good. So, I believe, my wife thinks: else why should she be so fond of him? Did we not know boys who never went out of bounds, and never were late for school, and never made a false concord or quantity, and never came under the ferule ; and others who were always playing truant, and blundering, and being whipped; and yet, somehow, was not Master Naughtyboy better liked than Master Goodchild? When Master Naughtyboy came to dine with us on the first day of his ruin, he bore a face of radiant happiness—he laughed, he bounced about, he caressed the children ; now he took a couple on his knees ; now he tossed the baby to the ceiling; now he sprawled over a sofa, and now he rode upon a chair; never was a penniless gentleman more cheerful. As for his dinner, Phil's appetite was always fine, but on this day an ogre could scarcely play a more terrible knife and fork. He asked for more and more, until his entertainers wondered to behold him. " Dine for to-day and to-morrow too ; can't expect such fare as this every day, you know. This claret, how good it is ! May I pack some up in paper, and take it home with me ? " The children roared with laughter at this admirable idea of carrying home wine in a sheet of paper. I don't know that it is always at the best jokes that children laugh :—children and wise men too.

When we three were by ourselves, and freed from the company of servants and children, our friend told us the cause of his gaiety. "By George !" he swore, " it is worth being ruined to find such good people in the world. My dear, kind Laura "—here the gentleman brushes his eyes with his fist—" it was as much as I could do this morning to prevent myself from hugging you in my arms, you were so generous, and—and so kind, and so tender, and so good, by George. And after leaving you, where do you think I went ? "

" I think I can guess, Philip," says Laura.

" Well," says Philip, winking his eyes again, and tossing off a great bumper of wine, " I went to her, of course. I think she is the best friend I have in the world. The old man was out, and I told her about everything that had happened. And what do you think she has done ? She says she has been expecting me—she has ; and she has gone and fitted up a room with a nice little bed at the top of the house, with everything as neat and trim as possible ; and she begged and prayed I would go and stay with her—and I said I would, to please her. And then she takes me down to her room ; and she jumps up to a cupboard, which she unlocks ; and she opens and takes three-and-twenty pounds out of a—out of a tea—out of a tea-caddy— confound me !—and she says, 'Here, Philip,' she says, and—Boo ! what a fool I am ! " and here the orator fairly broke down in his speech.

CHAPTER XVI.

IN WHICH PHILIP SHOWS HIS METTLE.

HEN the poor Little Sister proffered her mite, her all, to Philip, I dare say some sentimental passages occurred between them which are much too trivial to be narrated. No doubt her pleasure would have been at that moment to give him not only that gold which she had been saving up against rent-day, but the spoons, the furniture, and all the valuables of the house, including, perhaps, J. J.'s bricabrac, cabinets, china, and so forth. To perform a kindness, an act of self-sacrifice ;—are not these the most delicious privileges of female tenderness ? Philip checked his little friend's enthusiasm. He showed her a purse full of money, at which sight the poor little soul was rather disappointed. He magnified the value of his horses, which, according to Philip's calculation, were to bring him at least two hundred pounds more than the stock which he had already in hand; and the master of such a sum as this, she was forced to confess, had no need to despair. Indeed, she had never in her life possessed the half of it. Her kind dear little offer of a home in her house he would accept sometimes, and with gratitude. Well, there was a little consolation in that. In a moment that active little housekeeper saw the room ready; flowers on the mantel-piece; his looking-glass, which her father could do quite well with the little one, as he was always shaved by the barber now; the quilted counterpane, which she had herself made :—I know not what more improvements she devised; and I fear that at the idea of having Philip with her, this little thing was as extravagantly and unreasonably happy as we have just now seen Philip to be. What was that last dish which Pætus and Arria shared in common? I have lost my Lempriere's dictionary (that treasury of my youth), and forget whether it was a cold dagger *au naturel*, or a dish of hot coals *à la Romaine*, of which they partook; but, whatever it was, she smiled, and delightedly received it, happy to share the beloved one's fortune.

Yes: Philip would come home to his Little Sister sometimes : sometimes of a Saturday, and they would go to church on Sunday, as he used to do when he was a boy at school. "But then, you know," says Phil, "law is law; study is study. I must devote my whole energies to my work—get up very early."

"Don't tire your eyes, my dear," interposes Mr. Philip's soft, judicious friend.

"There must be no trifling with work," says Philip, with awful gravity. "There's Benton the Judge : Benton and Burbage, you know."

"Oh, Benton and Burbage!" whispers the Little Sister, not a little bewildered.

"How do you suppose he became a judge before forty?"

"Before forty who? law, bless me!"

"Before *he* was forty, Mrs. Carry. When he came to work, he had his own way to make : just like me. He had a small allowance from his father : that's not like me. He took chambers in the Temple. He went to a pleader's office. He read fourteen, fifteen hours every day. He dined on a cup of tea and a mutton-chop."

"La, bless me, child! I wouldn't have you to do that, not to be Lord Chamberlain—Chancellor what's his name? Destroy your youth with reading, and your eyes, and go without your dinner? You're not used to that sort of thing, dear; and it would kill you!"

Philip smoothed his fair hair off his ample forehead, and nodded his head, smiling sweetly. I think his inward monitor hinted to him that there was not much danger of his killing himself by over-work. "To succeed at the law, as in all other professions," he continued, with much gravity, "requires the greatest perseverance, and industry, and talent; and then, perhaps, you don't succeed. Many have failed who have had all these qualities."

"But they haven't talents like my Philip, I know they haven't. And I had to stand up in a court once, and was cross-examined by a vulgar man before a horrid deaf old judge; and I'm sure if your lawyers are like them I don't wish you to succeed at all. And now, look! there's a nice loin of pork coming up. Pa loves roast pork; and you must come and have some with us; and every day and all days, my dear, I should like to see you seated there." And the Little Sister frisked about here, and bustled there, and brought a cunning bottle of wine from some corner, and made the boy welcome. So that, you see, far from starving, he actually had two dinners on that first day of his ruin.

Caroline consented to a compromise regarding the money, on Philip's solemn vow and promise that she should be his banker whenever necessity called. She rather desired his poverty for the sake of its precious reward. She hid away a little bag of gold for her darling's use whenever he should need it. I dare say she pinched and had shabby dinners at home, so as to save yet more, and so caused the Captain to grumble. Why, for that boy's sake, I believe she would have been capable of shaving her lodgers' legs of mutton, and levying a tax on their tea-caddies and baker's stuff. If you don't like unprincipled attachments of this sort, and only desire that your womankind should love you for yourself, and according to your deserts, I am your very humble servant. Hereditary bondswomen! you know, that were you free, and did you strike the blow, my dears, you were unhappy for your pain, and eagerly would claim your bonds again. What poet has uttered that sentiment? It is perfectly true, and I know will receive the cordial approbation of the dear ladies.

Philip has decreed in his own mind that he will go and live in those chambers in the Temple where we have met him. Van John, the sporting gentleman, had determined for special reasons to withdraw from law and sport in this country, and Mr. Firmin took possession of his vacant sleeping-chamber. To furnish a bachelor's bed-room need not be a matter of much cost; but Mr. Philip was too good-natured a fellow to haggle about the valuation of Van John's bedsteads and chests of drawers, and generously took them at twice their value. He and Mr. Cassidy now divided the rooms in equal reign. Ah, happy rooms, bright rooms, rooms near the sky, to remember you is to be young again! for I would have you to know that when Philip went to take possession of his share of the fourth floor in the Temple, his biographer was still comparatively juvenile, and in one or two very old-fashioned families was called " young Pendennis."

So Philip Firmin dwelt in a garret; and the fourth part of a laundress and the half of a boy now formed the domestic establishment of him who had been attended by housekeepers, butlers, and obsequious liveried menials. To be freed from that ceremonial and etiquette of plush and worsted lace was an immense relief to Firmin. His pipe need not lurk in crypts or back closets now: its fragrance breathed over the whole chambers, and rose up to the sky, their near neighbour.

The first month or two after being ruined, Philip vowed, was an uncommonly pleasant time. He had still plenty of money in his pocket; and the sense that, perhaps, it was imprudent to take a cab or drink a bottle of wine, added a zest to those enjoyments which they by no means possessed when they were easy and of daily occurrence. I am not certain that a dinner of beef and porter did not amuse our young man almost as well as banquets much more costly to which he had been accustomed. He laughed at the pretensions of his boyish days, when he and other solemn young epicures used to sit down to elaborate tavern banquets, and pretend to criticize vintages, and sauces, and turtle. As yet there was not only content with his dinner, but plenty therewith; and I do not wish to alarm you by supposing that Philip will ever have to encounter any dreadful extremities of poverty or hunger in the course of his history. The wine in the jug was very low at times, but it never was quite empty. This lamb was shorn, but the wind was tempered to him.

So Philip took possession of his rooms in the Temple, and began actually to reside there just as the long vacation commenced, which he intended to devote to a course of serious study of the law and private preparation, before he should venture on the great business of circuits and the bar. Nothing is more necessary for desk-men than exercise, so Philip took a good deal; especially on the water, where he pulled a famous oar. Nothing is more natural after exercise than refreshment; and Mr. Firmin, now he was too poor for claret, showed a great capacity for beer. After beer and bodily labour, rest, of course, is necessary; and Firmin slept nine hours, and looked as rosy as a girl in her first season. Then such a man, with such a frame and health, must have a good appetite for breakfast. And then every man who wishes to succeed at the bar, in the senate, on the bench, in the House of Peers, on the Woolsack, must know the quotidian history of his country; so, of course, Philip read the newspaper. Thus, you see, his hours of study were perforce curtailed by the necessary duties which distracted him from his labours.

It has been said that Mr. Firmin's companion in chambers, Mr. Cassidy, was a native of the neighbouring kingdom of Ireland, and engaged in literary pursuits in this country. A merry, shrewd, silent, observant little man, he, unlike some of his compatriots, always knew how to make both ends meet; feared no man alive in the character of a dun; and out of small earnings managed to transmit no small comforts and subsidies to old parents living somewhere in Munster. Of Cassidy's friends was Finucane, now editor of the *Pall Mall Gazette;* he married the widow of the late eccentric and gifted Captain Shandon, and Cass himself was the fashionable correspondent of the *Gazette,* chronicling the marriages, deaths, births, dinner-parties of the nobility. These Irish gentlemen knew other Irish gentlemen, connected with other newspapers, who formed a little literary society. They assembled at each other's rooms, and at haunts where social pleasure was to be purchased at no dear rate. Philip Firmin was known to many of them before his misfortunes occurred, and when there was gold in plenty in his pocket, and never-failing applause for his songs.

When Pendennis and his friends wrote in this newspaper, it was impertinent enough, and many men must have heard the writers laugh at the airs which they occasionally thought proper to assume. The tone which they took amused, annoyed, tickled, was popular. It was continued, and, of course, caricatured by their successors. They worked for very moderate fees: but paid themselves by impertinence, and the satisfaction of assailing their betters. Three or four persons were reserved from their abuse; but somebody was sure every week to be tied up at their post, and the public made sport of the victim's contortions. The writers were obscure barristers, ushers, and college men, but they had omniscience at their pens' end, and were ready to lay down the law on any given subject—to teach any man his business, were it a bishop in his pulpit, a Minister in his place in the House, a captain on his quarter-deck, a tailor on his shopboard, or a jockey in his saddle.

Since those early days of the *Pall Mall Gazette*, when old Shandon wielded his truculent tomahawk, and Messrs. W—rr—ngt—n and P—nd—nn—s followed him in the war path, the *Gazette* had passed through several hands ; and the victims who were immolated by the editors of to-day were very likely the objects of the best puffery of the last dynasty. To be flogged in what was your own schoolroom—that, surely, is a queer sensation ; and when my Report was published on the decay of the sealing-wax trade in the three kingdoms (owing to the prevalence of gummed envelopes,—as you may see in that masterly document) I was horsed up and smartly whipped in the *Gazette* by some of the rods which had come out of pickle since my time. Was not good Dr. Guillotin executed by his own neat invention? I don't know who was the Monsieur Sanson who operated on me ; but have always had my idea that Digges, of Corpus, was the man to whom my flagellation was entrusted. His father keeps a ladies' school at Hackney; but there is an air of fashion in everything which Digges writes, and a chivalrous conservatism which makes me pretty certain that D. was my scarifier. All this, however, is naught. Let us turn away from the author's private griefs and egotisms to those of the hero of the story.

Does any one remember the appearance some twenty years ago of a little book called "Trumpet Calls"—a book of songs and poetry, dedicated to his brother officers by Cornet Canterton? His trumpet was very tolerably melodious, and the cornet played some small airs on it with some little grace and skill. But this poor Canterton belonged to the Life-Guards Green, and Philip Firmin would have liked to have the lives of one or two troops at least of that corps. Entering into Mr. Cassidy's room, Philip found the little volume. He set to work to exterminate Canterton. He rode him down, trampled over his face and carcase, knocked the "Trumpet Calls" and all the teeth down the trumpeter's throat. Never was such a smashing article as he wrote. And Mugford, Mr. Cassidy's chief and owner, who likes always to have at least one man served up and hashed small in the *Pall Mall Gazette*, happened at this very juncture to have no other victim ready in his larder. Philip's review appeared there in print. He rushed off with immense glee to Westminster, to show us his performance. Nothing must content him but to give a dinner at Greenwich on his success. Oh, Philip! We wished that this had not been his first fee; and that sober law had given it to him, and not the graceless and fickle muse with whom he had been flirting. For, truth to say, certain wise old heads which wagged over his performance could see but little merit in it. His style was coarse, his wit clumsy and savage. Never mind characterizing either now. He has seen the error of his ways, and divorced with the muse whom he never ought to have wooed.

The shrewd Cassidy not only could not write himself, but knew he could not—or, at least, pen more than a plain paragraph, or a brief sentence to the point, but said he would carry this paper to his chief. "His Excellency" was the nickname by which this chief was called by his familiars. Mugford—Frederick Mugford was his real name—and putting out of sight that little defect in his character, that he committed a systematic literary murder once a week, a more worthy good-natured little murderer did not live. He came of the old school of the press. Like French marshals, he had risen from the ranks, and retained some of the manners and oddities of the private soldier. A new race of writers had grown up since he enlisted as a printer's boy—men of the world, with the manners of other gentlemen. Mugford never professed the least gentility. He knew that his young men laughed at his peculiarities, and did not care a fig for their scorn. As the knife with which he conveyed his victuals to his mouth went down his throat at the plenteous banquets which he gave, he saw his young friends wince and wonder, and rather relished their surprise. Those lips never cared in the least about placing his *h*'s in right places. They used bad language with great freedom—(to hear him bullying a printing office was a wonder of eloquence)—but they betrayed no secrets, and the words which they uttered you might trust. He had belonged to two or three parties, and had respected them all. When he went to the Under-Secretary's office he was never kept waiting; and once or twice Mrs. Mugford, who governed him, ordered him to attend the Saturday reception of the Ministers' ladies, where he might be seen, with dirty hands, it is true, but a richly embroidered waistcoat and

fancy satin tie. His heart, however, was not in these entertainments. I have heard him say that he only came because Mrs. M.
would have it; and he frankly owned that he "would rather
'ave a pipe, and a drop of something 'ot, than all your ices and
rubbish."

Mugford had a curious knowledge of what was going on in the
world, and of the affairs of countless people. When Cass brought
Philip's article to his Excellency, and mentioned the author's name,
Mugford showed himself to be perfectly familiar with the histories
of Philip and his father. "The old chap has nobbled the young
fellow's money, almost every shilling of it, I hear. Knew he never
would carry on. His discounts would have killed any man. Seen
his paper about this ten year. Young one is a gentleman—passionate
fellow, hawhaw fellow, but kind to the poor. Father never was a
gentleman, with all his fine airs and fine waistcoats. I don't set
up in that line myself, Cass, but I tell you I know 'em when I
see 'em."

Philip had friends and private patrons whose influence was great
with the Mugford family, and of whom he little knew. Every year
Mrs. M. was in the habit of contributing a Mugford to the world.
She was one of Mrs. Brandon's most regular clients; and year after
year, almost from his first arrival in London, Ridley, the painter, had
been engaged as portrait painter to this worthy family. Philip and
his illness; Philip and his horses, splendours, and entertainments;
Philip and his lamentable downfall and ruin, had formed the subject
of many an interesting talk between Mrs. Mugford and her friend
the Little Sister; and as we know Caroline's infatuation about the
young fellow, we may suppose that his good qualities lost nothing
in the description. When that article in the *Pall Mall Gazette*
appeared, Nurse Brandon took the omnibus to Haverstock Hill,
where, as you know, Mugford had his villa;—arrived at Mrs. Mugford's, *Gazette* in hand, and had a long and delightful conversation
with that lady. Mrs. Brandon bought I don't know how many
copies of that *Pall Mall Gazette.* She now asked for it repeatedly
in her walks at sundry ginger-beer shops, and of all sorts of news-
vendors. I have heard that when the Mugfords first purchased the
Gazette, Mrs. M. used to drop bills from her pony-chaise, and dis-
tribute placards setting forth the excellence of the journal. "We
keep our carriage, but we ain't above our business, Brandon," that

good lady would say. And the business prospered under the management of these worthy folks; and the pony-chaise unfolded into a
noble barouche; and the pony increased and multiplied, and became
a pair of horses; and there was not a richer piece of gold-lace round
any coachman's hat in London than now decorated John, who had
grown with the growth of his master's fortunes, and drove the
chariot in which his worthy employers rode on the way to Hampstead, honour, and prosperity.

" All this pitching into the poet is very well, you know, Cassidy,"
says Mugford to his subordinate. " It's like shooting a butterfly with
a blunderbuss; but if Firmin likes that kind of sport, I don't mind.
There won't be any difficulty about taking his copy at our place.
The duchess knows another old woman who is a friend of his "
("the duchess" was the title which Mr. Mugford was in the playful
habit of conferring upon his wife). " It's my belief young F. had
better stick to the law, and leave the writing rubbish alone. But he
knows his own affairs best, and, mind you, the duchess is determined
we shall give him a helping hand."

Once, in the days of his prosperity, and in J. J.'s company, Philip
had visited Mrs. Mugford and her family—a circumstance which the
gentleman had almost forgotten. The painter and his friend were
taking a Sunday walk, and came upon Mugford's pretty cottage and
garden, and were hospitably entertained there by the owners of the
place. It has disappeared, and the old garden has long since been
covered by terraces and villas, and Mugford and Mrs. M., good
souls, where are they? But the lady thought she had never seen
such a fine-looking young fellow as Philip; cast about in her mind
which of her little female Mugfords should marry him ; and insisted
upon offering her guest champagne. Poor Phil ! So, you see, whilst,
perhaps, he was rather pluming himself upon his literary talents, and
imagining that he was a clever fellow, he was only the object of a
job on the part of two or three good folks, who knew his history,
and compassionated his misfortunes.

Mugford recalled himself to Philip's recollection, when they met
after the appearance of Mr. Phil's first performance in the *Gazette*.
If he still took a Sunday walk, Hampstead way, Mr. M. requested
him to remember that there was a slice of beef and a glass of wine
at the old shop. Philip remembered it well enough now : the ugly
room, the ugly family, the kind worthy people. Ere long he learned

what had been Mrs. Brandon's connection with them, and the young man's heart was softened and grateful as he thought how this kind, gentle creature had been able to befriend him. She, we may be sure, was not a little proud of her protégé. I believe she grew to fancy that the whole newspaper was written by Philip. She made her fond parent read it aloud as she worked. Mr. Ridley, senior, pronounced it was remarkably fine, really now; without, I think, entirely comprehending the meaning of the sentiments which Mr. Gann gave forth in his rich loud voice, and often dropping asleep in his chair during this sermon.

In the autumn, Mr. Firmin's friends, Mr. and Mrs. Pendennis, selected the romantic seaport town of Boulogne for their holiday residence; and having roomy quarters in the old town, we gave Mr. Philip an invitation to pay us a visit whenever he could tear himself away from literature and law. He came in high spirits. He amused us by imitations and descriptions of his new proprietor and master, Mr. Mugford—his blunders, his bad language, his good heart. One day, Mugford expected a celebrated literary character to dinner, and Philip and Cassidy were invited to meet him. The great man was ill, and was unable to come. "Don't dish up the side-dishes," called out Mugford to his cook, in the hearing of his other guests. "Mr. Lyon ain't a coming." They dined quite sufficiently without the side-dishes, and were perfectly cheerful in the absence of the lion. Mugford patronized his young men with amusing good-nature. "Firmin, cut the goose for the duchess, will you? Cass can't say Bo! to one, he can't. Ridley, a little of the stuffing. It'll make your hair curl." And Philip was going to imitate a frightful act with the cold steel (with which I have said Philip's master used to convey food to his mouth), but our dear innocent third daughter uttered a shriek of terror, which caused him to drop the dreadful weapon. Our darling little Florence is a nervous child, and the sight of an edged tool causes her anguish, ever since our darling little Tom nearly cut his thumb off with his father's razor.

Our main amusement in this delightful place was to look at the sea-sick landing from the steamers; and one day, as we witnessed this phenomenon, Philip sprang to the ropes which divided us from the arriving passengers, and with a cry of "How do you do, General?" greeted a yellow-faced gentleman, who started back, and, to my thinking, seemed but ill inclined to reciprocate Philip's friendly greeting. The General was fluttered, no doubt, by the bustle and interruptions incidental to the landing. A pallid lady, the partner of his existence probably, was calling out, " Noof et doo domestiques, Doo!" to the sentries who kept the line, and who seemed little interested by this family news. A governess, a tall young lady, and several more male and female children, followed the pale lady, who, as I thought, looked strangely frightened when the gentleman addressed as General communicated to her Philip's name. " Is that him?" said the lady in questionable grammar; and the tall young lady turned a pair of large eyes upon the individual designated as " him," and showed a pair of dank ringlets, out of which the envious sea-nymphs had shaken all the curl.

The general turned out to be General Baynes; the pale lady was Mrs. General B.; the tall young lady was Miss Charlotte Baynes, the General's eldest child; and the other six, forming nine, or "noof," in all, as Mrs. General B. said, were the other members of the Baynes family. And here I may as well say why the General looked alarmed on seeing Philip, and why the General's lady frowned at him. In action, one of the bravest of men, in common life General Baynes was timorous and weak. Specially he was afraid of Mrs. General Baynes, who ruled him with a vigorous authority. As Philip's trustee, he had allowed Philip's father to make away with the boy's money. He learned with a ghastly terror that he was answerable for his own remissness and want of care. For a long while he did not dare to tell his commander-in-chief of this dreadful penalty which was hanging over him. When at last he ventured upon this confession, I do not envy him the scene which must have ensued between him and his commanding officer. The morning after the fatal confession, when the children assembled for breakfast and prayers, Mrs. Baynes gave their young ones their porridge: she and Charlotte poured out the tea and coffee for the elders, and then addressing her eldest son Ochterlony, she said, " Ocky, my boy, the General has announced a charming piece of news this morning."

" Bought that pony, sir?" says Ocky.

" Oh, what jolly fun !" says Moira, the second son.

" Dear, dear papa ! what's the matter, and why do you look so?" cries Charlotte, looking behind her father's paper.

That guilty man would fain have made a shroud of his *Morning Herald.* He would have flung the sheet over his whole body, and lain hidden there from all eyes.

"The fun, my dears, is that your father is ruined : that's the fun. Eat your porridge now, little ones. Charlotte, pop a bit of butter in Carrick's porridge ; for you mayn't have any to-morrow."

" Oh, gammon," cries Moira.

" You'll soon see whether it is gammon or not, sir, when you'll be starving, sir. Your father has ruined us—and a very pleasant morning's work, I am sure."

And she calmly rubs the nose of her youngest child who is near her, and too young, and innocent, and careless, perhaps, of the world's censure as yet to keep in a strict cleanliness her own dear little snub nose and dappled cheeks.

" We are only ruined, and shall be starving soon, my dears, and if the General has bought a pony—as I dare say he has ; he is quite capable of buying a pony when we are starving—the best thing we can do is to eat the pony. M'Grigor, don't laugh. Starvation is no laughing matter. When we were at Dumdum, in '36, we ate some colt. Don't you remember Jubber's colt—Jubber of the Horse Artillery, General ? Never tasted anything more tender in all my life. Charlotte, take Jany's hands out of the marmalade ! We are all ruined, my dears, as sure as our name is Baynes." Thus did the mother of the family prattle on in the midst of her little ones, and announce to them the dreadful news of impending starvation. " General Baynes, by his carelessness, had allowed Dr. Firmin to make away with the money over which the General had been set as sentinel. Philip might recover from the trustee, and no doubt would. Perhaps he would not press his claim ? My dear, what can you expect from the son of such a father ? Depend on it, Charlotte, no good fruit can come from a stock like that. The son is a bad one, the father is a bad one, and your father, poor dear soul, is not fit to be trusted to walk the street without some one to keep him from tumbling. Why did I allow him to go to town without me ? We were quartered at Colchester then : and I could not move on account of your brother M'Grigor. ' Baynes,' I said to your father, ' as sure as I let you go away to town without me, you will come to mischief.' And go he did, and come to mischief he did. And through his folly I and my poor children must go and beg our bread in the streets—I and my seven poor, robbed, penniless little ones.   Oh, it's cruel, cruel !"

Indeed, one cannot fancy a more dismal prospect for this worthy mother and wife than to see her children without provision at the commencement of their lives, and her luckless husband robbed of his life's earnings, and ruined just when he was too old to work.

What was to become of them ? Now poor Charlotte thought, with pangs of a keen remorse, how idle she had been, and how she had snubbed her governesses, and how little she knew, and how badly she played the piano. Oh, neglected opportunities ! Oh, remorse, now the time was past and irrecoverable ! Does any young lady read this who, perchance, ought to be doing her lessons ? My dear, lay down the story-book at once. Go up to your school-room, and practise your piano for two hours this moment ; so that you may be prepared to support your family, should ruin in any case fall upon *you*. A great girl of sixteen, I pity Charlotte Baynes's feelings of anguish. She can't write a very good hand ; she can scarcely answer any question to speak of in any educational books ; her pianoforte playing is very very so-so indeed. If she is to go out and get a living for the family, how, in the name of goodness, is she to set about it ? What are they to do with the boys, and the money that has been put away for Ochterlony when he goes to college, and for Moira's commission ? "Why, we can't afford to keep them at Dr. Pybus's, where they were doing so well ; and they were ever so much better and more gentlemanlike than Colonel Chandler's boys ; and to lose the army will break Moira's heart, it will. And the little ones, my little blue-eyed Carrick, and my darling Jany, and my Mary, that I nursed almost miraculously out of her scarlet fever. God help them ! God help us all !" thinks the poor mother. No wonder that her nights are wakeful, and her heart in a tumult of alarm at the idea of the impending danger.

And the father of the family ?—the stout old General whose battles and campaigns are over, who has come home to rest his war-worn limbs, and make his peace with heaven ere it calls him away—what must be his feelings when he thinks that he has been entrapped by a villain into committing an imprudence which makes his children penniless and himself dishonoured and a beggar ? When he found what Dr. Firmin had done, and how he had been cheated, he went away, aghast, to his lawyer, who could give him no help. Philip's mother's trustee was answerable to Philip for his property. It had been stolen through Baynes's own carelessness, and the law bound him to replace it. General Baynes's man of business could not help him out of his perplexity at all ; and I hope my worthy reader is not going to be too angry with the General for what I own he did. *You* never would, my dear sir, I know. No power on earth would induce *you* to depart one inch from the path of rectitude; or, having done an act of imprudence, to shrink from bearing the consequence. The long and short of the matter is, that poor Baynes and his wife, after holding agitated, stealthy councils together—after believing that every strange face they saw was a bailiff's coming to arrest them on Philip's account—after horrible days of remorse, misery, guilt—I say the long and the short of the matter was that these poor people determined to run away. They would go and hide themselves anywhere—in an impenetrable pine forest in Norway—up an inaccessible mountain in Switzerland. They would change their names ; dye their mustachios and honest old white hair ; fly with their little ones away, away, away, out of the reach of law and Philip ; and the first flight lands them on Boulogne Pier, and there is Mr. Philip holding out his hand and actually eyeing them as they get out of the steamer! Eyeing them? It is the eye of heaven that is on those criminals. Holding out his hand to them? It is the hand of fate that is on their wretched shoulders. No wonder they shuddered and turned pale. That which I took for sea-sickness, I am sorry to say was a guilty conscience : and where is the steward, my dear friends, who can relieve us of that?

As this party came staggering out of the Custom-house, poor Baynes still found Philip's hand stretched out to catch hold of him, and saluted him with a ghastly cordiality. "These are your children, General, and this is Mrs. Baynes?" says Philip, smiling, and taking off his hat.

"Oh, yes! I'm Mrs. General Baynes!" says the poor woman; "and these are the children—yes, yes. Charlotte, this is Mr. Firmin, of whom you have heard us speak ; and these are my boys, Moira and Ochterlony."

"I have had the honour of meeting General Baynes at Old Parr Street. Don't you remember, sir?" says Mr. Pendennis, with great affability to the General.

"What, *another* who knows me?" I dare say the poor wretch thinks; and glances of a dreadful meaning pass between the guilty wife and the guilty husband.

"You are going to stay at any hotel?"

"'Hôtel des Bains!'" "'Hôtel du Nord!'" "'Hôtel d'Angleterre!'" here cry twenty commissioners in a breath.

"Hotel? Oh, yes! That is, we have not made up our minds whether we shall go on to-night or whether we shall stay," say those guilty ones, looking at one another, and then down to the ground; on which one of the children, with a roar, says—

"Oh, ma, what a story! You said you'd stay to-night; and I was so sick in the beastly boat, and I *won't* travel any more!" And tears choke his artless utterance. "And you said Bang to the man who took your keys, you know you did," resumes the innocent, as soon as he can gasp a further remark.

"Who told *you* to speak?" cried mamma, giving the boy a shake.

"This is the way to the 'Hôtel des Bains,'" says Philip, making Miss Baynes another of his best bows. And Miss Baynes makes a curtsey, and her eyes look up at the handsome young man—large brown honest eyes in a comely round face, on each side of which depend two straight wisps of brown hair that were ringlets when they left Folkestone a few hours since.

"Oh, I say, look at those women with the short petticoats! and wooden shoes, by George! Oh! it's jolly, ain't it?" cries one young gentleman.

"By George, there's a man with earrings on! There is, Ocky, upon my word!" calls out another. And the elder boy, turning round to his father, points to some soldiers. "Did you ever see such little beggars?" he says, tòssing his head up. "They wouldn't take such fellows into our line."

"I am not at all tired, thank you," says Charlotte. "I am accustomed to carry him." I forgot to say that the young lady had one of the children asleep on her shoulder; and another was toddling at her side, holding by his sister's dress, and admiring Mr. Firmin's whiskers, that flamed and curled very luminously and gloriously, like to the rays of the setting sun.

"I am very glad we met, sir," says Philip, in the most friendly manner, taking leave of the General at the gate of his hotel. "I hope you won't go away to-morrow, and that I may come and pay my respects to Mrs. Baynes." Again he salutes that lady with a *coup de chapeau*. Again he bows to Miss Baynes. She makes a pretty curtsey enough, considering that she has a baby asleep on her shoulder. And they enter the hotel, the excellent Marie marshalling them to fitting apartments, where some of them, I have no doubt, will sleep very soundly. How much more comfortably might poor Baynes and his wife have slept had they known what were Philip's feelings regarding them !

We both admired Charlotte, the tall girl who carried her little brother, and around whom the others clung. And we spoke loudly in Miss Charlotte's praises to Mrs. Pendennis, when we joined that lady at dinner. In the praise of Mrs. Baynes we had not a great deal to say, further than that she seemed to take command of the whole expedition, including the general officer, her husband.

Though Marie's beds at the " Hôtel des Bains " are as comfortable as any beds in Europe, you see that admirable chambermaid cannot lay out a clean, easy conscience upon the clean, fragrant pillow-case ; and General and Mrs. Baynes owned, in after days, that one of the most dreadful nights they ever passed was that of their first landing in France. What refugee from his country can fly from himself? Railways were not as yet in that part of France. The General was too poor to fly with a couple of private carriages, which he must have had for his family of "noof," his governess, and two servants. Encumbered with such a train, his enemy would speedily have pursued and overtaken him. It is a fact that, immediately after landing at his hotel, he and his commanding officer went off to see when they could get places for— never mind the name of the place where they really thought of taking refuge. They never told, but Mrs. General Baynes had a sister, Mrs. Major MacWhirter (married to MacW. of the Bengal Cavalry), and the sisters loved each other very affectionately, especially by letter, for it must be owned that they quarrelled frightfully when together ; and Mrs. MacWhirter never could bear that her younger sister should be taken out to dinner before her, because she was married to a superior officer. Well, their little differences were forgotten when the two ladies were apart. The sisters wrote to each other prodigious long letters, in which household affairs, the children's puerile diseases, the relative prices of veal, eggs, chickens, the rent of lodging and houses in various places, were fully discussed. And as Mrs. Baynes showed a surprising knowledge of Tours, the markets, rents, clergymen, society there, and as Major and Mrs. Mac. were staying there, I have little doubt, for my part, from this and another not unimportant circumstance, that it was to that fair city our fugitives were wending their way, when events occurred which must now be narrated, and which caused General Baynes at the head of his domestic regiment to do what the King of France with twenty thousand men is said to have done in old times.

Philip was greatly interested about the family. The truth is, we were all very much bored at Boulogne. We read the feeblest London papers at the reading-room with frantic assiduity. We saw all the boats come in : and the day was lost when we missed the Folkestone boat or the London boat. We consumed much time and absinthe at cafés; and tramped leagues upon that old pier every day. Well, Philip was at the " Hôtel des Bains " at a very early hour next morning, and there he saw the General, with a woe-worn face, leaning on his stick, and looking at his luggage, as it lay piled in the porte-cochère of the hotel. There they lay, thirty-seven packages in all, including washing-tubs, and a child's India sleeping-cot ; and all these packages were ticketed M. LE Général Baynes, Officier Anglais, Tours, Touraine, France. I say, putting two and two together ; calling to mind Mrs. General's singular knowledge of Tours and familiarity with the place and its prices ; remembering that her sister Emily—Mrs. Major MacWhirter, in fact—was there ; and seeing thirty-seven trunks, bags, and portmanteaus, all directed " M. le Général Baynes, Officier Anglais, Tours, Touraine," am I wrong in supposing that Tours was the General's destination ? On the other hand, we have the old officer's declaration to Philip that he did not know where he was going. Oh, you sly old man ! Oh, you grey old fox, beginning to double and to turn at sixty-seven years of age ! Well ? The General was in retreat, and he did not wish the enemy to know upon what lines he was retreating. What is the harm of that, pray ? Besides, he was under the orders of his commanding officer, and when Mrs. General gave her orders, I should have liked to see any officer of hers disobey.

" What a pyramid of portmanteaus ! You are not thinking of moving to-day, General ? " says Philip.

" It is Sunday, sir," says the General ; which you will perceive was not answering the question ; but, in truth, except for a very great emergency, the good General would not travel on that day.

" I hope the ladies slept well after their windy voyage."

" Thank you. My wife is an old sailor, and has made two voyages out and home to India." Here, you understand, the old man is again eluding his interlocutor's artless queries.

" I should like to have some talk with you, sir, when you are free," continues Philip, not having leisure as yet to be surprised at the other's demeanour.

" There are other days besides Sunday for talk on business," says that piteous sly-boots of an old officer. Ah, conscience! conscience! Twenty-four Sikhs, sword in hand, two dozen Pindarries, Mahrattas, Ghoorkas, what you please—that old man felt that he would rather have met them than Philip's unsuspecting blue eyes. These, however, now lighted up with rather an angry, " Well, sir, as you don't talk business on Sunday, may I call on you to-morrow morning."

And what advantage had the poor old fellow got by all this doubling and hesitating and artfulness ?—a respite until to-morrow morning ! Another night of horrible wakefulness and hopeless guilt, and Philip waiting ready the next morning with his little bill, and, " Please pay me the thirty thousand which my father spent and you owe me. Please turn out into the streets with your wife and family, and beg and starve. Have the goodness to hand me out your last rupee. Be kind enough to sell your children's clothes and your wife's jewels, and hand over the proceeds to me. I'll call to-morrow. Bye, bye."

Here there came tripping over the marble pavement of the hall of the hotel a tall young lady in a brown silk dress and rich curling ringlets falling upon her fair young neck—beautiful brown curling ringlets, *vous comprenez*, not wisps of moistened hair, and a broad clear forehead, and two honest eyes shining below it, and cheeks not pale as they were yesterday; and lips redder still; and she says, " Papa, papa, won't you come to breakfast? The tea is ——" What the precise state of the tea is I don't know—none of us ever shall—for here she says, " Oh, Mr. Firmin ! " and makes a curtsey.

To which remark Philip replied, " Miss Baynes, I hope you are very well this morning, and not the worse for yesterday's rough weather."

"I am quite well, thank you," was Miss Baynes's instant reply. The answer was not witty, to be sure; but I don't know that under the circumstances she could have said anything more appropriate. Indeed, never was a pleasanter picture of health and good-humour than the young lady presented; a difference more pleasant to note than Miss Charlotte's pale face from the steamboat on Saturday, and shining, rosy, happy, and innocent, in the cloudless Sabbath morn.

"A Madame,
"Madame le Major MacWhirter,
　　"à Tours,
　　　"Touraine,
　　　　"France.

　　　　　　"*Tintelleries, Boulogne sur-Mer,*
　　　　　　　"*Wednesday, August* 24, 18—.

"DEAREST EMILY,—After suffering *more dreadfully* in the *two hours'* passage from Folkestone to this place than I have in four passages out and home from India, except in that terrible storm off the Cape, in September, 1824, when I certainly did suffer most cruelly on board that horrible troopship, we reached this place last Saturday evening, having a *full determination* to proceed immediately on our route. *Now,* you will perceive that our minds are changed. We found this place pleasant, and the lodgings besides most neat, comfortable, and well found in everything, *more reasonable* than you proposed to get for us at Tours, which I am told also is damp, and might bring on the general's *jungle fever again.* Owing to the hooping-cough having just been in the house, which, praised be mercy, all my dear ones have had it, including dear baby, who is quite well through it, and recommended sea air, we got this house *more reasonable* than prices you mention at Tours. A whole house : little room for two boys ; nursery ; nice little room for Charlotte, and a *den for the General.* I don't know how *ever* we should have brought our party safe all the way to Tours. *Thirty-seven* articles of luggage, and Miss Flixby, who announced herself as perfect French governess, acquired at Paris —perfect, *but perfectly useless.* She can't understand the French people when they speak to her, and goes about the house *in a most bewildering way. I am the inter-preter ;* poor Charlotte is much too timid to speak when I am by. I have rubbed up the old French which we learned at Chiswick at Miss Pinkerton's ; and I find *my Hindostance* of great help : which I use it when we are at a loss for a word, and it answers *extremely well.* We pay for lodgings, the whole house —— francs per month. Butchers' meat and poultry plentiful but dear. A grocer in the Grande Rue sells excellent wine at fifteenpence per bottle ; and groceries pretty much at English prices. Mr. Blowman at the English chapel of the Tintelleries has a fine voice, and appears to be *a most excellent clergyman.* I have heard him only once, however, on Sunday evening, when I was so agitated and *so unhappy in my mind* that I own I took little note of his sermon.

"The cause of that agitation *you know*, having imparted it to you in my letters of July, June, and 24th of May, ult. My poor simple, guileless Baynes was trustee to Mrs. Dr. Firmin, before she married that most unprincipled man. When we were at home last, and exchanged to the 120th from the 99th, my poor husband was inveigled by the horrid man into signing a paper which put the doctor in possession of *all his wife's property;* whereas Charles thought he was only signing a power of attorney, enabling him to receive his son's dividends. Dr. F., *after the most atrocious deceit, forgery, and criminality of every kind,* fled the country; and Hunt and Pegler, our solicitors, informed us that the General was answerable *for the wickedness of this miscreant.* He is *so weak* that he has been *many and many* times on the point of going to young Mr. F. and giving *up everything.* It was only by my prayers, by my *commands,* that I have been enabled to keep him quiet; and, indeed, Emily, the effort has *almost killed him.* Brandy repeatedly I was obliged to administer on *the dreadful night* of our arrival here.

"For *the first person* we met on landing was Mr. Philip Firmin, *with a pert friend of his,* Mr. Pendennis, whom I don't at all like, though his wife is an amiable person like Emma Fletcher of the Horse Artillery : not with Emma's *style,* however, but still amiable, and disposed to be most civil. Charlotte has taken a great fancy to her, as she always does to every new person. Well, fancy our state on landing, when a young gentleman calls out, 'How do you do, General?' and turns out to be Mr. Firmin ! I thought I should have lost Charles in the night. I have seen him before going into action as calm, and sleep and smile as sweet, as *any babe.* It was all I could do to keep up his courage : and, but for me, but for my prayers, but for *my agonies,* I think he would have jumped out of bed, and gone to Mr. F. *that night,* and said, 'Take everything I have.'

"The young man I own has behaved in *the most honourable way.* He came to see us *before breakfast* on Sunday, when the poor General was so ill that I thought he would have *fainted over his tea.* He was too ill to go to church, where I went alone, with my dear ones, having, as I own, but very small comfort in the sermon : but oh, Emily, fancy, on our return, when I went into our room, I found my General on his knees with his Church service before him, crying, crying like a baby ! You know I am hasty in my temper sometimes, and his is *indeed an angel's* —and I said to him, 'Charles Baynes, be a man, and don't cry like a child !' 'Ah,' says he, 'Eliza, do *you* kneel, and thank God too ;' on which I said that I thought I did not require instruction *in my religion* from him or any man, except a clergyman, and many of these are *but poor instructors, as you know.*

"'He has been here,' says Charles ; when I said, 'Who has been here?' 'That noble young fellow,' says my General ; 'that noble, noble Philip Firmin.' Which noble his conduct I own it has been. 'Whilst you were at church he came again—here into this very room, where I was sitting, doubting and despairing, with the Holy Book before my eyes, and no comfort out of it. And he said to me, "General, I want to talk to you about my grandfather's will. You don't suppose that because my father has deceived you and ruined me, I will carry the ruin farther, and visit his wrong upon children and innocent people?" Those were the young man's words,' my General said ; and, 'oh, Eliza !' says he, 'what pangs of remorse I felt when I remembered we had used hard words about him,' which I own we had, for his manners are rough and haughty, and I *have heard things* of him which I do believe now can't be true.

"All Monday my poor man was obliged to keep his bed with a smart attack of his fever.   But yesterday he was quite bright *and well again*, and the Pendennis party took Charlotte for a drive, and showed themselves *most polite*.   She reminds me of Mrs. Tom Fletcher of the Horse Artillery, but that I think I have mentioned before.   My paper is full; and with our best to MacWhirter and the children, I am always my dearest Emily's affectionate sister,

"ELIZA BAYNES."

CHAPTER XVII.

BREVIS ESSE LABORO.

EVER, General Baynes afterwards declared, did fever come and go so pleasantly as that attack to which we have seen the Mrs. General advert in her letter to her sister, Mrs. Major MacWhirter. The cold fit was merely a lively, pleasant chatter and rattle of the teeth; the hot fit an agreeable warmth; and though the ensuing sleep, with which I believe such aguish attacks are usually concluded, was enlivened by several dreams of death, demons, and torture, how felicitous it was to wake and find that dreadful thought of ruin removed which had always, for the last few months, ever since Dr. Firmin's flight and the knowledge of his own imprudence, pursued the good-natured gentleman! What! this boy might go to college, and that get his commission; and their meals need be embittered by no more dreadful thoughts of the morrow, and their walks no longer were dogged by imaginary bailiffs, and presented a gaol in the vista! It was too much bliss; and again and again the old soldier said his thankful prayers, and blessed his benefactor.

Philip thought no more of his act of kindness, except to be very grateful, and very happy that he had rendered other people so. He could no more have taken the old man's all, and plunged that innocent family into poverty, than he could have stolen the forks off my table. But other folks were disposed to rate his virtue much more highly; and amongst these was my wife, who chose positively to worship this young gentleman, and I believe would have let him smoke in her drawing-room if he had been so minded, and though her genteelest acquaintances were in the room. Goodness knows what a noise and what piteous looks are produced if ever the master of the house chooses to indulge in a cigar after dinner; but then, you understand, *I* have never declined to claim mine and my children's right because an old gentleman would be inconvenienced: and this is what I tell Mrs. Pen. If I order a coat from my tailor, must I refuse to pay him because a rogue steals it, and ought I to expect to be let off? Women won't see matters of fact in a matter-of-fact point of view, and justice, unless it is tinged with a 'little romance, gets no respect from them.

So, forsooth, because Philip has performed this certainly most generous, most dashing, most reckless piece of extravagance, he is to be held up as a perfect *preux chevalier.* The most riotous dinners are ordered for him. We are to wait until he comes to breakfast, and he is pretty nearly always late. The children are to be sent round to kiss Uncle Philip, as he is now called. The children? I wonder the mother did not jump up and kiss him too. *Elle en était capable.* As for the osculations which took place between Mrs. Pendennis and her new-found young friend, Miss Charlotte Baynes, they were perfectly ridiculous; two school children could not have behaved more absurdly; and I don't know which seemed to be the younger of these two. There were colloquies, assignations, meetings on the ramparts, on the pier, where know I?—and the servants and little children of the two establishments were perpetually trotting to and fro with letters from dearest Laura to dearest Charlotte, and dearest Charlotte to her dearest Mrs. Pendennis. Why, my wife absolutely went the length of saying that dearest Charlotte's mother, Mrs. Baynes, was a worthy, clever woman, and a good mother—a woman whose tongue never ceased clacking about the regiment, and all the officers, and all the officers' wives; of whom, by the way, she had very little good to tell.

"A worthy mother, is she, my dear?" I say. "But, oh, mercy! Mrs. Baynes would be an awful mother-in-law!"

I shuddered at the thought of having such a commonplace, hard, ill-bred woman in a state of quasi authority over me.

On this Mrs. Laura must break out in quite a 'petulant tone—"Oh, how *stale* this kind of thing is, Arthur, from a man *qui veut passer pour un homme d'esprit!* You are always attacking mothers-in-law!"

"Witness Mrs. Mackenzie, my love—Clive Newcome's mother-in-law.   That's a nice creature; not selfish, not wicked, not——"

" Not nonsense, Arthur ! "

"Mrs. Baynes knew Mrs. Mackenzie in the West Indies, as she knew all the female army.   She considers Mrs. Mackenzie was a most elegant, handsome, dashing woman—only a little too fond of the admiration of our sex.   There was, I own, a fascination about Captain Goby.   Do you remember, my love, that man with the stays and dyed hair, who——"

" Oh, Arthur !   When our girls marry, I suppose you will teach their husbands to abuse, and scorn, and mistrust *their* mother-in-law.   Will he, my darlings ? will he, my blessings ? "   (This apart to the children, if you please.)   " Go !   I have no patience with such talk ! "

" Well, my love, Mrs. Baynes is a most agreeable woman ; and when I have heard that story about the Highlanders at the Cape of Good Hope a few times more" (I do not tell it here, for it has nothing to do with the present history), " I dare say I shall begin to be amused by it."

"Ah! here comes Charlotte, I'm glad to say.   How pretty she is ! What a colour !   What a dear creature ! "

To all which of course I could not say a contradictory word, for a prettier, fresher lass than Miss Baynes, with a sweeter voice, face, laughter, it was difficult to see.

" Why does mamma like Charlotte better than she likes us?" says our dear and justly indignant eldest girl.

" I could not love her better if I were her *mother-in-law*," says Laura, running to her young friend, casting a glance at me over her shoulder ; and that kissing nonsense begins between the two ladies. To be sure the girl looks uncommonly bright and pretty with her pink cheeks, her bright eyes, her slim form, and that charming white India shawl which her father brought home for her.

To this osculatory party enters presently Mr. Philip Firmin, who has been dawdling about the ramparts ever since breakfast.   He says he has been reading law there.   He has found a jolly quiet place to read law, has he ?   And much good may it do him !   Why has he not gone back to his law and his reviewing ?

" You must—you *must* stay on a little longer.   You have only been here five days.   Do, Charlotte, ask Philip to stay a little."

All the children sing in a chorus, "Oh, do, Uncle Philip, stay a little longer!" Miss Baynes says, "I hope you will stay, Mr. Firmin," and looks at him.

"Five days has he been here? Five years. Five lives. Five hundred years. What do you mean? In that little time of—let me see, a hundred and twenty hours, and, at least, a half of them for sleep and dinner (for Philip's appetite was very fine)—do you mean that in that little time, his heart, cruelly stabbed by a previous monster in female shape, has healed, got quite well, and actually begun to be wounded again? Have two walks on the pier, as many visits to the Tintelleries (where he hears the story of the Highlanders at the Cape of Good Hope with respectful interest), a word or two about the weather, a look or two, a squeezekin, perhaps, of a little handykin—I say, do you mean that this absurd young idiot, and that little round-faced girl, pretty, certainly, but only just out of the school-room—do you mean to say that they have—— Upon my word, Laura, this is too bad. Why, Philip has not a penny piece in the world."

"Yes, he has a hundred pounds, and expects to sell his mare for ninety at least. He has excellent talents. He can easily write three articles a week in the *Pall Mall Gazette*. I am sure no one writes so well, and it is much better done and more amusing than it used to be. That is three hundred a year. Lord Ringwood must be applied to, and must and shall get him something. Don't you know that Captain Baynes stood by Colonel Ringwood's side at Busaco, and that they were the closest friends? And pray how did *we* get on, I should like to know? How did *we* get on, baby?"

"How did we det on?" says the baby.

"Oh, woman! woman!" yells the father of the family. "Why, Philip Firmin has all the habits of a rich man with the pay of a mechanic. Do you suppose he ever sat in a second-class carriage in his life, or denied himself any pleasure to which he had a mind? He gave five francs to a beggar-girl yesterday."

"He had always a noble heart," says my wife. "He gave a fortune to a whole family a week ago; and" (out comes the pocket-handkerchief—oh, of course, the pocket-handkerchief)—"and—'God loves a cheerful giver!'"

"He is careless; he is extravagant; he is lazy;—I don't know that he is remarkably clever——"

"Oh, yes ! he is your friend, of course. Now, abuse him—*do*, Arthur ! "

"And, pray, when did you become acquainted with this astounding piece of news ? " I inquire.

"When? From the very first moment when I saw Charlotte looking at him, to be sure. The poor child said to me only yesterday, 'Oh, Laura ! he is our preserver !' And their preserver he has been, under Heaven."

"Yes. But he has not got a five-pound note ! " I cry.

"Arthur, I am surprised at you. Oh, men are awfully worldly ! Do you suppose Heaven will not send him help at its good time, and be kind to him who has rescued so many from ruin ? Do you suppose the prayers, the blessings of that father, of those little ones, of that dear child will not avail him ? Suppose he has to wait a year, ten years, have they not time, and will not the good day come ? "

Yes. This was actually the talk of a woman of sense and discernment, when her prejudices and romance were not in the way, and she looked forward to the marriage of these folks some ten years hence, as confidently as if they were both rich, and going to St. George's to-morrow.

As for making a romantic story of it, or spinning out love conversa·tions between Jenny and Jessamy, or describing moonlight raptures and passionate outpourings of two young hearts and so forth—excuse me, *s'il vous plait.* I am a man of the world, and of a certain age. Let the young people fill in this outline, and colour it as they please. Let the old folks who read lay down the book a minute, and remember. It is well remembered, isn't it, that time ? Yes, good John Anderson, and Mrs. John. Yes, good Darby and Joan. The lips won't tell now what they did once. To-day is for the happy, and to-morrow for the young, and yesterday, is not that dear and here too ?

I was in the company of an elderly gentleman, not very long since, who was perfectly sober, who is not particularly handsome, or healthy, or wealthy, or witty ; and who, speaking of his past life, volunteered to declare that he would gladly live every minute of it over again. Is a man who can say that a hardened sinner, not aware how miserable he ought to be by rights, and therefore really in a most desperate and deplorable condition ; or is he *fortunatus nimium,* and ought his statue to be put up in the most splendid and crowded thoroughfare of the town? Would you, who are reading this, for example, like to live *your* life over again? What has been its chief joy? What are to-day's pleasures? Are they so exquisite that you would prolong them for ever? Would you like to have the roast beef on which you have dined brought back again to table, and have more beef, and more, and more? Would you like to hear yesterday's sermon over and over again—eternally voluble? Would you like to get on the Edinburgh mail, and travel outside for fifty hours as you did in your youth? You might as well say you would like to go into the flogging-room, and take a turn under the rods: you would like to be thrashed over again by your bully at school: you would like to go to the dentist's, where your dear parents were in the habit of taking you: you would like to be taking hot Epsom salts, with a piece of dry bread to take away the taste: you would like to be jilted by your first love: you would like to be going in to your father to tell him you had contracted debts to the amount of $x + y + z$, whilst you were at the university. As I consider the passionate griefs of childhood, the weariness and sameness of shaving, the agony of corns, and the thousand other ills to which flesh is heir, I cheerfully say for one, I am not anxious to wear it for ever. No. I do not want to go to school again. I do not want to hear Trotman's sermon over again. Take me out and finish me. Give me the cup of hemlock at once. Here's a health to you, my lads. Don't weep, my Simmias. Be cheerful, my Phædon. Ha! I feel the co-o-old stealing, stealing upwards. Now it is in my ankles—no more gout in my foot: now my knees are numb. What, is—is that poor executioner crying too? Good-by. Sacrifice a cock to Æscu—to Æscula— . . . Have you ever read the chapter in "Grote's History?" Ah! When the Sacred Ship returns from Delos, and is telegraphed as entering into port, may we be at peace and ready!

What is this funeral chant, when the pipes should be playing gaily as Love, and Youth, and Spring, and Joy are dancing under the windows? Look you. Men not so wise as Socrates have their demons, who will be heard to whisper in the queerest times and places. Perhaps I shall have to tell of a funeral presently, and shall be outrageously cheerful; or of an execution, and shall split my sides with laughing. Arrived at my time of life, when I see a penniless young friend falling in love and thinking of course of committing matrimony, what can I do but be melancholy? How is a man to marry who has not enough to keep ever so miniature a brougham—ever so small a house—not enough to keep himself, let alone a wife and family? Gracious powers ! is it not blasphemy to marry without fifteen hundred a year? Poverty, debt, protested bills, duns, crime, fall assuredly on the wretch who has not fifteen —say at once two thousand a year; for you can't live decently in London for less. And a wife whom you have met a score of times at balls or breakfasts, and with her best dresses and behaviour at a country house ;—how do you know how she will turn out; what her temper is; what her relations are likely to be? Suppose she has poor relations, or loud coarse brothers who are always dropping in to dinner? What is 'her mother like ? and can you bear to have that woman meddling and domineering over your establishment? Old General Baynes was very well; a weak, quiet and presentable old man : but Mrs. General Baynes, and that awful Mrs. Major MacWhirter,—and those hobbledehoys of boys in creaking shoes, hectoring about the premises? As a man of the world I saw all these dreadful liabilities impending over the husband of Miss Charlotte Baynes, and could not view them without horror. Gracefully and slightly, but wittily and in my sarcastic way, I thought it my duty to show up the oddities of the Baynes family to Philip. I mimicked the boys, and their clumping blucher-boots. I touched off the dreadful military ladies, very smartly and cleverly as I thought, and as if I never supposed that Philip had any idea of Miss Baynes. To do him justice, he laughed once or twice; then he grew very red. His sense of humour is very limited ; that even Laura allows. Then he came out with a strong expression, and said it was a confounded shame, and strode off with his cigar. And when I remarked to my wife how susceptible he was in some things, and how little in the matter of joking, she shrugged her shoulders and said, "Philip not only understood perfectly well what I said, but would tell it all to Mrs. General and Mrs. Major on the first opportunity." And this was the fact, as Mrs. Baynes took care to tell me *afterwards.* She was aware who was her *enemy.* She was aware who spoke ill of her, and her blessed darling *behind our backs.* And "do you think it was to see *you* or any one belonging to your *stuck-up house,* sir, that we came to you so often, which we certainly did, day and night, breakfast and supper, and no thanks to you? No, sir! ha, ha!" I can see her flaunting out of my sitting-room as she speaks, with a strident laugh, and snapping her dingily gloved fingers at the door. Oh, Philip, Philip! To think that you were such a coward as to go and tell her! But I pardon him. From my heart I pity and pardon him.

For the step which he is meditating you may be sure that the young man himself does not feel the smallest need of pardon or pity. He is in a state of happiness so crazy that it is useless to reason with him. Not being at all of a poetical turn originally, the wretch is actually perpetrating verse in secret, and my servants found fragments of his manuscript on the dressing-table in his bedroom. *Heart* and *art, sever* and *for ever*, and so on; what stale rhymes are these? I do not feel at liberty to give in entire the poem which our maid found in Mr. Philip's room, and brought sniggering to my wife, who only said, "Poor thing!" The fact is, it was too pitiable. Such maundering rubbish! Such stale rhymes, and such old thoughts! But then, says Laura, "I dare say all people's love-making is not amusing to their neighbours; and I know who wrote not very wise love-verses when he was young." No, I won't publish Philip's verses, until some day he shall mortally offend me. I can recall some of my own written under similar circumstances with twinges of shame; and shall drop a veil of decent friendship over my friend's folly.

Under that veil, meanwhile, the young man is perfectly contented, nay, uproariously happy. All earth and nature smiles round about him. "When Jove meets his Juno, in Homer, sir," says Philip, in his hectoring way, "don't immortal flowers of beauty spring up around them, and rainbows of celestial hues bend over their heads? Love, sir, flings a halo round the loved one. Where she moves rise roses, hyacinths, and ambrosial odours. Don't talk to me about poverty, sir! He either fears his fate too much or his desert is small, who dares not put it to the touch and win or lose it all! Haven't I endured poverty? Am I not as poor now as a man can be—and what is there in it? Do I want for anything? Haven't I got a guinea in my pocket? Do I owe any man anything? Isn't there manna in the wilderness for those who have faith to walk in it? That's where you fail, Pen. By all that is sacred, you have no faith; your heart is cowardly, sir; and if you are to escape, as perhaps you may, I suspect it is by your wife that you will be saved. Laura has a trust in heaven, but Arthur's morals are a genteel atheism. Just reach me that claret—the wine's not bad. I say your morals are a genteel atheism, and I shudder when I think of your condition. Talk to *me* about a brougham being necessary for the comfort of a woman! A broomstick to ride to the moon! And I don't say that a brougham is not a comfort, mind you; but that, when it is a necessity, mark you, heaven will provide it! Why, sir, hang it, look at me! Ain't I suffering in the most abject poverty? I ask you is there a man in London so poor as I am? And since my father's ruin do I want for anything? I want for shelter for a day or two. Good. There's my dear Little Sister ready to give it me. I want for money. Does not that sainted widow's cruse pour its oil out for me? Heaven bless and reward her. Boo!" (Here, for reasons which need not be named, the orator squeezes his fists into his eyes.) " I want shelter; ain't I in good quarters? I want work; haven't I got work, and did you not get it for me? You should just see, sir, how I polished off that book of travels this morning. I read some of the article to Char——, to Miss ——, to some friends, in fact. I don't mean to say that they are very intellectual people, but your common humdrum average audience is the public to try. Recollect Molière and his housekeeper, you know."

" By the housekeeper, do you mean Mrs. Baynes? " I ask, in my *amontillado* manner. (By the way, who ever heard of *amontillado* in the early days of which I write?) " In manner she would do, and I dare say in accomplishments; but I doubt about her temper."

" You're almost as worldly as the Twysdens, by George, you are ! Unless persons are of a certain *monde*, you don't value them. A little adversity would do you good, Pen; and I heartily wish you might get it, except for the dear wife and children. You measure your morality by May Fair standards; and if an angel unawares came to you in pattens and a cotton umbrella, you would turn away from her. *You* would never have found out the Little Sister. A duchess—God bless her ! A creature of an imperial generosity, and delicacy, and intrepidity, and the finest sense of humour; but she drops her *h*'s often, and how could you pardon such a crime ? Sir, you are my better in wit and a dexterous application of your powers; but I think, sir," says Phil, curling the flaming moustache, " I am your superior in a certain magnanimity; though, by Jove, old fellow, man and boy, you have always been one of the best fellows in the world to P. F. ; one of the best fellows, and the most generous, and the most cordial,—

that you have: only you *do* rile me when you sing in that confounded
May Fair twang."

Here one of the children summoned us to tea—and "Papa was
laughing, and uncle Philip was flinging his hands about and pulling
his beard off," said the little messenger.

"I shall keep a fine lock of it for you, Nelly, my dear," says
uncle Philip. On which the child said, "Oh, no! I know whom
you'll give it to, don't I, mamma?" and she goes up to her mamma,
and whispers.

Miss Nelly knows? At what age do those little match-makers
begin to know, and how soon do they practise the use of their young
eyes, their little smiles, wiles, and ogles? This young woman, I
believe, coquetted whilst she was yet a baby in arms, over her nurse's
shoulder. Before she could speak, she could be proud of her new
vermilion shoes, and would point out the charms of her blue sash.
She was jealous in the nursery, and her little heart had beat for years
and years before she left off pinafores.

For whom will Philip keep a lock of that red, red gold which
curls round his face? Can you guess? Of what colour is the hair
in that little locket which the gentleman himself occultly wears?
A few months ago, I believe, a pale straw-coloured wisp of hair
occupied that place of honour; now it is a chestnut-brown, as far as
I can see, of precisely the same colour as that which waves round
Charlotte Baynes' pretty face, and tumbles in clusters on her neck,
very nearly the colour of Mrs. Paynter's this last season. So, you
see, we chop and we change: straw gives place to chestnut, and
chestnut is succeeded by ebony; and, for our own parts, we defy
time; and if you want a lock of my hair, Belinda, take this pair
of scissors, and look in that cupboard, in the band-box marked
No. 3, and cut off a thick glossy piece, darling, and wear it, dear,
and my blessings go with thee! What is this? Am I sneering
because Corydon and Phyllis are wooing and happy? You see I
pledged myself not to have any sentimental nonsense. To describe
love-making is immoral and immodest; you know it is. To describe
it as it really is, or would appear to you and me as lookers-on, would
be to describe the most dreary farce, to chronicle the most tautological
twaddle. To take a note of sighs, hand-squeezes, looks at the moon,
and so forth—does this business become our dignity as historians?
Come away from those foolish young people—they don't want us;

and dreary as their farce is, and tautological as their twaddle, you may be sure it amuses them, and that they are happy enough without us. Happy? Is there any happiness like it, pray? Was it not rapture to watch the messenger, to seize the note, and fee the bearer? —to retire out of sight of all prying eyes and read:—" Dearest! Mamma's cold is better this morning. The Joneses came to tea, and Julia sang. I did not enjoy it, as my dear was at his *horrid dinner*, where I hope he amused himself. Send me a word by Buttles, who brings this, if only to say you are your Louisa's own, own," &c. &c. &c. That used to be the kind of thing. In such coy lines artless Innocence used to whisper its little vows. So she used to smile ; so she used to warble ; so she used to prattle. Young people, at present engaged in the pretty sport, be assured your middle-aged parents have played the game, and remember the rules of it. Yes, under papa's bow-window of a waistcoat is a heart which took very violent exercise when that waist was slim. Now he sits tranquilly in his tent, and watches the lads going in for their innings. Why, look at grandmamma in her spectacles reading that sermon. In *her* old heart there is a corner as romantic still as when she used to read the " Wild Irish Girl " or the " Scottish Chiefs " in the days of her misshood. And as for your grandfather, my dears, to see him now you would little suppose that that calm, polished, dear old gentleman was once as wild—as wild as Orson. . . . Under my windows, as I write, there passes an itinerant flower-merchant. He has his roses and geraniums on a cart drawn by a quadruped—a little long-eared quadruped, which lifts up its voice, and sings after its manner. When I was young, donkeys used to bray precisely in the same way ; and others will heehaw so, when we are silent and our ears hear no more.

CHAPTER XVIII.

DRUM IST'S SO WOHL MIR IN DER WELT.

U R new friends lived for a while contentedly enough at Boulogne, where they found comrades and acquaintances gathered together from those many regions which they had visited in the course of their military career. Mrs. Baynes, out of the field, was the commanding officer over the General. She ordered his clothes for him, tied his neckcloth into a neat bow, and, on tea-party evenings, pinned his brooch into his shirt-frill. She gave him to understand when he had had enough to eat or drink at dinner, and explained, with great frankness, how this or that dish did not agree with him. If he was disposed to exceed, she would call out, in a loud voice : " Remember, General, what you took this morning !" Knowing his constitution, as she said, she knew the remedies which were necessary for her husband, and administered them to him with great liberality. Resistance was impossible, as the veteran officer acknowledged. "The boys have fought about the medicine since we came home," he confessed, "but she has me under her thumb, by George. She really is a magnificent physician, now. She has got some invaluable prescriptions, and in India she used to doctor the whole station." She would have taken the present writer's little household under her care, and proposed several remedies for my children, until their alarmed mother was obliged to keep them out of her sight. I am not saying this was an agreeable woman. Her voice was loud and harsh. The anecdotes which she was for ever narrating related to military personages in foreign countries with whom I was unacquainted, and whose history failed to interest me. She took her wine with much spirit, whilst engaged in this prattle. I have heard talk not less foolish in much finer company, and known people delighted to listen to anecdotes of the duchess and the marchioness who would yawn over the history of Captain Jones's quarrels with his lady, or Mrs. Major Wolfe's monstrous flirtations with young Ensign Kyd. My wife, with the mischievousness of her sex, would mimic the Baynes' conversation very drolly, but always insisted that she was not more really vulgar than many much greater persons.

For all this, Mrs. General Baynes did not hesitate to declare that we were "stuck-up" people ; and from the very first setting eyes on us she declared that she viewed us with a constant darkling suspicion. Mrs. P. was a harmless, washed-out creature, with nothing in her. As for that high and mighty Mr. P. and *his* airs, she would be glad to know whether the wife of a British general officer who had seen service in *every part of the globe*, and met the *most distinguished* governors, generals, and their ladies, several of whom *were noblemen* —she would be glad to know whether such people were not good enough for, &c. &c. Who has not met with these difficulties in life, and who can escape them ? "Hang it, sir," Phil would say, twirling the red moustache, "I like to be hated by some fellows ;" and it must be owned that Mr. Philip got what he liked. I suppose Mr. Philip's friend and biographer had something of the same feeling. At any rate, in regard of this lady the hypocrisy of politeness was very hard to keep up ; wanting us for reasons of her own, she covered the dagger with which she would have stabbed us : but we knew it was there clenched in her skinny hand in her meagre pocket. She would pay us the most fulsome compliments with anger raging out of her eyes—a little hate-bearing woman, envious, malicious, but loving her cubs, and nursing them, and clutching them in her lean arms with a jealous strain. It was "Good-by, darling ! I shall leave you here with your friends. Oh, how kind you are to her, Mrs. Pendennis ! How can I ever thank you, and Mr. P., I am sure ;" and she looked as if she could poison both of us, as she went away, curtseying and darting dreary parting smiles.

This lady had an intimate friend and companion in arms, Mrs. Colonel Bunch, in fact, of the —th Bengal Cavalry, who was now in Europe with Bunch and their children, who were residing at Paris for the young folks' education. At first, as we have heard, Mrs. Baynes' predilections had been all for Tours, where her sister was living, and where lodgings were cheap and food reasonable in proportion. But Bunch happening to pass through Boulogne on his way to his wife at Paris, and meeting his old comrade, gave General Baynes such an account of the cheapness and pleasures of the French capital, as to induce the General to think of bending his steps thither. Mrs. Baynes would not hear of such a plan. She was all for her dear sister and Tours; but when, in the course of conversation, Colonel Bunch described a ball at the Tuileries, where he and Mrs. B. had been received with the most flattering politeness by the royal family, it was remarked that Mrs. Baynes' mind underwent a change. When Bunch went on to aver that the balls at Government House at Calcutta were nothing compared to those at the Tuileries or the Prefecture of the Seine; that the English were invited and respected everywhere; that the ambassador was most hospitable; that the clergymen were admirable; and that at their boarding-house, kept by Madame la Générale Baronne de Smolensk, at the " Petit Château d'Espagne," Avenue de Valmy, Champs Elysées, they had balls twice a month, the most comfortable apartments, the most choice society, and every comfort and luxury at so many francs per month, with an allowance for children—I say Mrs. Baynes was very greatly moved. " It is not," she said, " in consequence of the balls at the Ambassador's or the Tuileries, for I am an old woman; and in spite of what you say, Colonel, I can't fancy, after Government House, anything more magnificent in any French palace. It is not for *me*, goodness knows, I speak: but the children should have education, and my Charlotte an entrée into the world; and what you say of the invaluable clergyman, Mr. X——, I have been thinking of it all night; but above all, above all, of the chances of education for my darlings. Nothing should give way to that—nothing !" On this a long and delightful conversation and calculation took place. Bunch produced his bills at the Baroness de Smolensk's. The two gentlemen jotted up accounts, and made calculations all through the evening. It was hard even for Mrs. Baynes to force the figures into such a shape as to make them accord with the General's income; but, driven away by one calculation after another, she returned again and again to the charge, until she overcame the stubborn arithmetical difficulties, and the pounds, shillings, and pence lay prostrate before her. They could save upon this point; they could screw upon that; they *must* make a sacrifice to educate the children. "Sarah Bunch and her girls go to Court, indeed! Why shouldn't mine go?" she asked. On which her General said, "By George, Eliza, that's the point you are thinking of." On which Eliza said, "No," and repeated "No" a score of times, growing more angry as she uttered each denial. And she declared before heaven she did *not* want to go to any Court. Had she not refused to be presented at home, though Mrs. Colonel Flack went, because she did not choose to go to the wicked expense of a train? And it was base of the General, *base* and *mean* of him to say so. And there was a fine scene, as I am given to understand; not that I was present at this family fight: but my informant was Mr. Firmin; and Mr. Firmin had his information from a little person who, about this time, had got to prattle out all the secrets of her young heart to him; who would have jumped off the pier-head with her hand in his if he had said "Come," without his hand if he had said "Go:" a little person whose whole life had been changed— changed for a month past—changed in one minute, that minute when she saw Philip's fiery whiskers and heard his great big voice saluting her father amongst the commissioners on the *quai* before the custom-house.

Tours was, at any rate, a hundred and fifty miles farther off than Paris from—from a city where a young gentleman lived in whom Miss Charlotte Baynes felt an interest; hence, I suppose, arose her delight that her parents had determined upon taking up their residence in the larger and nearer city. Besides, she owned, in the course of her artless confidences to my wife, that, when together, mamma and aunt MacWhirter quarrelled unceasingly; and had once caused the old boys, the Major and the General, to call each other out. She preferred, then, to live away from aunt Mac. She had never had such a friend as Laura, never. She had never been so happy as at Boulogne, never. She should always love everybody in our house, that she should, for ever and ever—and so forth, and so forth. The ladies meet; cling together; osculations are carried round the whole family circle, from our wondering eldest boy, who cries, "I say, hullo! what are you kissing me so about?" to darling baby, crowing and sputtering unconscious in the rapturous young girl's embraces. I tell you, these two women were making fools of themselves, and they were burning with enthusiasm for the "preserver" of the Baynes family, as they called that big fellow yonder, whose biographer I have aspired to be. The lazy rogue lay basking in the glorious warmth and sunshine of early love. He would stretch his big limbs out in our garden; pour out his feelings with endless volubility; call upon *hominum divumque voluptas, alma Venus;* vow that he had never lived or been happy until now; declare that he laughed poverty to scorn and all her ills; and fume against his masters of the *Pall Mall Gazette*, because they declined to insert certain love verses which Mr. Philip now composed almost every day. Poor little Charlotte! And didst thou receive those treasures of song; and wonder over them, not perhaps comprehending them altogether; and lock them up in thy heart's inmost casket as well as in thy little desk; and take them out in quiet hours, and kiss them, and bless heaven for giving thee such jewels? I dare say. I can fancy all this, without seeing it. I can read the little letters in the little desk, without picking lock or breaking seal. Poor little letters! Sometimes they are not spelt right, quite; but I don't know that the style is worse for that. Poor little letters! You are flung to the winds sometimes and forgotten with all your sweet secrets and loving artless confessions; but not always—no, not always. As for Philip, who was the most careless creature alive, and left all his clothes and haberdashery sprawling on his bed-room floor, he had at this time a breast-pocket stuffed out with papers which crackled in the most ridiculous way. He was always looking down at this precious pocket, and putting one of his great hands over it as though he would guard it. The pocket did not contain bank-notes, you may be sure of that. It contained documents stating that mamma's cold is better; the Joneses came to tea, and Julia sang, &c. Ah, friend, however old you are now, however cold you are now, however tough, I hope you, too, remember how Julia sang, and the Joneses came to tea.

Mr. Philip stayed on week after week, declaring to my wife that she was a perfect angel for keeping him so long. Bunch wrote from his boarding-house more and more enthusiastic reports about the comforts of the establishment. For his sake, Madame la Baronne de Smolensk would make unheard-of sacrifices, in order to accommodate the General and his distinguished party. The balls were going to be perfectly splendid that winter. There were several old Indians living near; in fact they could form a regular little club. It was agreed that Baynes should go and reconnoitre the ground. He did go. Madame de Smolensk, a most elegant woman, had a magnificent dinner for him—quite splendid, I give you my word, but only what they have every day. Soup, of course, my love ; fish, capital wine, and, I should say, some five or six and thirty made dishes. The General was quite enraptured. Bunch had put his boys to a famous school, where they might "whop" the French boys, and learn all the modern languages. The little ones would dine early ; the baroness would take the whole family at an astonishingly cheap rate. In a word, the Baynes' column got the route for Paris shortly before our family-party was crossing the seas to return to London fogs and duty.

You have, no doubt, remarked how, under certain tender circum-stances, women will help one another. They help where they ought not to help. When Mr. Darby ought to be separated from Miss Joan, and the best thing that could happen for both would be a *lettre de cachet* to whip off Mons. Darby to the Bastile for five years, and an order from her parents to lock up Mademoiselle Jeanne in a convent, some aunt, some relative, some pitying female friend is sure to be found, who will give the pair a chance of meeting, and turn her head away whilst those unhappy lovers are warbling endless good-byes close up to each other's ears. My wife, I have said, chose to feel this absurd sympathy for the young people about whom we have been just talking. As the days for Charlotte's departure drew near, this wretched, misguiding matron would take the girl out walking into I know not what unfrequented bye-lanes, quiet streets, rampart-nooks, and the like ; and la ! by the most singular coinci-dence, Mr. Philip's hulking boots would assuredly come tramping after the women's little feet. What will you say, when I tell you, that I myself, the father of the family, the renter of the old-fashioned house, Rue Roucoule, Haute Ville, Boulogne-sur-Mer—as I am going into my own study—am met at the threshold by Helen, my eldest daughter, who puts her little arms before the glass door at which I was about to enter, and says, "You must not go in there, papa ! Mamma says we none of us are to go in there."

"And why, pray ?" I ask.

"Because Uncle Philip and Charlotte are talking secrets there ; and nobody is to disturb them—*nobody !*"

Upon my word, wasn't this too monstrous? Am I Sir Pandarus

of Troy become ?　Am I going to allow a penniless young man to steal away the heart of a young girl who has not twopence half-penny to her fortune?　Shall I, I say, lend myself to this most unjustifiable intrigue ?

'" Sir," says my wife (we happened to have been bred up from childhood together, and I own to have had one or two foolish initiatory flirtations before I settled down to matrimonial fidelity)—" Sir," says she, " when you were so wild—so spoony, I think is your elegant word—about Blanche, and used to put letters into a hollow tree for her at home, I used to see the letters, and I never disturbed them. These two people have much warmer hearts, and are a great deal fonder of each other, than you and Blanche used to be.　I should not like to separate Charlotte from Philip now.　It is too late, sir. She can never like anybody else as she likes him.　If she lives to be a hundred, she will never forget him.　Why should not the poor thing be happy a little, while she may ?"

An old house, with a green old courtyard and an ancient mossy wall, through breaks of which I can see the roofs and gables of the quaint old town, the city below, the shining sea, and the white English cliffs beyond ; a green old courtyard, and a tall old stone house rising up in it, grown over with many a creeper on which the sun casts flickering shadows; and under the shadows, and through the glass of a tall gray window, I can just peep into a brown twilight parlour, and there I see two hazy figures by a table.　One slim figure has brown hair, and one has flame-coloured whiskers.　Look, a ray of sunshine has just peered into the room, and is lighting the whiskers up !

" Poor little thing," whispers my wife, very gently.　" They are going away to-morrow.　Let them have their talk out.　She is crying her little eyes out, I am sure.　Poor little Charlotte !"

Whilst my wife was pitying Miss Charlotte in this pathetic way, and was going, I dare say, to have recourse to her own pocket-handkerchief, as I live there came a burst of laughter from the darkling chamber where the two lovers were billing and cooing.　First came Mr. Philip's great boom (such a roar—such a haw-haw, or hee-haw, I never heard any other *two*-legged animal perform).　Then follows Miss Charlotte's tinkling peal ; and presently that young person comes out into the' garden, with her round face not bedewed with tears at all, but perfectly rosy, fresh, dimpled, and good-

CHARLOTTE'S CONVOY.

humoured. Charlotte gives me a little curtsey, and my wife a hand and a kind glance. They retreat through the open casement, twining round each other, as the vine does round the window; though which is the vine and which is the window in this simile, I pretend not to say—I can't see through either of them, that is the truth. They pass through the parlour, and into the street beyond, doubtless: and as for Mr. Philip, I presently see *his* head popped out of his window in the upper floor with his great pipe in his mouth. He can't "work" without his pipe, he says; and my wife believes him. Work indeed!

Miss Charlotte paid us another little visit that evening, when we happened to be alone. The children were gone to bed. The darlings! Charlotte must go up and kiss them. Mr. Philip Firmin was out. She did not seem to miss him in the least, nor did she make a single inquiry for him. We had been so good to her—so kind.' How should she ever forget our great kindness? She had been so happy —oh! so happy! She had never been so happy before. She would write often and often, and Laura would write constantly—wouldn't she? "Yes, dear child!" says my wife. And now a little more kissing, and it is time to go home to the Tintilleries. What a lovely night! Indeed the moon was blazing in full round in the purple heavens, and the stars were twinkling by myriads.

"Good-by, dear Charlotte; happiness go with you!" I seize her hand. I feel a paternal desire to kiss her fair, round face. Her sweetness, her happiness, her artless good-humour, and gentleness has endeared her to us all. As for me, I love her with a fatherly affection. "Stay, my dear!" I cry, with a happy gallantry, "I'll go home with you to the Tintilleries."

You should have seen the fair round face *then!* Such a piteous expression came over it! She looked at my wife; and as for that Mrs. Laura she pulled the tail of my coat.

"What do you mean, my dear?" I ask.

"Don't go out on such a dreadful night. You'll catch cold!" says Laura.

"Cold, my love!" I say. "Why, it's as fine a night as ever——"

"Oh! you—you *stoopid!*" says Laura, and begins to laugh. And there goes Miss Charlotte tripping away from us without a word more.

Philip came in about half an hour afterwards. And do you know I very strongly suspect that he had been waiting round the corner.

Few things escape *me*, you see, when I have a mind to be observant. And, certainly, if I had thought of that possibility and that I might be spoiling sport, I should not have proposed to Miss Charlotte to walk home with her.

At a very early hour on the next morning my wife arose, and spent, in my opinion, a great deal of unprofitable time, bread, butter, cold beef, mustard and salt, in compiling a heap of sandwiches, which were tied up in a copy of the *Pall Mall Gazette*. That persistence in making sandwiches, in providing cakes and other refreshments for a journey, is a strange infatuation in women; as if there was not always enough to eat to be had at road inns and railway stations! What a good dinner we used to have at Montreuil in the old days, before railways were, and when the diligence spent four or six and twenty cheerful hours on its way to Paris! I think the finest dishes are not to be compared to that well-remembered fricandeau of youth, nor do wines of the most dainty vintage surpass the rough, honest, blue ordinaire which was served at the plenteous inn-table. I took our bale of sandwiches down to the office of the Messageries, whence our friends were to start. We saw six of the Baynes family packed into the interior of the diligence; and the boys climb cheerily into the rotonde. Charlotte's pretty lips and hands wafted kisses to us from her corner. Mrs. General Baynes commanded the column, pushed the little ones into their places in the ark, ordered the General and young ones hither and thither with her parasol, declined to give the grumbling porters any but the smallest gratuity, and talked a shrieking jargon of French and Hindustanee to the people assembled round the carriage. My wife has that command over me that she actually -made me demean myself so far as to deliver the sandwich parcel to one of the Baynes boys. I said, "Take this," and the poor wretch held out his hand eagerly, evidently expecting that I was about to tip him with a five-franc piece or some such coin. *Fouette, cocher!* The horses squeal. The huge machine jingles over the road, and rattles down the street. Farewell, pretty Charlotte, with your sweet face and sweet voice and kind eyes! But why, pray, is Mr. Philip Firmin not here to say farewell too?

Before the diligence got under way, the Baynes boys had fought, and quarrelled, and wanted to mount on the imperial or cabriolet of the carriage, where there was only one passenger as yet. But the conductor called the lads off, saying that the remaining place was engaged by a gentleman who they were to take up on the road. And who should this turn out to be? Just outside the town a man springs up to the imperial; his light luggage, it appears, was on the coach already, and that luggage belonged to Philip Firmin. Ah, monsieur! and that was the reason, was it, why they were so merry yesterday—the parting day? Because they were not going to part just then. Because, when the time of execution drew near, they had managed to smuggle a little reprieve! Upon my conscience, I never heard of such imprudence in the whole course of my life! Why, it is starvation—certain misery to one and the other. "I don't like to meddle in other people's affairs," I say to my wife; "but I have no patience with such folly, or with myself for not speaking to General Baynes on the subject. I shall write to the General."

"My dear, the General knows all about it," says Charlotte's, Philip's (in my opinion) most injudicious friend. "We have talked about it, and, like a man of sense, the General makes light of it. 'Young folks will be young folks,' he says; 'and, by George! ma'am, when I married—I should say, when Mrs. B. ordered me to marry her—she had nothing, and I but my captain's pay. People get on, somehow. Better for a young man to marry, and keep out of idleness and mischief; and I promise you, the chap who marries my girl gets a treasure. I like the boy for the sake of my old friend Phil Ringwood. I don't see that the fellows with the rich wives are much the happier, or that men should wait to marry until they are gouty old rakes.'" And, it appears, the General instanced several officers of his own acquaintance; some of whom had married when they were young and poor; some who had married when they were old and sulky; some who had never married at all. And he mentioned his comrade, my own uncle, the late Major Pendennis, whom he called a selfish old creature, and hinted that the Major had jilted some lady in early life, whom he would have done much better to marry.

And so Philip is actually gone after his charmer, and is pursuing her *summâ diligentiâ?* The Baynes family has allowed this penniless young law student to make love to their daughter, or accompany them to Paris, to appear as the almost recognised son of the house. "Other people, when they were young, wanted to make imprudent marriages," says my wife (as if that wretched *tu quoque* were any answer to my remark!) "This penniless law student might have a good sum of money if he chose to press the Baynes family to pay him what, after all, they owe him." And so poor little Charlotte was to be her father's ransom! To be sure, little Charlotte did not object to offer herself up in payment of her papa's debt! And though I objected as a moral man and a prudent man, and a father of a family, I could not be very seriously angry. I am secretly of the disposition of the time-honoured *père de famille* in the comedies, the irascible old gentleman in the crop wig and George-the-Second coat, who is always menacing "Tom the young dog" with his cane. When the deed is done, and Miranda (the little sly-boots!) falls before my squaretoes and shoe-buckles, and Tom, the young dog, kneels before me in his white ducks, and they cry out in a pretty chorus, "Forgive us, grandpapa!" I say, "Well, you rogue, boys will be boys. Take her, sirrah! Be happy with her; and, hark ye! in this pocket-book you will find ten thousand," &c. &c. You all know the story: I cannot help liking it, however old it may be. In love, somehow, one is pleased that young people should dare a little. Was not Bessy Eldon famous as an economist, and Lord Eldon celebrated for wisdom and caution? and did not John Scott marry Elizabeth Surtees when they had scarcely twopence a year between them? "Of course, my dear," I say to the partner of my existence, "now this madcap fellow is utterly ruined, now is the very time he ought to marry. The accepted doctrine is that a man should spend his own fortune, then his wife's fortune, and then he may begin to get on at the bar. Philip has a hundred pounds, let us say; Charlotte has nothing; so that in about six weeks we may look to hear of Philip being in successful practice——"

"Successful nonsense!" cries the lady. "Don't go on like a cold-blooded calculating machine! You don't believe a word of what you say, and a more imprudent person never lived than you yourself were as a young man." This was departing from the question, which women will do. "Nonsense!" again says my romantic being of a partner-of-existence. "Don't tell ME, sir. They WILL be provided for! Are we to be for ever taking care of the morrow, and not trusting that we shall be cared for? *You* may call your way of thinking prudence. I call it *sinful worldliness*, sir." When my life-partner speaks in a certain strain, I know that remonstrance is useless, and argument unavailing, and I generally resort to cowardly subterfuges, and sneak out of the conversation by a pun, a side joke, or some other flippancy. Besides, in this case, though I argue against my wife, my sympathy is on her side. I know Mr. Philip is imprudent and headstrong, but I should like him to succeed, and be happy. I own he is a scapegrace, but I wish him well.

So, just as the diligence of Lafitte and Caillard is clearing out of Boulogne town, the conductor causes the carriage to stop, and a young fellow has mounted up on the roof in a twinkling; and the postilion says "Hi!" to his horses, and away those squealing greys go clattering. And a young lady, happening to look out of one of the windows of the intérieur, has perfectly recognized the young gentleman who leaped up to the roof so nimbly; and the two boys who were in the rotonde would have recognized the gentleman, but that they were already eating the sandwiches which my wife had provided. And so the diligence goes on, until it reaches that hill, where the girls used to come and offer to sell you apples; and some of the passengers descend and walk, and the tall young man on the roof jumps down, and approaches the party in the interior, and a young lady cries out "La!" and her mamma looks impenetrably grave, and not in the least surprised; and her father gives a wink of one eye, and says, "It's him, is it, by George!" and the two boys coming out of the rotonde, their mouths full of sandwich, cry out, "Hullo! It's Mr. Firmin."

"How do you do, ladies?" he says, blushing as red as an apple, and his heart thumping—but that may be from walking up hill. And he puts a hand towards the carriage-window, and a little hand comes out and lights on his. And Mrs. General Baynes, who is reading a religious work, looks up and says, "Oh! how do you do, Mr. Firmin?" And this is the remarkable dialogue that takes place. It is not very witty; but Philip's tones send a rapture into one young heart: and when he is absent, and has climbed up to his place in the cabriolet, the kick of his boots on the roof gives the said young heart inexpressible comfort and consolation. Shine stars and moon. Shriek grey horses through the calm night. Snore sweetly, papa and mamma, in your corners, with your pocket-handkerchiefs tied round your old fronts! I suppose, under all the stars of heaven, there is nobody more happy than that child in that carriage—that wakeful girl, in sweet maiden meditation—who has given her heart to the keeping of the champion who is so near her. Has he not been always their champion and preserver? Don't they owe to his generosity every-thing in life? One of the little sisters wakes wildly, and cries in the night, and Charlotte takes the child into her arms and soothes her. "Hush, dear! He's there—he's there," she whispers, as she bends over the child. Nothing wrong can happen with *him* there, she feels. If the robbers were to spring out from yonder dark pines, why, he would jump down, and they would all fly before him! The carriage rolls on through sleeping villages, and as the old team retires all in a halo of smoke, and the fresh horses come clattering up to their pole, Charlotte sees a well-known white face in the gleam of the carriage-lanterns. Through the long avenues the great vehicle rolls on its course. The dawn peers over the poplars: the stars quiver out of sight: the sun is up in the sky, and the heaven is all in a flame. The night is over—the night of nights. In all the round world, whether lighted by stars or sunshine, there were not two people more happy than these had been.

A very short time afterwards, at the end of October, our own little sea-side sojourn came to an end. That astounding bill for broken glass, chairs, crockery, was paid. The London steamer takes us all on board on a beautiful, sunny autumn evening, and lands us at the Custom-house Quay in the midst of a deep, dun fog, through which our cabs have to work their way over greasy pavements, and bearing two loads of silent and terrified children. Ah, that return, if but after a fortnight's absence and holiday! 'Oh, that heap of letters lying in a ghastly pile, and yet so clearly visible in the dim twilight of master's study! We cheerfully breakfast by candlelight for the first two days after my arrival at home, and I have the pleasure of cutting a part of my chin off because it is too dark to shave at nine o'clock in the morning.

My wife can't be so unfeeling as to laugh and be merry because I have met with an accident which temporarily disfigures me. If the dun fog makes her jocular, she has a very queer sense of humour. She has a letter before her, over which she is perfectly radiant. When she is especially pleased I can see by her face and a particular animation and affectionateness towards the rest of the family. On this present morning her face beams out of the fog-clouds. The room is illuminated by it, and perhaps by the two candles which are placed one on either side of the urn. The fire crackles, and flames, and spits most cheerfully; and the sky without, which is of the hue of brown paper, seems to set off the brightness of the little interior scene.

"A letter from Charlotte, papa," cries one little girl, with an air of consequence. "And a letter from Uncle Philip, papa!" cries another, "and they like Paris so much," continues the little reporter.

"And there, sir, didn't I tell you?" cries the lady, handing me over a letter.

"Mamma always told you so," echoes the child, with an important nod of the head; "and I shouldn't be surprised if he were to be *very rich*, should you, mamma?" continues this arithmetician.

I would not put Miss Charlotte's letter into print if I could, for do you know that little person's grammar was frequently incorrect; there were three or four words spelt wrongly; and the letter was so *scored* and *marked* with *dashes* under *every* other *word*, that it is clear to me her education had been neglected; and as I am very fond of her, I do not wish to make fun of her. And I can't print Mr. Philip's letter, for I haven't kept it. Of what use keeping letters? I say, Burn, burn, burn. No heart-pangs. No reproaches. No yesterday. Was it happy, or miserable? To think of it is always melancholy. Go to! I dare say it is the thought of that fog, which is making this sentence so dismal. Meanwhile there is Madame Laura's face smiling out of the darkness, as pleased as may be; and no wonder, she is always happy when her friends are so.

Charlotte's letter contained a full account of the settlement of the Baynes family at Madame Smolensk's boarding-house, where they appear to have been really very comfortable, and to have lived at a very cheap rate. As for Mr. Philip, he made his way to a crib, to which his artist friends had recommended him, on the Faubourg St. Germain side of the water—the "Hotel Poussin," in the street of that name, which lies, you know, between the Mazarin Library and the Musée des Beaux Arts. In former days, my gentleman had lived in state and bounty in the English hotels and quarter. Now he found himself very handsomely lodged for thirty francs per month, and with five or six pounds, he has repeatedly said since, he could carry through the month very comfortably. I don't say, my young traveller, that *you* can be so lucky now-a-days. Are we not telling a story of twenty years ago? Aye marry. Ere steam-coaches had begun to scream on French rails; and when Louis Philippe was king.

As soon as Mr. Philip Firmin is ruined he must needs fall in love. In order to be near the beloved object, he must needs follow her to Paris, and give up his promised studies for the bar at home ; where, to do him justice, I believe the fellow would never have done any good. And he has not been in Paris a fortnight when that fantastic jade Fortune, who had seemed to fly away from him, gives him a smiling look of recognition, as if to say, " Young gentleman, I have not quite done with you."

The good fortune was not much. Do not suppose that Philip suddenly drew a twenty-thousand pound prize in a lottery. But, being in much want of money, he suddenly found himself enabled to earn some in a way pretty easy to himself.

In the first place, Philip found his friends Mr. and Mrs. Mugford in a bewildered state in the midst of Paris, in which city Mugford would never consent to have a *laquais de place*, being firmly convinced to the day of his death that he knew the French language quite sufficiently for all purposes of conversation. Philip, who had often visited Paris before, came to the aid of his friends in a two-franc dining-house, which he frequented for economy's sake; and they, because they thought the banquet there provided not only cheap, but most magnificent and satisfactory. He interpreted for them, and rescued them from their perplexity, whatever it was. He treated them handsomely to caffy on the bullyvard, as Mugford said on returning home and in recounting the adventure to me. " He can't forget that he has been a swell : and he does do things like a gentleman, that Firmin does. He came back with us to our hotel— Meurice's," said Mr. Mugford, " and who should drive into the yard and step out of his carriage but Lord Ringwood—you know Lord Ringwood ? everybody knows him. As he gets out of his carriage—'What ! is that you, Philip ?' says his lordship, giving the young fellow his hand. ' Come and breakfast with me to-morrow morning.' And away he goes most friendly."

How came it to pass that Lord Ringwood, whose instinct of self-preservation was strong—who, I fear, was rather a selfish nobleman— and who, of late, as we have heard, had given orders to refuse Mr. Philip entrance at his door—should all of a sudden turn round and greet the young man with cordiality ? In the first place, Philip had never troubled his lordship's knocker at all ; and second, as luck would have it, on this very day of their meeting his lordship had been to dine with that well-known Parisian resident and *bon vivant*, my Lord Viscount Trim, who had been governor of the Sago Islands when Colonel Baynes was there with his regiment, the gallant 100th. And the General and his old West India governor meeting at church, my Lord Trim straightway asked General Baynes to dinner, where Lord Ringwood was present, along with other distinguished company, whom at present we need not particularize. Now it has been said that Philip Ringwood, my lord's brother, and Captain Baynes in early youth had been close friends, and that the Colonel had died in the Captain's arms. Lord Ringwood, who had an excellent memory when he chose to use it, was pleased on this occasion to remember General Baynes and his intimacy with his brother in old days. And of those old times they talked ; the General waxing more eloquent, I suppose, than his wont over Lord Trim's excellent wine. And in the course of conversation Philip was named, and the General, warm with drink, poured out a most enthusiastic eulogium on his young friend, and mentioned how noble and self-denying Philip's conduct had been in his own case. And perhaps Lord Ringwood was pleased at hearing these praises of his brother's grandson ; and perhaps he thought of old times, when he had a heart, and he and his brother loved each other. And though he might think Philip Firmin an absurd young blockhead for giving up any claims which he might have on General Baynes, at any rate I have no doubt his lordship thought, " This boy is not likely to come begging money from me !" Hence, when he drove back to his hotel on the very night after this dinner, and in the courtyard saw that Philip Firmin, his brother's grandson, the heart of the old nobleman was smitten with a kindly sentiment, and he bade Philip to come and see him.

I have described some of Philip's oddities, and amongst these was a very remarkable change in his appearance, which ensued very speedily after his ruin. I know that the greater number of story readers are young, and those who are ever so old remember that their own young days occurred but a very, very short while ago. Don't you remember, most potent, grave, and reverend senior, when you were a junior, and actually rather pleased with new clothes ? Does a new coat or a waistcoat cause you any pleasure now ? To a well-constituted middle-aged gentleman, I rather trust a smart new suit causes a sensation of uneasiness—not from the tightness of the fit, which may be a reason—but from the gloss and splendour. When my late kind friend, Mrs. ——, gave me the emerald tabinet waist-coat, with the gold shamrocks, I wore it once to go to Richmond to dine with her; but I buttoned myself so closely in an upper coat, that I am sure nobody in the omnibus saw what a painted vest I had on. Gold sprigs and emerald tabinet, what a gorgeous raiment! It has formed for ten years the chief ornament of my wardrobe; and though I have never dared to wear it since, I always think with a secret pleasure of possessing that treasure. Do women, when they are sixty, like handsome and fashionable attire, and a youthful appearance? Look at Lady Jezebel's blushing cheek, her raven hair, her splendid garments! But this disquisition may be carried to too great a length. I want to note a fact which has occurred not seldom in my experience—that men who have been great dandies will often and suddenly give up their long-accustomed splendour of dress, and walk about, most happy and contented, with the shabbiest of coats and hats. No. The majority of men are not vain about their dress. For instance, within a very few years, men used to have pretty feet. See in what a resolute way they have kicked their pretty boots off almost to a man, and wear great, thick, formless, comfortable walking boots, of shape scarcely more graceful than a tub!

When Philip Firmin first came on the town, there were dandies still; there were dazzling waistcoats of velvet and brocade, and tall stocks with cataracts of satin; there were pins, studs, neck-chains, I know not what fantastic splendours of youth. His varnished boots grew upon forests of trees. He had a most resplendent silver-gilt dressing-case, presented to him by his father (for which, it is true, the doctor neglected to pay, leaving that duty to his son). "It is a mere ceremony," said the worthy doctor, "a cumbrous thing you may fancy at first; but take it about with you. It looks well on a man's dressing-table at a country-house. It *poses* a man, you understand. I have known women come in and peep at it. A trifle you may say, my boy; but what is the use of flinging any chance in life away?" Now, when misfortune came, young Philip flung away all these magnificent follies. He wrapped himself *virtute suâ;* and I am bound to say a more queer-looking fellow than friend Philip seldom walked the pavement of London or Paris. He could not wear the nap off all his coats, or rub his elbows into rags in six months; but, as he would say of himself with much simplicity, "I do think I run to seed more quickly than any fellow I ever knew. All my socks in holes, Mrs. Pendennis; all my shirt-buttons gone, I give you my word. I don't know how the things hold together, and why they don't tumble to pieces. I suspect I must have a bad laundress." Suspect! My children used to laugh and crow as they sowed buttons on to him. As for the Little Sister, she broke into his apartments in his absence, and said that it turned her hair grey to see the state of his poor wardrobe. I believe that Mrs. Brandon put surreptitious linen into his drawers. He did not know. He wore the shirts in a contented spirit. The glossy boots began to crack and then to burst, and Philip wore them with perfect equanimity. Where were the beautiful lavender and lemon gloves of last year? His great naked hands (with which he gesticulates so grandly) were as brown as an Indian's now. We had liked him heartily in his days of splendour; we loved him now in his threadbare suit.

I can fancy the young man striding into the room where his lordship's guests were assembled. In the presence of great or small, Philip has always been entirely unconcerned, and he is one of the half-dozen men I have seen in my life upon whom rank made no impression. It appears that, on occasion of this breakfast, there were one or two dandies present who were aghast at Philip's freedom of behaviour. He engaged in conversation with a famous French statesman; contradicted him with much energy in his own language; and when the statesman asked whether monsieur was membre du Parlement? Philip burst into one of his roars of laughter, which almost breaks the glasses on a table, and said, "Je suis journaliste, monsieur, à vos ordres!" Young Timbury of the embassy was aghast at Philip's insolence; and Dr. Botts, his lordship's travelling physician, looked at him with a terrified face. A bottle of claret was brought, which almost all the gentlemen present began to swallow, until Philip, tasting his glass, called out, "Faugh! It's corked!" "So it is, and very badly corked," growls my lord, with one of his usual oaths. "Why didn't some of you fellows speak? Do you like corked wine?" There were gallant fellows round that table who would have drunk corked black dose, had his lordship professed to like senna. The old host was tickled and amused. "Your mother was a quiet soul, and your father used to bow like a dancing-master. You ain't much like him. I dine at home most days. Leave word in the morning with my people, and come when you like, Philip," he growled.   A part of this news Philip narrated to us in his letter, and other part was given verbally by Mr. and Mrs. Mugford on their return to London.   "I tell you, sir," says Mugford, "he has been taken by the hand by some of the tiptop people, and I have booked him at three guineas a week for a letter to the *Pall Mall Gazette.*"

And this was the cause of my wife's exultation and triumphant "Didn't I tell you?"   Philip's foot was on the ladder; and who so capable of mounting to the top?   When happiness and a fond and lovely girl were waiting for him there, would he lose heart, spare exertion, or be afraid to climb?   He had no truer well-wisher than myself, and no friend who liked him better, though, I dare say, many admired him much more than I did.   But these were women for the most part; and women become so absurdly unjust and partial to persons whom they love, when these latter are in misfortune, that I am surprised Mr. Philip did not quite lose his head in his poverty, with such fond flatterers and sycophants round about him.   Would you grudge him the consolation to be had from these sweet uses of adversity?   Many a heart would be hardened but for the memory of past griefs; when eyes, now averted, perhaps, were full of sympathy, and hands, now cold, were eager to soothe and succour.

CHAPTER XIX.

QU'ON EST BIEN À VINGT ANS.

FAIR correspondent—and I would parenthetically hint that all correspondents are *not* fair—points out the discrepancy existing between the text and the illustrations of our story; and justly remarks that the story dated more than twenty years back, while the costumes of the actors of our little comedy are of the fashion of to-day.

My dear madam, these anachronisms must be, or you would scarcely be able to keep any interest for our characters. What would be a woman without a crinoline petticoat, for example? an object ridiculous, hateful, I suppose hardly proper. What would you think of a hero who wore a large high black-satin stock cascading over a figured silk waistcoat; and a blue dress-coat, with brass buttons, mayhap? If a person so attired came up to ask you to dance, could you refrain from laughing? Time was when young men so decorated found favour in the eyes of damsels who had never beheld hooped petticoats, except in their grandmother's portraits. Persons who flourished in the first part of the century never thought to see the hoops of our ancestors' age rolled downwards to our contemporaries and children. Did we ever imagine that a period would arrive when our young men would part their hair down the middle, and wear a piece of tape for a neckcloth? As soon should we have thought of their dyeing their bodies with woad, and arraying themselves like ancient Britons.

So the ages have their dress and undress ; and the gentlemen and ladies of Victoria's time are satisfied with their manner of raiment; as no doubt in Boadicea's court they looked charming tattooed and painted blue.

The times of which we write, the times of Louis Philippe the king, are so altered from the present, that when Philip Firmin went to Paris it was absolutely a cheap place to live in ; and he has often bragged in subsequent days of having lived well during a month for five pounds, and bought a neat waistcoat with a part of the money. "A capital bed-room, *au premier*, for a franc a day, sir," he would call all persons to remark, " a bedroom as good as yours, my lord, at Meurice's. Very good tea or coffee breakfast, twenty francs a month, with lots of bread and butter. Twenty francs a month for washing, and fifty for dinner and pocket-money—that's about the figure. The dinner, I own, is shy, unless I come and dine with my friends ; and then I make up for banyan days." And so saying Philip would call out for more truffled partridges, or affably filled his goblet with my Lord Ringwood's best Sillery. "At those shops," he would observe, "where I dine, I have beer : I can't stand the wine. And you see, I can't go to the cheap English ordinaries, of which there are many, because English gentlemen's servants are there, you know, and it's not pleasant to sit with a fellow who waits on you the day after."

"Oh ! the English servants go to the cheap ordinaries, do they ?" asks my lord, greatly amused, "and you drink *bière de Mars* at the shop where you dine ?"

"And dine very badly, too, I can tell you. Always come away hungry. Give me some champagne—the dry, if you please. They mix very well together—sweet and dry. Did you ever dine at Flicoteau's, Mr. Pecker ?"

"*I* dine at one of your horrible two-franc houses ?" cries Mr. Pecker, with a look of terror. "Do you know, my lord, there are actually houses where people dine for two francs ?"

"Two francs ! Seventeen sous !" bawls out Mr. Firmin. " The soup, the beef, the rôti, the salad, the dessert, and the whitey-brown bread at discretion. It's not a good dinner, certainly—in fact, it is a dreadful bad one. But to dine so would do some fellows a great deal of good."

"What do you say, Pecker? Flicoteau's ; seventeen sous. We'll make a little party and try, and Firmin shall do the honours of his restaurant," says my lord, with a grin.

"Mercy!" gasps Mr. Pecker.

"I had rather dine here, if you please, my lord," says the young man. "This is cheaper, and certainly better."

My lord's doctor, and many of the guests at his table, my lord's henchmen, flatterers, and led captains, looked aghast at the freedom of the young fellow in the shabby coat. If *they* dared to be familiar with their host, there came a scowl over that noble countenance which was awful to face. They drank his corked wine in meekness of spirit. They laughed at his jokes trembling. One after another, they were the objects of his satire; and each grinned piteously, as he took his turn of punishment. Some dinners are dear, though they cost nothing. At some great tables are not toads served along with the *entrées?* Yes, and many amateurs are exceedingly fond of the dish.

How do Parisians live at all? is a question which has often set me wondering. How do men in public offices, with fifteen thousand francs, let us say, for a salary—and this, for a French official, is a high salary—live in handsome apartments; give genteel entertainments; clothe themselves and their families with much more sumptuous raiment than English people of the same station can afford; take their country holiday, a six weeks' sojourn, *aux eaux*; and appear cheerful and to want for nothing? Paterfamilias, with six hundred a year in London, knows what a straitened life his is, with rent high, and beef at a shilling a pound. Well, in Paris, rent is higher, and meat is dearer; and yet madame is richly dressed when you see her; monsieur has always a little money in his pocket for his club or his café; and something is pretty surely put away every year for the marriage portion of the young folks. "Sir," Philip used to say, describing this period of his life, on which and on most subjects regarding himself, by the way, he was wont to be very eloquent, "when my income was raised to five thousand francs a year, I give you my word I was considered to be rich by my French acquaintance. I gave four sous to the waiter at our dining-place:—in that respect I was always ostentatious:—and I believe they called me Milor. I should have been poor in the Rue de la Paix: but I was wealthy in the Luxembourg quarter. Don't tell me about poverty, sir! Poverty is a bully if you are afraid of her, or truckle to her. Poverty is good-natured enough if you meet her like a man. You saw how my poor old father was afraid of her, and thought the world would come to an end if Dr. Firmin did not keep his butler, and his footman, and his fine house, and fine chariot and horses? He was a poor man, if you please. He must have suffered agonies in his struggle to make both ends meet. Everything he bought must have cost him twice the honest price; and when I think of nights that must have been passed without sleep—of that proud man having to smirk and cringe before creditors—to coax butchers, by George, and wheedle tailors—I pity him; I can't be angry any more. That man has suffered enough. As for me, haven't you remarked that since I have not a guinea in the world, I swagger, and am a much greater swell than before?" And the truth is that a Prince Royal could not have called for his *gens* with a more magnificent air than Mr. Philip when he summoned the waiter, and paid for his *petit verre*.

Talk of poverty, indeed! That period, Philip vows, was the happiest of his life. He liked to tell in after days of the choice acquaintance of Bohemians which he had formed. Their jug, he said, though it contained but small beer, was always full. Their tobacco, though it bore no higher rank than that of caporal, was plentiful and fragrant. He knew some admirable medical students; some artists who only wanted talent and industry to be at the height of their profession: and one or two of the magnates of his own calling, the newspaper correspondents, whose houses and tables were open to him. It was wonderful what secrets of politics he learned and transmitted to his own paper. He pursued French statesmen of those days with prodigious eloquence and vigour. At the expense of that old king he was wonderfully witty and sarcastical. He reviewed the affairs of Europe, settled the destinies of Russia, denounced the Spanish marriages, disposed of the Pope, and advocated the Liberal cause in France with an untiring eloquence. "Absinthe used to be my drink, sir," so he was good enough to tell his friends. "It makes the ink run, and imparts a fine eloquence to the style. Mercy upon us, how I would belabour that poor King of the French under the influence of absinthe, in that café opposite the Bourse where I used to make my letter! Who knows, sir, perhaps the influence of those letters precipitated the fall of the Bourbon dynasty! Before I had an office, Gilligan, of the *Century*, and I, used to do our letters at that café; we compared notes and pitched into each other amicably."

Gilligan of the *Century*, and Firmin of the *Pall Mall Gazette*, were, however, very minor personages amongst the London newspaper correspondents. Their seniors of the daily press had handsome apartments, gave sumptuous dinners, were closeted with ministers' secretaries, and entertained members of the Chamber of Deputies. Philip, on perfectly easy terms with himself and the world, swaggering about the embassy balls—Philip, the friend and relative of Lord Ringwood—was viewed by his professional seniors and superiors with an eye of favour, which was not certainly turned on all gentlemen following his calling. Certainly poor Gilligan was never asked to those dinners, which some of the newspaper ambassadors gave, whereas Philip was received not inhospitably. Gilligan received but a cold shoulder at Mrs. Morning Messenger's Thursdays; and as for being asked to dinner, "Bedad, that fellow, Firmin, has an air with him which will carry him through anywhere!" Phil's brother correspondent owned. "He seems to patronise an ambassador when he goes up and speaks to him; and he says to a secretary, 'My good fellow, tell your master that Mr. Firmin, of the *Pall Mall Gazette*, wants to see him, and will thank him to step over to the Café de la Bourse.'" I don't think Philip, for his part, would have seen much matter of surprise in a Minister stepping over to speak to him. To him all folk were alike, great and small; and it is recorded of him that when, on one occasion, Lord Ringwood paid him a visit at his lodgings in the Faubourg St. Germain, Philip affably offered his lord-ship a *cornet* of fried potatoes, with which, and plentiful tobacco of course, Philip and one or two of his friends were regaling themselves when Lord Ringwood chanced to call on his kinsman.

A crust and a carafon of small beer, a correspondence with a weekly paper, and a remuneration such as that we have mentioned, —was Philip Firmin to look for no more than this pittance, and not to seek for more permanent and lucrative employment? Some of his friends at home were rather vexed at what Philip chose to consider his good fortune; namely, his connection with the news-paper, and the small stipend it gave him. He might quarrel with his employer any day. Indeed no man was more likely to fling his bread and butter out of window than Mr. Philip. He was losing precious time at the bar; where he, as hundreds of other poor gentlemen had done before him, might make a career for himself. For what are colonies made? Why do bankruptcies occur? Why do people break the peace and quarrel with policemen, but that

barristers may be employed as judges, commissioners, magistrates ?·
A reporter to a newspaper remains all his life a newspaper reporter.
Philip, if he would but help himself, had friends in the world who
might aid effectually to advance him. So it was we pleaded with
him, in the language of moderation, urging the dictates of common
sense. As if moderation and common sense could be got to move
that mule of a Philip Firmin ; as if any persuasion of ours could
induce him to do anything but what he liked to do best himself !

"That *you* should be worldly, my poor fellow" (so Philip wrote
to his present biographer)—"that you should be thinking of money
and the main chance, is no matter of surprise to me. You have
suffered under that curse of manhood, that destroyer of generosity in
the mind, that parent of selfishness—a little fortune. You have
your wretched hundreds" (my candid correspondent stated the sum
correctly enough ; and I wish it were double or treble ; but that is
not here the point :) "paid quarterly. The miserable pittance numbs
your whole existence. It prevents freedom of thought and action.
It makes a screw of a man who is certainly not without generous
impulses, as I know, my poor old Harpagon : for hast thou not
offered to open thy purse to me ? I tell you I am sick of the way
in which people in London, especially good people, think about
money. You live up to your income's edge. You are miserably
poor. You brag and flatter yourselves that you owe no man
anything ; but your estate has creditors upon it as insatiable as any
usurer, and as hard as any bailiff. You call me reckless, and
prodigal, and idle, and all sorts of names, because I live in a single .
room, do as little work as I can, and go about with holes in my
boots : and you flatter yourself you are prudent, because you have a
genteel house, a grave flunkey out of livery, and two greengrocers
to wait when you give your half-dozen dreary dinner parties.
Wretched man ! You are a slave : not a man. You are a pauper,
with a good house and good clothes. You are so miserably prudent,
that all your money is spent for you, exept the few wretched shillings
which you allow yourself for pocket-money. You tremble at the
expense of a cab. I believe you actually look at half-a-crown before
you spend it. The landlord is your master. The livery-stablekeeper
is your master. A train of ruthless, useless servants are your
pitiless creditors, to whom you have to pay exorbitant dividends
every day. I, with a hole in my elbow, who live upon a shilling

dinner, and walk on cracked boot soles, am called extravagant, idle, reckless, I don't know what; while you, forsooth, consider yourself prudent. Miserable delusion! You are flinging away heaps of money on useless flunkeys, on useless maid-servants, on useless lodgings, on useless finery—and you say, 'Poor Phil! what a sad idler he is! how he flings himself away! in what a wretched, disreputable manner he lives!' Poor Phil is as rich as you are, for he has enough, and is content. Poor Phil can afford to be idle, and you can't. You must work in order to keep that great hulking footman, that great rawboned cook, that army of babbling nursery-maids, and I don't know what more. And if you choose to submit to the slavery and degradation inseparable from your condition;—the wretched inspection of candle-ends, which you call order;—the mean self-denials, which you must daily practise—I pity you, and don't quarrel with you. But I wish you would not be so insufferably virtuous, and ready with your blame and pity for *me*. If I am happy, pray need you be disquieted? Suppose I prefer independence, and shabby boots? Are not these better than to be pinched by your abominable varnished conventionalism, and to be denied the liberty of free action? My poor fellow, I pity you from my heart; and it grieves me to think how those fine honest children —honest, and hearty, and frank, and open as yet—are to lose their natural good qualities, and to be swathed, and swaddled, and stifled out of health and honesty by that obstinate worldling their father. Don't tell *me* about the world; I know it. People sacrifice the next world to it, and are all the while proud of their prudence. Look at my miserable relations, steeped in respectablity. Look at my father. There is a chance for him, now he is down and in poverty. I have had a letter from him, containing more of that dreadful worldly advice which you Pharisees give. If it weren't for Laura and the children, sir, I heartily wish you were ruined like your affectionate—P. F.

"N.B., PS.—Oh, Pen! I am so happy! She is such a little darling! I bathe in her innocence, sir! I strengthen myself in her purity. I kneel before her sweet goodness and unconsciousness of guile. I walk from my room, and see her every morning before seven o'clock. I see her every afternoon. She loves you and Laura. And you love her, don't you? And to think that six months ago I was going to marry a woman without a heart! Why, sir, blessings be on the poor old father for spending our money, and rescuing me·

from that horrible fate! I might have been like that fellow in the
'Arabian Nights,' who married Amina—the respectable woman, who
dined upon grains of rice, but supped upon cold dead body. Was it
not worth all the money I ever was heir to to have escaped from
that ghoul? Lord Ringwood says he thinks I was well out of that.
He calls people by Anglo-Saxon names, and uses very expressive
monosyllables; and of Aunt Twysden, of Uncle Twysden, of the girls,
and their brother, he speaks in a way which makes me see he has
come to just conclusions about them.

"PS. No. 2.—Ah, Pen! She is such a darling. I think I am
the happiest man in the world."

And this was what came of being ruined! A scapegrace, who,
when he had plenty of money in his pocket, was ill-tempered, imperious, and discontented; now that he is not worth twopence, declares
himself the happiest fellow in the world! Do you remember, my
dear, how he used to grumble at our claret, and what wry faces he
made when there was only cold meat for dinner? The wretch is
absolutely contented with bread and cheese and small-beer, even that
bad beer which they have in Paris!

Now and again, at this time, and as our mutual avocations permitted, I saw Philip's friend, the Little Sister. He wrote to her
dutifully from time to time. He told her of his love affair with Miss
Charlotte; and my wife and I could console Caroline, by assuring
her that this time the young man's heart was given to a worthy
mistress. I say console, for the news, after all, was sad for her. In
the little chamber which she always kept ready for him, he would ·
lie awake, and think of some one dearer to him than a hundred poor
Carolines. She would devise something that should be agreeable to
the young lady. At Christmas time there came to Miss Baynes a
wonderfully worked cambric pocket-handkerchief, with " Charlotte "
most beautifully embroidered in the corner. It was this poor widow's
mite of love and tenderness which she meekly laid down in the place
where she worshipped. "And I have six for him, too, ma'am," Mrs.
Brandon told my wife. " Poor fellow! his shirts was in a dreadful
way when he went away from here, and that you know, ma'am." So
you see this wayfarer, having fallen among undoubted thieves, yet
found many kind souls to relieve him, and many a good Samaritan
ready with his twopence, if need were.

The reason why Philip was the happiest man in the world of ·

MORNING GREETINGS.

course you understand. French people are very early risers; and, at the little hotel where Mr. Philip lived, the whole crew of the house were up hours before lazy English masters and servants think of stirring. At ever so early an hour Phil had a fine bowl of coffee and milk and bread for his breakfast; and he was striding down to the Invalides, and across the bridge to the Champs Elysées, and the fumes of his pipe preceded him with a pleasant odour. And a short time after passing the Rond Point in the Elysian fields, where an active fountain was flinging up showers of diamonds to the sky,—after, I say, leaving the Rond Point on his right, and passing under umbrageous groves in the direction of the present Castle of Flowers, Mr. Philip would see a little person. Sometimes a young sister or brother came with the little person. Sometimes only a blush fluttered on her cheek, and a sweet smile beamed in her face as she came forward to greet him. For the angels were scarce purer than this young maid; and Una was no more afraid of the lion, than Charlotte of her companion with the loud voice and the tawny mane. I would not have envied that reprobate's lot who should have dared to say a doubtful word to this Una: but the truth is, she never thought of danger, or met with any. The workmen were going to their labour; the dandies were asleep; and considering their age, and the relationship in which they stood to one another, I am not surprised at Philip for announcing that this was the happiest time of his life. In later days, when two gentlemen of mature age happened to be in Paris together, what must Mr. Philip Firmin do but insist upon walking me sentimentally to the Champs Elysées, and looking at an old house there, a rather shabby old house in a garden. "That was the place," sighs he. "That was Madame de Smolensk's. That was the window, the third one, with the green jalousie. By Jove, sir, how happy and how miserable I have been behind that green blind!" And my friend shakes his large fist at the somewhat dilapidated mansion, whence Madame de Smolensk and her boarders have long since departed.

I fear that baroness had engaged in her enterprise with insufficient capital, or conducted it with such liberality that her profits were eaten up by her boarders. I could tell dreadful stories impugning the baroness's moral character. People said she had no right to the title of baroness at all, or to the noble foreign name of Smolensk. People are still alive who knew her under a different name. The

baroness herself was what some amateurs call a fine woman, especially
at dinner-time, when she appeared in black satin and with cheeks
that blushed up as far as the eyelids. In her *peignoir* in the morning,
she was perhaps the reverse of fine. Contours which were round at
night, in the forenoon appeared lean and angular. Her roses only
bloomed half an hour before dinner-time on a cheek which was quite
yellow until five o'clock. I am sure it is very kind of elderly and
ill-complexioned people to supply the ravages of time or jaundice,
and present to our view a figure blooming and agreeable, in place of
an object faded and withered. Do you quarrel with your opposite
neighbour for painting his house front or putting roses in his balcony?
You are rather thankful for the adornment. Madame de Smolensk's
front was so decorated of afternoons. Geraniums were set pleasantly
under those first-floor windows, her eyes. Carcel lamps beamed from
those windows : lamps which she had trimmed with her own scissors,
and into which that poor widow poured the oil which she got somehow and anyhow. When the dingy breakfast *papillotes* were cast of
an afternoon, what beautiful black curls appeared round her brow!
The dingy *papillotes* were put away in the drawer: the *peignoir*
retired to its hook behind the door: the satin raiment came forth,
the shining, the ancient, the well-kept, the well-wadded : and at the
same moment the worthy woman took that smile out of some cunning
box on her scanty toilet-table—that smile which she wore all the
evening along with the rest of her toilette, and took out of her mouth
when she went to bed and to think—to think how both ends were to
be made to meet.

Philip said he respected and admired that woman : and worthy
of respect she was in her way. She painted her face and grinned at
poverty. She laughed and rattled with care gnawing at her side.
She had to coax the milkman out of his human kindness : to pour
oil—his own oil—upon the stormy épicier's soul : to melt the
butterman : to tap the wine-merchant : to mollify the butcher : to
invent new pretexts for the landlord : to reconcile the lady boarders,
Mrs. General Baynes, let us say, and the Honourable Mrs. Boldero,
who were always quarrelling : to see that the dinner, when procured,
was cooked properly; that François, to whom she owed ever so
many months' wages, was not too rebellious or intoxicated ; that
Auguste, also her creditor, had his glass clean and his lamps in order.
And this work done and the hour of six o'clock arriving, she had to

carve and be agreeable to her table; not to hear the growls of the discontented (and at what table-d'hôte are there not grumblers?); to have a word for everybody present; a smile and a laugh for Mrs. Bunch (with whom there had been very likely a dreadful row in the morning); a remark for the Colonel; a polite phrase for the General's lady; and even a good word and compliment for sulky Auguste, who just before dinner-time had unfolded the napkin of mutiny about his wages.

Was not this enough work for a woman to do? To conduct a great house without sufficient money, and make soup, fish, roasts, and half a dozen entrées out of wind as it were? to conjure up wine in piece and by the dozen? to laugh and joke without the least gaiety? to receive scorn, abuse, rebuffs, insolence, with gay good-humour? and then to go to bed wearied at night, and have to think about figures and that dreadful, dreadful sum in arithmetic—given 5*l.* to pay 6*l.*? Lady Macbeth is supposed to have been a resolute woman: and great, tall, loud, hectoring females are set to represent the character. I say No. She was a weak woman. She began to walk in her sleep, and blab after one disagreeable little incident had occurred in her house. She broke down, and got all the people away from her own table in the most abrupt and clumsy manner, because that drivelling, epileptic husband of hers fancied he saw a ghost. In Lady Smolensk's place Madame de Macbeth would have broken down in a week, and Smolensk lasted for years. If twenty gibbering ghosts had come to the boarding-house dinner, madame would have gone on carving her dishes, and smiling and helping the live guests, the paying guests; leaving the dead guests to gibber away and help themselves. "My poor father had to keep up appearances," Phil would say, recounting these things in after days; "but how? You know he always looked as if he was going to be hung." Smolensk was the gayest of the gay always. That widow would have tripped up to her funeral pile and kissed her hands to her friends with a smiling "Bon jour!"

"Pray, who was Monsieur de Smolensk?" asks a simple lady who may be listening to our friend's narrative.

"Ah, my dear lady! there was a pretty disturbance in the house when *that* question came to be mooted, I promise you," says our friend, laughing, as he recounts his adventures. And, after all, what does it matter to you and me and this story who Smolensk was?

I am sure this poor lady had hardships enough in her life campaign, and that Ney himself could not have faced fortune with a constancy more heroical.

Well. When the Bayneses first came to her house, I tell you Smolensk and all round her smiled, and our friends thought they were landed in a real rosy Elysium in the Champs of that name. Madame had a *Carrick à l'Indienne* prepared in compliment to her guests. She had had many Indians in her establishment. She adored Indians. *N'était ce la polygamie*—they were most estimable people the Hindus. Surtout, she adored Indian shawls. That of Madame la Générale was ravishing. The company at Madame's was pleasant. The Honourable Mrs. Boldero was a dashing woman of fashion and respectability, who had lived in the best world—it was easy to see that. The young ladies' duets were very striking. The Honourable Mr. Boldero was away shooting in Scotland at his brother, Lord Strongitharm's, and would take Gaberlunzie Castle and the duke's on his way south. Mrs. Baynes did not know Lady Estridge, the ambassadress? When the Estridges returned from Chantilly, the Honourable Mrs. B. would be delighted to introduce her. "Your pretty girl's name is Charlotte? So is Lady Estridge's—and very nearly as tall;—fine girls the Estridges; fine long necks—large feet—but your girl, Lady Baynes, has beautiful feet. Lady Baynes, I said? Well, you must be Lady Baynes soon. The General *must* be a K.C.B. after his services. What, you know Lord Trim? He will, and must, do it for you. If not, my brother Strongitharm shall." I have no doubt Mrs. Baynes was greatly elated by the attentions of Lord Strongitharm's sister; and looked him out in the *Peerage*, where his Lordship's arms, pedigree, and residence of Gaberlunzie Castle are duly recorded. The Honourable Mrs. Boldero's daughters, the Misses Minna and Brenda Boldero, played some rattling sonatas on a piano which was a good deal fatigued by their exertions, for the young ladies' hands were very powerful. And madame said, "Thank you," with her sweetest smile; and Auguste handed about on a silver tray—I say silver, so that the convenances may not be wounded—well, say silver that was blushing to find itself copper—handed up on a tray a white drink which made the Baynes boys cry out, "I say, mother, what's this beastly thing?" On which madame, with the sweetest smile, appealed to the company, and said, "They love orgeat, these dear infants!" and resumed her picquet with old M. Bidois—that odd old gentleman in the long brown coat, with the red ribbon, who took so much snuff and blew his nose so often and so loudly. One, two, three rattling sonatas Minna and Brenda played; Mr. Clancy, of Trinity College, Dublin (M. de Clanci, madame called him), turning over the leaves, and presently being persuaded to sing some Irish melodies for the ladies. I don't think Miss Charlotte Baynes listened to the music much. She was listening to another music, which she and Mr. Firmin were performing together. Oh, how pleasant that music used to be! There was a sameness in it, I dare say, but still it was pleasant to hear the air over again. The pretty little duet *à quatre mains*, where the hands cross over, and hop up and down the keys, and the heads get so close, so close. Oh, duets, oh, regrets! Psha! no more of this. Go downstairs, old dotard. Take your hat and umbrella and go walk by the sea-shore, and whistle a toothless old solo. "These are our quiet nights," whispers M. de Clanci to the Baynes ladies, when the evening draws to an end. "Madame's Thursdays are, I promise ye, much more fully attended." Good night, good night. A squeeze of a little hand, a hearty hand-shake from papa and mamma, and Philip is striding through the dark Elysian fields and over the Place of Concord to his lodgings in the Faubourg St. Germain. Or, stay! What is that glowworm beaming by the wall opposite Madame de Smolensk's house?—a glowworm that wafts an aromatic incense and odour? I do believe it is Mr. Philip's cigar. And he is watching, watching a window by which a slim figure flits now and again. Then darkness falls on the little window. The sweet eyes are closed. Oh, blessings, blessings be upon them! The stars shine overhead. And homeward stalks Mr. Firmin, talking to himself, and brandishing a great stick.

I wish that poor Madame Smolensk could sleep as well as the people in her house. But care, with the cold feet, gets under the coverlid, and says, "Here I am; you know that bill is coming due to-morrow." Ah, atra cura! can't you leave the poor thing a little quiet? Hasn't she had work enough all day?

END OF VOL. I.